MIXED BLOOD

RENOIR

MEREDIAN
PICTURES & WORDS

MEREDIAN
PICTURES & WORDS

INSPIRING IMAGINATION

✿ Created with Vellum

For my darling bride, and Muse.

And for Narnia!

CONTENTS

1

WHAT MAKES US WHAT WE ARE

Louth wasn't much of a town. It had been scratched out of the bush solely because of its proximity to a deep sweeping bend on the river that was a natural harbour. As a port it served the surrounding sheep farming properties.

There was a saying that the young New South Wales colony rode on the sheep's back. Wool handling centres like Louth were pivotal in the transport of the bales that were building what would be the wealth of the nation.

But it was rough. Roughly built, and mostly populated by rough men who lived and worked in hard conditions.

Five labourers were sweating over a stack of crates that had been unloaded from the paddle steamer that wallowed at the dock, a steamer that was now being reloaded with bales of precious wool.

That was the true tide of Louth. Not the rise and fall of the water, but the ebb of supplies into the town, and the flow of wool back out.

Among the items most recently arrived was a large wheeled traction engine. The big machine was destined for a farm several miles away. It needed a team of horses to move it – a team that had already been hitched up and were being led away by two men on horseback.

The older of the two – James Arnold by name - was almost bald, but sported a thick silver beard. Bushy black brows gave a hint as to what his hair must have been like in younger days. He rode on one side of the team, his dark companion on the other.

As they rode past the sweating labourers one of the five looked up and spat contemptuously on the ground behind the riders.

The older horseman had noticed from the corner of his eye. He reined his horse to a halt and turned to face the docker.

"You got a problem, mate?" he asked casually.

The docker growled, "I reckon you've got a problem – lettin' one of those bastards ride beside ya like he was as good as a white man. You *are* a white man, aren't ya?"

Arnold looked at him impassively. When he replied his voice was quiet but certain. "Magpie does the same work as I do. Works just as hard, just as long. Longer sometimes. Damn right he rides alongside me."

The man standing on the ground sneered. "Magpie. That'd be right. Half black, half white. Worst kind of bastard. Can't trust 'em, you know," he warned.

Magpie had halted the team of horses and rode back alongside Arnold. He pushed his hat back on his head and grinned amiably.

"Oh, I dunno," he said. "There's worse kinds of bastards. There's lazy bastards, vicious bastards, mean bastards. And ignorant bastards."

"You don't call me ignorant, you piece of black shit!" He pulled a pistol from his waistband and brandished it at the riders. "I ought to blow you right off that nag!"

The labourer was clearly uncomfortable with the two mounted men looking down on him. A couple of his workmates also looked tense, as much threatened as threatening.

James Arnold pulled a rifle from a holder at the back of his saddle. He laid the gun casually across his lap, but it was clearly pointed in the direction of the belligerent docker.

The horseman's voice was still quiet. "You don't want to be waving that thing about. Guns have got a funny way of going off."

Another of the labourers, Lewis Heath, had drawn his pistol. His companions started to reach for theirs.

"There's five of us, two of you. You wouldn't stand a chance," said Heath.

Magpie drew his own pistol and aimed it squarely at Heath's head. "Maybe not, but we'd go down fighting. You volunteering to die for your friend's big mouth? Any of you?"

The dockers looked nervously at each other.

"Sorry, Rourke," mumbled one as he put his gun away.

The man called Rourke, who had started the exchange, turned his back on the teamsters and jammed his pistol into the waistband of his pants. His companions also turned back to their work.

Rourke glanced up but didn't meet the eyes of either horseman. "Just piss off, mate," he growled.

Magpie grinned as he shook his head. "You're no mate of mine."

"Not mine either," added Arnold as they rode back to gee up their team and get the traction engine rolling forward again.

Rourke pulled his pistol out again and aimed it at Magpie's back. Arnold turned in his saddle. He'd been expecting treachery and was still holding his rifle. His shot smashed into Rourke's shoulder before the pistol could be fired.

The docker fell to the ground screaming. Neither horseman looked back as they cantered away.

"There's bastards you know you can't trust, hey James?" said Magpie casually.

"Sad but true, my friend."

❧

FAR TO THE southeast of the river port, a well-appointed house stood in the middle of lush pastureland. It was home to wealthy squatter James Robertson and his family.

On a balmy afternoon Robertson sat working at his writing desk. His daughter Davinia reclined on a couch, feigning sleep. Barely more than twenty, the young woman had a cultivated air of haughtiness, from her carefully applied make-up to the rather theatrical pose.

Her brother Phillip, a couple of years older, ignored his sister as he usually did. He stood in front of the window that looked out over the property, but showed no interest in the view. His attention was focused on cleaning a good quality pistol. He was a keen hunter.

The door of the room opened and the Robertson's manservant Ali came in. He had been with James Robertson for a long time, and rarely felt the need to knock before entering.

He almost seemed to glide across the carpeted floor. "A communication has arrived for you, sir," he said and handed to the squatter a tray on which lay an unopened envelope. The Indian stepped back and waited patiently for any instruction.

Robertson opened the envelope briskly and read quickly. None of his movements appeared rapid, but he moved with great economy. Every action was precise and to the point.

"Interesting," he said.

"What is?" asked Davinia, opening one eye. She'd heard Ali enter but had paid no attention to him.

Her father made a small vague gesture with the letter as he reread it. He took up a pen and started making notes on a pad.

Phillip watched him, curious. "Who's it from, Father?"

"Kaminski."

The young man's forehead creased as he rifled through his memory. "Polish fellow? Worked for us some time ago? A horseman, wasn't he?"

"A horse thief, more likely," suggested Davinia with a sarcastic smile.

The squatter nodded absently, not looking up. "Very likely so, Davinia. Good with horses though. Especially wild ones."

The girl's smile now took on a distinctly wicked look as she said, "I remember he was a bit wild himself."

None of the men reacted. If that disappointed her she didn't show it. "I thought you didn't like him, Father. That's why he left, isn't it?"

Robertson shrugged and replied, "He left because he thought he could do better for himself elsewhere."

Davinia gave a small derisive laugh, prompting the squatter to put down his pen and give both his offspring a studious look. Phillip hoped his father didn't notice his reflex rolling of the eyes at the prospect of another little 'life and business lesson'.

"My liking or disliking the man is irrelevant. He was good at his job and did what he was told. Any feelings about each other, good or bad, are of no consequence. Nor should they ever be. Look at Ali here. His family has served my family for many years now, here and before we left Ahmednagar. I greatly appreciate his efficiency, not to mention the many little special talents he's cultivated. But I could hardly say I like the man. And I daresay the feeling is mutual, eh Ali?'

The Indian looked genuinely puzzled. "*Like* you, sir?" There was no trace of anger in his voice, but the whole idea was clearly alien to him.

Davinia pouted, "That's different, Father. Ali is a native..."

"Which does not preclude him from having many admirable qualities and abilities, my dear. All the more so when they are employed to my advantage."

"What does the Polish fellow want?" asked Phillip, hoping to return to the point of the conversation. He assumed that any former employee writing to his father must want something.

Robertson looked thoughtfully at the letter on his desk. "He writes from quite some way inland. It seems he'd been working at one of those little port towns along the Darling River. He tells me there's gold nearby."

His daughter smiled dreamily. "I like gold. It's pretty. I like pretty things."

The young man was of a far more practical mind, asking, "So why is he telling you? Why isn't he making himself rich?"

"A reasonable question, my boy. It seems that, unlike in some other parts of the country, the gold isn't simply lying about waiting to be picked up by a lucky passer-by. A certain amount of effort and equipment is required to extract a worthwhile quantity." He looked at the notes he'd been making. "Kaminski also apparently has a certain amount of concern about a local tribe of natives. He expresses the hope I may be able to... facilitate something."

Phillip looked at his father, his curiosity aroused. When Robertson Senior appeared to have turned his attention back to jotting notes the young man prompted, "Well?"

"Mm?" The older man looked up. "Oh, an opportunity worth investigating, certainly. Gold is a powerful commodity."

THE HOUSE in Italy was small, but furnished and decorated well enough to indicate a reasonable level of prosperity. The parlour was compact, but comfortable.

Two men in their sixties sat facing each other. The house's owner, Angelo Pasquale, was clearly nervous. He was more discomfited by the man facing him – Don Chiabatoni – than by the two burly men standing behind his visitor. One of the men held a large wicker basket of the kind used locally for carrying fruit at the market.

Don Chiabatoni leaned forward, his fingers steepled. "Angelo, I am truly sorry it has come to this. Our children were promised to each other since their early years. I have been patient. My Rosa has been patient. I know Vittorio is your only son – I have seen that he must learn your business. It is good that he has committed himself to this. The Pasquale house has produced fine food for as long as any of us can remember."

Angelo gave an uncertain but genuine smile at the compliment. He was proud of the family reputation, but he was sure that Don Chiabatoni had not come to deliver pleasantries. As if in confirmation of this, his guest's expression darkened.

"How is our patience rewarded, Angelo? While we wait, thinking Vittorio is a good man, thinking he is only doing the best he can by his family while he prepares to become a part of our family – while we do this, your son debases himself by entering into a... relationship with a strumpet who works at the tavern. A creature who is not of our family – not even our blood!"

Pasquale's shock was genuine. If this was true... he shared the Don's outrage, but his son? Surely not...

"It is true, Angelo. Your Vittorio has been found in disgrace with the Irish baggage who Giorgio set to work cleaning his kitchen when she came begging for employment. How could I now let him besmirch my beautiful Rosa? He has dishonoured her! He has dishonoured *me*!"

The colour had drained from Angelo's face. He reached towards the other man, but stopped short of grasping his hand.

"Don Chiabatoni, let me talk to Vittorio, I beg you. He is a good

man – he will listen to his father! There will be no more of this relationship you speak of..."

Chiabatoni held up a hand for silence. "I know this, Angelo," he
said. "I have ensured this."

With the raised hand he gestured to the man behind him holding
the wicker basket. The silent man lifted the lid from the basket and
tipped its contents onto the floor.

There was a dull thump and a flash of red hair as the Irish girl's
head rolled across the floor.

Angelo could barely breathe as he murmured, "Vittorio..."

The Don stood. "Angelo, there are debts between our houses that
go back many, many years. I have convinced some of the more – hot-
blooded members of my family that your son should live. However it
would we best, I think, if he were to do so a long way away. Let him
pursue your business interests for you, but ensure he does so as far
from here as possible. It would be unfortunate if my boys gave way to
their passions."

The two large men behind him shifted slightly. The movement
was small but unquestionably menacing. Angelo gripped the edge of
his chair.

Chiabatoni continued, "Vittorio will find no friends, no allies in
this, my town. You know this."

Pasquale all but fell to his knees, gazing helplessly at a picture of
his son on a side table. In a voice barely more than a croak he said, "I
know this. It... it shall be as you say."

THE FIRST RAYS of the dawn just barely lit a small clearing in woodland in the craggy hills of Crete. An old stone building stood uphill a little way, its ancient walls seeming to absorb the thin light into their deep shadows. Ottoman soldiers, encamped in the woods, were stirring as they made ready for the day's action.

Not yet out of his teens, Orhan Keilbren looked troubled as he cleaned his rifle while talking to his much older comrade Kamal.

"How many more days can these Cretan rebels hold out?" the youth asked plaintively. "We have them hopelessly outnumbered!"

The veteran soldier shrugged. "Yes, but the walls of the Arkadi Monastery are strong. There may only be two or three hundred of them, but they are well armed. Our commanders believe there is much ammunition stored in there to sustain their fight."

"So we keep throwing our bullets and ourselves at their walls."

"As we are commanded to, yes." The old soldier sighed. "For myself, I would as soon burn the place to the ground. The monastery and all those in it! Then we'd be over this tiresome siege!"

The young man looked at him, shocked. "But there are women and children in there! Hundreds of them!"

The veteran shrugged. "Their choice. If they surrender they'll be spared. If they wish to stand alongside the rebels then they must be willing to fall alongside them. Come, Orhan, it will be our turn to throw our bullets at their walls shortly."

The attack was not long in beginning. Crouching in cover, Keilbren was still struggling to see clearly in the dim morning light. He could barely make out the shape of one of his Turkish comrades running from the doorway of the monastery, having just lit the fuse of a bomb.

Orhan joined in trying to provide covering fire, but as the bomber neared his line in the woods a Cretan bullet, fired from somewhere high on the stone wall, hit him. The young Turk dashed out into the exposed ground and grabbed his comrade. At a crouching run he carried the fallen man back towards relative safety.

Just as he reached the line of the woods the bomb exploded, throwing the two of them flat. For several seconds the young soldier could neither see nor hear. He shook his head to clear his senses, his first attention going to the wounded man he lay on top of. Unconscious but breathing, he realised with relief.

He rolled to one side and looked back up the hill. Ottoman troops were streaming into the gaping hole that had been torn in the stonework.

Inside the walls, an abbot looked fearfully across the courtyard as the Turks started to pour in, putting rebels to the sword as they came. He ducked back into the church, pulling a heavy door shut behind him.

The elderly man pushed through the women and children crowding the room, muttering prayers as he went, until he reached a smaller door in the opposite wall. He slipped through that, and made his way as rapidly as his shaking legs allowed down a winding staircase. As he went he pulled a burning torch from its sconce on the stairwell wall.

Breathing hard, he half staggered, half ran into the crypt. The vault was full of barrels. The abbot stopped for a moment. He crossed himself and looked upwards. Maybe it was to heaven, or maybe it was to the rebels, or the Turks, or to the innocents he imagined screaming in the room above.

A prayer on his lips, he tore the cover off the nearest barrel. It was full of black powder.

Outside, Orhan had managed to get to his feet. He steadied himself, preparing to run and join his comrades fighting. He'd barely taken a step when the monastery was ripped apart by a massive explosion.

The youth fell back to his knees, holding his rifle limply in front of him.

VITTORIO PASQUALE SHUFFLED along in a line of people making their way onto a steamship. The ship was battered-looking but supposedly seaworthy, not that Vittorio cared very much. The events of the past few days had left him numb. So numb that his eyes barely registered the couple playing chess on a barrel at the dockside.

The woman, an attractive blonde perhaps in her late forties, looked a little pale and unwell, but was doing her best to hide it from her companion. She put down the chess piece she'd held.

"I believe, my gallant Cossack, that you are deliberately letting me win." Her accent identified her as English.

Her companion assumed an air of affronted dignity. "An Azov would never allow himself to deliberately lose, madam! You underestimate your own ability."

She smiled affectionately at him. "Hmm, I don't know about that," she said.

"Come, dear Christina!" he replied. "Did you not secretly learn much of the information that enabled your British navy and her allies to take Kerch? Information that the great "Intelligence Officer" Cattley took the credit for? He could not let a woman steal his precious recognition. Ah, but I know the truth." The Cossack smiled ruefully. "For was Gregori Volkoff not the source of some of that information?"

Christina squeezed his arm gently. "Had I known what the cost to you would be, I wonder would I have acted as I did? Especially as the capture of the city achieved so little. Sevastopol was still supplied with food and ammunition, which I'd thought to restrict."

He shrugged in response. "You were not to know the harvest of 1854 would be the best in a generation. And you *do* underestimate your efforts. It took nearly a quarter of our army just to protect those alternative supply lines. Deployed elsewhere, those 35,000 men could have turned the war in Crimea."

She laughed – a light cheerful sound that masked her illness. "Ah, that wonderful game 'What If?' Oh, *kotchinka*, so many what ifs. What if you'd not forgiven my betrayal of your secrets, saved me from your commanders and fled west to Austria? What if Captain Gregori

Volkoff of the Azov Host hadn't been such a fine soldier that whatever army he chose to join wanted his services so badly they accepted his wife as part of the package?"

Ex-Captain Volkoff returned the smile. "His darling and resourceful wife, whose skills won respect of their own..."

"What if our luck had failed in any of our narrow escapes in so many battles, so many wars, over twenty years?"

He took his wife's hand in a firm but tender clasp. "Then we would have died as we have lived for those twenty years. Together. I made my choice, Christina, as you made yours, and I have never regretted it."

"Nor I, my love, neither have I. I'm just tired. Tired of the fighting. Thank you for agreeing to this new start. A new land, a land of golden opportunity they're saying."

"We will make our own opportunity, *kotchinka*. We have our last souvenirs of our one last battle to parlay into that opportunity. But as you say, not with the fighting. Not any more. Come, we must gather our belongings and board the vessel. Oh, and Christina? Checkmate."

THE SUN BEAT down from high overhead on a sandy beach in a small cove, fringed by low scrub and mangroves. It was in the far north of the colony of Queensland, although nobody within days' march of this spot would likely have recognised the name.

It was the hour of day when even the birds were quiet, trying to shelter from the worst of the heat.

A man groaned. He was battered and bruised, lying amongst a tangle of fishing line and bamboo. He was a Makassar, and for years he'd plied his trade as a fisherman in the waters north of Australia.

He opened his eyes, groaned again and shielded them from the sun. He rolled over, and gingerly made it to his knees. Muttering under his breath, he started to explore among the tangled mess around him, probing with long fingers until he located two very specific lengths of bamboo.

One was a flute – the man played a few experimental notes and grinned broadly at the realization that the instrument was intact. The other object was a blowpipe. He didn't test this, but gave it a thorough examination until he was satisfied it was undamaged.

Next, he rummaged and searched until he located a small parcel wrapped in a broad leaf. He unfolded it carefully. It held darts for the blowpipe. His expression changed to a frown. The seawater had ruined many of the darts. He carefully examined all of them, preserving those that looked like they may still have a smear of poison on their tip. These he carefully rewrapped in the driest portion of leaf.

With a heavy sigh he got to his feet. After looking wistfully out to sea for a moment, he turned and started to trudge painfully toward the shelter of the bushes.

Three dark tribesmen stepped from the cover, holding spears. The fisherman stopped – between the sun's glare and his injuries, he hadn't noticed the men as he would normally have expected to. By their posture, the natives were clearly tense, if not actually threatening.

The fisherman instinctively went to bring up his blowgun, but thought better of it. Instead, he grinned broadly and opened his palms towards the men. He spoke in Yanuwa - a native dialect he had some experience of.

"Greetings!" he said. "I mean you no harm. I want you to mean me no harm. My name is Asbul."

The three men were clearly surprised at his speech. They were struggling to understand him, although by their faces it was clear that they could make out at least some of what he was saying.

"Asbul," he repeated, and then spoke more slowly. "I am Asbul. No harm you. No harm me." He reinforced his words with gestures, carefully gauging their reactions. "I know a little of your language, or something like it. I fish in the waters that way." He pointed north. "For years I have regularly traded with a couple of different families somewhere... ah... that way, I think."

He pointed along the coast to the west. He grumbled to himself in his own language, "It might help if I had a better idea of where I am..."

One of the tribesmen addressed the fisherman. The dialect was similar, but far from identical. "This tribe, we are Kuthant. We also trade with men from that way," he said, repeating Asbul's gesture of pointing northwards.

"If you are a trader, where are your wares?" asked another of the spearmen.

His two companions looked at him disdainfully. The one who'd spoken first admonished him, "Look at the mess. It's obvious the fisherman has been wrecked."

Asbul was able to follow some of their exchange.

"Not wrecked," he said. "Attacked. I was attacked by pirates."

The three Kuthant looked at him blankly.

"Pirates... um... bad men on the water. They left me to drown as my boat burned. Maybe I can make it home with some other trader from my own islands. Are you returning to your – umm – trading place?"

The first of the Kuthant speakers introduced himself as Karumbari. "We won't return for some time yet. We left a while ago, and are well along the walkabout track that will eventually take us back there."

Like a number of the Aboriginal tribes, the Kuthant were wanderers. Not nomads who walked randomly from place to place as conditions required, but following a trail that had been reprised for generations. They gathered goods as they travelled, following growing and breeding seasons across many miles of country in a circuit that extended from the Gulf of Carpentaria down to an area near the banks of the Darling River.

The fisherman and the three tribesmen squatted together on the beach, drawing pictures in the sand and talking, as best they could.

Asbul scratched his head and said in Makassar, "This is no good. I'm used to navigating by sea, and they navigate by land. Our reference points are too different." In Yanuwa he said, "About the best I can work out is that it's a long way, and dangerous to try to go on my own, eh?"

Karumbari nodded.

The fisherman thought for a few moments then asked, "Can I travel with you? Eventually we'll come back to a point where I should meet some of my own people. Or maybe we'll run into some other group or tribe who are heading in the right direction before you do."

Asbul grinned his wide toothy grin. This time it was answered in kind by the three Kuthant tribesmen. As they relaxed and finally lowered their spears more of the tribe slowly started to emerge from the mangroves. The fisherman looked about and smiled at his new adopted family.

~

THE WARMTH of the mid-afternoon was radiating back up from the soil of a vegetable garden in a southern part of China.

Li Wei Sun knelt amongst the rows of plants. He had been carefully removing burnt and damaged leaves from the cabbages, but had stopped when his father Li Xuedong had come out to lecture him. Although the older Li stood over him, doing his best to loom threateningly, Wei Sun showed no sign of being intimidated or compromised.

He glared up at his father and snapped, "I have no interest in going to Australia! I have no interest in scraping for gold!"

The older man matched his glare. With contempt in his voice he replied, "You have no interest in anything except your plants! For five years – more! You have no interest in anything. You were a good soldier, Wei Sun. You provided well for us!"

"And you know what happened."

"Yes, yes. You have told the tale so many times. You rode into Nanjing and saw nothing but death..."

"One hundred thousand people, father. Men, women, children. Dead by their own hands rather than face our army!"

The old man was implacable. "That is to their shame, not yours. You did not kill them."

"No," said Wei Sun bitterly. "They died from their fear of us. And with good reason. The troops I rode with – the 'loyal' Chinese Qing and foreign mercenary alike – when they saw that there was no one left in the city for them to kill they turned their violence on those who lived in the nearby villages. Was this what it means to be a soldier? A warrior? To be a rapist, a murderer, a thief?"

Li Xuedong looked at his soldier with a mix of disapproval and disbelief. "To be a soldier is to follow orders! Such is the way of war. And to be paid – well paid, to provide for your family. Look at us now, Wei Sun – what sort of life do we have? The proud family Li – relying on your vegetables." The last word dripped with contempt.

The son remained unmoved. "Perhaps the money I made as a soldier would sustain us all still if you and Han were to gamble less, or better."

"Still your tongue!" snapped the father. "Your brother and I do our best to parlay your meagre contributions into something more substantial." He leaned down and narrowed his eyes, staring balefully at his son. "There is no argument. Our honoured ancestors present this opportunity to us. Your passage to this Cook Town has been arranged. I have made payment, and guaranteed the remainder."

"You had no right to..."

"I have every right! I am your father! You will honour me! You will obey me!"

Wei Sun bowed his head. It was the first time since the old man had come into the garden to make his announcement that he did not meet his father's eyes.

"You may command my obedience. You cannot command my honour."

Li Xuedong pursed his lips. "Then obey me. Go to Australia. You spend your time here scrabbling in the dirt. Go and scrabble in the dirt of the place where there is gold and wealth in the earth. When the debt to Master Wu is paid..."

"Who?" demanded Wei Sun.

"Wu. The fine man who has given you this opportunity."

"I thought it came from our honoured ancestors."

The older man ignored the wry interruption. "He must be paid to transport you and provide for you. To send men to supervise you."

The former soldier looked up at his father, at least skeptical. More frankly, he was deeply distrustful of his family's 'benefactor'. Xuedong ignored him.

"These things are expensive for Master Wu, but I have made this arrangement! To restore the Li family's honour and fortune!"

"And Han? What is his contribution to this worthy cause?"

"Your brother's place is here, to support me. You have experience of white men and their ways – you will manage there amongst them."

The gardener spat on the ground, subconsciously careful to aim between plants. "Experience, yes. Of the white mercenaries in the army of the Qing. The rapists, the murderers..."

"Again Nanjing! Well, so that is your experience! Learn from it. Be cautious. Hold to your honour. Remember that your first responsibility and loyalty is to your family. I no longer ask you to make me proud."

The younger man gave a contemptuous snort and replied, "No, you merely ask me to make you rich. You and Han and this Wu."

"Just so," answered his father with a decisive nod, before turning and walking away. He didn't even look back as he said, "You will leave on the day after tomorrow."

As he watched his father walk away Wei Sun grabbed a spade. For a moment he brandished it like a spear, then with a wordless snarl jammed the implement into the earth with force and feeling.

Six weeks had passed since Li Xuedong had issued his ultimatum to his son. Master Wu's boat wheezed its way past Cooktown harbour on its way to Sydney.

Already moored in Cooktown at just that moment was a steamer that had arrived from the south soon after sunrise. Most of the passengers had already disembarked. The wealthier among them were still assembling their belongings as they were unloaded.

Among that number was Quentin Johnson, a distinguished looking white man in his fifties. He leant on his cane as his household sorted their goods onto two wagons. His wife, who in turn was closely watched by their twenty-year-old daughter Pearl, more closely attended to the actual supervision.

The actual loading was being done by their twelve-year-old son Robert and the household staff. This was a team of three: the Asian cook Chung and two well dressed dark men – a tall young West Indian named Micah, and Adhilasa, an older fellow of distinguished African appearance.

While his family worked, Quentin counted out a handful of banknotes that he handed to one of the three businessmen standing beside him.

"You charge a high price for your wagons, Mister Dillon," said Johnson without rancour.

"Supply and demand, mate. Supply and demand. You look like you can afford it, anyway," replied Dillon with an eye on the wad of cash.

Quentin smiled a little wanly. "Appearances can be sadly deceiving, sir. I'm afraid the last outpouring of wrath and rainwater which the good Lord saw fit to visit upon our fair New Orleans has all but done for me and my family."

The three businessmen looked at him blankly.

"We were wiped out by floods. Not for the first time," the American explained.

The men nodded, now comprehending. Johnson's rather florid style of speech wasn't something they were used to.

One of them, Keith Cox, tried to cheer their customer up, suggesting, "Well, you'll make it up on the Palmer alright, mate. Plenty of gold there for anyone that wants to go get it."

"And there's plenty who do!" added Dillon.

Johnson nodded. "So I gather. It's that population that interests me, not so much the gold itself. My business is hostelry. There was a time when the Johnsons owned and operated the finest eating, drinking and entertainment facilities in the southern US of A."

"Sounds fancy, alright," admitted the third man.

"Yes sir, Mister Thomas. But one great storm too many has driven me and my loved ones to seek a new start in a new land."

Thomas was casting a surly eye on the activities around the wagons. He said, "You ought to be told, there's a lot of us here who don't take kindly to the idea of slaves."

That got a genuinely indignant reaction from Johnson. "Sir, those men are not slaves! They do an honest day's work for an honest day's pay!"

Cox gave the working men a suspicious look. "Yeah, well," he said, "I reckon you want to watch the darkies around your womenfolk."

Johnson in turn gave Cox a withering glare, and in a cold voice said, "I trust those men implicitly. Young Micah – the Caribbean lad there - has grown up with my Pearl since his own poor mother died. That's when I took Chung on as a cook in her place. I've raised the boy like my own – he's a bright young man. He already does much of my bookkeeping for me. I hope my young Robert turns out as well as he grows up."

Thomas was still dubious. "I thought your side fought for slavery in the War?"

The American stood tall. "Sir, I ask you, is every man in this country a convict?"

"Of course not!" said Thomas defensively.

"Then kindly do not assume that every man south of the Mason Dixon line supports that vile trade in human flesh! I, and many like me, have taken it upon ourselves wherever possible to assist the unfortunate. Purchase their freedom. Offer real employment for them as wants it."

"That sounds fair," Thomas admitted.

"I hope so, sir, I truly do. Look at Adhilasa there. Stolen from his family in Africa as a boy. Sold off to work in one of the sugar plantations in Barbados. When he grew into a tall strong man he was sold again to a ship's captain. Travelled the world, learned to read and write. He managed to jump ship, as they so prosaically put it, when docked in New York."

Johnson was a born storyteller, very much in the Mark Twain mould. The three Australians were captivated by his story.

"Hang on," said Cox. "New York? Didn't you say you were from New Orleans? Are they the same place?"

Quentin chuckled and replied, "No sir, they are not. New York has its own sorry history. Two hundred years ago New Amsterdam, as it was called then, was home to one of the largest slave markets of any Dutch colony in the world. Time has not healed all of those wounds, and when the War Between the States became a sad reality there were plenty of volunteers from the black population of New York to fight for the Union cause. Adhilasa was one of those proud volunteers."

Just at this point Adhilasa walked over to stand quietly beside the little group. As his employer briefly paused for breath he spoke, "Mister Johnson, we're just about loaded, sir. Are you ready to take your leave of these gentlemen? I don't believe the day will get any cooler for us to travel in."

Quentin smiled benignly and threw a genial arm around the black man's shoulders. "Soon enough, Adhilasa, soon enough. These good folks have expressed an interest in your story."

The African looked slightly puzzled, and amused as he asked, "My story?"

Dillon nodded enthusiastically. "Yeah. Your... boss here was telling us you went off to fight in the Union army. What happened?"

"Nothing good, sir. I was part of a group led by a man more fond of hard liquor than he was of his men. At Petersburg we were attempting to rescue a division of men - black and white, pinned down in the massive crater of an exploding mine. Our commander, I later learned, was hiding in a bomb shelter with a bottle of medicinal rum. The Confederates had regrouped their rifles and cannons and drove us into that damned pit. Four thousand brave men died that day. Most of those left had little choice but to surrender. I suppose I was lucky. Plenty of black soldiers were shot out of hand under such circumstances. The officer facing us decided that would be a waste of valuable property, so we 'nigros' were rounded up and sent off to be sold. Again.'"

The three Australian businessmen looked suitably stunned, perhaps as much by Adhilasa's erudition as the story itself – a story that Johnson now took up again.

"And it was on a slaver's block in Louisiana that I found him. I looked in his eye, heard some of his story as the peddler in human misery told it, and knew that this was a worthy man. I paid the price that was asked, and offered Adhilasa the freedom to follow whatever path he saw fit. To my undying honour, he chose to remain with me. He's been my strong right arm at my establishments as my own health has, well, declined somewhat."

Johnson brandished his cane, a little wistfully before fixing a steely look on Cox and continuing, "And he has been a powerful good influence in the upbringing of my children. *All* of them. "

Clearly the remark about 'watching the womenfolk' had hit a nerve. Dillon, determined to look like the community leader he aspired to be, grasped Quentin's hand and shook it firmly.

"Welcome to Cooktown, sir. Welcome to our country," he said.

With only a bare moment of hesitation he turned to Adhilasa and extended his hand.

"And the same goes for you."

The distinguished African gave a small nod and smile, and shook the proffered hand.

~

THE SETTING SUN created long shadows across the small clearing. It was a small area in the bush a little way off one of the main tracks out of Louth. Their team of horses securely hitched to a nearby tree, James Arnold and Magpie were setting up camp for the evening. Their well-loaded wagon sat at the edge of the clearing.

Silently an Aboriginal man stepped from the trees leading his own horse. Magpie acknowledged him with a cheerful nod as the man began to assist them.

Arnold looked up and noticed him. "Ah – evening, Mundil," he said.

The tribesman readily accepted the contraction of his real name – Thonkumundil. He always found James' attempts at pronunciation funny, but liked the man too much to laugh openly at him. His English was rather better than Arnold's Burundji – the Balyarta people's dialect the tribesman spoke. The shortened version of his name was a good compromise.

Mundil often worked with the two horsemen. He was a good rider himself, which was unusual among his own tribe, and he enjoyed the men's company. The share of their income that they passed on to him had originally been immaterial to him, but he'd found that it was useful for providing some useful 'extras' for his tribe –food and basic medicines for emergencies. He resolutely avoided introducing his kinfolk to some of the more dangerous options – he felt a responsibility to protect those who didn't know what was bad for them. What they didn't know could hurt them.

"Want a bite to eat?" asked the white man.

Mundil lifted a haunch of wallaby from his horse and replied, "Brought me own. Want some?"

Arnold grinned. "Looks good! Hey, Magpie! You got a fire going yet? Mundil's brought tucker. Better than the tinned stuff!"

An hour or so later the three men were seated around the fire finishing off what had been a very satisfying meal.

Arnold stretched comfortably and said to Mundil, "You right to look after the horses and wagon for a bit while we ride back into Louth?"

"Sure," replied the native. "You going to the pub?"

Magpie grinned and said, "James been missing his woman again."

Arnold assumed as dignified air as he could muster and replied, "We are going because you and I could both do with a few drinks before we haul that load out to Wilson's station. Cattenach's beer might be only two cuts better than swill, but it's the best in town."

"And Rebecca might just happen to be there, eh?"

Arnold shrugged at his old friend's jibe. His action was non-committal but his smile revealed the truth.

Mundil though shook his head and looked concerned. "You two looking for another fight with Cattenach."

The half-caste shook his head emphatically and replied, "I don't go looking for no fights. I just want a quiet drink."

"Same here," said James. "And to enjoy the company."

Mundil looked unconvinced. "You know Cattenach don't want no blackfellas in his bar. He serve you cos your money's good – better'n a lot of the fellas he gets in there. And cos if he don't serve you, you break the place up. And anybody he gets to try to throw you out."

James and Magpie looked at each other with looks of injured innocence that would have fooled nobody, smiled and shrugged.

IT HAD BEEN a few hours since they'd left Cooktown for the goldfields of the Palmer River. After New Orleans the Johnsons thought they knew about heat and humidity, but this had been something quite different.

The two wagons were stopped at the side of the track. Adhilasa was tending to the horses of the leading wagon, in which sat Quentin, his wife and daughter Pearl. Micah had already alighted from the driving position of the second wagon. Chung was helping young Robert to the ground.

The boy was chattering excitedly. "Did you see the size of that butterfly? The big blue one? Wow! And the colours of some of those birds that flew past!"

His mother tried to smile as she squirmed uncomfortably on her seat. "Quentin," she said, "I really do think we should have waited to travel with some other folks. We may have been able to go at a more – ouch – leisurely pace."

Clearly the bouncing of the wagon along the rough track had been causing bruises in places that Mrs. Johnson would rather not talk about.

Her husband smiled sympathetically and said, "My darling, we might have left earlier and travelled with some of the folks from our own ship had you and Pearl not insisted on quite so much shopping before our departure." Although the words were critical, his tone was gentle rather than scolding. It was obvious that Quentin Johnson habitually indulged his family.

"Couldn't we have waited overnight, Daddy?" asked Pearl, who was only slightly less uncomfortable than her mother.

"Strike while the iron is hot, my darling girl!" he replied. "The sooner we arrive the sooner we can begin the grand adventure that will be the New Johnson Hotel! We'll start simple, but with quality! Real good entertainment. A decent standard of food and drink for our customers."

As he spoke, Quentin reached back and patted one of the barrels packed behind him.

Just then Robert caught a glimpse of movement among the scrub lining the track. He tugged on the cook's sleeve and pointed. Chung peered into the bushes, a worried look on his face.

His concern was well justified. From a spot several yards away from where he was looking a spear flew out of cover and lodged in Mrs. Johnson's breast. She was dead before she'd had the chance to make a sound. Sprayed with her mother's blood, Pearl screamed "Mamma!" and grabbed at the weapon.

Adhilasa rushed around the horses to see what was happening. As he did, Quentin stood, turning to reach for a rifle. His grasping hand never found its mark. A hail of spears erupted from the covering bush. One lodged in Pearl's side. Johnson was hit by several and fell dead among the pile of new provisions.

From the limited cover of the wagon Adhilasa reached up and plucked Pearl down into his arms. The girl was sobbing and mumbling incoherently. The words "Mamma... Papa..." were all that could be made out.

Another hail of spears flew towards the second wagon, but Micah, Chung and Robert were already sheltered behind it. A dreadful cry from many voices arose from the surrounding bush – clearly the precursor to an attack. Adhilasa clutched Pearl as closely to himself as he could. Shielding her with his own body he made a crouching run to join the others.

Suddenly a crowd of black men burst from the scrub. They were Merkins – a small tribe who had been developing a fearsome reputation on the Palmer goldfields as savage cannibals. Having thrown their spears they were now armed only with clubs, short things of hard wood that they brandished as they formed into a rough semi-circle around their intended victims. They kept a careful distance back though.

The leader of the Merkin called to Adhilasa, recognizing the older man as a leader. "Why are you with these people? You are our colour! Let us have them, and the yellow man. You can go, or you can stay with us and feast well!"

It was probably a good thing for the man that Adhilasa didn't understand a word of what he'd said. Several of the tribesmen were giving puzzled looks to the two black Americans, reflecting their leader's thoughts.

Realising that he hadn't been understood, the Merkin leader gestured for Adhilasa and Micah to move away from the others. Adhilasa didn't take his eyes off the man. He gently laid Pearl on the ground, and then slowly started to walk towards the man who'd spoken to him.

The Merkin leader smiled. Several of his men licked their lips as they gazed at the children and at Chung. The flesh of Asian people had become a favourite delicacy among the tribe, much to the terror of the Chinese gold seekers and market gardeners along the Palmer River.

Adhilasa suddenly moved in a blur, catching the Merkin leader in a choke with his right arm. He turned, holding the man as a shield, clearly well positioned to break the tribesman's neck. One of the other Merkins moved to grab Adhilasa from behind. Spotting the movement, Chung drew a long carving knife from a scabbard at his waist and threw it. The man fell dead, probably not even knowing what killed him.

The cook moved quickly to retrieve his knife then stand protectively over the now silent Pearl. Several of the tribesmen took a wary step or two back. Others were still looking at Micah and Adhilasa in bafflement.

One shouted at Micah, "You there! And the old one – what's wrong with you? Don't protect them!"

The Merkin leader tried to speak, but the grip on his throat was so tight he could barely gurgle.

Tears in his eyes, Micah stood so that his body shielded Robert. He reached into the second wagon and pulled out a repeating rifle for himself, and a pistol that he handed to the boy.

Several of the Merkin rushed at the leading wagon, dodged the flailing hooves of the frightened horses and smashed the wheels with their clubs. It collapsed at such an angle that even had the defenders been able to scramble onto the second wagon there was no room for them to maneuver an escape.

Adhilasa shouted, "I don't know if you can understand me, but I want you to back off. Otherwise I swear I will tear this man's head off!"

His words were mysterious to the Merkin but his meaning was clear. Several of them shouted defiant responses. Half a dozen of them tried to rush Chung. More were about to follow when Micah opened fire, cutting down several of them. That frightened a few into backing off, but others continued to advance, more warily. A few hurled their clubs, achieving nothing more than disarming themselves.

Dodging one of the thrown clubs, Robert ducked under the wagon behind Micah. The boy fired a few shots out past Micah's legs. One of the Merkin fell, a knee shattered by the lad's bullet.

The tribesmen who had approached Chung were regretting their adventure. One reeled away, his jaw smashed by a blow from the edge of Chung's hand. Two more had their faces, arms and chests slashed by the carving knife in the cook's other hand while another writhed on the ground after a mighty kick that ensured he would never father children.

One small group of Merkins had crept around behind the rear wagon – the one that was still intact. Two of them dived under it, trying to reach Robert. The boy turned in time and managed to shoot both attackers, but the momentum of their lunges carried their bloodied bodies towards him. Robert crawled backwards in panic, trying to disentangle himself from their arms.

Several of the Merkins grabbed the side of the wagon and tried to tip it up. The horses reared and kicked in their harnesses. With a terrible groan the axles snapped and wheels collapsed. The air was torn by a terrible scream as the wagon crashed down onto Robert.

The whole scene descended into hellish chaos. With a guttural cry Adhilasa snapped the Merkin leader's neck. He swung the man's body like a club at other attackers, finally hurling the corpse headfirst into the face of an advancing cannibal. The former soldier lunged, grabbing two more tribesmen, one by the throat and the other by the hair. He slammed their heads together, fracturing both skulls before either man could effectively use a club.

Micah stood with his back to the wrecked wagon, almost blinded by tears as he fired the rifle wildly. From the ground near his feet Chung scooped up Robert's pistol and another from the debris, then fired over the wagon into the group who'd caused the collapse.

As Adhilasa reeled, gasping for breath, one of the Merkins grabbed the body of their fallen leader and started to drag it away. Two more rushed to help him with the corpse.

Just as suddenly as they'd appeared, the surviving Merkins seemed to melt back into the bush. A few bullets were fired after them.

After the conflagration the sudden absence of noise was eerie. Micah and Chung stared into the silent trees. Adhilasa knelt beside Pearl. The others looked down at him, but he simply shook his head. Micah started to weep uncontrollably. The cook laid a gentle hand on his shoulder. Adhilasa stood and embraced the young West Indian.

Chung stepped away, and warily stared in the direction where the Merkins had fled. For a while the only sound was that of Micah's sobbing.

Eventually Chung spoke, without turning his watchful gaze away from the bush. "What do we do now?"

Adhilasa drew himself upright, fighting to regain some composure. "First, we give our loved ones a decent burial. We do not leave them for those heathen savages to despoil in any way. Then we see what we can carry away from our supplies. The wagons are ruined, but at least we have horses."

The West Indian struggled to pull himself together, following the older man's example. "And then?" he asked.

The former slave squared his shoulders and pointed down the track. "Then we follow the road laid out before us, my friends."

~

Bob Cattenach's bar in Louth was one of the roughest elements of a rough town. The structure itself was little better than a slab hut, the clientele were mostly either the rough end of the town's population or new arrivals who didn't yet know any better, and the publican himself was a dishonest rogue. All that kept him from being recognised as an outright villain was the innate cowardice that prevented him from actually getting his own hands dirty.

There were several customers this evening, mostly seated at various tables around the single room. Magpie sat at one table on his own, reading a newspaper. At a nearby table James was deep in close conversation with a middle-aged blonde woman.

She was still attractive – more striking than pretty, but there was an air of weariness about her that no amount of cosmetics could successfully mask. Her figure was still good, and the dress she wore fitted snugly in some places and gapped enticingly enough in others to emphasize that fact. Her make-up and outfit left little doubt as to her occupation.

Bob Cattenach was standing behind his bar, engrossed in furtive conversation with three surly men. One of them was the dock labourer Lewis Heath. He was flanked by his very large brother Norman and a scrawny ferret-faced individual named Kev Seiman. All four cast frequent glares toward Magpie and Arnold.

If James was aware of their attentions he gave no indication of it, deeply engrossed in conversation with the woman Rebecca.

"James, do we have to have this conversation every time you come into town?" she asked in low tones.

"It's not every time!" he protested.

"It feels like it! Look, it doesn't matter how much I... care about you. I have to work here. I have to live, I have to eat, I have to have a roof over my head and a bed under my arse."

Arnold's voice was quiet but plaintive. "Rebecca, all I'm asking is..."

She cut him off sharply. "All you're asking is for me to 'take a night off' every time you're in town. It's not that bloody simple! I get seen spending a whole evening with you, word gets around I work for free with you, and next every bastard will expect it!"

"It's not like that!"

"You might know that, and I might know that, but no one else does." She sighed and placed her hand on his arm. Her voice was very quiet. "You're a good man James Arnold, I know that, and you know that I know. I'll see you later on, when the bar's closed, back at my place. But here, on my territory, you've got to respect my position. You get up and go back to your horses and your black mates and your sleeping under a tree, but I've got to stay here in this town."

"We could get..."

"James!" she interrupted him sharply again. "Do not ask me that again! What would it change? I can't live rough the way you do. You can't afford to keep me. Everyone in Louth knows who I am and what I do. My job is my choice, and frankly, I'm good at it."

In spite of himself, Arnold grinned. He knew she was right. Rebecca patted his hand and said, "I'll see you tonight," before getting up and walking to another table, where she coquettishly sat down beside a man who'd arrived on the previous day's boat.

The publican removed a rum bottle and several tumblers from in front of the three men at the bar and gave a nod towards Magpie. Rebecca had taken the newcomer by the arm and was leading him out of the bar. As she left the Heath brothers and Kev made their move.

Led by the lumbering Norman, the three stood between Magpie's and Arnold's tables.

Lewis glared down at James and said, "John Rourke's shoulder's still a mess. He still ain't able to come back to work."

The horseman looked up and asked casually, "Who's John Rourke?"

"Man you shot a few weeks back, remember?" snarled the smaller Heath.

James nodded slowly. "Ah yeah, I remember something about him. Suppose he won't be waving a gun around with that hand for a while then, eh?"

"He won't be working for a long while, neither!" snapped Lewis.

Magpie finished his drink and looked up from his paper. "Long enough to learn his lesson, maybe?"

Lewis turned on his heel to face him. "You know Mister Cattenach doesn't like darkies in his bar."

The half-caste looked Lewis squarely in the eye, but only shrugged. The docker jerked an angry thumb over his shoulder to the big man behind him.

"This is my brother Norman. Just come into town. He doesn't like sharing a bar with darkies, either."

"I just don't like darkies at all, Lewis," growled the ox-like figure, who then turned toward James. "I don't think much of darkie lovers, either."

"Neither do I," added Kev as he reached behind his back.

Cattenach called out from the bar, "Oi! Kev! No guns inside the bar, I said!"

Seiman smiled as he produced a knife from his waistband. It was a nasty-looking knife and a nastier-looking smile. "No guns here, Mister C."

Before the ratty man could do anything with the blade Magpie pulled a boomerang from his boot and clubbed hard on Kev's wrist. The sharp weapon clattered to the floor.

With a snarl Norman lunged at Magpie, but the horseman was far too quick for him. He jumped from his chair and landed a series of hard punches with both hands to the big man's face.

Lewis bent down and grabbed Arnold from behind, wrapping his arms around him to pinion the horseman to his chair. James surprised him by not struggling. The two of them watched Magpie and Norman circling each other warily. Kev stood to one side, clutching his wrist and moaning.

Norman took a few wild swings. One of them caught Magpie's shoulder a glancing blow – just enough to knock him slightly off balance. The half-caste dodged around a vacant table to put a bit of distance between himself and the much bigger man.

Taking advantage of the distraction Arnold snapped his head

back, cracking his skull hard into Heath's mouth. Lewis fell away, spitting blood and broken teeth. The horseman spun up out of his chair and finished the job with a thumping right hand to the jaw.

The other patrons were backing up and keeping as well clear of the fight as they could. Norman had gotten tangled with a chair as he'd tried to reach over the table to grab Magpie. That gave the smaller man the opportunity to dart forward and unleash another flurry of punches to the face.

The big man reeled backward, bumping into Seiman as he passed. Wincing but angry, Kev made a grab for Magpie's face and eyes with his good hand. The dark horseman planted one hard blow into the pit of Seiman's stomach, doubling the man over and dropping him to his knees.

It was a lucky landing for the ferret faced man – he'd gone down within easy reach of where his knife had landed. He reached for it with his good hand. Then Arnold stomped down hard, grinding his heel on Kev's fingers.

By now Magpie was landing blows at will. Norman staggered and reeled, finally tripping and landing awkwardly. He tried to crawl under a table for some protection, but couldn't squeeze his bulky frame into the space. Magpie shaped to kick the fallen man, but instead he gestured dismissively and walked away.

The half-caste casually went about resetting his table and two chairs, picking up the newspaper that had been strewn on the floor. Meanwhile Arnold strolled to the bar. He casually pushed a couple of coins across the counter.

"Same again," he ordered, sounding as though absolutely nothing out of the ordinary had occurred in the past few minutes.

The barman looked unhappy, but he took the coins and handed over the two beers. Without another word James carried the drinks to the table Magpie had set up. He sat down, and the two horsemen, smiling, raised their glasses in a wordless toast.

The other customers gradually resumed their seats, several of them sniggering quietly at how the hulking Heath brother had been well beaten by the much smaller Magpie. Nobody made their mirth obvious – Norman was too obviously furious and he was still, despite his battered features, a very big threatening man.

After struggling to his feet Norman Heath staggered to the bar, wiping a mess of blood and snot from his nose with the back of a beefy arm. Kev followed in his wake, moaning and trying to cradle both hands with a very dazed Lewis propped against his shoulder.

Bob Cattenach looked nervous. "Boys, I..." he began.

"Shut up!" growled Norman. "Gimme two bottles of rum. And don't you never ask for no more favours, right?"

Tight-lipped, Cattenach handed over the bottles. He didn't dare ask for any payment. The three men lurched out of the bar, a thin line of crimson still stringing from the big man's nose.

Magpie turned a page casually.

"Any good news?" asked his companion.

"You seen the age of the papers we get here? Mate, if there was, it's old news now!"

HOURS HAD PASSED. The Heath brothers were riding along a narrow rough track out of town. Both swayed unsteadily in their saddles. Lewis' face sported a large bandage around his jaw. Norman's was badly bruised, but not so much that he couldn't swig from the rum bottle he clutched.

"You sure this is the way to where the bastards live?" slurred the big man.

His brother's horse was slightly ahead. The smaller man looked back over his shoulder and said, "Blacks' camp is out here a bit further. I reckon that's where we'll find 'em." The bandage muffled his voice.

Norman growled, "I hate bloody darkies. And that little bastard got a cheap shot on me."

As he'd worked his way through the rum he'd convinced himself more and more that he'd been the victim in the exchange with Magpie. His brother knew better than to argue with him, whatever the reality of the situation. Wisely he just said, "Yeah, that's right, Norm. He did."

"Damn right he did! Then he bloody turned and walked away like I was a piece of dirt on the floor. They laughed. I heard the bastards laugh at me."

"No one laughs at you, Norm," said Lewis supportively.

"I heard 'em. The bastards in the bar – they was laughin' at me. 'Cause the little black bastard got a cheap shot in on me."

The brothers rode in silence for a while, Norman stewing in his own cocktail of rum and bitterness. Eventually the leading Lewis held up his hand, and pointed to a glow visible some way away through the trees. A campfire.

"There. Right where I said."

The two men dismounted as quietly as they could, although the larger man half fell off his horse.

"I thought these buggers moved round all over the place?" asked the big brother, whose knowledge of the 'darkies' he disliked was sketchy at best.

"This lot don't," replied Lewis. "Been here as long as the town, anyway. Like they own the place. Quiet, mate – they'll hear us."

"So? Let 'em! Reckon they own the place, huh? Soon fix that!"

Lewis was at least trying to move stealthily, creeping between the trees a little clumsily. His brother either couldn't or wouldn't make such an effort, crashing through the bush and then flinging his empty rum bottle ahead of him.

The clearing that the Heath brothers were approaching had been home to the Balyarta – Thonkumundil's tribe - for a few years. As Lewis had alluded to, they were not one of the nomadic types of tribes, preferring to settle in one place until circumstances like dwindling resources or aggressive intruders compelled them to move on.

The brothers' clumsy approach could hardly have gone unnoticed by the alert Balyarta. The tribespeople were aware that they were unpopular with some elements in the town. It hadn't yet come to much, but they knew enough to live cautiously. Hearing the approach of the white men and the hostility in their voices, several of the Balyarta men were rousing their families, moving them out of their bark shelters and into the cover of surrounding bush. One man grabbed a fallen branch that was still well endowed with leaves and rushed over to the fireplace, intending to beat out the flames.

He didn't get there in time. Norman burst into the clearing at a staggering run, two pistols drawn and firing wildly. And not firing into the air. The tribesman by the fireplace fell dead. One of the women shrieked and reeled into the cover of the trees clutching at her shoulder. Others fell, or continued fleeing wounded.

Lewis stepped into the clearing at a much more deliberate pace than his brother. He held an old shotgun at his hip. Its blast brought more shrieks from fleeing Balyarta as pellets struck home. The white man muttered at the inconvenience of having to reload while his beefy brother emptied his pistols into the darkness of the woods.

By the time the shotgun was ready and Norman had started to fumble for more ammunition of his own, the clearing was empty of any life but the Heaths.

"Did you see the little bastard?" demanded Norman.

"Nah. Nor the white one, neither. Maybe they're not back yet."

The big man gave an ugly grin. "Gonna get a surprise when they get here then, eh? Bugger!"

He'd dropped all of his ammunition. He cursed again when he realised that between the darkness and Cattenach's rough rum his grasping fingers couldn't find any of it.

His brother was starting to look nervously into the darkness of the surrounding trees. "Come on mate, hurry up!" he said. "One shotgun ain't much use if they start chucking spears from where we can't see 'em. I reckon we oughta get going."

"Bugger that! I want to wait for them two from the pub!"

The smaller man was clearly losing his nerve. He was marginally less drunk than Norman. He started to back up, the way he'd come.

As he moved he said, "If you want a few of them big pointy sticks between yer ribs that's your look-out, mate. I'm heading back into town."

Norman spent a few moments groping in the dirt for his bullets. He looked up, looked around, and realised that being left alone in the dark as the fire dwindled really wasn't a good idea.

Muttering profanities he hauled himself to his feet and staggered after Lewis.

As the fire died down, the clearing was left quiet and bereft of life.

∼

IT WAS JUST PAST DAWN. Sitting at the dock at Cooktown was a run-down steamship that had limped and wheezed its way there from Italy, with a passenger load of desperate people. Most of them had spent something close to the last of whatever they owned to risk the journey to a place that they knew little about. It was the other end of the earth, and it had gold. For many of them, the chance was enough.

Vittorio Pasquale had met and befriended the Volkoffs during the voyage. He and Gregori were very carefully assisting Christina ashore, one man on either side of her. The Englishwoman was so sick she could barely walk. The men's eyes met over her head as they supported her down the gangplank. Vittorio shook his head sadly. The Cossack could only shrug resignedly.

With great care they guided Christina to a rough seat in the shade of one of the dock buildings. Gregori squatted beside his wife. Pasquale tactfully stepped away.

Volkoff leaned in close to his wife and quietly asked, "How do you feel, beloved? This has been a terrible journey for you."

Christina managed a weak smile. "And to think, when we met I'd just sailed through the Strait of Kerch in a rotting English warship which made that vessel look like a floating palace!"

"The English do not know how to treat women," said Volkoff grimly.

His wife looked for a moment as though she was going to argue, but clearly didn't have the strength. Instead she mustered another smile and replied, "Not like a gallant Cossack captain I know."

The ex-captain responded with a small bow, his grim demeanour softening only slightly into mere seriousness. "I must see to unloading our goods, such as they are. Please be safe."

"I'll be fine here. You've brought me out of the worst of the sun. You go and take care of things, especially our – French package."

For the first time in what seemed like a long while, Volkoff wore a small smile as he answered his beloved. "After all that we have endured obtaining them, bringing them here, you may be sure of that. They are our currency. Our best and only currency, even here."

"Until we find gold, my love. Only until then. And then, no more guns. No more weapons, no more war."

"No more war. Yes..."

There was no more certainty in Gregori Volkoff's voice than in his mind or heart. He had been a soldier since his teens. Wars, many and varied, were what he knew. His beloved Christina had been at his side for twenty years of them, her charm and agile mind a fine foil for his tactical skill. They'd both made a career out of overcoming the odds, but it was military matters they understood. What else did they – he – truly know how to do?

His wife, it seemed, had no such qualms. She grabbed at his arm, gripping with such little strength as she could muster. "With gold, you can stop being a soldier, Gregori. You are not so young any more. *We* are not so young. It's time to find better things. To enjoy the rest of our lives. Do something good!"

The Cossack gently stroked the hand grasping him until, eventually, her fingers relaxed. Whether that was the result of his tenderness, or her exhaustion, was impossible to say.

"Yes, my Christina. It shall be as you say. Wait for me here, please."

With a wry smile that said more eloquently than words that she had little choice but to sit and wait, she nodded, then watched her husband walk back to the boat.

With long strides he crossed the gangplank leading up from the dock to the deck. As he boarded, he saw the Italian, Pasquale, leaning on a handrail and watching him. The Cossack opened his mouth to speak, but Vittorio got in first.

"It is not the *male de mare* – the sickness of the sea. You know that, don't you, my friend?"

"Of course. The Azov Cossack Host are sailors, as well as soldiers. I do not know what disease it is, but I do know that it is not seasickness which is taking my beloved from me."

The Russian leaned on the rail beside Vittorio, both men staring straight ahead, looking through, rather than at, the building by which Christina sat quietly.

"It may have struck during our long voyage, but I think that timing is only coincidence. I have seen disease spread like wildfire throughout a village, but this sickness, it seems to have travelled no further than your wife. I feel that this – this is something that has come from within. Perhaps..."

"Where it has come from is of no importance. It has come," Volkoff interrupted, not releasing his grip of the railing. "And it shows no sign of going. Thank you for your companionship. Your help. You and our musical friends, the *Senors* Buitrito, have made this journey something more bearable." His nose wrinkled, and he turned to look back across the deck. "Speaking of whom..."

His acute sense of smell had caught the distinctive spicy whiff of a scented pomade. Approaching them were two broad-shouldered men, their familial link obvious in the features of their tanned faces. Faces so weathered that it was really only the colour of their thick manes of hair: glossy black and silvery grey, that clearly distinguished the ages of father and son.

The two men each bore one end of a large steamer trunk. The younger man, Cristiano, grinned broadly at the Italian merchant he'd befriended, and called, "*Hola, amigo!*" He indicated the trunk. "Our costumes. Senor Johnson's Hotel will see us at our splendid best!"

His father, Guillermo, however, saw the expressions on the faces of the two men at the handrail. He hissed through his teeth, "Cristiano! *Silenzio, stupido!*"

Putting down his end of the trunk and motioning for his son to do the same, he addressed the two sombre figures, "It is the woman, yes? Signora Christina? Her condition is worse?"

The former soldier shrugged, without making eye contact. The merchant nodded sadly and replied, "Very much so, yes, Guillermo."

"I'm so sorry..." the younger Buitrito began, but his father cut him off with a gesture.

They took up the trunk and made for the gangplank. As they passed the others, Guillermo laid a brief consoling hand on Gregori's shoulder. Cristiano opened his mouth to speak but was silenced by a movement of his father's head.

The musicians descended to the dock, followed off the boat by the two men they'd befriended.

The group were watched keenly by a trio of businessmen, eagerly awaiting their opportunity to swoop. Dillon, Cox and Thomas were honest enough men, but experience taught that new arrivals in Cooktown were the best prospects. The longer a man stayed in the region, the less funds he was likely to have to spend. There was money to be made at the Palmer River goldfields, but it was hard-won, and eluded many. The reliable profits lay in servicing those optimistic miners at the outset of their efforts. The supplies and provisions offered by these three men were at least of good quality, which was more than could be said for some of their competitors.

The younger Buitrito, swept up in the excitement of arrival, was enthusiastically making plans as the little group placed their baggage on the ground together. "We all travel together, yes? We have instruments and costumes to carry to Senor Johnson's. Father and I will need a wagon anyway. You, Senor Pasquale, you too have much to carry. And the lady should travel in as much comfort as we can offer. Between us, I am sure we can afford something!"

The Italian merchant nodded, appreciating the sense of the young man's suggestion. The gesture was echoed by the Russian ex-soldier, who carefully laid down what he'd been carrying – a longish box securely wrapped in oilskins.

"I must go to Christina," he said. "I will leave – arrangements – to you."

Fetching up the box again, evidently reluctant to entrust it to the others, he strode off towards the shaded verandah where his wife sat.

"Well, that seems agreed, then," said Vittorio with a shrug. "Young Senor Buitrito and I will negotiate a wagon for us all." He turned to the older musician, and as if instinctively sensing where such responsibility could be safely entrusted asked, "Would you please stay here and keep an eye on everyone's property?"

"Si. As you say, of course."

An astute observer may have caught the barest hint of a reflex military click of Guillermo's heels as he answered the merchant.

That same observer may also have been struck by the way the musician stood with arms folded only loosely, his eyes alert, scanning all of the area around him, even glancing back towards the boat at times. The Spaniard missed nothing of the activity on or near the dock.

He saw Volkoff carefully lean his box against the wall beside his wife, and crouch to talk quietly with her.

He saw his son and the Italian merchant engage in earnest conversation with three men, evidently traders themselves. He nodded approval. There was an air of respectability about these three that was lacking in some of the others standing singly or in groups about the area. They weren't 'touting' for business like some of those, were well dressed without being flashy, and even at a distance he could tell that they met his son's gaze directly. A man's eyes told you all you needed to know about his character, a fact he'd spent years impressing upon Cristiano.

It was a lesson well learned, and Guillermo's son was pleased to shake the hand of the wagon dealer Dillon.

"Struck me as a bloody good bloke, that Mister Johnson. I reckon you'll do well working in his new place. Be a pleasure to give you blokes the same deal as I done him."

"Likewise," said Thomas, seller of tinned and dried foods (not Vittorio Pasquale's first choice of provender, but he was realistic about his new environment, he hoped). "You be sure to say g'day for us to him and – all his family."

If Thomas still harboured any misgivings about the Johnson's multi-racial assemblage, or the evident trust the hotelier held them in, he didn't utter them. This collection of Europeans would probably fit right on in with the Americans' open-armed attitude, he figured.

"Si, senor. With pleasure," agreed Cristiano, shaking the man's hand.

The young guitarist glanced over towards the Cossack, and with a worried nod of his head directed Vittorio's attention in the same direction.

Gregori had dropped to one knee, his wife's pale hand resting on his shoulder. It seemed clear she didn't have the strength to grasp as she might have liked.

Softly she was saying, "Sorry to be a burden, *kotchinka*."

"You are not, and have never been, a burden to me, beloved."

"How kind of you to say so, sir."

Even now, she was teasing him gently, playing the 'proper' Englishwoman to his gallant officer. He smiled in spite of himself – she could always find a way to lighten his heart.

Suddenly she gasped, but her smile widened as she did so. She was looking out over his shoulder, her eyes glistening.

"Gregori! I can see our gold!"

Volkoff turned his head to follow her gaze. The morning sun was a brilliant golden ball through the trees, coloured perhaps by smoke from fireplaces in some dockside premises. Pedantically he began to explain, "No, my dear. It is only…"

A little strength came into her hand and she squeezed his shoulder. "It is our gold, *kotchinka* – our gold." She sighed deeply. "Do some good," she said in a clear voice.

Then, smiling, she died, still gazing at the rising sun.

Guillermo stood rigidly beside the pile of belongings. He had seen enough death in his own life to recognize it immediately.

His son had less of the same sombre experience, but enough to also be aware of what had happened. He ran towards the couple, Vittorio instinctively following behind.

Volkoff stood, and with a gesture cut off their approach. He strode over to them, and laid a firm hand on the Italian's arm.

Calmly he said, "Signor Pasquale, I must arrange a burial. Would you do me the service of enquiring of the local gentlemen if there is a man of God in this settlement?"

Cristiano's mouth opened and closed ineffectually. He was unnerved by the Russian's reserve and matter-of-fact attitude.

In truth, Pasquale was similarly disconcerted, sharing more than a little of the Spaniard's emotional nature. But he was able to get out the words, "The beautiful signora – she is…?"

"A burial, *spaceeba*," Volkoff repeated quietly.

With difficulty, Vittorio reined his emotions under control. If this man could have the discipline to do what must be done for his wife, then he would do no less, to honour them both.

"Of course," he said. "A man of God...? Ah! A priest, yes! The lady – what was her faith?"

The Cossack officer looked back to where the body of Christina sat, her back against a wooden wall, her still-smiling face lit by the sun. "Her faith?" he repeated. "Considerable..."

A NEW ARRIVAL may assume that Louth was no more than a lawless backwater. The settlement sometimes gave that appearance, but it was, very definitely, subject to the laws of the Colony of New South Wales. And those laws were enforced, for the most part, as much as common sense and limited manpower would allow.

That limited manpower was a small company of native troopers under the command of two white men: John McCartney and Jack Walters.

Jack Walters was the wrong man for the job in many ways. A loner who expected the worst from everyone he met, and was seldom disappointed. McCartney as Sergeant, the 'officer-in-charge', quickly realized that Walters was best deployed as his out-rider, routinely patrolling the roads and tracks that wove around the fringes of the area under their authority.

In the town itself, Jack on a bad day could cause more trouble than he'd prevent. He'd really only joined the force for the money, and the prospect of working in solitude. The colour of a man's skin didn't matter much to him – he'd rather not have anything to do with any of the bastards.

McCartney was similarly inclined to not pay much attention to someone's skin tone so much as their behaviour. He wasn't a gregarious fellow, but he didn't avoid human contact. People could be interesting, even if many of them were ultimately pretty bloody aggravating.

He was better at his job than he gave himself credit for. Calm, measured, and wanting a quiet life for himself and his community. This, he reasoned, offered the best prospect of everyone living longer and happier.

This morning found him in his comfortably untidy office, engrossed in reading a lengthy, official-looking letter. Standing not quite at attention nearby was the native trooper who'd delivered the mail, widely known as Possum due to his apparently (deceptively) sleepy nature. If he was inclined to grin at his sergeant's irritated mutterings, he shrewdly restrained the impulse.

"A new Gold Warden? What do you want to send a Gold Warden

here for?" McCartney asked, apparently to the empty air. "Stupid question, McCartney – obvious someone's found gold nearby. News to me. Of course, it would be. Why would anyone tell me? I'm just the poor bastard who's supposed to keep 'law and order' around here. 'Law and order'. Equipped with a cupboard-full of clapped out muskets that should have been scrapped years ago, and a squad of black boys who couldn't shoot straight even if the guns could."

Possum didn't react, but the sergeant looked over at him anyway. "I'd apologise, Possum, if it wasn't true. Not your fault. I haven't the spare ammunition to train you. Or the time. Nor really the inclination, I suppose. At least you and your mates mean well. I think." He turned back to the letter. "So, I'm to keep this very quiet. Walters is to take 'greater responsibility' for this locality. That'll be fun for him, and every other poor bugger here. Meanwhile, I'm to trot up the road somewhere with this Warden Robertson and help him to 'establish a new settlement' – where? Hard Rock Creek? Where the hell is Hard Rock Creek? Possum – you heard of it?"

"No, boss. There's a creek a bit of a way north. Could be it. Never heard it called nothin', but."

"Anything to justify the name 'Hard Rock', do you know?"

"All rock's hard I reckon, boss."

The sergeant laughed. Possum was so straight-faced it was impossible to tell if he was joking, but McCartney was amused anyway.

Suddenly there was a knock at the door. At a gesture from McCartney, the trooper went to open the door while the sergeant folded up the letter and slipped it under his battered enamel mug.

In walked a dishevelled, dusty figure, untrimmed untidy hair, greying beard likewise. He could have been any sort of rough bushman, only the white collar about his faded and patched black shirt gave away his profession.

The bearded man scowled and leaned his clenched fists heavily on the Sergeant's desk. "There's a problem wi' the Balyarta," he announced, in a rich Scottish brogue.

"Good morning to you, too, Mister McGregor. A problem with the natives. Now that *is* a surprise. What have they done now?" The policeman was used to the preacher's customary rudeness, and knew better than to take it personally.

"Ye've never had a problem with the Balyarta, and well ye know it. They keep themselves tae themselves and bother no-one."

"Well, who is it that raids the stations outside of town? Who hides in the bush and chucks spears at passing riders? Who steals food off wagons after whacking the drivers?" asked McCartney levelly.

The Scot's scowl deepened as he replied, "I've told ye before. That's mostly they thieving Beeargahs. The Balyarta are by and large a quiet, settled people. The Beeargahs prey on them just as much, if not more than they do on our settlers."

McCartney sighed. "Mister McGregor, they all look the same to me. Fly like a crow, look like a crow, get called a crow. If you can tell them apart, then good luck to you. Now what's your problem? I'm busy," he said, waving the letter that had so discomfited him.

"They're gone."

"Pardon?" McCartney's eyebrows raised in genuine surprise. From the corner of his eye he noticed Possum's similar reaction.

The preacher explained. "I rode out tae their camp this morning. I've been bringing them the Word of the Lord, and a bit of flour and sugar and the like. This morning, the place was deserted. The camp-fires burned down, not kicked out as normal. The only people there were the dead yins in the trees."

"What?!" That sudden graphic image disconcerted McCartney.

"Dinna fash yerself - it's what they do with their dead. Set them up in a tree for the birds tae make a meal of. Disturbed me a bit when I first found out, too, but then I realized feeding crows was nae much different from feeding worms.

The bemused sergeant turned to his trooper. "Possum, is this true?"

Possum nodded. "Yes sir. Not for everyone, but some families."

Peter McGregor shook his head shortly to himself, getting back to his point. He had enough self-awareness to know that, as short tempered as he could be, he also was also prone to being distracted.

As patiently as he could, he tried to explain, "The Balyarta are a sedentary people."

The policeman looked at him blankly. Taking his fists off the desk, McGregor sighed as he stood erect. He realized that, like most whites in Australia, McCartney knew almost nothing about the people whose country they'd moved into.

"They dinna move around much. They stay in one spot. They hunt a little, and gather what they can, and grow things. Far as I can make out, they were camping on that spot long before this town was built, and had every intention of being there long after we're gone. They wouldnae up and go without being well pushed." He paused. "I think..." He leaned over the desk, closer to the sergeant, and lowered his voice to an ominous rumble. "I think some of they corpses were fresh."

If he was hoping for a sharp reaction, he was disappointed. McCartney appeared to be no more than mildly interested as he replied, "Well, you did reckon that other lot - whatever you called them - 'preyed' on them. Maybe it was one raid too many."

The Scot reached into his pocket and dropped a couple of spent bullets on the desk, saying in a low voice, "Beeargah dinna use guns."

McCartney shrugged. "Just about everyone else around here does, though. Look, Mister McGregor - I'm sorry you've lost some of your flock. My advice to you is to leave them alone and they'll come home, wagging their tails behind them. Or not. These people really are nomads when you get right down to it. Quite frankly I haven't the resources to check the movements of everyone in Louth to see if they've been making a bit of mischief among the blacks. If it keeps you awake at night, talk to Walters when I'm gone."

That brought the preacher up with a start. "You're leaving Louth?" he asked in surprise.

McCartney wearily waved the letter advising him of his new responsibilities. "For my sins, I'm to provide 'support and security' as a new settlement is established at Hard Rock Creek."

"And where might that be?"

"It might be on the moon as far as I know. Possum here thinks it may be a creek some way north of us. I presume our esteemed new Gold Warden Mister Robertson will enlighten me when he arrives."

Almost without thinking, McGregor crossed himself. "Gold, ye say? No good may come o' this."

McCartney grimaced as he replied, "I won't argue with you there. Bloody stuff causes nothing but trouble. The root of all evil, doesn't the Book say?"

"The love of money is the root of all evil," the preacher corrected. "It does have a powerful effect on men, aye."

"I must ask you not to repeat what I've told you, I'm afraid. Think of this office as a confessional, if you would."

The Scot nodded. "Aye, alright. The less folk as know the longer we might delay the troubles this'll surely bring."

The trooper frowned uncertainly as his sergeant shrugged and said balefully, "I hope you're right, padre."

A PORT the size and importance of Sydney receives a wide variety of traffic. Vessels, cargo and crew of many shapes, sizes and qualities. But surely at the bottom end of anyone's assessment of that range would have been the rusting, decrepit ironclad boat currently moored at one of the outlying docks.

This particular unsanitary scow was newly arrived from what was still called the Far East, despite its relative proximity to Australia.

Dubious as the quality of the cargo was, many of the crew were, frankly, far worse. The captain, Wu, was an unscrupulous villain. As far as Wu was concerned, the most worthless commodity on his vessel was the crew. He had a handful of trusty overseers – hard, experienced sailors, most of whom had been with him for years. The subjects of their 'discipline', undisguised cruelty for the most part, were the coolies who made up most of Wu's workforce.

A motley band, many of them were illiterate peasants or refugees from other fates. Wu gathered them up from whatever port he happened to be in. Their lives were cheap as far as he was concerned, and there was a high turnover of both deaths and desperate escapes.

On this steamy Sydney afternoon, the former farmer and one-time soldier Li Wei Sun was one of the gang sweating to unload a small mountain of heavy bales. The 'gold exploration' that Wu had described to Li Xuedong had been a total fabrication, designed to appeal to the old man's greed. Their work was supervised by two of Wu's henchmen – his long-standing enforcer Fang, and the recently-recruited former Turkish soldier Orhan Keilbren.

The heavy-set Burmese Fang, cutlass hanging at his waist and whip in hand, watched their labours with a mix of contempt and amusement. Standing a little way away, young Keilbren was paying less attention to the coolies' activities. Trembling and sweating profusely, he fidgeted nervously with the hilt of the katana he wore at his side. He too had a whip, but it was coiled and slung carelessly over one shoulder. He'd been known to use it, but seldom effectively.

A straggly procession of coolies was coming up from the hold through a wide hatch on the deck. Most had bamboo poles across their shoulders, heavily laden with baskets and bales of goods.

But among the mostly cowering labourers, one man was conspicuously different. He carried his burden with ease, and himself with
dignity. Lighter-skinned than most of his fellows, his complexion
suggested his mixed heritage almost as clearly as his name: Pierre de
la Fontaine.

While his bamboo pole bore a load as heavy as any of his
comrades, he also had slung over one shoulder something like a
bedroll – a coarse blanket wrapped and tied around an obviously
meagre collection of possessions.

Fang noticed the paler man, snarled and flicked his whip at
Pierre's shoulder.

"What that you carry?" he growled.

De la Fontaine stopped, and turning to look impassively at the
Burmese, replied simply, "My property."

"You were not told to bring your own worthless chattels on deck!
Your orders just to bring Master Wu's goods to shore! I will not stand
for this, Frenchman!" the burly overseer snarled, and cracked his
whip on Pierre's bare shoulder.

That barely provoked a flinch. Instead, the paler coolie inhaled
deeply, laid the bamboo pole and baskets down on the deck, and
calmly turned his back on Fang.

Infuriated, the overseer slashed his whip across Pierre's back.
Again, there was scarcely a reaction, the son of a Frenchman kneeling
to reach into his pack.

Quietly he said, "You know, Fang, I'm tired of listening to you
telling us what you won't stand for. I don't mind taking orders, but
you know - I really don't like bullies."

Ignoring another lash across his back, Pierre quickly stood and
turned, now wielding a dao – a fairly small but lethal Chinese sabre
he'd kept well-hidden throughout the voyage. A backhand slash of
the unexpected blade caught the whip and tore it from Fang's
surprised grasp.

The burly enforcer growled as he drew his cutlass, "You stinking
ex-soldiers, you make me sick. Think you're tough. Think you can
fight 'cause you learned to march in line..."

There was a smile on de la Fontaine's face as he advanced in a crouch. A smarter man than Fang would have taken a warning from that smile, even as the man with the dao said, "Actually, I don't think I can fight - I know I can."

The coolies started to drop their loads and gather around to watch the fight. Fang was larger than his opponent, and more aggressive. Like its wielder, the cutlass was the larger and heavier of the weapons. But the dao was in the hands of a much better fighter – faster and more skillful. De la Fontaine was dodging the slashes of the Burmese and had already inflicted several cuts of his own.

Uncertainly, the young Turk Keilbren took a step towards de la Fontaine. Approaching from behind, he silently drew the Japanese sword at his waist.

Before he could complete whatever action he might have contemplated, Li Wei Sun intervened, hurling a heavy bale at the youth. The clumsy missile struck the katana awkwardly, snapping the blade. Orhan and Wei Sun stared at each other, neither moving.

Pierre shot a quick glance to the Chinese coolie and called a grateful, "Thanks!" before dodging another slash of the cutlass. He dived and rolled under Fang's blade, then with a deft movement slashed the dao across the big overseer's bulging hamstrings, severing them.

Fang collapsed with a shrill cry, still clutching his cutlass but unable to move into any position to use it.

"Now you can really not stand for me!" said Pierre with a satisfied grin.

Dao still in one hand, he quickly snatched up his bedroll with the other. He could hear a commotion from the hold as more of Wu's trusties started to realize what had been happening.

Still grinning, he gave something like a salute to the man who'd assisted him, and said, "Time to be off, I think!"

Wei Sun didn't return the smile, but he came to a quick decision, nodded in agreement, and the two men sprinted down the gangplank onto the dock.

Young Orhan stared at the moaning Fang. Nobody had offered

any assistance, nor seemed likely to. Keilbren appeared to linger in an agony of indecision for a moment, then turned and ran down the gangplank after the two escapees.

A few minutes' sprint was enough for the two ex-prisoners to need to duck into an alleyway to catch their breath. There'd been no lack of labouring exercise on the boat, but neither had actually run for quite some time.

Offering a small bow, the Chinese man introduced himself. "Li Wei Sun."

The polite gesture was returned with a smile. "Pierre de la Fontaine." He extended a hand. "I think we can relax. I don't think Wu will regard us as worth so much time and money as to organize a chase."

His new compatriot nodded and bent to inhale deeply, replying, "Not when there are so many more who are less trouble."

As if on cue, the Turkish overseer ran into the alley.

"Of course, I could be wrong," Pierre said with a shrug, and moved to reach into his roll.

The young pursuer managed to gasp out the words, "Wait! I..." before Wei Sun hit him with a chopping blow that sent him flying.

Pierre began to advance on him, brandishing his dao. On his back, Keilbren tried to squirm away as best he could, palms raised.

"No! No! I'm not here to bring you back! I swear!"

Now there was a grimness to de la Fontaine's smile. "I don't think you'd have much chance of it, my friend."

The young man stammered, "I... I've had enough of Wu, and Fang, and the rest of them."

Wei Sun glowered at him and snapped, "So, why follow us?"

"I don't know! I guess... I guess I was inspired, watching you stand up to Fang - and me, when you thought I was threatening your friend."

Pierre's grin softened slightly. "Oh, so you weren't, then? You had your sword out to give it some air?"

"Yes. No. I don't know. I didn't know what to do. Fang's supposed to be my officer - I should help him, but I hated him!"

"You're no bad judge of character, then," conceded Pierre.

Orhan took a deep breath, trying to compose himself. "Wu hired me because I was a soldier, but Fang and some of the other overseers hated anyone with a military background."

That drew a contemptuous snort from Li Wei Sun. His father had made passing mention of Wei Sun's history to Wu. He may have found himself in a similar position to the Turk, but the elder Li had only spoken disparagingly of his son's 'lack of discipline'. He was only a disappointing commodity. And certainly, he'd kept his own counsel around the rogue, preferring to watch and wait, hoping for an opportunity to escape with some shred of honour intact.

"That's because they were pirates," he said bitterly. "Working for Wu is a less risky occupation for them, that's all. You were a soldier?"

The young Turk gathered himself together a little - not easy from his position on the ground. "My name is Orhan Keilbren. My former rank & regiment - probably don't matter any more..."

Pierre's smile had now lost much of its aggression. "And what are you running from, Orhan?"

"A Turkish soldier does not run! He..."

Wei Sun interrupted his protest. "Does not usually carry a katana. Does not seek employment in the waterfronts of Shanghai. If he is an honourable soldier he does not do the bidding of a creature such as Wu."

"How long have you been using the opium?" Pierre asked.

Keilbren was about to protest, but then looked away and said nothing.

"It's how Wu and his thugs kept you in line, isn't it?" de la Fontaine continued. "Fed your need, kept you desperate and obedient? You're not the only man it's ever happened to. How did you come to this? What happened to you?"

"I saw... something I couldn't face. I tried, but in the end, I fled Crete. I was going to go home, but could not face my family - the women and children of my village. I could not imagine seeing them without seeing those who died in that monastery. I travelled east. I worked where and how I could - I shoot well, and handle a sword well. Or at least, I did. But I couldn't escape the memories. They haunt my nights..."

Pierre sighed, and finished the young man's exposition for him. "And somewhere someone gave you something that dulled the pain and helped you sleep." At a slow nod from the Turk, he continued. "What now? You've just about reached the end of the earth, my young friend."

"I don't know. Following you was... an impulse. An instinct maybe. Where will you two go?"

"We two?" asked Pierre in some surprise.

Orhan shrugged and said, "I assumed you were comrades in arms. Wu told us you both fought in the army of the Qing."

"Really?" said Pierre, surprised. He and Wei Sun looked at each other. "I hadn't realized. I never heard you mention it."

Wei Sun replied in a low voice, "It is not something to make light conversation of. You, Turk, are not the only one to have seen - difficult things."

For once, the smile had disappeared from Pierre's face. Looking thoughtfully at the Chinese man he said, "You were at Nanjing. As was I."

Without a word or movement of warning, Li leapt at Pierre's throat, knocking the dao aside with his arm as he dived. Taken by surprise, Pierre fell and desperately tried to break the grip around his neck. They wrestled for a few moments. Orhan threw himself into Wei Sun's side and helped break his grip. Rolling clear, Pierre regained his dao and held it defensively.

"What the hell...?" he spluttered.

Wei Sun looked furious as he shouted, "You were one of those murderous mercenaries! The wanton Europeans who wreaked their shameful havoc on the villages! Used men for target practice! Used women for that and worse!"

Pierre didn't flinch at the hurled accusation. Calmly he answered, "I was a mercenary, yes, like my father before me. I was in such an army at Nanjing, yes! I saw the horrors that Hong Xiuquan's followers did to each other and to themselves. And yes, I saw what you saw outside the city walls. Do not presume to make me a part of it, though! I could no more stop it than you could. Certain individual acts, yes - I did what I could..."

"So you say now!"

"Look at me, man! Look hard! I have my father's name, but my mother was not French! No more than you!"

Wei Sun slumped slightly in Orhan's grasp. "Perhaps... I have wronged you."

"Oh, 'perhaps', you think. I sympathize with your anger, Li Wei Sun. Do not make me the object of it."

Chastened, the former farmer bowed his head. "I... am sorry."

The three men got to their feet, some of the tension dissolving. Pierre's smile reappeared.

"So, to take up Orhan's point - what do we do now?" he asked.

The other two looked at him in surprise.

"We?" said the Turk.

"If two heads are better than one, three must be better again, eh? Young Keilbren, I think you are a good man at heart. Whatever horrors you've witnessed, believe me when I tell you this man and I have seen their equal." He held up a hand to silence the interruption that he saw coming. "Nor is that a challenge to compare nightmares. All that achieves is to reinforce and magnify them."

Orhan nodded slowly in dawning understanding.

Pierre continued. "You jumped to assist me a moment ago. I will do my best to assist you, if you wish it, to overcome your addiction."

The Chinese member of the ill-assorted trio stood stiffly. "And I?" he asked.

In response to the Frenchman's shrug, an implicit invitation to make up his own mind, he maintained a thoughtful silence for some moments.

Finally, he said, "My father abandoned me to Wu's 'care', but my family remains my family. I must do something to satisfy the debt he incurred. I came to this country told to seek gold. Perhaps I should persist with that. Alongside you, if you share the ambition."

"A good thought," agreed Pierre. "Some discreet questions to find out the best opportunity - some new find that hasn't been gouged clean yet maybe - then use our collective wits and skills to equip ourselves and travel." He clapped Orhan on the shoulder. "We'll have you sweating the poison out of your body before you know it, my young friend, and we'll get rich into the bargain!"

THE COLOURS of the dawn were still in the sky above the outskirts of Louth as Magpie yawned and stretched. He was sitting up in the branches of a gum tree, his back propped against the trunk. Two horses were tethered below him.

He swung his legs around to dangle from the branch, and pulled a strip of dried meat from his shirt pocket. Chewing contentedly, he smiled as he looked down from his perch to a small, neat shack across the dusty track that served as a road.

The door of the shack opened and James Arnold stepped out, with more than a little reluctance, as far as Magpie could see. The reason was immediately obvious – James was still holding the hand of an attractive blonde woman who was following him outside.

"Damn it, Rebecca," Arnold swore softly, "I hate slippin' away at dawn like this. I always feel like... like we're ashamed of each other or something."

The blonde reached to stroke his beard, turning him to face her. "We both know that's not true," she said. "But you do know why..."

"Yeah, yeah. We've talked about it enough. Maybe one day..." He smiled faintly. "I better go. We've gotta get out to Wilson's station and back before the next cargo boat comes in."

Rebecca smiled warmly. "Off you go. I've got things to do round here before I have to work tonight."

It took her no effort to pull James into an embrace. They shared a lingering kiss.

Meanwhile, Magpie dropped lightly from the tree and unhitched the horses. Pulling a battered hat from his back pocket, Arnold crossed the track to join his business partner, who grinned broadly and waved to Rebecca. The older man turned and waved his hat before jamming onto his head. The woman laughed and blew him a kiss. With a fond wave to both men she went back inside.

"Good night, James?" asked Magpie.

"Yep. Thanks for hangin' around out here."

"No problem, mate."

James looked thoughtfully at his friend as they mounted their horses. "Good woman'd do you a world of good, Magpie."

"Not much chance mate. Too black for the white women, too white for the lubras. Well, for any of the ones I'd touch, anyway." Despite his words, there was no bitterness in Magpie's voice as they rode off.

Stubbornly, Arnold disagreed. "I reckon you're bein' too harsh - on yourself and maybe women in general. Reckon there's some good ones out there'd appreciate you."

The darker man shrugged. "No offence to you and Rebecca, mate, but the way I live ain't no life for a woman, and I got no plans to settle down for a while yet."

"Yeah, well, I suppose I have got a couple of years on you," James admitted, truthfully. "Man's gotta have a bit of an eye to his future, but."

Magpie shook his head. "Don't like lookin' too far forward. Any more than I like lookin' back."

The older man sighed resignedly, and they rode on in companionable silence.

∾

THE SPRAWLING Robertson house was a hive of activity. A pile of trunks and cases stood near the door. Young Phillip leaned three or four good hunting rifles against a steamer trunk. His father walked up and lay a document case on top of the same trunk. He looked at his son and gave what was meant to be an encouraging smile, although the effect was diminished by a lack of practice.

"Well, you may at least find some variety in your hunting. Take that as a positive thing."

"I'm not trying to find 'positive things', Father. I'm trying to find sensible things. One sensible thing. A sensible reason."

"I suppose 'because I say so' isn't enough for you."

"Hardly. You did raise me to think for myself, remember?"

"Mmm. I thought I'd also raised you to be obedient."

"Not blindly. Not without question."

Robertson senior gave a wry smile. "My mistake."

Ali entered the porch, carrying a large wicker hamper. Given the size of the hamper, it was obvious that the wiry Indian was stronger than he looked.

"Ah, Ali - our kitchen essentials?" the patriarch asked, giving his manservant an amiable pat on the shoulder.

"Indeed, sir. Enough to set up adequately."

"Good. We can start loading the carts, I think."

With a nod Ali took the hamper out the front door.

Phillip stood with his hands on his hips, still looking cross. "See, that's what I mean. Why set up an 'adequate' kitchen when we already have an excellent one? Why ride miles north to carve a place out of some God-forsaken spot on the map when you've already done that here? And done it well! You've proved your point," he said, gesturing through the porch towards the substantial main body of the house.

"Thank you for your approval, son." Robertson kept most of the irony out of his voice.

Both men picked up cases and started carrying them out to the two carts outside. The two Robertsons and Ali seemed to automatically slip into well-coordinated activity. The pile of luggage was quickly being relocated, packed securely onto the vehicles that would be taking it north. Father and son talked as they worked, Ali maintaining his characteristic reserve.

"You haven't answered me, father. Why do all this? We're already comfortable here. The money is good. You've got connections - influence. What can Hard Rock Creek offer that you don't already have?"

"I don't believe I've ever suggested that it's possible to have too much wealth, or too much power and influence. You're right, Phillip, we do have a satisfactory life here, and were no further opportunities to have ever arisen I daresay I would have been as content as you evidently are."

The young man nodded as his father continued to offer more explanation than he had perhaps expected to. It was almost as though James Robertson was considering his own motivation aloud to himself.

"But the opportunity has arisen. This property has been good to us, yes. Probably the most enduringly successful of my - ventures. But as potent a commodity as wool is in this colony, gold is significantly better."

Phillip looked askance over the case he was carrying. "Better in what way? It's more difficult, surely..."

"Reward for effort, Phillip. Reward for effort," his father explained. "The price of gold buys more than the price of wool, buys it more quickly, and with less questions asked."

Ali, carrying a box of bottles, stepped around them smoothly as the pair re-entered the house. All three men carried out their tasks with an almost balletic efficiency.

"More what, though?" the young man pressed. "You've already admitted we have all we need."

As they walked in, neither man noticed Phillip's sister Davinia standing just inside the house, arms folded and an expression of undisguised annoyance marring her pretty face as she listened to her father sigh.

"All we need isn't necessarily the same as all we want. Ask your sister."

"So this is all my fault, is it?" she snapped.

"Good morning, dear," James said without missing a beat. "Good of you to join us. I trust you've packed."

"No, I have not packed! If you want to go charging off into the wild country, that's fine. I wish you success - much of it! And much wealth from it! But it seems absurd that I should have to go with you. I can remain here and - look after things."

Phillip snorted derisively in response. "Waiting to spend the new wealth without having to go to any trouble yourself."

The elder Robertson stopped in the doorway and looked at his daughter sternly, saying, "Davinia, I would not be - happy to leave you here unattended."

Davinia waved an airy hand. "Ali can watch over me."

The manservant glanced up momentarily while picking up a trunk. His expression was, as usual, non-committal, but he managed to radiate his displeasure at Davinia's suggestion.

Robertson frowned and said firmly, "No. I expect to require Ali's services myself. This is not open to debate, young lady. You will accompany us. You will pack, now. You have thirty minutes. Anything not packed then will remain here - not including you. Once your own things are loaded, you and Phillip will ride into town and arrange supplies for the journey - a list is on my desk. I will stress again - be discreet!"

The girl stamped her foot. "This is so unfair!"

With more patience than he felt, James replied, "I'm sure I remember you saying "I like gold" - you did, didn't you?"

"Yes, but..."

"The closer you are to its source, the more of it is likely to find its way to you. I can hardly expect that we'll be the only ones there looking for it."

His son frowned in surprise. "I thought you'd kept this a secret," he said.

"As much as possible, yes, but that can't last forever. In my new position as Gold Warden all finds are supposed to go through me. I expect to make a small but reasonable percentage, but the digger must see some reward as encouragement."

His daughter continued to pout but sounded thoughtful as she mused aloud, "I suppose I can make something of the situation, if you insist..."

With that, she spun on her heel and flounced out towards her own room.

Her proposition had triggered a thought in her brother. With a pensive scratch of his chin he asked, "And what of the property while we're gone? Maybe I should stay?"

"No," replied James with a shake of his head. "While I'd be less concerned than I would be leaving Davinia unattended, I'd still rather have you with me, at least at the outset of this enterprise. Amos is a good foreman - he'll run the property well enough for a time. Gold strikes are not noted for being long term propositions, Phillip."

"So, we get in, make what we can as quick as we can..."

"While retaining this comfortable security to return to. Exactly. It may be a couple of years, with luck. Once the new settlement is established it should be possible for you to pay an occasional call on Amos to keep an eye on the family interests. But for now, those interests are best served at Hard Rock Creek."

With an air of finality, Robertson picked up a steamer trunk and walked out.

Phillip was balancing his guns on another trunk ready to lift them when Davinia strolled back into the room.

She called out, "Ali, take my bags out to the cart!"

"That was quick," Phillip remarked, looking at her wryly. "Of course, you were already packed, weren't you? Just trying to extract some last-minute concessions from Father?"

"Making the most of my resources, Phillip dear. You should learn that."

∽

THE MIDDAY SUN beat down on what was becoming a well-worn track from Cooktown to the fledgling Palmer River settlement. Four new worthies were on their way to try their luck on the goldfields.

The Cossack Gregori Volkoff drove their wagon at a steady pace, not enough to disturb baggage or passengers. The Buitritos nestled among the bags, father and son both strumming their guitars. Vittorio Pasquale was perched at the rear of the wagon, engrossed in a book.

As they rounded a sharp bend, Volkoff's eyes narrowed. At the side of the road ahead was wreckage. Two wagons, apparently only partially stripped of goods. The Russian slowed the horses to a stop, and gazed around warily. Guillermo did likewise. Cristiano, with his back to the discovery, played on until his father kicked him in the shin.

"Wha...?" the young man began, before being silenced by a gesture from his sire, who pointed over his shoulder.

Vittorio had looked up at their wagon's halt, and seeing the cause, had jumped down to investigate. Curious by nature, he was trotting towards the nearest of the ruined vehicles, a puzzled expression on his face.

"Stop!" cried Guillermo, who tapped Volkoff's arm and indicated the rifle propped at the driver's side. "You go with him, I think. Cristiano and I will cover you."

Gregori was surprised to realize that the two musicians had each produced a pistol from somewhere, but nodded. He was quickly at the side of the Italian, who was puzzled by his sudden escort.

"What's wrong?" he asked. "I mean, besides the obvious." He indicated the damaged wagon. "There's no-one here."

"Don't assume that," the Russian replied.

Now moving cautiously, the two men approached the wreck. Volkoff knelt to pick up a spear tip from the side of the track. There were clear traces of blood still visible in the dirt. He turned the broken blade over in his hand as he began to examine the wagon more closely. He had no way of recognizing the broken fragment as a

Merkin weapon – he'd never so much as heard of the small, savage tribe, but he knew danger when it was near.

Meanwhile Vittorio walked cautiously toward the trees fringing the road. He spotted a small clearing a short way into the bush, and peered between the trunks.

Recoiling suddenly, he called, "Some dead black men here!"

"Are you sure they're dead?" Volkoff quizzed.

"By the look of the wounds I can see, I certainly hope so! Bizarre... they're stacked like so much corded wood..."

From behind the Italian a pistol cracked, and a bullet whanged off a tree trunk a little to his left. Volkoff dropped to one knee, his rifle at the ready, facing the direction he knew the shot had been aimed at.

His gun still smoking, Cristiano called from the wagon, "Time to go!"

He and his father scanned different parts of the surrounding bush, instinctively operating as a team. Guillermo fired a shot into a patch of scrub, provoking a brief cry.

To the surprise and annoyance of his companions, Pasquale stopped to snatch up a cask from the wrecked wagon. He'd recognized the maker's mark of a good quality brandy. But now he ran back to their own vehicle.

The former captain of the Azov Host followed at a slower pace, cautiously hunched as he backed up, rifle moving as he watched the trees. "How many?" he called.

The older Spaniard shrugged. "Several, I think. Maybe more."

Vittorio had already stowed the cask and clambered aboard the wagon. Gregori followed close behind, and nudged the merchant.

"You drive," he ordered.

There was no argument. The Italian grabbed the reins and chivvied the horses into a rapid departure. One of the belligerent Merkin stepped out from behind a tree, spear raised. The threat died with the man, thanks to Volkoff's skill with the rifle.

The four Europeans were quickly out of range of even the most well thrown spears. As their wagon clattered along the track, it passed four small wooden crosses at the edge of the tree line. Guillermo spotted the pitiable memorials, and nudged the other two gunmen, who exchanged wordless glances.

Vittorio was concentrating on the task of driving, watching the road, and hadn't seen the crosses. As they rounded another bend he called back over his shoulder to the two Spaniards, "I didn't know you were carrying guns."

The older musician shrugged and said, "Country like this, everyone carries guns."

Cautiously Pasquale replied, "You know how to use them, too, I think."

If he hoped for any illumination of his travelling companions' past, he was disappointed. Father and son exchanged brief glances.

"Maybe later," muttered the older man.

Perhaps by way of distraction, Cristiano asked the driver, "You say there were bodies stacked? Who would do such a thing, and why?"

Vittorio looked deeply troubled as he replied, "I can't help thinking it reminded me of a larder."

ON THE FRINGE of the business district that was already growing in Sydney Town was a sturdy stone building that housed several well-appointed offices. Among them was one with walls extensively adorned with a range of militaria – weapons, artwork, and several framed citations.

An ostentatiously large desk faced the door. After a brisk knock, the door swung open and a uniformed man entered, snapping off a sharp salute. The grizzled soldier stood at the threshold, awaiting acknowledgement from his commanding officer.

William Andrews sat behind the desk, leaning back with hands behind his head and a rather vacant smile on his lean face. He might have been stoned, or drunk, by his expression, but he nodded at his adjutant to enter properly.

"Yes, Finlay?"

Approaching no closer than necessary, Michael Finlay handed Andrews a sealed envelope. He knew from experience to wait patiently while the officer opened and read the message.

After an appropriate pause, he ventured to ask, "Orders, sir?"

"Not as such, Finlay, not as such. We don't get 'orders' any more since we left Her Majesty's service. But it's certainly an interesting offer of work." After a lengthy pause he continued, "It's the Governor's pleasure to send our little group north. A new settlement is being established some distance north of the Darling River, and while it's in its infancy the 1st Riverview Infantry Company are invited to provide support to the new Gold Warden who'll be in charge there. The fee is - attractive."

The burly adjutant looked surprised, and a little displeased. "Goldfields duty, Captain Andrews? That's work for the troopers, surely! Use the black boys! They're happy enough to ride shotgun over their own kind or anyone else for a few coppers and some tea and sugar!"

Both men spoke in the cultured tones of well-educated British men, only slightly coarsened by their shared long experience in various rough corners of the Empire.

Suppressing a chuckle, Andrews replied, "Unlike our own stalwart men, eh Finlay? No, it seems that this new Warden has some important connections. And furthermore, it's being suggested as a potential opportunity to test out our new shipment of Martini Henrys."

"Testing the new rifles, sir? So, trouble is anticipated?"

"Oh, there seems to be some suggestion of some rogue blackfellas in the district. We're to discourage them from interfering in the acquisition of gold, and the collection of the Colony's due percentage, of course."

Finlay smiled in anticipation of the eagerly-awaited new equipment. "Twenty men with good breech-load rifles should discourage them right enough sir!" he said jovially.

A sudden stern expression crossed Andrews' face. "It would of course be preferable to bring enlightenment to the heathens - to cleave them to the bosom of Mother Church." He caught his breath, and just as suddenly relaxed back into the distracted smile. "But discouragement by force of arms will work just as nicely. Go and advise the men, without too much detail, if you please. This is apparently to be kept very quiet for now. Make the necessary arrangements for travel."

Finlay saluted again and left smartly, closing the door behind himself.

An audible giggle came from under the desk. Andrews looked sternly in the direction of his lap.

"And before you ask, no - you will not be accompanying me. I have orders to follow, and the Lord's work to do."

He reached under the desk to ruffle a handful of curly hair. "Don't fret my dear - I'm sure I'll be back before your sentence is fully served."

MAGPIE, Thonkumundil and Arnold were making their way along a track outside of Louth. They led a team of horses hauling a wagon full of supplies, including a large boiler. The white man kept glancing towards the tree line, looking slightly puzzled.

"Hey Mundil!" he said. "Where's your mates? There's usually someone from the campsite spotted us by now - some of the kids at least."

The tribesman was also looking concerned as he answered, "I just been thinking the same thing. Somebody usually wants to come out and see what I brung them this time."

Magpie grinned as he said, "That's why you work with us, isn't it? Get a few extras in for the family? Nothing wrong with that, mate - beats digging up grubs or chasing wallabies all the time."

"Wallaby last night was good but, eh?" replied Mundil with a grin.

Arnold laughed and agreed, "Sure was! Better you than me for hunting the buggers though!" He turned serious, his concerns deepening. "Reckon we better check in on the camp." Bringing the team to a halt, he turned to his partner and said, "Magpie, you want to keep an eye on the load while Mundil and I go have a look-see?"

"No worries, James."

Arnold and Thonkumundil cantered their horses through the bush cautiously. Few horsemen could have followed their passage.

Reaching the clearing that was home to the Balyarta campsite, they immediately realized that it was deserted. Dismounting, the two men scouted around. Arnold checked hearths and inside humpies, while Mundil examined the ground itself.

"Men in boots been here, Mister Arnold," observed the native.

James was digging some shotgun pellets from a tree trunk as he replied, "Doesn't surprise me."

Now truly worried, he looked over at his friend. The native gestured up into another tree. Looking up, the horseman saw a black body draped among the branches. A crow cawed somewhere nearby.

"New?" asked the white man.

Mundil nodded. They both looked up, keen eyes examining the corpse.

"Bullet wounds," said Arnold. Looking around, he gestured and said, "At least a couple more."

They were silent for a moment, before the horseman continued contemplatively, "Well, whoever did it can't have gotten all of them. Somebody has to have moved the bodies."

"Reckon you're right, Mr. Arnold," agreed his companion.

"We better go looking for the survivors."

The native shook his head. "Nah. We got that wagon full of stuff we left on the track to deliver first. We take on a job, I want to finish it. You taught me that. Balyarta never travel real fast, or real far. We find 'em after."

Arnold looked at him uncertainly, but knew from past experience the man wouldn't change his mind. Instead, he said, "Fair enough. So, let's get a move on, hey?"

They rode off together, and explained to Magpie what they'd found, and the proposed course of action.

The half-caste shrugged and said to Mundil, "Long as you're sure, mate. We'll be quick as we can then get back here."

Just as they were about to spur the team into action there was the sound of hoofbeats approaching quickly. The two regular teamsters immediately had guns at the ready, then relaxed as they recognized the figure galloping around the bend.

His time in the bush had made the Scottish preacher a capable rider. He reined in his steed, which trotted up to stand by the wagon.

McGregor exchanged curt nods with all three horsemen. He tilted his head towards the campsite. "Ye've been in tae see...?"

Arnold nodded. Too many words seemed superfluous. "Yeah. You knew about it?"

"Aye. Rode out this morning and found the place deserted. Found a few bullets, too, so I headed back tae town tae see Sergeant McCartney."

James couldn't restrain a snort of distaste. "I'm sure he was very helpful."

"Even less than I'd expected," the preacher said grimly.

Magpie only shrugged. "He doesn't give a bugger about black people, except when he's got a problem with 'em."

"Aye well, he's nae the only one like that," said McGregor. "Tae be fair I suppose McCartney seems tae feel that way about everyone - black or white. But that's why I came back - tae see if I can find anything that might force him tae take a bit more notice."

"You'd have found some more bullets if you'd looked in a body or two," said Arnold.

The Scot looked grim. "I should have thought of that. I'll see if I can get yon spalpeen Walters tae take an interest in murder while McCartney's playing nursie tae his new Gold Warden."

The half-caste teamster shook his head emphatically at that, and said, "The only way Jack Walters would take an interest in the murder of a black man is if he did it himself. Probably any man, come to think of it."

With a gesture of reluctant agreement, McGregor began, "Magpie, I'm truly sorry about what's happened tae yuir people..."

"They're not my people."

"Aye, I know ye're half white, I was told that's how ye got yuir name..."

Magpie continued shaking his head and repeated, "They're not my people. They're Balyarta - Thonkumundil's mob. My mother was Bidjigal. Different people."

Some understanding dawned on the preacher. "Like they Beeargah," he said.

"No! Not like them buggers!" Magpie snapped. "Bidjigal didn't move round much either. They were from over that way, near the coast. Balyarta people have always lived around this place."

Arnold nodded and tried to explain to the other white man, "It's not just that they're not related, they're a whole different race. As far as they're concerned the Balyarta are no more related to Magpie's tribe, or that marauding pack of scavengers the Beeargah, than they are to you and me."

"Aye, aye - I understand that. All God's children, but nae every family gets along, do they? Sorry, I'd just thought the lad was a local. My apologies," he said with obvious sincerity.

James was looking thoughtful. "You said something before about gold?"

"Aye. McCartney was blethering about having tae look after a new Gold Warden somewhere called Hard Rock Creek. Ever heard of it?"

The three teamsters exchanged puzzled looks and shrugs.

"Near here? New one on me. If there's gold been found we'll all know about it soon enough I reckon," said Arnold.

"That's true enough," agreed the preacher bitterly. "What's tae be done about Thonkumundil's people though?"

James shrugged again. "Mundil reckons he'll find 'em easy enough after we've delivered this lot to old man Wilson. Bastard thing's heavy and it's got some expensive fragile stuff for his missus, so we don't travel real quick, but he's a bloody good tracker."

The Scot scratched at his beard, and said, "I was thinking more about justice for whoever murdered them."

There was no irony in Magpie's voice as he replied, "Ain't no justice for the blackfella, Mister Mac - you oughta know that by now. Not unless we do it ourselves."

"Careful, laddie. There's a difference between justice and revenge."

"In your rules maybe. Blackfellas got their own rules."

Thonkumundil nodded silently. He and McGregor looked warily into each other's eyes for a moment. There was respect there, and a degree of understanding, but here was also warning. The preacher turned back to Magpie.

"And what about ye? Whose rules do ye live by?"

There was little mirth in the half-caste's grin as he answered, "Depends on what's working."

"God's Law always works."

Arnold tapped the team horses into activity, and grunted, "Tell that to the poor bastards up those trees," before pointedly riding away from further discussion.

"I know you mean right, Mister Mac, but there ain't many like you," said Magpie sympathetically before riding after James.

Mundil only nodded before goading his horse to follow his two companions. McGregor watched them go. He looked towards the campsite, and sighed heavily at the realization of how much he couldn't do.

As he turned his horse to ride back to Louth, he mused aloud to himself, "How many do there have tae be, I wonder?"

THE 'SETTLEMENT' which had grown up near the Palmer River gold strike was still only a primitive affair. A few wooden structures, some more substantial than others, stood among a sprawl of tents.

Standing in a solemn group outside one of those tents were the Buitritos, Gregori Volkoff and the Italian merchant, Vittorio Pasquale. The latter had just handed out a round of fine glasses full of brandy. This was the spirit contained in the cask reclaimed from the wrecked wagon they'd passed. He laid a sympathetic hand on the shoulder of the bereaved Cossack.

"To absent friends," he said, raising his glass.

The other three quietly shared in the toast. As they stood, each lost in his own thoughts, they were approached by a tall, distinguished-looking black man. It was the man who'd taken the name Adhilasa Johnson.

He offered a welcoming smile, extending his hand as he said, "I'd join you gentlemen in that sentiment, if I were a drinking man. Welcome to Palmer River. I..."

He stopped short, the words dying in his throat as he saw the small cask from which the brandy had been drawn. His voice was suddenly as cold and hard as his eyes as he asked, "Where did you get that?"

Oblivious to the change in tone, Vittorio patted the barrel with some affection. "We found it with a couple of damaged wagons several miles back along the track," he explained.

"Did you find... anything else?"

The merchant shook his head, puzzled by the question. "There was quite a bit of stuff, but this was all I had time to salvage. There were several natives looking threatening, my friends saw them."

The former slave's expression didn't change as he looked about the quartet. He repeated Vittorio's word. "Threatening. Indeed."

Guillermo met his stare, eye to eye, and quietly said, "We saw the crosses. They look - not disturbed."

The Italian blinked, perplexed. "Crosses?" he asked, before a sudden flash of insight struck him, closely followed by acute discomfort. "They were your wagons? You lost - friends? *Famiglia*?"

Adhilasa softened. This man's contrition was clearly genuine – he was a fellow who clearly had no talent for hiding his emotions. He wouldn't last five minutes in a poker game. "Family, yes," he replied.

The younger Spaniard raised his glass and diplomatically added to the toast, "To your loss, too, then."

Pasquale indicated the cask. "I apologise about the..."

The tall black man waved the thought away. "Better it be appreciated than swilled by those barbarians. They're cannibals, I'm told by those who've been here for a while."

"*Manaya!*" exclaimed the merchant. "I would rather not go back, even for more of this excellent spirit."

Warming to Vittorio, Adhilasa's smile returned as he nodded and again extended his hand. "Let me introduce myself, and I'll tell you what I can about this little piece of heaven we find ourselves in."

THE DISTRICT CALLED The Rocks wasn't one of Sydney Town's most salubrious areas, but it did have some quiet spots where it was possible to simply watch over the harbour and enjoy some stillness.

Li Wei Sun and Orhan Keilbren had found one such location. They sat on a low stone wall, looking out over the water as the sky darkened into early evening. The Turk was pale, and at unguarded moments trembled slightly, but he was holding himself together bravely. His companion had said little throughout the afternoon, but even silence could be encouraging, when accompanied by the right gestures and actions.

As distracted as both men appeared, they both immediately turned at the sound of soft footsteps behind them. They relaxed when they recognized the figure approaching confidently.

"Bonjour, my friends! And how is the young warrior?"

Orhan forced a smile and said, "I am... managing, thank you, Pierre."

That won a supportive nod from Wei Sun, who agreed, "He has done well. There are dens to tempt him, even here."

"But those dens are good sources of information, so we needed to be there," the Turk added.

"Oui. Well done, my friend. And the information you found?"

"There are options," said Wei Sun. "There is still gold to be had around Ballarat, as well as the fields closer to the Murray River."

The Frenchman pondered. "Mmm. Beechworth. I've heard of it, and of the large nugget found at... what was it? Dunolly? But these are well-established fields. Little opportunity left for three poor itinerants like us."

"There are Chinese communities in all of those well-established fields. We may find a place for ourselves there," suggested Wei Sun, without conviction.

"As what? Farmers?" scoffed Keilbren.

"There are worse things in life than being a farmer! Far worse!"

Pierre raised a placating hand. "Very true, very true. But Orhan does have a point. Worthy an occupation as farming may be, it is - *unlikely* to make us the wealth we agreed to seek. Especially those of us lacking both experience and inclination, eh? And furthermore, those Chinese enclaves are likely to be the home of more men like Wu. Personally, I have no taste for getting closer to any more such men than necessary."

"Yes!" agreed the Chinaman emphatically. "What of other places? There are newer discoveries, further north, where we may find some opportunity."

"Oui. My very thought. Certainly, I've heard of some good finds in the north of Queensland. A long journey for us, though, and we aren't all that well equipped for such a thing."

Orhan looked downcast. The prospect of a long difficult journey, scavenging or on bare rations, only added to his unhappiness. But Pierre gave an encouraging smile.

"However, I did happen to overhear something interesting in a store. An argument between a young man and a very attractive young lady who I was happy to discover is his sister. They were obtaining supplies for a journey north with their father, who is evidently about to become Gold Warden at a place called Hard Rock Creek."

Wei Sun looked thoughtful. "Not a name I have heard in our - enquiries."

"Nor I, mon ami. This was, I think, a major part of what they were arguing about. The youth was not happy at her mentioning the gold in public. Apparently, their father is adamant that as few people as possible know the real reason for their leaving town. I suspect it's a good thing neither of them noticed I was kneeling behind a barrel at the side of the store, hoping to find affordable old stock. They'd sent the shopkeeper out to a back room to fetch something, and I got the impression that if there was any sign that he'd caught the girl's care-less remark, then the man would be in trouble."

"Have you any idea of how far away this Creek is?" quizzed Wei Sun.

"No. Clearly it's some distance, judging by the supplies they were buying. But I can't imagine that it's anywhere completely remote - not for the man to be taking his family on the journey. I suggest we get ourselves some horses and some basic supplies." He was smiling mischievously. "I've learned where this family live. We keep a careful eye on them without drawing attention to ourselves, and when they travel we follow - at a discreet distance."

Now Orhan was smiling. "With our experience we should be able to keep them in sight without being seen ourselves."

His companions exchanged glances, quietly amused by the reference to 'our experience'.

"*Certainment*," agreed Pierre.

THE SUN HUNG low in the sky over the Palmer River. The scrub outside the goldfields 'tent city' was still surprisingly dense in places, but it was little impediment to the Kuthant. Their extensive travels took them through a wide variety of different environments in different parts of Australia, and they'd developed a talent for moving lightly and quietly.

It had been quite a while since their circuitous trade route had brought them here, and they were aware that things had changed. Their noses and ears alerted them first. The tribesman who was leading their steady progress through the bush held up a cautious hand. Several of his companions, including the Makassar Asbul, gathered at his shoulder, peering through the trees.

Visible some way ahead was the fringe of the sprawl of tents, among which, as it chanced, were those of Vittorio Pasquale and Adhilasa Johnson.

The lead tribesman said warily, "This was not here last time we came this way."

One of his brothers, a cautious fellow named Walan, observed, "White men. We should travel carefully. Go around them if we can."

Karumbari had more of what might be called an entrepreneurial spirit. "Maybe not," he said. "Maybe there's something worth trading here."

"With white men? Dangerous," warned Walan.

The Makassar fisherman, a natural linguist, had by now mastered enough of the Kuthant dialect to understand and be understood. Enthusiastically he offered, "I can talk to them - I speak their language."

Karumbari gestured toward Walan and in heavily accented English replied, "Us two, too, a little," earning a grin from Asbul.

Clicking his tongue uncertainly, the tribesman who'd been leading the way said in his own language, "I'm not sure about this."

In the same dialect, Walan replied, "Some white men we've met were good, but others..."

While the Kuthant were deeply engrossed in this quiet conversation, young Micah Johnson, his own mind wandering, almost walked into their distracted midst. The youth shouted wildly and dropped the fossicking equipment he was carrying, trying to unsling the rifle over his shoulder.

Most of the tribesmen were already starting to back away quickly, melting into the scrub as Micah fumbled with the gun. Asbul sprang forward, and with one movement disarmed the young man. With his second movement he sent the West Indian flying, yelling in alarm as he hit the ground. But before the fisherman could advance on the sprawling youth, the cook Chung appeared at a run to block his way.

Dropping his own equipment, he growled, "Oh no you don't..."

A brief fight ensued, the likes of which the Kuthant tribe had never seen. Neither, for that matter, had Micah. Over the years, Chung had shown him a few unusual martial techniques, but this was an extraordinary exhibition as the Makassar demonstrated agile, powerful moves of his own. Both men abruptly found themselves sprawled on the ground.

Grinning broadly, evidently enjoying the challenge, Asbul called out, "Hey! You're good!"

Chung stared at him, shocked at being addressed in English.

Drawn by Micah's shout, Adhilasa, Cristiano and Vittorio arrived at a run from their tents, the latter two armed with rifles. The Kuthant had mostly disappeared back into the bush, but a couple remained barely visible, watching out for their new ally.

Raising his hand to stop his friends' advance, Chung called, "Wait! I... don't think these are the same people we fought before."

"Indeed?" asked Adhilasa, raising a suspicious eyebrow. He'd known Chung a long time, but this was such a different environment to anything he'd known in his adventurous life.

Just beginning to pick himself up off the ground, Micah, as puzzled as his mentor, asked, "What do you mean?"

The cook was looking thoughtfully at Asbul. "I mean, the men who killed our family threw spears from the cover of an ambush. None of them looked like they could fight hand to hand - not like this - and there was no sign of anyone speaking English."

The Italian merchant looked askance at the Makassar – a man of a race he'd never seen before. "English?" he asked.

Asbul almost shouted his reply, "I speak English! I speak lots of t'ings! I been trading with lots of different folks long time now." He looked at the man he'd been fighting moments before, an expression of genuine concern on his face. "You say someone kill your family? Where dis happen?"

Adhilasa gestured eastwards and replied, "A day or two's ride that way."

The fisherman shook his head. "We been coming from dat way," he said pointing north. "And de Kut'ant don't usually kill people - bad for business!" he added, the grin tentatively returning.

Looking wryly at this seemingly eccentric character, Adhilasa repeated the surprising term, "Business?"

"Sure. Kut'ant – good people I wit' - dey traders. Dey walk from up dere, down, around and back again. Dey collect stuff dey need, and more besides. Dat stuff dey trade wit' different people dey meet along de way, get more t'ings for demselves, more t'ings to trade as dey go along."

The Italian was intrigued, in spite of himself. He shook his head in bemusement. "That makes sense to me. But most people I've met in this country have reckoned the black men are just primitive savages."

Dusting himself off, Micah said bitterly, "A good description of the ones we met, that's for sure!"

The young Spaniard Cristiano shrugged and replied, "Goes to show - never take anything for granted."

He held his hand out to Asbul, who shook it, still grinning. Cautiously, Vittorio made the same move.

Several of the Kuthant started to emerge from cover, emboldened by the change in atmosphere. Chung took a step towards them, hands open in a gesture of peace. Asbul looked towards his adopted tribe and nodded reassuringly. He had a good feeling about these men, and was used to trusting his instincts.

Pasquale's own merchant instincts were asserting themselves. "If these fellas are trading in food then it occurs to me you could do some business here."

The Makassar was talking to the Kuthant in their language. "See, Karumbari - we might do alright here."

"Could do," his friend agreed.

The leading tribesman was more cautious, but did also recognize a new opportunity. Warily he said, "Alright, but we should be careful."

Asbul turned back to the tent-dwellers. Identifying Vittorio as a natural trader, he said, "Got some dried fish, roots and herbs."

Before the Italian could reply, Chung interjected, "Well I'm interested! Anything to make meals a bit more interesting than the tinned and dried stuff I've had to work with!"

Adhilasa smiled at his friend's enthusiasm, and explained to the natives, "My old friend is an artist always on the look-out for inspiration." He chuckled and continued, "I hope Palmer River can provide something worthwhile in return."

Karumbari looked puzzled by the adopted American's phrase. He turned to Asbul and gestured helplessly.

"He says he hopes Palmer River can offer us a good trade."

"Ah!" the tribesman said, and replied in English, "Reckon we can always find something."

The fisherman explained further to Vittorio and his friends, "What dey can't use, dey find somebody who will, and trade wit' dem."

Cristiano looked approving. "A good system. Do the best by everyone."

IT WAS early afternoon in Louth. It would be nice to say the town had turned on its best to impress its important new arrivals, but Louth didn't really have a 'best' to turn on. Furthermore, James Robertson had very deliberately kept his arrival as quiet as possible. The great majority of residents were still oblivious to any suggestion of gold there, far less the appointment of a Gold Warden.

The new appointee and his two offspring stood outside the Wool-pack Inn - the closest thing Louth had to an up-market hotel. Yet another heated Robertson family discussion had been underway, with the usual result. Each generation was as intransigent as the other, but ultimately, James controlled the finances. The young Robertsons were looking decidedly unimpressed by their new surroundings.

Responding to his father's instruction of what they should be doing next, Phillip snorted in derision. "Look around town, Father? That *is* an enticing prospect." He looked up and down the street dismissively before adding, "Still, at least it shouldn't take long."

His sister's gaze was no less contemptuous. She didn't move from the spot where she stood, arms folded, looking about coldly. "If we avoid the nastier-looking places it should take us... just about... yes, done. Now what shall we do?"

Their attitude made no dent on their father's demeanour. Casu-ally he replied, "Quite frankly, I don't care. I have people to meet this afternoon and until I have a temporary office set up I'm obliged to use the lounge of our lodgings. I don't require your assistance at the meetings, and I would have thought you would prefer not to remain cooped up in your rooms..."

Phillip shrugged. "When you put it that way... Come on, Vin. If we're going to be stuck here for a while we'd better work out what our options are."

Glowering, Davinia had one last barbed question for her sire. "That's a point Father - how long will we be stuck here?"

By now even James Robertson's patience was wearing thin. He had more important concerns than his petulant children. "We have just arrived. We will be here only as long as necessary, that much I will say to you. Among the men I'm intending to meet today are those who will construct our home and my office once I've chosen a site. I expect Kaminski to also be here this afternoon, and I'll arrange to go with him to have a look at this Hard Rock Creek."

He was looking squarely at his daughter as he continued, "I expect you to not cause trouble while I'm away. Or while I'm here for that matter."

Davinia looked slightly huffy at that, but didn't meet her father's eyes. Instead she turned to her sibling and said, "Alright Phillip - let's see what delights we can find."

The young man nodded. He checked that his pistol was loaded, conspicuously spinning the chamber. His father laid a warning hand on his shoulder.

"Phillip - my instruction not to cause trouble applies to you, too."

With an effort at dignity, Phillip answered, "Understood. I won't cause trouble. I might ask around and see what's worth hunting around here."

Robertson Senior nodded in approval. "I'm sure you can find something to shoot."

"Or at least, shoot at," was Davinia's snide addendum as she turned and flounced away.

Her brother directed a mirthless smile at a point between her shoulder blades, then followed a few steps behind.

A voice came from a few paces behind James Robertson, remarking drily, "So you brought the whole cheerful family, I see."

Without turning the new Warden replied, "Of course, Kaminski. I'm hardly going to leave them behind on the property."

The Polish-born horseman gave a short derisive laugh that was more like a bark. All trace of his origins had been lost from his accent, erased by spending almost his entire life in the rough country of Australia. He'd watched his parents struggle to scrape a living as farmers using 'old country' techniques on unsuitable land. The experience had hardened him.

He was as pragmatic as flint, and accepted the apparent family commitment in his own wry way. "Fair enough. You might find your-self without a property to go back to."

Robertson turned to face his former employee, but the movement was casual. "I hardly think so. But your concerns are noted."

Kaminski shook his grizzled head. A little younger than Robert-son, years of exposure to harsh weather had made him look consider-ably older. "No concern of mine," he corrected. "My only concern is what I found by the creek bed north of here."

"The small fragment you sent looked promising," admitted James, knowing his arrival here was evidence enough of his genuine interest.

"Yeah - I reckon so. It'll be bloody hard to crack, mind you."

The newly appointed authority nodded, and moved them both into the shade of the Woolpack. He made sure they were well away from any open windows, and discreetly watched for casual passers-by before continuing.

"Which is why, as you pointed out, a well-equipped operation will be required. Making the most of my new official position will make some more resources available to us, although, as yet, my actual role is not public knowledge. Tell me about this native 'problem' you alluded to."

Appreciating his boss' caution, Kaminski kept his voice low. "There's a couple of black tribes near here. One's a pretty quiet mob that live a little way out of town. They don't get up to much. The problem's a bunch of hard-heads called the Beeargah. Not exactly vicious, unlike some I've heard of in other parts. But aggressive. They'd rather steal than hunt, I think, and they don't mind a fight."

"Sounds like plenty of men you and I have both known."

"True enough. A few men have gone missing, but it's hard to tell around a place like this whether they've just headed elsewhere, or if something else has happened. There's a couple have blamed the Beeargah, but nobody's cared enough to raise much fuss."

Nodding his understanding, Robertson replied thoughtfully, "So, it's not unknown for a man to disappear unexpectedly. That could be a useful thing to keep in mind. On the subject of usefulness, I see my first official appointment of the afternoon approaching. Will you stay and meet Sergeant McCartney of the local police?"

"We've met," was the toneless reply.

"Under not too difficult circumstances, I trust? I'm likely to require co-operation between you."

"It'll be right. I rode out with some of his black boys once, looking for a lost little girl."

Robertson shook his head sadly and reflected, without a trace of irony, "What sort of parent would bring a young innocent out to country like this? Did you find her?"

"Not... as such. Some of her clothes, just."

The Warden looked thoughtful. "These Beeargah you mentioned, perhaps?"

Kaminski was non-committal. "They got blamed," he admitted. "By some folks at least."

"And yet nothing was done? No demands to execute the murderous swine?"

There was a shrug in response. "No proof. And there's more than a few of them. I don't reckon the two coppers in charge would have fancied their chances. There's a preacher-man type hanging around, put in a good word for the blacks, too. He managed to stop the town getting too worked up at them."

Looking over Kaminski's shoulder, Robertson noticed the police sergeant starting to cross the road. He signalled briskly for the uniformed man to join them in the shade, and as he approached, held out a steady hand, saying, "You are Sergeant McCartney I presume. James Robertson. How do you do?"

They shook hands.

"As well as can be expected, Warden, thanks."

"You know Marusz Kaminski, I believe? He'll be working for me."

The two men exchanged wary nods as Robertson continued. "Mister Kaminski used to work for me, and is the gentleman who alerted me to the presence of gold north of here."

"So, it's you we have to thank..." McCartney muttered.

Robertson smiled diplomatically. "Now now, Sergeant. Don't be ungracious. I'm sure we can find ways of turning this discovery to everyone's advantage. If we adjourn inside I can have my man prepare refreshments. He's Indian - he prepares an excellent cup of tea."

The Warden spotted the look that flitted across the policeman's face, and knew he'd found a weak spot already. Good. Everyone had them, and it was always good to know just how to use them.

The sergeant didn't hide his enthusiasm "That sounds bloody marvellous, I must admit."

"Excellent," exclaimed the new man in town. "Will you join us, Marusz?"

Kaminski flinched, slightly suspicious at the uncharacteristic use of his forename.

"Ali's still with you, then? Not for tea, no," he replied.

"I'm sure the Woolpack can offer something stronger, until my own supplies can be properly unpacked." Robertson was smiling, but it was clear that the Warden wouldn't accept 'no' as an answer.

Tight-lipped, the horseman said, "Alright then." "Boss," he added quietly, following the other two into the hotel.

Soon the three were seated in the private lounge of the Woolpack, Ali standing discreetly near the door to intercept any other visitors, or hotel staff. Kaminski stared wordlessly into his tumbler of rum, making mental notes as the other two sipped tea from decent china cups as they talked.

Robertson's tone was casual, but his body language reinforced his determination that his words be taken to heart. "So, I've impressed upon you the importance of discretion, I trust. It will make both of our jobs easier if we avoid a 'rush' until we have a good degree of order established. None of your - men have any local ties, do they? I've found in the past that can lead to some reluctance to follow certain orders."

"I know what you mean," agreed the police officer. "No, these boys are all from further south, beyond Dunlop Station."

"So, they're reliable then."

McCartney snorted into his tea. "I wouldn't call them that! But they'll do what they're told, as best they can. Usually. Mind you, Mister Robertson, they're not any sort of private army you can use for any old business of your own. I'm trying to get them to respect the white man's laws - I don't want to teach them to break them."

The squatter gave a serious nod and replied, "I assure you, sergeant, I wouldn't ask you to do anything I'm not prepared to do myself. But I am, after all, only one man. My staff are loyal, but their numbers are small. And I do have my family to consider."

The sergeant raised surprised eyebrows and said, "You brought your family out here?"

"My son and daughter are quite old enough, and capable of looking after themselves, Sergeant, but thank you for your concern."

"And your wife?"

"Has been dead for a number of years - no, don't apologise, you weren't to know. And I'm quite recovered from the loss, thank you. So, given the unpredictable nature of these Beeargah and some of the stories I've already heard of them, I appreciate the reassurance of your presence."

McCartney shook his head in warning. "Don't be too reassured. We'll be well outnumbered, especially in the early days of establishing the new settlement."

He received a shrewd smile in response. "Precisely why I've arranged further support for you."

Suspicion obvious in his voice, the policeman probed, "Support?"

Robertson explained with satisfaction, "A small group of men who were, until recently, Her Majesty's loyal troops will be stationed with us - temporarily at least. I expect they'll arrive within a few days."

"Mercenaries? Bloody soldiers? That's all I need!"

"I sincerely hope it doesn't come to your 'needing' them, Sergeant. I expect law enforcement to remain firmly your responsibility. Think of the military men as a resource to be used if required. A well-armed resource. More tea, please Ali."

Almost unconsciously, the policeman handed his cup to Ali for refilling. "Yes, well, that'd certainly be handy if we did run into trouble with the Beeargah," he admitted.

Kaminski had been listening intently, and now, his curiosity piqued, asked, "How well armed, exactly?"

His employer smiled. "We shall know when they get here, but I understand they have some quite new equipment they'll be happy to field test should the need arise."

The under-staffed, under-resourced, under-appreciated law enforcement officer sighed a little wistfully. "New equipment. I'd like to see some of that."

The Warden waved a lugubrious hand. "You shall, Sergeant, you shall."

EARLY THAT EVENING, the subjects of the Warden's enthusiasm were pitching tents and unloading their wagons in a clearing in the bush. They were within sight of the rough road that led from Sydney to Louth.

Casually confident in the ability of his men, Andrews didn't bother to watch them work. He stood with hands on hips and looked at the surrounding area.

"It's hardly God's Own Country, is it, Finlay?" he asked wryly.

Struggling to carry a large box of equipment, the adjutant just managed to puff out, "No, sir."

"Oh! Let me help you with that, lad!" the captain exclaimed, and cheerfully took one end of the box, earning a gasp of thanks. "Always be mindful of the welfare of the troops. Loyalty is best earned, not ordered."

Finlay was clearly sincere as he replied, "Indeed, sir."

"Thinking of the men's welfare - their spiritual welfare - I think I may deliver one of my little sermons this evening."

The adjutant made a brave effort at diplomacy. "Oh - ah - good..."

His commander didn't notice the hesitation. "What do you think I should make my topic this evening?"

It was an awkward question for Finlay. Well-regarded as Andrews was in many ways amongst the company, his 'little sermons' weren't popular. Most of the men knew hypocrisy when they heard it, even if the word itself was unfamiliar.

"Er... something about piety and restraint, sir?" Finlay offered, at length.

"Hmm... No, I'm sure I've done that."

They put the crate down and walked back to the wagon in silence, Andrews deep in thought. He took a well-used Bible from the wagon. Holding it in one hand, eyes closed, the captain let the book fall open, and pulled from his pocket a small dark object with which he poked at the page, randomly selecting a verse.

He opened his eyes and smiling, said, "Leviticus Chapter 19 - yes, I can do something with that."

The Bible slipped slightly in his grasp. As he went to grab it he dropped the small object. His adjutant went to helpfully pick it up and then recoiled in distaste, if not quite horror.

"What in God's name is that?! Er, sir," he added apologetically.

"Finlay! You know my thoughts on taking the Lord's name in vain!"

Andrews chuckled, to suggest he was at most only partly serious. He genuinely liked his loyal adjutant, and the teasing was good-natured. He picked the dark object up himself, and held it out for Finlay's reluctant examination.

"You haven't seen my little souvenir before, Finlay? My apologies. Do you recall that group of natives up in the Blue Hills that we were called on to bring into line?"

"The Blue...? Oh, yes - the Blue Mountains, sir. Yes, sir?"

"One of their old chaps was gesturing at me and jabbering in a most unpleasant manner. One of our trackers explained it to me. It's some sort of heathen curse-casting spell. 'Pointing the bone' it's apparently called."

"Can't be having with them cursing you, sir," said Finlay loyally.

"My very thought, my friend! It's not as if *he* was young enough to actually enjoy the girl I'd chosen! So, I thought, 'point your bone at me, will you, you old reprobate? Well, you won't do that again!' And made damn sure he wouldn't."

"Ah," Finlay nodded, knowing his commander's proclivities. "Not, perhaps, a bit harsh, sir? Cutting his finger off?" he wondered carefully.

Andrews smiled benignly as he reminisced. "Well, he was hardly going to use it, was he? Not once I'd taken the silly old sod's guts out with my bayonet."

～

On a track well out of Louth, Thonkumundil was moving cautiously through undergrowth, looking at the ground and at low branches. James Arnold and Magpie, also on foot, followed behind him, leading their team of horses and a single loaded wagon.

They'd delivered their load, and had collected from the client some 'rubbish' to be disposed of. They knew from experience, though, that one man's rubbish could be another's treasure. Useful-ness was often a product of patience and ingenuity.

"This way, I reckon," Mundil called over his shoulder. A few paces more, and he held up a hand. "Wait here," he said, and ran quietly into the bush.

Arnold folded his arms and looked concerned. "Y'know, up until now I reckon we've seemed more worried than he's been."

His teamster partner shrugged. "They're his people, James. He knows 'em better than we do. They're survivors. They've lasted a long time."

"Maybe so, but this isn't the same world they survived in for most of that time. *We're* here," James said, more aware than most white men of what had been, and likely would be, the impact of European settlement.

Mundil suddenly emerged from the bush. He'd heard Arnold's comment, and answered phlegmatically, "Bad stuff come, bad stuff go. People survive." He jerked a thumb over his shoulder. "Found 'em. Come on."

Very soon after, the three men entered a clearing in a patch of otherwise dense scrub. What may have recently been a small area of comparatively sparse growth was being made larger and more habit-able by the Balyarta people.

A shrewd eye would quickly spot why the place had been chosen. It was level, but defensible. Several scattered granite rocks dotted the area. One of these, tall as a man, stood at the eastern edge. Not far beyond it, past the cleared perimeter, was a large granite outcrop, more than twice the height of a big man. It had a substantial flat top sloping away from the clearing. Rough scrub remained around its base.

The Balyarta weren't a large tribe, but most of them were busy. Some were constructing a bark shelter on the northern perimeter, edging a shallow slope which then dropped sharply into dense bush. Others were sweeping the new encampment area with branches and small uprooted shrubs. Several shrubs remained within the clearing, as did a couple of large fallen branches.

Some of the people were squatting around a fire, including a few with plant-leaf dressings on wounds.

The teamsters were arriving at the south-western edge of the new encampment. Three of the elders of the tribe were waiting to greet them, including the man who was the closest thing they had to a leader, a grey-haired old warrior now called Samuel. He'd adopted the Biblical name after his conversion to the faith espoused by Peter McGregor.

The man beside Samuel was the first to call out to the new arrivals. He spoke in the Balyartas' own tongue – the dialect called Burundji. "Thonkumundil! We thought you'd find us!"

Mundil's response, in the same language, was scolding. "Your trail wasn't hard to follow. That was risky."

Samuel's reply wasn't defensive, merely matter-of-fact, as he said, "We were in a hurry! We can move on a lot more carefully if that's what we decide to do."

James Arnold interrupted. He understood Burundji better than he actually spoke it, but made the effort to try. "Never mind that - what happened? Is everyone okay?" he asked.

Out of courtesy, Samuel replied in English. His incongruous accent was evidence of who he'd learned the language from. "Nae everyone, Mister Arnold."

"We saw bodies..."

"Aye, two. And a few more with injuries but not too bad, the Guid Lord be praised."

"Yeah, well..." James Arnold's opinion of religion was clear.

Magpie spoke in Burundji, respecting the elders. "But what happened? Who did it?"

"Two white men, from the town I think. Nobody we know," explained one.

"They didn't say anything?" the half-caste probed.

"Nothing we noticed. We were busy," said the elder wryly.

"Busy running away," Thonkumundil replied bitterly.

"Yes. Surviving," defended the other greybeard.

"So, how far will you run?" asked Magpie, concerned.

One of the elders turned and cast thoughtful eyes about the clearing behind them, before saying, "Here looks good, for now."

"For now. But how long?" There was more than a trace of cynicism in Arnold's voice.

Old Samuel shrugged and replied, "For as long as we can."

"Until someone else comes along and shoots us up?" demanded Thonkumundil.

Samuel turned on the horseman and demanded in his own language, "What else would you have us do?" After a deep sigh, he added in his richly accented English, "A long time since Balyarta had tae be warriors."

LOUTH STILL LAY some way ahead, but it was a clear morning, so the three Asian companions rode at a relaxed pace, barely a canter. Pierre was a little way in front, unobtrusively watching the bush at the sides of the track.

Behind him, Orhan and Wei Sun were deep in conversation. The Turk was wielding his broken katana with one hand, making experimental movements at Li's direction. He'd been about to discard the fractured weapon, but had been convinced to reconsider.

"That's right," encouraged Wei Sun. "Remember, there is no tip to your blade, so stabbing will only work at a very precise angle. With most of the curve now gone, your movement must change. Shorter blade means shorter movement."

"So, the idea is to chop, rather than slice?"

"Exactly. And you must aim for targets where that sort of attack is most effective - the hands, the ankles, the neck."

The young man nodded, his actions immediately reflecting the advice. "I see. And with handle and blade almost the same length it feels like there is more power concentrated in the blow."

"Just so," agreed his tutor. "There is less distance between you and your opponent but the force you can apply is greater. The same is also true of your defence. You parry and block with the back of the blade - you are not positioned or equipped to deflect blows as you would with a longer blade like the Frenchman's dao or your katana as it was."

"I'm grateful, Wei Sun, and impressed. I was resigned to throwing away my blade, for all that I'd come to like it since acquiring it."

The Chinese ex-soldier smiled and explained a little history. "These *ninjato* - the proper name for such a weapon, were first made of damaged blades collected from battlefields. Being broken is not the same as being useless."

"So I'm learning, my friend, so I am learning."

They rode on, a bond of friendship subtly strengthened.

AN AIR of tense desperation hung over the tent city at the edge of the Palmer River goldfield. Disease had struck. It had arrived suddenly, and was spreading quickly.

Outside the tent occupied by Adhilasa and Micah, a conference of sorts was taking place. The Americans were joined by Volkoff, Pasquale, and the Makassar fisherman Asbul. There was little activity to see as they looked about. The Kuthant tribe huddled together under trees nearby, watching nervously. Several miners sat or lay outside their tents, clearly unwell. Chung knelt beside one such man, mopping sweat from the miner's forehead.

Adhilasa watched his old friend's labours. "The fever's spreading. The longer we stay here, the more likely we are to have to trust ourselves to Chung or one of the other angels of mercy trying to help."

"Help!" muttered the Cossack dispiritedly. "I would if I could, but I have seen more than enough sickness that I can do nothing to help. I dig more graves than I dig for gold - that's all the help I can offer."

"Not that searching for gold has been bringing much joy either," added Micah. "I mean, there's still some there, I think, but with so many men here..."

"Over a hundred thousand, so I heard at the Mining Warden's office," reported Adhilasa. "I wonder how many know about the new strike reported in the south? We wouldn't, if I hadn't happened to have been right beside him when the message about a new Warden there arrived from Sydney. I think our Warden may be keeping it quiet deliberately. We'll wake up one morning and find his office abandoned."

The young West Indian gestured helplessly, and said, "You couldn't blame him - look around! If we want to go and try our luck at this new place, we should work out how we're going to get there."

Vittorio scratched at his chin. He'd decided to let his stubble grow out into a beard – less of his face to be sunburned, he'd reasoned. He'd been applying his mind to the options available to them, and there didn't seem to be many. "I suppose we take our chances heading back to Cooktown and try to get a ship south, then head back inland," he said.

Adhilasa looked unhappy at the prospect. "I don't mind a fight when it's necessary, but I admit I don't like the idea of running the gauntlet of those damned Merkin again," he said.

The Italian tried to sound positive, replying, "We made it here without seeing them."

"We didn't," the tall black man reminded him quietly.

He hadn't meant to sound thoughtless, so Vittorio shifted uncomfortably. "I know," he said, then went on to concede, "And I know they've been getting more aggressive lately. I think they've been picking off diggers too sick to properly defend themselves."

That was certainly true. There had been more evidence that the Merkin had developed a particular taste for the flesh of the Chinese people who lived at the fringes of the settlement, growing food to service other miners. They'd never intended to be a food source themselves.

Micah growled angrily, "If they're eating sick men I hope they get the disease themselves and it wipes out every damned one of them."

His long-time mentor nodded sympathetically, and said, "Every chance of that happening. But we don't know how long it might take. And it might just make them even meaner. I have to admit that my preference would be to head south rather than back east."

Asbul had been listening attentively, but so far had said nothing as he pondered his new friends' concerns. Suddenly he asked, "How far sout' you fellas want to go?"

"The Darling River," replied Adhilasa.

"Never heard of it," said the fisherman.

"Until recently, neither had I," the black man admitted. "I'm told it's big. Big enough for paddle steamers to be carrying wool and supplies along it."

"Paddle steamers?!" exclaimed Micah. "That'd feel like home!" he said, fondly recalling life with the Johnsons.

"What's a paddle steamer?" asked Asbul, mystified.

Micah was smiling at the memory as he said, "The most beautiful boat ever made. I loved watching them go by. Fine wood walls and floors, chandeliers, beautiful women, the band playing while the big wheel churns..."

Bemused, Asbul asked, "A boat wit' wheels?"

"One, anyway," said Adhilasa with a smile. "A big one, on the side of the vessel."

"And it rolls over de water?"

"Through it," Micah explained. "It's a bit like the spokes of the wheels are all oars."

Asbul looked thoughtful, and as understanding dawned, he nodded excitedly. "I reckon I'd like one of dem!"

Grinning broadly, he ran over to his Kuthant friends and started an animated conversation. More of the tribe got involved in the discussion. By his gestures, it was clear that Asbul was trying to describe a paddle steamer – no easy task for a man who'd never seen one. The Europeans and Americans watched, intrigued.

"You look at them, and you think of the Merkins. Couldn't be much more different, eh?" said Vittorio.

Adhilasa nodded in agreement, while Gregori added quietly, "I think that some of the things we were told on the way to this country may have been... misguided. These local black men are not 'all the same'."

An eyebrow raised, Adhilasa turned to Volkoff and said, "No more than all Cossacks are, I'm sure."

Gregori only nodded.

Abruptly, Asbul trotted back to the group beside the tent, and grinning broadly said, "Boys - I reckon we can help you!" Quite unfazed by the dubious reactions of some of the group, he continued, "A big boat wit' wheels isn't somet'ing you forget. Karumbari and Walan reckon dey seen boats like dat when dey were camped along-side a real big river."

It dawned on Adhilasa that they might be onto something. "Do they know how far away?" he asked.

"Somewhere between one and two changes of de moon, dereabouts." Seeing the blank look on the Italian merchant's face, Asbul explained, "Dat's how dey measure distances. Same as I do at sea. What does 'a mile' look like, anyway?"

Vittorio grinned in sudden understanding. "I see what you mean. A month of walking - maybe two. A lot less if we're riding, hey?"

The observant Volkoff shook his head. "Asbul's friends don't ride."

"We can, though," said Micah. "Why don't we just ride due south? Sounds like this river should be too big to miss."

His mentor put a cautionary hand on his shoulder, curbing the young man's impatience. "Do you have any idea of the country we'd be travelling through? No - neither do I. Can horses even get through the whole way? We couldn't carry that much food with us. Yes, we can hunt, but do you know what else is safe to eat - which plants are poisonous? I think if the Kuthant are willing, I'll travel with them. Learn as I go."

"We might take horses as far as we can," suggested Volkoff. "Ride only at the pace the Kuthant can walk at, so we don't lose them - but we're not all as used to long marches as they are."

Pasquale, a man whose background was quite unlike his new companions', looked grateful for the suggestion as he asked, "What do you think, Asbul? Will they mind if some of us travel with them?"

The fisherman's voice turned serious. "Dis sickness is scaring dem real bad. It got no Kut'ant so far and I reckon dey're going to go real soon before it does. Dey walk wit' me all de way from de beach where dey found me. So long as nobody's sick I reckon dey not mind, if everyone behaves demselves." Grinning he added, "No touching de women!"

"Not much fear of that!" laughed Micah.

"So, you're intending to join us?" Adhilasa asked his charge.

The young man looked back to the east, where his family lay buried. "It seems the best of a range of bad options."

Looking at him sternly, Volkoff said, "You might feel differently about the women after a time."

"The young man has discipline," said Adhilasa.

Gregori answered levelly, "He is still a young man."

Micah met his gaze and said, "I've been taught to be a gentleman."

They looked into each other's eyes, unblinking for some moments, before the Cossack turned to Adhilasa and said simply, "Yes. It is good."

By now, Vittorio was looking thoughtful. "I wonder how many others will want to travel with us?" he mused.

"Not too many, I hope," said Asbul. "I don't know how hard de way going to be, but if it's like de way we come to get here, I don't reckon dere'll be a lot of tucker to go round."

Adhilasa looked thoughtful. He mused, "Hmm... On the one hand, I don't like the idea of abandoning men to die here. However..."

"Travel lightest, travel fastest," was the veteran Volkoff's advice.

"Just the four of us, then? And Chung, if he's willing?" asked Micah.

"Perhaps two more," suggested the Russian.

Micah gave a wry smile. "What happened to 'travel lightest'?"

"From what I've seen, I think our Spanish friends may prove valuable travelling companions," was the reply.

Enthusiastically Asbul said, "Kut'ant would like it if dey bring deir guitars!"

"I'll talk to them," volunteered Pasquale.

Warningly, Adhilasa said, "We *will* be travelling light! Weapons, a blanket. No trunks full of costumes! Only what can be carried easily."

"And guitars!" insisted the Makassar.

With only a little reluctance, the older American conceded, "Seems entertainment might be the price of passage."

After a moment of thought he then said, "I'll talk to Chung. He may not be willing to leave off trying to tend to the sick men."

Micah waved a confident hand. "We're family. He'll stay with you and I."

In response Adhilasa shrugged. He was inclined to agree, but he'd seen Chung's earnestness in treating the sick. But Asbul laughed.

"He learn to cook some new tucker if he comes wit' us!"

Adhilasa looked at the Kuthants' self-appointed spokesman. He presented himself as a simple, jovial fellow, but there was definitely a shrewd, observant mind at work there.

"You know, that might just be enough to convince him!" he agreed with a smile.

.ooo.

2

THE GATHERING

Orhan Keilbren was sitting on the ground, his back against a tree, his head between his knees. Wei Sun and Pierre stood a little way away from him, the Frenchman holding the reins of their three horses. Wei Sun offered some of the handful of berries he was holding.

"You're sure they're safe?" Pierre's question was casual.

"I have watched several types of birds eat these. That is usually a good sign."

"Right enough," Pierre replied, taking a couple of berries and eating them. "A pity Orhan wasn't always so observant, or careful about what he consumed."

"I don't believe young Keilbren's current distress is related to anything he's eaten recently."

"Not at all, no. I said 'consumed', not eaten, and I don't think it's anything he's had recently."

"It is an evil, insidious master," observed the ex-farmer.

"Mm. And one whose grip isn't easily broken. Not without great willpower and perhaps a satisfactory distraction."

The two men walked over to the tree.

Pierre squatted beside the young man, and gently asked, "How do you feel?"

The Turk was sweating and trembling, mumbling, "She is so beautiful... so beautiful." Suddenly he looked up and grabbed Pierre's arm, although he seemed to look through, not at the Frenchman. "She is beautiful, isn't she? Beautiful?" Keilbren demanded.

Pierre patted Orhan's hand and said, "Yes. Striking. But she and her family are making much better time than us, my friend. We are travelling slowly for your sake, but we do have to keep moving or risk losing track of them."

"No! No! We must catch them up!" cried the young man, struggling to stand.

Wei Sun placed a restraining hand on his shoulder. "Be calm. We will reach them. You want to meet her honourably, do you not?"

Pierre put his hand on Orhan's other shoulder. "Being the best you possibly can be, yes?"

Keilbren looked at each of them in turn, and nodded slowly and painfully. "Best. Yes," he croaked.

～

No WHITE MAN would call it a track. Winding through dense scrub, a narrow path was being trodden down by a procession of the Kuthant and their new companions, never more than three abreast. Walan led the way, accompanied by the ever-watchful Guillermo.

After more wary tribesmen came some family groups. The cook Chung walked amongst them, holding a handful of leaves while he conversed, via Karumbari, with some of the tribe's women.

At the back of this group was Cristiano. The younger Spaniard was bearing a substantial pack on his back, but was still able to strum his guitar, to the delight of some children walking with him.

Immediately behind the musician were Vittorio, Micah, Asbul and two of the Kuthant tribesmen, each leading a pair of laden horses. For the Kuthant, this was a novel way of carrying goods – indeed, carrying goods in such quantity was a novelty – and they were still determining whether it was really effective.

The sweating Italian looked around, trying to peer through heavy scrub. "Are we lost?" he wondered aloud.

Cristiano grinned and called back over his shoulder in reply, "Does it count as lost if you don't know where you're going in the first place?"

That got a laugh from Asbul, who tried to reassure his new friends. "We not lost. Kut'ant know where dey're going."

Micah, though, was a little less certain, and a little more serious, when he asked, "But are they going to the same place as us?"

Asbul laughed again, and, pointing to Cristiano, said, "We don't know where we going anyway, he said. So we must be!"

Micah looked back at the two natives leading the horses behind the Makassar. They were engaged in their own conversation. He couldn't understand a word of it, but it seemed casual and non-threatening. The Kuthants suddenly burst into laughter at their own private joke, and one gave the young man a cheery wave as if to say, "Don't mind us!" – it reassured him, a little.

Some of the tribal elders, male and female, followed the horses. Adhilasa was amongst them, practicing his pronunciation of some of the Kuthant dialect. Most of his new companions were polite enough not to giggle very often, although when they did, he usually joined in.

At the rear of the procession were more of the tribe's brawnier young men. They weren't 'warriors'. The Kuthant never considered any of their number as such. But they could be handy in a fight. And in their midst was the ever-watchful Cossack, for whom fighting had been a way of life.

JAMES ROBERTSON and his erstwhile horse breaker were riding north from Louth at a steady canter. They were approaching the area of Hard Rock Creek, although Kaminski had not yet given a clear description of their precise destination. Even the name 'Hard Rock' was something of the unimaginative Pole's own devising, based entirely on the most distinguishing characteristic he'd noticed about the small outcrop where he'd chanced on a vein.

He'd been doing emergency repairs to a bit of broken riding equipment. He carried a few small tools from habit, and had simply used a convenient large stone as an anvil on which to hammer some stirrup iron. One blow had slipped off its target, chipping off a chunk of dark rock. As soon as Marusz had seen the glint of the exposed vein, he'd set about the stone with hammer blows, trying to bring more to light. He'd achieved just enough to be convinced that there was a good lode there to be found, but also to realise that getting at it effectively would take more and better tools than he could afford. There were other, similar rocks in the area. Some were also promising, but just as resistant to the meagre tools that Kaminski could bring to bear.

Keeping any sign of impatience in check, Robertson said, "Quite a distance from Louth. We've ridden hard for some time. There will have to be plenty of good quality ore to justify the trouble of bringing the equipment you've suggested."

"You doubt me?" was the answering grunt.

"If I doubted you, Marusz, I'd hardly have brought myself and my family this far. I wouldn't have called in a substantial percentage of the favours I'm owed by his Lordship the Governor," James explained with more patience than he felt.

"Don't forget, it's my find!" said Kaminski defensively. It was a particularly hot day, and both men were feeling the effects of the weather.

The squatter sighed, and answered, "Which is why you're my foreman. We have a deal. You'll be paid, and you'll receive a generous percentage of our workings."

Both lapsed back into disgruntled silence. They rounded a sharp bend in the track, and pulled up suddenly. They'd glimpsed a few natives crossing the track some way ahead, disappearing into the bush. And with them, apparently, a white man.

The two exchanged puzzled looks. Being as watchful as they could, guns at the ready, they rode on slowly. At a signal from the Warden, the pair dismounted, and started to cautiously make their way into the fringing scrub.

"I don't like this!" Kaminski muttered. "First decent reef I found was along this way."

"Really – how decent?" asked Robertson mildly.

"Enough for me to write to you about it."

The squatter signalled for silence as they crept on. Through the trees they could see ahead at a distance, a small clearing. Clearly a campsite around a well-built fire, one substantial shelter had been constructed and other small ones in various stages of completion were visible at the fringe. A number of natives could be seen. Men, women and children busy with domestic pursuits: cooking, wood-working, drowsing and playing.

Very quietly, Robertson said, "They seem rather less aggressive than you indicated."

Kaminski frowned. "They're not the Beeargah. From what I've heard I didn't think they settled down in one spot like this. I reckon this is some other mob."

Cautiously the two approached the edge of the encampment. Suddenly, a figure stepped out from behind a tree and confronted them. A white man with rifle in hand, although it wasn't pointed at them yet. A flicker of movement to their right, another to their left – two natives had appeared, holding spears that looked like they could be thrown very quickly.

The grizzled white man spoke. "Can I help you blokes?"

The squatter promptly rose to his full height, and in a clear, almost-cheerful voice said, "Good afternoon. My name's Robertson. I'm new to these parts. Could I have your name, please?"

Caught off-guard by the rather incongruous question, the man facing them automatically replied, "James Arnold." Recovering himself, he continued after a pause, "And what brings you here, Mr. Robinson?"

"That's Robertson. My horse does actually." He smiled slightly at his own joke - although it hadn't put Arnold at his ease completely it had at least lessened the tension, he thought.

Pressing the situation, he continued, "Seriously though, I'm travelling on Government business. I'm actually quite pleased to find you here."

Arnold's suspicions were immediately restored by the term 'government business'. He lived independently in the bush by very deliberate choice, after all. Glowering, he asked, "Why?"

"Well, as you're visiting these natives, I presume you have a grasp of their language. I don't. You can talk to them for me."

There was more than a trace of sarcasm in the teamster's voice as he asked, "What would you like me to say?"

Robertson took a thoughtful pose for a moment, then replied, "Explain that this land is under the power of His Majesty's government. It's intended that a settlement will be constructed here as soon as possible, with a view to exploration for the gold that's been reported."

"Gold?! News to me!" Arnold interrupted.

"Really?" said Robertson in apparent surprise. "I'd wondered whether that may have been the reason for your being here."

"Not bloody likely! I..."

Robertson cut him off. "Fine. Please explain to these people that they are required to move along as quickly as possible. I propose to open this area up to diggers immediately. A camp will be established. Equipment will be set up, and more substantial structures will follow, including an office and residence for the Gold Warden, and facilities for a contingent of troopers to maintain order."

The teamster shook his head angrily. "You can't just kick these people off this land and start slapping up tents and buildings."

"Actually, I can. A substantial claim has been staked for this area by the Hard Rock Mining Company, and as Warden I have a responsibility, indeed, an obligation to enforce that claim."

"So you're the Warden, hey? There's a surprise! But the Balyarta people already live here. Some Mining Company can't just own the place out from under them."

Unnoticed by any of the three white men, Magpie had quietly ridden to the edge of the encampment, coming from the creek. He'd dismounted from his horse , waved silently to the Balyarta folk by the fire, and started to approach, listening to the conversation. His first response was curiosity, but then a look of shock crossed his face as he drew nearer. He stopped for a moment, recovered himself, and approached very slowly and warily as Robertson continued speaking in his best authoritative voice.

"Are you familiar with the term *Terra Nullius*? No? It means 'empty land'. In the eyes of the law that's what this has been. A claim has been staked, there is no record of prior ownership, so the claim stands."

Arnold continued to try to protest. "But these people..."

"Are not recognized by the laws of the colony as being here and possessing this property."

"But you can see them...!" was the exasperated reply.

"But the law, which I am bound to enforce, can't." The squatter had adopted his most reasonable 'I'd-like-to-help-you-but-my-hands-are-tied' voice. "I'm sorry Mister - Arnold, wasn't it - had you lodged a prior claim to the land I would of course be obliged to recognize and defend it. But you haven't, have you?"

Just as Arnold was about to make an angry reply, his teamster partner appeared at his shoulder, his approach so silent he startled even the tribesmen still standing as silent witnesses to the tense exchange.

Quietly Magpie said, "Mister Robertson. Kaminski. Didn't think I'd be seeing you again."

Kaminski put his hand on his gun, but said nothing. Robertson betrayed a momentary flicker of reaction, but kept his voice level as he replied, "Magpie. The feeling is mutual."

Far more surprised by the words than Magpie's sudden appearance – he knew just how stealthy the half-caste could be – Arnold asked, "You know this joker?"

"Too bloody well. I worked for him for years..."

"Treat you crook, did he?"

Robertson, who hadn't taken his eyes off Magpie, was quick to answer first. "Hardly. You grew up in my household, didn't you?"

"I was a kid, amongst your stockmen and shearers."

"You were fed, and clothed, and taught. You were paid for the work you did."

"Yeah - same as the rest of us!" added Kaminski venomously. "Then you turned round and took off, didn't you?"

Magpie glared now at the Pole. "I remember you, too. You'd no sooner rode in than you talked about taking off yourself, often enough. You never did, eh? Too busy sniffing round the boss's daughter?"

In response Kaminski snarled, but the squatter showed no reaction at all.

He simply replied, "As a matter of fact, Mister Kaminski did leave my employ to further his ambitions - just as you did. We've only recently renewed our acquaintanceship. By chance, I found him in the area when I came to take up my appointment as Warden. And now I chance to find you here too - what a small world! I'm afraid if you've made yourself at home amongst these people I'll expect you to move on with them. Of course, if you're willing to work for me, I'm sure I can find a position for you. The same goes for you, Mister Arnold."

His bland expression was at stark variance to the other faces around him. Kaminski looked mightily unimpressed, Arnold scowled suspiciously, the two Balyartas were puzzled and troubled by the obvious tension, and Magpie's face mirrored his anger.

"These people are my friends! No way I'm gonna betray them..." he began.

His former employer only shrugged. "I didn't say anything about betrayal. I've offered you work, you've refused - so far. These people are to move on. Whether you go with them or not frankly doesn't matter to me. Mister Arnold, if you're looking for work, you'll find my temporary office in Louth - ask at the Woolpack - until I get quarters built here. That will be soon."

The new Warden turned on his heel, as best he could among the scrubby undergrowth, and strode back to his horse without a backward glance. Kaminski gave the encampment a last look which suggested that he was thinking of ways to enforce the 'move on' order, then set off after his boss.

By the time they'd reached the sharp bend in the track the Pole had caught up with Robertson.

"Who the hell is the Hard Rock Mining Company?" he asked, peevishly.

"I am, of course."

"What about all that legal stuff you were telling them? Is it true?"

"Does it matter? Who's going to stop us?"

∼

IN THE EARLY EVENING, the exchange with the new Gold Warden was still being discussed around the Balyarta campfire. The gist of the conversation had been relayed to everyone, analyzed and talked about. Ultimately it was left to the small group of elders to determine what to do next.

That little coterie, including by invitation Magpie and James Arnold, sat together in a circle, eating and talking.

Arnold's deeply felt outrage had only intensified with time and reflection. "I reckon we call his bluff. Sit tight" he said.

Magpie, surprisingly, didn't share his friend's attitude. "James Robertson isn't a bloke who bluffs. Besides, if there really is gold somewhere round here…"

He let his voice trail off. His implication was clear. If there was gold in the area, as soon as word got around the landscape would change in very many ways, and none of them for the better as far as the Balyarta were concerned.

"Yeah, true," admitted James. "That stuff does funny things to blokes' heads."

Mundil's smile had no mirth in it as he said, "Most white buggers bloody crazy anyway. Anything makes 'em worse is something we want to be well out of."

The Balyarta had been cautious in their dealings with the men who'd come to their country in recent years, with good reason. Few had treated them well, which is why the few who'd done so, like James Arnold and Peter McGregor, were so esteemed.

One of the older women, Keewuk, whose English was still only sketchy, had been looking thoughtfully around the campsite where the rest of the tribe were settling down for the night. In her Burundji dialect she observed, "We've got a lot of people carrying injuries and wounds. They didn't get much rest in the rush away from home. It would be better to rest and heal."

"Aye," agreed Samuel, using English as a respectful courtesy to his friend James. "Even if this isn't tae be our new home, we do need some time tae recover strength tae move on."

James' reply was still angry. "Again with the 'moving on'. Somewhere along the way you've got to stand up to bastards that throw their weight around. Gold Warden or whatever he's calling himself."

Once more, Magpie shook his head in disagreement. "I know you're right, James, but Robertson's a bloke to tread real careful with."

The veteran teamster looked at his partner askance, the measure of the half-caste's caution finally starting to sink in. "Never seen a bloke spook you before, mate," he said with concern.

"It's not that. I just know how... ruthless he can be."

Old Samuel eyed their friend and ally shrewdly. "Ye've done yuir own share of moving on, haven't ye?"

Magpie didn't say anything in reply, but his uncomfortable expression was all the answer Samuel required.

Missing the implications in the unfamiliar language, and concerned for the welfare of her own children, Keewuk continued, "I think if we try to move too far or too fast now, people will die."

Samuel replied, in their own tongue, "And if we don't move on, and this man is as dangerous as Magpie fears, I think people may die."

The woman's long-time partner, Yallaroi, took her side. "But we can wait for a bit, surely," he said.

The half-caste nodded, thoughtfully. "I reckon so. Robertson's out of his home turf. No matter what he says, even he has to take some time to get organized to 'enforce' his law."

"Mmm," mused Arnold, still unhappy but reading the prevailing mood. "But everybody keeps an eye out. Really watches out for trouble."

"And we keep a low profile for a bit," added Magpie.

"You two?" asked Mundil, wryly.

"Yeah, us too. Robertson will want to at least look like he's playing by the rules."

Thonkumundil scoffed. "Whose rules? His own?"

Magpie shrugged. He knew more about how James Robertson operated than he liked. "Probably. But we can try not to give him any more excuse to be a bastard, at least while the people heal up."

Arnold looked dubiously at his uncharacteristically cautious friend. "He strikes me as a bloke who doesn't need an excuse."

"You're right, but maybe he's got to be a bit more careful now he's got his flash new job to protect. Maybe..."

He sounded no more certain than he felt.

IT WAS about the same time of the early evening, but a few days later and still many miles distant. A small fire had been set under a rocky overhang. Above the fire, a sizeable pot had been suspended, in which water seethed around chunks of wallaby carcass - mostly bone.

Chung was stirring the pot with a long-bladed knife while he talked with a few Kuthant folks, male and female. He managed a smattering of their dialect, but mostly the conversation was translated each way by Walan.

"So, even when there's almost no decent meat left on the bones, you crack them to release the marrow and boil them down like this to dissolve the sinews and stuff into a stock. Good stuff for keeping the strength up."

His audience nodded. This made sense, and if time permitted certainly seemed preferable to trying to suck the marrow from just the long bones.

A little way away, Guillermo and Cristiano were playing an old Spanish folk tune on their guitars. Most of their companions sat around them. Some, like Vittorio, were clapping in time. Others accompanied the music with carved rhythm sticks, shaped specially for the purpose. Asbul was clicking a pair of these. He'd been delighted to find a new instrument as portable as his trusty flute – percussion was as important a part of music as melody, he knew.

At the far end of the overhang, where the rock 'ceiling' started to curve upwards, sat Adhilasa, Volkoff and Karumbari. The three chatted comfortably in the sometimes-fractured English they shared. It was a reasonably secure position, but wary as ever, the Russian had ensured Micah and a few keen-eyed tribesmen kept watch from discreet positions nearby.

While they talked, the Kuthant man was painting up on the surface of the rock. He'd used a few different ochres and ground bits of various stones and plants to give himself a palette of surprising range, that he mixed with saliva and applied with the well-chewed end of a stick.

Gregori was explaining some of the strategy he'd learned across his long career as a soldier. "The fourth brigade of the army of the Vosges were *francs-tireurs*," he explained.

The proudly multi-lingual Adhilasa shook his head. "I'm sorry. My Kuthant is improving, my friend, but that one's beyond me. I can't even put it into English."

The Cossack thought for a moment. "Um - guerillas. Civilian fighters? An army of volunteers who fought, er, outside the rules of war."

Karumbari didn't stop painting, but his voice conveyed his bafflement as he asked, "War has rules for you?"

Something close to a smile crossed Volkoff's face. "Perhaps better to say there are traditional ways of organizing for war. Formations, battle lines. *We* did not always use such things. We used the terrain - the countryside itself - as a weapon."

For Karumbari this was so obvious as to be puzzling. Why was this worth mentioning, as if it were some revelation? "Yes," he said. "Any other way and you'd be fighting against the land as well as your enemy."

Gregori nodded. "You'd be surprised how many generals and commanders fail to see that sense! Their weakness. At Chatillon there were less than 400 of us, but we surprised and over-ran more than a thousand Prussians."

"Good odds to overcome," said Adhilasa admiringly, reflecting on his own experiences.

The Cossack smiled at the recollection, and said, "I am proud that I helped Ricciotti Garibaldi devise our strategy. We captured many of their men, their officers, their horses, even their ammunition and arms. And best of all, lost only six of our own men in the process."

The Kuthant spat into a little mound of a chalky white dust, then said sympathetically, "Six is a lot to lose."

"Not from a force of four hundred," Volkoff replied.

Karumbari looked at him. "How big is four hundred?"

Thinking he realised the problem, Adhilasa tried to explain, "Many times the number of your people, Karumbari."

Volkoff, though, perceived his own mistake, and apologetically said, "Yes. I see that six would be a great loss to you, my friend."

Karumbari continued with his work. "Loss of one is great to somebody."

Both Gregori and Adhilasa reacted sharply to this simple observation. Almost as one voice, the pair responded, "Yes..."

A thoughtful silence ensued as they watched the painting take shape. It was a simple gathering of human figures, in a close circle. Each individual was depicted in a different colour.

JAMES ROBERTSON HAD ESTABLISHED a temporary office for himself in the Woolpack. Not as luxurious as he'd like, but comfortable and quite adequate. This morning, two men were busy in the room. The Gold Warden was perusing some legal papers he'd drafted, making sure he'd covered contingencies. His manservant was continuing what seemed a Herculean task of getting the room and its fittings satisfactorily clean.

Shaking his head as he rubbed at a particularly stubborn stain on the woodwork, Ali observed, "I do not think the staff here take their responsibilities seriously."

His employer smiled without looking up from his paperwork. "Good help is hard to find. That's why you're appreciated, old man." The valet didn't react to this rare expression of something like affection. From long experience, James didn't expect him to, and continued equably, "It's as I told the children. This arrangement is only temporary. It won't take long to have our own premises out by the creek, which you can maintain properly. I'll send young Phillip out with Kaminski tomorrow to look at potential building sites."

Ali gave a small nod to indicate his appreciation of the prospect. There was a knock at the office door. Ali opened it slightly, with a crisply polite, "Yes?"

The heavy door muffled the reply, but Ali turned to his employer and announced, "Mister and Mrs. Gillespie to see you, sir."

"Ah – the builder! Show them in, please Ali," said the Warden genially as he stood up to greet his visitors.

Into the office came a large bluff Englishman in a suit more serviceable than stylish, and a strikingly beautiful coloured woman.

The man extended a large, calloused hand and introduced himself. "Charles Gillespie, at yer service. This is my wife, Jade."

Robertson returned the clasp. "A pleasure to meet you." Turning to Jade he added, "And to meet you, young lady. Please forgive my impertinence, but I'm trying to place your nationality."

The girl – surely, she was only a little more than that? – smiled demurely while her grinning husband replied on her behalf. "Bit of an all-sorts, my girl is. Met her on one of the Pacific Islands as I sailed down here a few years back. Not sure exactly, but I reckon she's part Indian, part white, and part a few types of Polynesian."

Unashamedly admiring, James said, "Well, I must say that the sum of those parts is very lovely indeed. Pardon my presumption, sir, but may I ask Jade, are there any more like you at home?"

The builder chuckled amiably. He was well used to men's reaction to his wife. His own had been exactly the same, after all. He figured he was just fortunate enough to have met her first. "No offence taken, mate. I know how lucky I am. Ain't no-one quite like her, I reckon."

Smiling, Robertson agreed, "I dare say not. Ali, please fetch drinks while we get down to business. What will you have?"

"Whiskey and water," said the builder.

"Just water, please," said his wife.

Ali gave the couple a small bow and left the room. Robertson indicated chairs for the Gillespies, and resumed his own seat at his desk.

"To business," the Warden said briskly. "As it happens we were just discussing my new premises before you arrived. I'll need both accommodation and an office. In the first instance it needn't be anything grand, just serviceable. I'm confident I'll soon be in a position to ask you to construct something more substantial."

Gillespie's forehead creased. "I'm sorry, Mister Robertson, you've given me very little to work with here. What sort of office are we talking about?"

Tapping his fingers on the desk idly, James framed a careful reply. "For now, can I just say a government office? I'll need desk space and storage space - secure."

"Secure?" the builder repeated.

"I'll be acquiring a substantial safe, but I'd like both the office and the house itself to be as secure as possible. Double lock doors, perhaps bars on the windows?"

Charles Gillespie rocked back on his chair, his lips pursed. After a few moments' thought, he said, "The way you're talking, I'd make a guess this might be a gold office. I worked on one of them down south soon after I arrived in the country. You've kept this quiet."

The Warden inclined his head slightly. Gillespie wasn't stupid, clearly, so with appropriate respect in his voice he replied, "I'd be very grateful if you'd do the same. I suggest that your discretion may be - well worth your while."

The Englishman gave a happy guffaw. "Hey, I'm happy to be able to stake a claim ahead of a crowd! I'll need a team to help with the construction, but..." He thought for a moment. "If I arrange it right I ought to be able to fit the more obvious security features myself at the end of the job, when I've paid everyone off. You might have to come up with a story about why you're building a big house way out of town."

"Mm. I see your point."

There was a single quick knock at the office door, and Ali entered with a tray bearing a tall glass of cold water, a small jug containing more water, and two tumblers of whiskey. He passed around the drinks with his usual quiet efficiency, serving his employer last, as protocol required.

As he took his glass, Robertson asked, "Ali, why might a man build a house in the bush, miles from anywhere - other than for the reason you know I have?"

The valet gave the smallest of shrugs and replied, tapping his head, "Why do white men do many of the things they do?"

Jade Gillespie smiled at the gesture. "I think the heat makes some of them a little crazy," she said.

"Poor men go crazy," said Robertson, returning her smile. "Men with money are regarded as eccentric. Ali, dear lady, you both may offer a solution. In the event of curious questions before I'm ready to give answers we may describe the project as an eccentric whim. I don't expect it to take long before the first claims return very generously, at which point - well, it would be hard to keep the news quiet, eh?"

"You're right there!" said the jovial builder. "Well, I reckon we can do business, Mister R. Your secret's safe with me – us," he corrected, with a polite gesture to his wife. "Where is this place to be built?" he asked.

The Warden steepled his fingers, but smiled as he said, "All in good time. Once I have a clearer idea of the area myself, I'll get you to help me select the best site. Please make a start on the drawings - we'll stay in touch."

"I'm looking forward to it!" enthused Gillespie.

"As am I," said Jade in a much softer voice.

"Soon, then," said Robertson. He smiled, and extended his hand first to the lady and then to her husband. The Gillespies smiled back, and politely departed.

Ali closed the door behind them, turning to see his employer idly pacing the room as he drained his glass.

"Very attractive woman," said the Warden.

"Indeed sir? I couldn't say I'd noticed."

James tried not to laugh, out of some respect for his long association with the Indian. "Really?" he said. "I wonder about you sometimes Ali. Jade Gillespie is a very interesting woman."

"Your interest is duly noted, sir," said Ali, non-committal as ever.

❦

DESPITE TALKING WELL into the night, the teamsters were working as efficiently as usual next morning. A combination of experience and attitude could be thanked.

Arnold and Thonkumundil were hitching up the team, while Magpie tied packs to his own and James' horses. Samuel stood beside them, trying to radiate reassurance. It wasn't quite working.

"I don't like the feeling that we're running out on you," said Arnold.

"Ye're not. Ye be doing your job, as ye should."

The white man shook his head. "We can get by without the money for a while. Especially if we're staying close by you."

Mundil looked up from adjusting a harness. "It's not about money, boss. You made a commitment to Mister Sutherland. Like you told me - let someone down now, bad for business in future."

"Andrew Sutherland's a good bloke. He'd understand..."

"Yeah, he probably would, when you tell him," agreed Magpie. "But if you're gonna ride out to his property and talk to him, we might as well ride out there and do the job, eh?"

Samuel put a hand on the older teamster's shoulder and said, "James Arnold, ye go and be true tae yuir word. I know ye mean well by us, but we can look out for ourselves. We will be careful and keep watch."

Still trying to protest, Arnold said, "Well, the job doesn't need the three of us."

His final knot tied, Magpie clambered onto his horse. "Sorry mate, but you reckoned it would when you took it on - a bloody big wagon load, you and him reckoned - won't be any lighter or easier. Think of it this way, three of us doing the work will make it quicker and we can be back here sooner.

Watching Mundil settle onto his own horse, James finally conceded. "Yeah. Yeah, alright. Come on." As he mounted his horse he looked down at Samuel, concern etched on his face. "Everyone takes care, right?"

A HOT SUN was high in the sky. Men and horses were soaked with sweat as they struggled with a difficult creek crossing. The actual water was shallow, but the banks were steep and slippery.

Micah and Chung had just made it across. They stood, holding the reins loosely, men and beasts getting their breath back. On the far bank, Adhilasa and Cristiano held several more horses, waiting their turn. They watched, concerned, as Volkoff and Pasquale stood near the top of the far bank, hauling on ropes and reins to assist a horse struggling up the slope.

Guillermo stood below, in the creek itself, setting a rope harness around the next horse in line, ready to assist with its climb.

The Kuthant tribe were arrayed on either side of the creek, watching, but keeping a wary distance from the animals. One of the men who'd made it across was sitting in a patch of bracken, nursing an injured leg. He was being tended by Asbul, who'd prepared a quick poultice, and was laying that on a gash below the man's knee.

"I was trying to help and the vicious thing kicked me!" complained the injured fellow.

"Not vicious. Scared and upset," the Makassar tried to explain.

"Upset? I'm upset! I think my leg is broken!"

"No, you just got a cut and a bad bruise. These leaves settle it for now, and I'll make up another good poultice to rest on it tonight."

Suddenly there was a shout from Volkoff as the rope slipped in his sweaty hands, and the horse stumbled. As the beast fell, some of its load came loose and crashed down the creek bank. Among the spillage was the Cossack's precious box, the top of which jarred off.

Guillermo lunged forward and reassured the horse as it regained its feet. His gentle voice calmed the animal while it fought for balance, stamping hooves on the rocky creek bed. Quickly it settled, with a final shake of its head, almost like a fighter recovering from a blow. The Spaniard patted its rump as it made the climb on the second attempt, Volkoff back on the securing rope.

With the horse safe, Guillermo started passing the fallen boxes up to Gregori and Vittorio. The guitarist went to press the lid back on Volkoff's box, and for the first time noticed the contents. He gave a little whistle of surprise and admiration at the long rifle, offering an approving nod to the Russian as he passed up the container.

"Chassepot. Fine piece of work," Guillermo said quietly.

"The best rifles ever made," Volkoff answered, a little defensively.

As he passed more boxes up to the two men on the bank, the Spaniard continued casually reviewing the weapons. "Fast loading, accurate over an excellent range. You may be right."

The Cossack looked at him in surprise. "You know their capabilities?""A little. We saw a small number in Piribebuy."

"Where?" asked Vittorio, who hadn't been following the conversation, not having noticed the guns.

Handing up the last of the fallen crates, Guillermo explained only briefly. "The mountains of Paraguay. A story for another time. This is hot work and the creek is hardly cooling. I would rather we were done and done quickly!"

The Russian nodded agreement as he retied the load on the now-placid horse. He discreetly ensured his rifles were secure, and that particular box was masked by others.

Adhilasa was leading another horse down the gentler slope into the creek. At the same time, Vittorio tossed the guide rope back down to the Spaniard in the creek bed. The process continued, the teamwork consolidating with every obstacle encountered on the journey.

ARNOLD and his team were making good time, leading their horses to Sutherland's outlying property. They were nearing the outskirts of Louth, when they were hailed by a lone horseman riding towards them. Both parties reined in their mounts.

The maverick preacher Peter McGregor tipped his battered wide-brimmed hat in greeting.

"Well met, gentlemen!" he called. "Especially ye, Thonkumundil - I was hoping tae find some clue of where yuir people are. How is everyone?"

Mundil acknowledged the concern with a grateful nod. "Mostly okay, Mister Mac. Lost a couple, like you thought, but most of the rest not hurt too bad."

"I'll pray for the souls of those who've passed. Is there owt I can do for the living?" asked the Scot.

Magpie had an answer. "There's some pellet wounds I'm worried might be getting infected. I've tried pouring a bit of rum on them."

McGregor snorted, "The most useful thing ye could do with that devil's brew."

"Especially the bilge that gets served up in this town! It's probably doing more harm than good," was James Arnold's wry comment.

The preacher didn't disagree. "Aye, well, I can find something better. Where are Samuel and the rest?"

Arnold opened his mouth to answer, but paused. He craned his neck to peer down the road behind McGregor. "You make sure nobody follows you out there."

"Aye, I'll do my best. But nobody else here is interested in the Balyarta."

Magpie looked grimly at the preacher, before describing the tribe's new location. Bitterly he said, "Somebody was, Mister Mac, somebody was..."

MARUSZ KAMINSKI WAS BACK on the track near what he'd called Hard Rock Creek. This time his riding companion was the younger 'Mister Robertson'. With the Warden's encouragement, the Pole had agreed to accompany Phillip on a hunting expedition.

The father had some hope it may foster a better attitude to his new situation, making the boy less tiresome to live with. Davinia would be even more difficult, of course.

Both riders had their guns at the ready, and were scanning the surrounding bush as they travelled.

"So, this will be home. Well, Mister K, you've impressed my father, anyway," said the young man, casually.

"Not you?"

"Gold doesn't hold as much appeal for me," Phillip admitted.

Kaminski grunted, irritated. "You were born well off. It means a lot more to men who've had to struggle. A soldier like me. Son of a soldier like your father."

"Hmph. I don't know that my grandfather had to struggle so much in India."

The Pole grunted again, and replied, "All soldiers struggle, even officers. Especially when they're in a foreign country. You never knew India, did you?"

"Not at all. Grandfather had come to Australia and left the service before I was born. I'd like to go there someday though. I hear the hunting was great. Elephants, tigers..."

That lifted Kaminski's surly demeanour slightly. With a small grin he said, "I reckon kangaroos have their own challenges."

"I suppose so," said Phillip, for whom the grazing marsupials had been among his most frequent targets around their property. Wild ones may prove more interesting, he hoped. "You've seen some around here? We're not wasting our time?"

"Heat of the day, they're less likely to be moving around - you know that. Tougher hunting, better hunting. Keep an eye out in the shade under trees."

Phillip was watching to the left of the track, Marusz to the right.

Suddenly the older man cinched his horse over, hard into the side of his companion's animal.

He raised his rifle and growled, "Trouble!"

A group of about ten Beeargah native men rushed aggressively from the cover of the trees, and blocked the road in front of the horsemen. A few were armed with battered old muskets, and the rest brandished spears and clubs. They were dressed in an odd assortment of native attire and ill-fitting stolen clothes such as shirts, vests and trousers.

One of the Beeargah, who spoke fragmentary English, shouted, "Stop there! Give us money!"

"Get the hell out of our way!" was Kaminski's angry response.

"You stop there! Give us money! Give us food!" the man repeated his demand.

Phillip leaned to his companion and quietly warned, "Behind us."

A smaller group of natives had moved from cover to cut off the track behind the white men. Phillip covered them as best he could with his rifle, without taking his attention from the larger group in front.

"How many behind me?" asked the Pole softly.

"Six."

"Less than in front. That's the way we go then. On my signal, wheel."

"What signal?" asked Phillip, puzzled.

Kaminski's reply was to shoot one of the spear-carrying Beeargah as he turned his horse. Taken by surprise, Robertson was a little slower to get his horse around. Admittedly, too, he was a somewhat less able horsemen than the experienced Pole. Nonetheless he got the animal turned, and was close enough to his companion to hear his instruction.

"Aim for the buggers with the spears. I don't reckon those guns are much threat."

As if to confirm that suspicion, one of the Beeargah flung his musket like a boomerang at the riders. Phillip swayed and dodged the weapon as the pair rode straight at the six natives. Following the

directive, he let off a shot which wounded one of the men brandishing spears.

Even as the riders burst through the thin rank of tribesmen,
Robertson looked down at the man he'd wounded, and was surprised
by what he was wearing. What he'd thought was an oversized necker-
chief was actually a knitted woolen shawl.

There were angry, frustrated shouts from behind them. A few
spears were thrown, but the closest one came to damaging effect was
to lodge in one of Phillip's saddle bags.

Even as they rode away at speed, Phillip cast a thoughtful glance
back over his shoulder. The shawl had been incongruous, but more –
it had struck a faint chord of memory.

IT WAS EARLY that evening when the Robertson family were gathered in what was doing service as their living room upstairs in the Woolpack. James was pacing the room, Phillip stood, holding a drink, and Davinia perched on the arm of a chair, radiating anger. That wasn't unusual for her, admittedly.

"You're quite sure of this?" asked the Warden.

"Absolutely!" replied his son, emphatically. "It looked that damned odd - I just thought it was a scrap of cloth at first, then when I was closer I realized it was a knitted shawl. I remembered that Sergeant describing what the girl was wearing when she went missing."

His father nodded. "Yes. Amongst other things, her mother's shawl, grey with tasseled edges."

"If it's not the same one it looks a lot like it. And that seems an unlikely coincidence."

Davinia tossed her head back, and snapped, "So! The savages did take the child!"

The squatter seemed surprisingly non-committal. His shrewd mind was already assessing a range of possibilities. "Mmm..." he intoned, unconsciously.

Phillip looked at his father suspiciously. "You're thinking," he said.

"Yes, I am. I'm thinking that I... I'm sorry, son - *we* should be taking this information to Sergeant McCartney, and strongly suggesting that action should be taken."

His daughter folded her arms and nodded once, decisively. "Definitely. Shoot the bastards."

The Warden was more restrained. "It may come to that. Certainly, this proves it would be in the best interests of our new community to remove the native presence."

At least one of his offspring caught the note of calculated satisfaction in his voice.

~

THE PROCESSION of the Kuthants and their oddly-assorted travelling companions had continued south. Although they didn't know it, they were within a day or two of reaching Louth. For now, though, they were continuing to make their way through thick bush, picking their way as best they could to lead the pack-horses through gaps between trees.

There was a leading group of a half-dozen Kuthant men, including Karumbari and Walan, together with most of the more senior of their companions: Adhilasa, Guillermo, Volkoff, Vittorio and Asbul. The women and children followed. At the rear were the rest of the men-folk, with Chung, Cristiano and Micah leading the horses that placidly trampled down ferns and low vegetation, some of which they took the opportunity to munch as they went.

After a brief discussion with their guides, Asbul reported, "We getting close, Karumbari t'inks."

Vittorio looked about. He might as well have been in deepest darkest Africa, he thought. "How would you tell? All this time we've travelled, the countryside still looks the same. I mean, I can tell bush from desert, but once we're back amongst these trees, it's all the same to my eyes!"

Adhilasa nodded sympathetically. "Which is why we're with these folks."

He was rather less bewildered than the merchant, but he did appreciate his friend's frustration. It was, he knew, still a totally strange environment for the Italian.

"Si," agreed Guillermo, "I am learning, but they recognize trails and paths I can still only just make out."

His friends' support reassured Pasquale, or at least reduced his discomfort. Grinning, he said, "I think our friends can read trees like I read street signs at home."

Karumbari paused to allow Asbul to catch up with him, and quietly spoke to the fisherman in Kuthant. Gregori was listening closely, trying to be unobtrusive.

"Water? Near here? Is that it?" the Cossack asked in surprise.

The Makassar gave him an admiring grin. "Hey, you getting good! We close to a creek, or a river – running water."

He spoke again to Karumbari, who replied in equally low tones.

Asbul translated, "Little running water, dat leads into bigger running water. Dat's where he's seen de boat with de wheel."

That made sense to Vittorio. "So, we follow this creek to the Darling River, then what? East or west, do we know?"

Gregori had already thought of a strategy. He suggested, "See if Karumbari or Walan know which way the boats are usually heading when we get there. Follow the opposite direction till we see one coming towards us. Then ask the people on the boat - subtly I think - about this gold strike."

"Good plan," said Adhilasa approvingly.

The trader Vittorio was thoughtful. He gave voice to his concern. "Given how much time we've taken to get here, I'd reckon there's a good chance plenty of people know about it. Someone would have had to have been really devious to have kept it quiet so long."

'ANY PORT IN A STORM', it's sometimes said. Similarly, on a blazingly hot afternoon, any bar can be welcome, even Cattenach's in Louth. Uncomfortably sweat-soaked as they were, that temptation lay just before the three Asian companions who'd made their way north from Sydney.

"Is it wise to ply our young friend with alcohol when he - and we - have worked so hard to help him overcome his addiction on the way here?" asked Wei Sun.

Pierre's amiable nature was being affected by the heat. He snapped, "I'm not going to 'ply' him with anything! I know you don't drink, Orhan can make up his own mind, but I am dry and dusty from travelling and I want a drink - a strong one!"

Wei Sun shrugged, accepting the comment casually. He followed the others' example, and tied the reins of his weary horse to a convenient rail. Orhan grinned, but stopped suddenly before they entered the bar. He pointed up the street.

A group of horsemen were heading in their direction, the animals ridden at a resolute canter. More than half the riders wore blue coats, and most of those were dark-skinned. As they came closer, the faces of two of the white men were recognizable and familiar.

"It's the man we followed up here - the man in charge of the gold. And that's his son," observed Orhan, who added in sudden excitement, "And look behind them!"

Not far behind the troopers rode Davinia. She'd contrived to ride rather more decorously than the men in front of her, conscious as ever of attracting attention.

Wei Sun scowled disapprovingly. He didn't like the look of the sergeant and his squad of troopers and their civilian escort, which included Marusz Kaminski as well as the two Robertson males.

"The girl rides with them," he complained.

"After them, at least. Well, we've already seen she didn't sit demurely in their carriage all the way from Sydney. Orhan certainly noticed," he added with a grin.

That was entirely true. "She moves well. With grace," said the Turk, admiringly.

Wei Sun nodded, perhaps grudgingly, as he said, "And a suggestion of power. Like a young tigress, I think."

"Mm..." was the dreamy response.

Pierre's thoughts were in a quite different direction. Aloud he mused, "Have you noticed there's not a lot of gold-hungry men streaming into town? I think that devious fellow has succeeded in keeping his cards remarkably close to his chest."

At a signal from the Warden, the mounted party stopped right outside Cattenach's. The Robertsons and Kaminski quickly dismounted and rushed into the bar, the latter pushing Wei Sun aside roughly as he passed. De la Fontaine put a restraining hand on his friend's arm, then led the three Asians in quietly following the men inside. Sergeant McCartney and his troopers waited restlessly outside, still on their horses.

The crowd in the bar were hardly Louth's finest. It was a little more than half full. Mostly Cattenach's regulars, they were a motley collection of sots, petty crooks, and men desperately down on their luck. Not all rogues, but for the most part, hard men and hard drinkers. Two women had been 'circulating', unenthusiastically touting for business. Rebecca wasn't one of them – she preferred an evening shift, when at least some of the clientele were less horrible options.

Robertson stood on a bench, rapping a glass like a bell, ensuring he could be seen and heard by all present. When he was sure he had everyone's attention, he introduced himself, carefully not mentioning his official title. Very few people knew of that yet, which was exactly how he wanted it. He indicated his son and Kaminski.

"Gentlemen, these two fellows are prepared to swear they've seen evidence that the local savages did definitely take that little girl!"

Phillip wore an appropriate look of righteous anger, but a keen observer might wonder if there were something slightly furtive – guilty, even - about Kaminski's expression.

A wave of anger rippled around the audience, as expected. As they stirred, Davinia slipped quietly in and stood just inside the doorway, behind Pierre. She was watching her father, but also casting her eyes appraisingly around the room. Clearly the youngest man in the room, apart from her brother, Orhan attracted her approval. Not just for his age, he was genuinely good-looking. Perhaps sensing her gaze, or more likely keeping his own watch on the pretty girl, the Turk met her eye briefly, smiled nervously, then looked away. Davinia smiled to herself, clearly making a mental note.

Meanwhile, her father had continued speaking. "I've got Sergeant McCartney and some of his boys outside, but I don't know how many of these fellows we'll be up against. A gang of them attacked my men yesterday..." he said, brandishing the spear that had lodged in Phillip's saddlebag.

"Damn right, Mr. Robertson! They're a rough lot, alright!" exclaimed Kaminski.

Giving the Pole a gesture of thanks, James looked around the room. "I'd be grateful to any man that chose to ride alongside us, and bring his gun!"

"How grateful?" called ratty Kev Seiman.

The squatter looked at him sternly and asked, "What price do you put on a little girl's life?"

Two of the men nearest Seiman scowled and jabbed the scrawny man in the ribs. The men, Miller and Boyd, both growled angrily as Kev looked sheepishly at his glass.

Others in the crowd were less obviously mercenary than Seiman. "Yeah, we'll go with you mate!" shouted a tall, lean Irishman named O'Dea, leading to a sudden chorus of agreement that brought a satisfied smile to Robertson's face.

"You bet!" agreed Jansen, a beefy Swede not long arrived in Louth, but uncritically keen to fit in.

Orhan turned to his two companions, enthusiastically encouraging, "We should go, too!"

Wei Sun looked doubtful. "I'm not sure about this man..."

The Frenchman looked just as uncertain, but said quietly, "I think our friend wants to impress the young lady. But I do think it may be in our interests to be on the right side of this man Robertson. Let's ride with them and see what happens, eh?"

Wei Sun shrugged and nodded, accepting de la Fontaine's reasoning.

"We'll join you, sir!" Keilbren loudly declared, and smiled broadly at Davinia.

She returned the smile with a satisfied nod. Her father looked similarly pleased, acknowledging the three Asians with a gracious nod of his own. Not all of the crowd were quite so happy, like occasional dockhands Martin and Hardy, whose limited experience of Chinese traders further south had been harsh and negative.

More than half the customers spilled out of the bar. Pierre and his companions found themselves alongside men like Miller, Boyd, Jansen and O'Dea, who acknowledged them variously with nods or clipped introductions. Hardy and Martin kept their distance.

Kev Seiman was among those who didn't go outside, positioning himself defensively at the bar, close to Bob Cattenach, who, of course, couldn't possibly leave his business, however loud his declarations of support for a clearly wealthy potential customer.

As Robertson walked out to join his 'posse', he caught Davinia's arm, asked her quietly, "What do you think you're doing, following us?"

She shrugged. "I was bored. Phillip went off on his hunting expedition without me, so this time..."

"And look what happened with Phillip," answered her father sharply. "It was more luck than good judgement that he didn't come home with this spear lodged in himself. I doubt even you'd enjoy having one of these things stuck in you."

Davinia looked out at the men in the street, particularly watching the handsome young Turk. Lazily she replied, "I'm sure I can find someone to look out for me."

"I'm sure you can. But I'd rather the men riding with me were looking out for themselves first and foremost." He sighed and shook his head. "I can't stop you. Try not to get yourself killed. And try not to get anyone killed who's actually of use to me!"

"Oh! And I'm not?" she replied in some irritation.

James looked at her thoughtfully before replying, "Not at present, no. But I did at least ask you to be careful."

The patriarch turned away and walked out. Davinia glowered at his back for a moment, then followed him. Outside, they found Sergeant McCartney looking down from his horse, in earnest conversation with Peter McGregor.

"The witnesses are very clear and specific about what they saw, Mister McGregor," the policeman explained patiently.

It provoked an angry response. "Aye, maybe so, but it proves nothing! Alright, it proves ye need tae be askin' questions of the natives. But not ridin' out with a small army of angry armed men!"

Robertson took it upon himself to interrupt. "Padre, the sergeant hasn't made these men angry. Nor have I. That fault rests with whoever took the unfortunate child. And it does appear that the savages who attacked my son were in some way involved."

The Scot repeated the words, with a deliberate shift in emphasis. "Aye – 'in some way'! If it was the Beeargah yuir boy ran into, they're scavengers! They could have found yon scarf, even if it is the same one. All I'm saying is that ye're going off half-cocked..."

The squatter had already walked away, leaving the preacher fuming, and was preparing to climb onto his horse, which stood alongside the already-mounted Kaminski.

Meanwhile Davinia had taken Orhan aside. The two were exchanging quiet words while his two travelling companions looked on from a distance, radiating distrust.

Led by the two Robertson men, the ragtag posse began to move off. They were strung out unevenly behind the troopers, the three Asians near the end of the group.

Davinia hung back for a few cautious moments, to allow the men to ride into danger first. Even as the girl goaded her horse into motion, McCartney was making a final effort to placate McGregor.

"I can't make promises for Mister Robertson and his friends but as far as I'm concerned, you're welcome to come with us and try to talk to the natives - get some answers."

"Och, aye, I'd love tae - but I've got Mrs. Daniels' wee bairn tae deliver!" He shook with agitated annoyance. "Shall I tell it tae hurry up - or tae wait?"

The sergeant rolled his eyes sympathetically. "As much chance of getting a baby to stop on request as... as... as I have of getting these fellows to stop here now their blood's up. I'm sorry Mister McGregor. Follow us if and when you can. You might hope - pray - things don't get out of hand."

He spurred his horse, keen to catch up with his troopers. It was a challenge to control them most of the time anyway. He didn't need such authority as he had to be eroded by James Robertson.

Angrily the preacher watched him go. McGregor's fist was clenched in frustration around his small black Bible.

A LITTLE EARLIER, a few miles away, the Kuthant and their companions were making their way along a substantial bush track. Unlike many they'd travelled, it was wide enough to accommodate several walking side by side.

Chung, Asbul and Vittorio were walking and talking together. The cook had been walking with his nose in the air.

"I reckon we're getting near the creek," he said. "I've been smelling water for a little while."

The Italian looked at him, bemused. "Smelling water? I know some of the Kuthant have been able to find water where I wouldn't have thought there was any, but you can smell it?"

Chung nodded. "I've been trying to learn as much as I can from them, not just food things."

"So have I," said Vittorio, "I think smelling water is a bit beyond me, though."

"It shouldn't be. You can recognize different herbs and stuff in Italian cooking, can't you?"

"Of course."

"Same thing. A matter of practice. Concentrate, and pick up the subtleties."

The two men started to very deliberately sniff at the air, and both reacted with surprise at the same moment.

"Smoke?" asked Vittorio.

Chung nodded, but before he could say anything, the young Kuthant, Bowra, came running up to the group. He'd been travelling ahead as one of the forward scouts for the group. He started chattering quickly in his own dialect.

Almost immediately Asbul translated, "There's another tribe camped up ahead. Don't look like they've been there long. Young Bowra says Walan's surprised because he don't remember them being there before."

A little huddle quickly formed – the Kuthant elders and their foreign co-travellers.

"So, what do we do?" asked Micah, the youngest of the group, talking over the top of the low-voiced elders' discussion amongst themselves.

Adhilasa motioned towards that cohort and replied, "Follow their lead. They've done well by us so far."

The others nodded their agreement. Asbul had been following the elders' conversation. "We been following de way dey always gone - de way dey know. Dey prefer to stick with dat if dey can. Dere's a place udder side of de creek dey get real good tucker, and pitjuri dey can trade."

"What's pitjuri?" asked Chung, perhaps anticipating a new culinary exploration.

"Plant makes strong medicine if you treat it right," explained the fisherman. "Good to kill pain." He brandished his blowpipe, a gleam in his eye. "Good for udder stuff too. Mix in with de stuff I been making up as we travel and it be real good. Had some of dat and dem damn pirates woulda been in trouble!" he reflected with a broad grin.

Asbul listened in again to the Kuthant conversation, and put in a few of his own comments. He turned back to the companions. "Reckon a couple of us go into dis here camp and talk. Make sure dey okay with us passing t'rough."

"That sounds fair," said Adhilasa. "Who goes?"

Asbul looked thoughtful, and spoke again with the elders. There was some debate, pointing, shaking and nodding of heads before he reported, "Walan, Karumbari, me. Reckon you two, so dey know we not all one tribe." He indicated Micah and Adhilasa as he conveyed that last proposal.

"I'd like to go," said Chung.

"As would I," agreed Volkoff.

The Makassar shook his head, though. "Better wait till we seen dem and talked to dem. Dunno how dey might feel about white fellas. And you know some of dese mobs reckon you Chinese make good tucker."

"I can look after myself," the cook reminded him grimly.

Asbul grinned in response, "Hey, I know dat, man! But be good to not fight if we don't have to."

"The man makes good sense," said Adhilasa, folding his arms. "Micah, I suppose you might keep a gun handy, but not obvious."

His protégé nodded, quietly pleased at the responsibility. A few hand clasps were exchanged, and the little 'diplomatic party' assembled. They got their heads together immediately. It was important to have some strategies planned before meeting a new group - friends or foes.

AN HOUR OR SO LATER, the new campsite of the Balyarta tribe held five new faces. The 'emissaries' stood surrounded by a group of men and women who regarded them with more caution than suspicion. The atmosphere was already becoming amiable – Asbul was a natural diplomat. Not least because of his remarkable facility for languages.

Burundji, the Balyarta tongue, was different again to what he'd encountered previously, but again, there had been enough similarities and commonalities for him to understand and be understood. Imperfectly, but enough for goodwill on both sides to be established.

After an extended discussion, the Makassar turned to Adhilasa, who he'd come to regard as an 'elder' of sorts in his own right. He explained, "So, it sounds alright. Dey happy for us to travel t'rough, dey not man-eaters like dem buggers you met up nort', so Chungy safe."

"And our lighter-skinned comrades...?" asked the American, cautiously.

"Aye, well – we had some problems with white fellas not far from here - that's how come we move and set up new camp here. We ken not every white man's a bad man, no more than every black one's a good yin. We learn tae take every person as we find them," replied Samuel, totally unexpectedly.

There'd been no indication that any of this new tribe spoke any English, so the patriarch's casual explanation came as a shock. As did the incongruous accent!

Asbul recovered first, and grinning as usual, simply accepted that there'd been no reason for anyone to assume anything about each other's origins or language.

"Dese fellas got right idea, I reckon!" he said.

Young Micah smiled in agreement. "You're right. Sounds pretty smart."

Samuel acknowledged their praise with a polite bow. "We been lucky. We met a couple of good white men. Learned some good things. Then we learn there some real bad yins too, but cannae blame the innocent for the sins of the unrighteous. Everyone, black or white, got tae take responsibility for their own actions."

Adhilasa raised an eyebrow. He would privately admit to being surprised, but more importantly, he was impressed.

"Indeed!" he agreed. "Can I suggest Micah and one of our Kuthant friends go back and give the 'all clear' to the others? The rest of us might stay here and start trying to improve communication."

There was a vigorous nod of agreement from Asbul. In the Kuthant dialect he said to his companions, "This is good. Karumbari, will you and Micah go and tell the rest of the people it's safe, and bring them on?"

At the same time, Samuel was addressing those of his people less fluent in English. "It's alright. We can make them welcome. I think we may learn from them. The people can benefit."

There were signs of general agreement, even as Karumbari moved to stand beside Micah, ready to go back to his own tribe.

"We'll be back soon!" averred Micah, and extended his open hand towards the Balyarta.

The fellow beside Samuel, a younger man named Kumbu, who was quite new to the circle of elders, responded to the gesture, and took the West Indian's hand in a firm grip. They exchanged smiles.

With good cause for optimism, Karumbari and Micah turned and trotted away into the bush, back in the direction they'd come from. Their erstwhile companions accompanied their new hosts into the centre of the encampment.

All three were soon at the centre of huddles of interested Balyarta people. Walan was already talking trade. His English was more fragmentary than that of the Balyarta, but his earnestness was unfeigned. There was a good reason why he had a reputation among his own tribe as their most effective trade negotiator.

Asbul and Adhilasa had attracted a mostly younger audience, at least in part by shrewd diplomatic design. The Makassar had caught attention by trilling on his trusty flute, then launched into a display of juggling, playfully tossing an assortment of stones, sticks and various utensils. He was swiftly surrounded by a circle of excited children, and some equally delighted parents. Laughing, the older American soon joined in the fun with some sleight of hand tricks. Small pebbles were inexplicably produced from behind ears, or vanished and reappeared from hand to hand, as if by magic.

Suddenly the entertainment was disrupted by a commotion at the southernmost edge of the encampment. Three of Robertson's volunteers came crashing through the undergrowth between trees, brandishing their pistols.

The Balyarta looked alarmed, a couple of them quickly grabbing and raising their spears.

A shot rang out from another part of the tree fringe, and one of the spear-toting men fell dead. Beside a tree, the native trooper Ghurruk grinned over his smoking musket. Grinned, that is, until Sergeant McCartney clipped him hard in the ear.

"Ghurruk! No bloody shooting till I give the order, I said!"

The trooper protested, "That fella gonna throw spear at Mista Martin, boss!"

"Only maybe - and it would have been Martin's own stupid fault!"

Before the argument could continue, several of the posse and the troopers opened fire.

Kaminski's voice rang out from among the trees, "That's it, men! Get the child-murdering bastards!"

A little way behind the Pole, Phillip tugged at his father's arm. Uncertainly, he said, "I'm... ah... I'm not sure that these are the right people...?"

The Warden stared straight ahead, into the encampment. Tonelessly he replied, "I am."

Neither Robertson had noticed Pierre de la Fontaine within earshot of this quiet exchange. The former mercenary raised his eyebrows momentarily, and backed discreetly away to look for his two companions. He would soon find them, and with a few well-chosen words, lead them away, unnoticed by anyone.

The Balyarta were desperately taking such cover as they could, many of them trying to edge away in the direction that Micah and Karumbari had taken.

One of the volunteers, a surly youth named Hardy, stepped forward to take aim at the back of a retreating native. He stopped in mid-stride, a startled look on his face, and grabbed at his neck. He gave a sharp jerk and looked at his hand. A small tuft of feathers was just visible between his fingers. His eyes rolled back in his head as he collapsed to the ground.

A little way away, Asbul was running for a tree. He was reloading his blowpipe, even as he shinned up the trunk into the sheltering branches. He wasn't grinning now.

Alerted by the sounds of gunfire, Micah was running back towards the Balyarta campsite. At his heels were Volkoff, Chung, Pasquale, the two Spaniards and a half-dozen Kuthant, led by Karumbari, wielding a pistol. The other natives were armed with short spears and boomerangs – not the throwing type, but hard-edged weapons used for hand-to-hand fighting.

The Cossack called after the hot-headed youngster, "Wait! Move cautiously! We should see who is shooting at who. Spread out and split up - four groups of three. Chung, go with Cristiano, and Vittorio, with Micah please. Guillermo, you take two of our friends, yes?" He rested a hand on Karumbari's shoulder and concluded, "You with me."

The native nodded, then addressed his tribesmen in their own language, following the tactical lead. "You, with the young musician and the cook. You two with the old hawk. Moolbong, you got a calm head, you go with the bearded trader and the handsome boy. And you, Bowra, come with me."

"We've got to hurry!" Micah implored. "Adhilasa may be in trouble!"

Gregori was implacable, replying, "And we will do him no good by simply running into a hail of bullets. Keep to cover, watch, listen, and strike only when you are sure of your target."

At a gesture from the Cossack, the four groups separated. Guillermo and his two allies moved to the left, followed by his son with Chung and the rangy native Baza. Before they split up, the elder Buitrito called, "You listen for my signal, si?"

"Si," agreed the younger musician, cocking two Colt revolvers.

Volkoff instructed Micah, "You follow the track you used before. We will cover from your right."

"Right," agreed the young man, and started to move off, repeating rifle at the ready and the Kuthant spearman Moolbong at his shoulder.

Volkoff briefly paused the nervous-looking Pasquale, and cautioned him, "Watch the young man."

The Italian swallowed uncomfortably, nodded, and moved off, holding his pistol awkwardly. In the course of their long journey south from Palmer River he'd learned a lot of things about his companions, and himself. One of those things was the frank admission that, unlike some of the others, he was not a born fighter.

Karumbari and Bowra were already making their way through the trees. Gregori quickly followed them, clutching a handgun. He'd considered unpacking one of his treasured chassepot rifles. But in this country, this situation, surely that would be unnecessary. They were of more value in perfect condition, and his pistol was an old and trusted friend.

Shots were still audible ahead – Micah was trying to balance speed with stealth, when there was a sudden disturbance from the bush nearby. The youth brought his rifle up, ready to fire, but Moolbong grabbed his arm. He'd had a better view of who was approaching. A group of Balyarta women and children emerged from the scrub. Some of them were wounded, although all could still walk.

One of the lead women, Koolwunnung, tried to explain. But she spoke in Burundji, incomprehensible to any of the three men. She recognized Micah from his recent visit, though, and desperately resorted to the little English she could assemble in her agitation.

"Troopers. White men. Town. Surprise. Bad."

It was enough. Vittorio and Moolbong quickly checked for any serious injuries. Reassured, they then managed, with some difficulty and a lot of gestures, to explain where to find the rest of the Kuthant. Micah was almost hopping from foot to foot with impatience by the time they moved off again.

As they moved, Vittorio gave thanks for one small relief. "Well, at least we know the gunshots aren't betrayal by our new friends."

Volkoff's trio were the first to get within sight of the encampment. Karumbari, leading, held up a cautionary hand. Instinctively, all of them crouched low. That was good, as a bullet ricocheted off a tree beside the Cossack and whirred over Bowra's head. The three men threw themselves behind the shelter of a low ridge of earth. Looking up cautiously, they took in the scene before them.

Even to the Kuthants' keen eyes, nobody was immediately visible – nobody moving, at least. Three or four Balyarta bodies lay near the edge of the encampment, and one was near the centre. Also in plain sight were the bodies of the volunteer manhunters Hardy and O'Dea, the latter with a spear in his side. Shots rang out at any suggestion of movement from the surrounding bush, but it was at first impossible to be sure where from, or who was shooting.

Watching patiently and carefully, Bowra started to notice a few white men – less adept natural bushmen than most of the troopers – in positions of cover. He nudged his elder Karumbari, who gave a gesture of acknowledgement before silently conveying the observations to Volkoff.

The policeman McCartney, himself in what he hoped was a safe position, looked pensively at the corpses of Hardy and O'Dea. A few of his troopers were nearby.

Quietly he addressed them. "I think we'd better try to finish this mess off, lads. See if you can flush 'em out. Try not to make a massacre out of it please."

Possum nodded, and at the sergeant's instruction, gave some directions: a few to hold their positions alongside him, Ghurruk and Big Billy to swing left, Little Billy and Meataxe to swing right.

Moving silently, the pair on the left flank chanced to approach the low slope near the large shelter, at just the right angle to see that, behind it, Adhilasa was protecting some of the children he'd been entertaining only minutes before.

Elbowing Big Billy in the ribs, Ghurruk grinned unpleasantly and started to aim his musket at the unsuspecting Adhilasa. Suddenly there was a musical whistle from among the trees. It was a fragment of a tune that Guillermo and Cristiano had been teaching the Kuthant on their travels.

Startled, Adhilasa looked up and around. He was just in time to see Ghurruk scream as a bullet shattered both his musket and the hand clutching it. The American quickly hurled a rock he'd been holding. His aim was good enough to stun Big Billy, who'd been distracted by his mate's distress.

A few angry troopers broke ranks and burst from cover, as did some of the hot-headed posse. Meataxe (who wasn't mad, just misunderstood) led a ragged rush towards where he'd spotted a few Balyarta figures hiding. Others were looking, a little more cautiously, for where that last excellent shot had come from.

A couple headed in Adhilasa's direction, prompting Micah to stand up from his position on the fringe of the clearing and fire a volley of shots that scattered them.

But while the young man's attention was in that direction, he was spotted by Jansen. Before the Swede could shoot, though, he was fired on by Vittorio. The shot was wild, but it was enough to put the Scandinavian off. Before he could collect his wits, Karumbari had also fired from cover – more successfully, his bullet splintering Jansen's rifle barrel, deflecting to lodge in the man's arm and cause him to drop the weapon.

Still at a hopefully safe distance, Davinia had been keeping a concerned watch on Orhan before he and his friends quietly disappeared. The handsome Micah had also caught her eye, though, and she was visibly relieved when he escaped injury.

Her father, meanwhile, was also watching events unfold with a look of concern on his face. Things were not going to plan, and he wasn't pleased.

Beside him, Kaminski scowled. "I didn't expect them to be armed!" he gritted.

"Or to be quite so good with the guns," added the Warden, thoughtfully. He cupped his hands around his mouth, and without breaking cover called loudly, "This is Commissioner Robertson. We are here to investigate the abduction and possible murder of a child. You are firing on officers of the law. If you do not put down your weapons we'll regard you as accessories to that crime..."

The outraged Pasquale interrupted, shouting, "This is how you investigate, is it? Shoot first, and question the corpses? I suppose you get the answers you want that way, eh?"

Young Phillip Robertson possessed a streak of conscience his father didn't have, and looked uncomfortable at the shouted question.

So too did Sergeant McCartney, who muttered bitterly to himself, "I really did *not* want to be drawn into a serious fight..."

The self-described Commissioner, however, continued unperturbed. "We have witnesses who can testify that these black men were seen carrying the missing child's effects. Clearly, they are involved in the crime. We came here to find out what they know, when they reacted by throwing a spear at one of my men..."

Suddenly his impromptu speech was interrupted by a new voice from another part of the encircling bush – the unexpected voice of the half-caste Magpie.

"Robertson! You couldn't lie straight in a coffin!"

If the Warden's reaction was one of surprise, that of his daughter was even more so. Nobody had mentioned around her the presence of a familiar figure from her childhood.

Magpie turned to the other two teamsters, crouched nearby, and said to them softly, "Reckon we got here just in time."

"Damn glad we go quiet!" said Mundil, with feeling.

Kaminski's voice was similarly low as he growled to his employer, "It's that damned half-breed!". The unnecessary observation was ignored.

The half-breed in question shouted to his former boss again. "I don't know what cock and bull story you've dreamed up. I know you wanted the Balyarta out of your way - I'll bet your 'witnesses' are mates of yours. Right?"

Frustrated, but glad of the interruption to the shooting, McCartney tried to intervene, calling out, "Magpie - I know these darkies are mates of yours, but this is police business. If the gunmen are friends of yours, get them to put up their weapons."

Then an unexpected voice boomed from the limited shelter of the ditch near the centre of the encampment – a deep voice with an American accent.

"Officer! I don't know who this 'Magpie' is, but I do know your men have a strange way of 'finding things out'. Micah, and my other friends, keep your weapons handy and your heads down - I don't think I trust all of the Commissioner's men."

"I wouldn't bloody trust any of them!" called Arnold in impulsive agreement.

Adhilasa smiled slightly at the endorsement from an unknown quarter. Encouraged, he went on, "Officer, if you really only want to ask questions, it'd be best done without so many drawn weapons and drawn nerves. If you take your trigger-happy men and leave, I think I can arrange for someone to come see you and talk to you."

Up in his tree, Asbul looked a little dubious at Adhilasa's presumption, speaking on behalf of people he'd barely met.

Similarly perturbed, and puzzled, Arnold nudged Thonkumundil and asked, "Who the hell is that?"

There was only a shrug in reply. The three teamsters started to creep discreetly in the direction of the American voice.

Long familiar with Adhilasa's oratory skill, Chung quietly observed to Cristiano, "Well and good, if it works. This standoff could get nasty. I'm not sure how many of them there are."

"Si, amigo. But they don't know how many of us there are, either."

A similar thought had already crossed McCartney's mind. Too many unknowns. He moved carefully, closer to Robertson, and asked, "Do you want this to get out of hand? More men killed?"

"I want..." The Warden forced himself to bite down on his anger. "I want to see justice done, of course. But you're right - without unnecessary loss of life."

Before the policeman could say anything more, Robertson shouted, "Alright - we'll do it your way, for now. But be warned, if no-one has presented themselves to Sergeant McCartney in Louth within twenty-four hours, or if their answers are not satisfactory, we will track these people down again. And we will respond, with serious force this time."

There was no immediate response, from anyone. Unhappily, McCartney seized the little opportunity he saw, and called out, "My troopers! Come on boys - to me. But keep your eyes open and your pistols cocked."

Grudgingly, Robertson conceded agreement, adding his own instruction: "You men who rode with me, you too. I don't like it any more than you do, but we'll back off. For now. Back the way we came."

Davinia had seen and heard enough. She slipped away to her horse, and lit out for Louth as quickly as possible.

Meanwhile the troopers and volunteers followed their orders. Their adversaries silently, watchfully maintained their positions, an unseen, unexpected threat. The raiders picked up the bodies of Hardy and O'Dea, and helped their wounded back into cover and towards their tethered horses.

Kaminski grabbed Robertson's sleeve. "This is bull..."

James pulled from the grip without fuss and said quietly, "Don't imagine this is over. This is an unexpected complication, that's all."

The two men joined the group very cautiously making their way back to the road. As he went, Robertson, determined to have the last word, called back over his shoulder, "Twenty-four hours!"

Only when they were quite sure that the bush surrounding the campsite was clear of enemies did any of the defenders break cover. The three teamsters were the first to enter the clearing. Arnold strode over to angrily confront Adhilasa, still standing protectively in front of the children, one of whom clutched his trouser leg.

"I don't know who you are, mister, but you've got a hell of a nerve, volunteering to hand some of these people over to that bastard Robertson," he railed, even as Mundil knelt to talk softly with the children.

More of the Balyarta emerged cautiously, some dropping from tree branches just as Asbul did.

Samuel walked towards Adhilasa with his hand outstretched, and said, "I watch ye throw yuirself over these children. Ye are a brave mon. Thank ye."

Adhilasa shook the proffered hand, and gave a small bow of acknowledgement.

Arms folded, Arnold looked at the Balyarta elder, somewhat mollified but still suspicious. "I'll take your word for it, Samuel," he said grudgingly.

Mundil looked up and reassured him, "Is okay, James. The kids reckon this fella look after 'em when the shots started flyin'. Him an' his friends."

At a small signal from Adhilasa, Asbul and the others started to approach.

Magpie had been standing back, watching and listening. Now he stepped forward and put his hand on the tall American's shoulder. "Thank you for that. But James is right. Robertson is a bastard who can't be trusted. This whole missing child thing is bull."

"Really?" There was no surprise in Adhilasa's voice.

Arnold grunted, "Oh, a girl is missing, right enough, but these people have nothing to do with it."

Vittorio had been listening as he approached, and now said carefully, "Can you be sure of that? Of every one of them?"

"Course I can...!" snapped the white teamster, but Magpie interrupted him.

"Hang on, James - this fella's right. We can be pretty damn sure, but maybe, just maybe, one of the Balyarta boys did do something. I don't reckon he'd tell us, or anyone else, hey?"

Samuel nodded reluctant agreement. "Afraid ye might be right, Mister Magpie. I dinna reckon so, but nae man is completely without sin." The elder stepped into his position of authority easily. "Us older yins better talk about this, then have words with all the people. Mister Adhilasa, I reckon ye done the right thing trying tae get the shooting tae stop. We lost too many good people already lately. But we gotta be sure we *are* right before we go see the boss trooper. Thonkumundil, ye sit with us, please?"

Mundil and Samuel gathered several Balyarta elders, including

Koolwunnung who, with her injured charges, had been fetched back to camp by Micah and Kumbu. The little 'council' sat together under a tree, some way from the others. The rest of the Balyarta knew to keep a respectful distance, and the new arrivals followed their lead.

Vittorio took the diplomatic initiative and offered his hand to the three teamsters. "Vittorio Pasquale, trader and, more recently, it seems, explorer," he said with an earnest smile.

It was an effective icebreaker, and soon introductions and conversations were being widely exchanged among the Balyarta, the Kuthant, and the various international travellers.

Vittorio was standing with hands on hips, looking rueful as he pondered the recent turn of events. "We were looking for a goldfield, but it seems we've found a field of trouble," he lamented.

"Trouble indeed," was the gloomy agreement of the grizzled man who'd just arrived at his side. With a small bow and a faint, automatic military click of his heels the Cossack introduced himself to Magpie and Arnold. "What is it that we have walked in on?" he asked.

James Arnold looked balefully in the direction the attackers had departed. Bringing his temper under control, he explained, "The word is there's been gold found somewhere round here. That bastard Robertson - the one giving the orders - a few days back he came by and told the Balyarta to get out. He's got himself made Gold Warden somehow."

Magpie pulled a face and added, "Either bought the job or twisted his way in somehow. Bastard's always been good at getting others to do his dirty work for him."

"Sounds like you have a history with this man," observed Adhilasa.

The half-caste looked wry. "Yeah. I was... on his payroll for years. Did all sorts of jobs for him, down south. A couple of them I'm not real proud of. But then he sent a bunch of us to clear off a tribe of blackfellas that he reckoned was worryin' sheep in his big back paddock."

"Your people?" asked Vittorio.

"No. I'm Bidjigal, or my mam was. This was some tribe of wanderers. Traders maybe."

Adhilasa nodded in understanding. "Like these good folks we've been travelling with - the Kuthant."

"Yeah, there's plenty of tribes like them out there," confirmed the teamster. "These fellas were just in the wrong place at the wrong time, in Robertson's way. Just like the Balyarta now. The bastard sent us out to clear 'em away from anywhere near his property, by 'whatever means necessary' he said. Well, on the ride down there I lit out when it finally dawned on me to ask myself why I would shoot other black men, my mother's tribe or not."

"There's plenty of those damn troopers never bothered to think that way," remarked Arnold bitterly.

"Yeah, I know, just so long as they get paid," admitted Magpie. "Not all of 'em, but more than enough. But me, I don't reckon it's right. And I gotta live with myself. My father's people never had or would accept me - most of 'em anyhow, James. Was a few blackfellas tribes along the way didn't take to me either, but these Balyarta, I reckon they were good people long before Mister Mac started preachin' to them."

"Mister Mac?" quizzed Volkoff.

Arnold answered, sounding unimpressed. "McGregor. Scottish preacher. Been making it his business to fill their heads with his Gospel."

"There's nothing wrong with preaching the Gospel," was the good Catholic Pasquale's terse reply.

It was Magpie who interrupted to head off a potential argument, adding, "And he's made it his business to fill their bellies too, when necessary. And fill their heads with some learnin', too. You gotta admit James, he done better teachin' a lot of 'em English than we ever done."

"That explains the - surprising accent that Samuel has," said Adhilasa.

"Samuel. Yeah. Named for some bloke in the Bible," grumbled Arnold, still tetchy. "What was wrong with his own name?"

"Samuel the prophet was a fine man, and a good leader to his people," Adhilasa pointed out. "A man has the right to choose his own name, and there are many worse he could have taken for himself."

"Fair enough. His choice, as you say," admitted James, finally succumbing to diplomacy.

～

EVEN AS THE bullets were flying in earnest at the campsite, the three Asian companions had reined in their horses beside the main track, a considerable distance closer to Louth. They gazed back in the direction they'd ridden from.

"Well, that was interesting," said Pierre.

"So, now you will tell us why you so quietly led us away from the incident you'd led us into?" asked Wei Sun.

The Frenchman stroked his chin. "I think you were right to not trust our Warden, Wei Sun. Something I overheard leads me to think those tribespeople may not have been involved in the crime they were accused of. I suspect he had some other reason for wanting to attack them."

"So?" replied Orhan, irritated at missing an opportunity to display his bravery in front of the girl.

"So, as much as you may want to impress the young lady, you must ask yourself is that more important than being a party to injustice?"

The Turk was silent, but looked uncomfortable. The jab at his conscience had found its mark. He left it to their Chinese companion to respond.

"You know we have all seen too much injustice, too much abuse of the innocent, already. Let us not be involved in any more."

"Alright, you've made your point," Keilbren admitted. "So, what do we do now?"

"Well, we came here looking for gold," Pierre mused. "I suspect, from Mister Robertson's interest in the area, that we are on the right track. My suggestion is that we make camp somewhere near here and start quietly exploring."

"What about those natives?" asked Orhan.

"I hope that if we don't disturb them, they won't disturb us."

"They seemed capable of defending themselves. Let's hope they're not aggressive, or think attack may be a better form of defence. They appear to have allies," said Wei Sun.

"Useful ones," agreed Pierre. "All the more reason for us to keep a low profile while we're prospecting, hey?"

His Chinese companion gave a hesitant nod. "Mmm. Easier if we had a better idea what we were looking for. The man has kept the details of the gold strike very much to himself - an extraordinary effort, really."

The Frenchman replied thoughtfully, "I have the feeling Mister Robertson is not an ordinary man."

"It seems to run in the family, then!" laughed Orhan. "His daughter is certainly out of the ordinary! As to the gold, I guess we find this 'Hard Rock Creek' and look for a likely spot to start panning before anyone else does."

"That sounds reasonable," said Wei Sun. "Although I wonder, if it were that simple, why Robertson would not have already commenced to do so..."

"That's worth thinking about. Let's get back into town. In the morning we can pack our belongings, and see what supplies we can afford. While we're about that we can keep our ears open for any fragments of information."

"You have a flair for that, it seems, Pierre!" said the Turk with a laugh.

"It's stood us in good stead so far," admitted Wei Sun, as the trio started back to Louth again.

THE SKY WAS DARKENING over the Balyarta campsite, and a fire had been lit. Discussion amongst the elders of both tribes, independently and together, had been long, and sometimes heated. At different points some of their other friends and travelling companions had been invited to contribute.

Meanwhile, the communities had mingled. Shared trauma facilitated that. It also helped that there were individuals on all sides who were very willing to offer their own specialized help, with healing, food, construction or child-minding.

One thing that had been mutually agreed very early in discussion was the need for security – a concept known by the Balyarta only in a theoretical sense. Now, an armed 'sentry' was positioned at each compass point. Quiet, but watchful. And armed. Cristiano, Micah, Walan and Chung were currently 'on duty', the latter a little reluctantly, having spent the recent part of the afternoon talking food with the women now preparing a meal for everyone. He'd wanted to be a part of that process – and indeed he was, with his advice and suggestions having been seized on.

The elders' private discussions had broken up. Some of them, from both tribes, now sat by the fire with the men they regarded as the 'elders' of their visitors: Adhilasa, Asbul, Gregori, Guillermo and Vittorio. The three teamsters were also in the group – Thonkumundil was almost regarded as an elder in his own right anyway, and the Balyarta had learned to value the insights and experience of his partners.

Samuel had been explaining to the group the results of his peers' earlier talks. "So, my friends, we are as sure as we can be that nobody of the Balyarta had anything tae do with this lost child." He addressed Adhilasa directly, and asked, "Are ye content with that?"

"I am. What of you, my friends?"

The Spaniard and the Cossack nodded silently.

Arnold shrugged. "I always said it was bull."

Magpie laughed. "Typical James bloody Robertson!" he said.

After a brief discussion Karumbari spoke for his people, simply replying, "Yes."

Asbul had been part of that consultation, and explained further: "Kut'ant reckon dese good fellas. I reckon more important, dey figure if you say okay it's good enough for dem, Mister Adhilasa. Dey trust you plenty."

Some of the Kuthant elders nodded in confirmation. Adhilasa gave a modest bow of thanks.

Vittorio smiled. "You do make an impression, my friend. I hope the Gold Warden is as impressed. What can we do to convince him?"

"Won't make no difference," replied Magpie, shaking his head. "Robertson wants them gone to make way for some mining company, and what he wants he'll find a way to get."

Gregori had been considering tactical options, as was his wont. "If the police can be convinced of these people's innocence that may deprive him of some leverage."

The half-caste looked unconvinced. "McCartney couldn't give a bugger about a black man's innocence. I reckon he'll do whatever Robertson tells him. Even if he was a bit reluctant, wave some money or grog in front of his troopers and most of them'd shoot anyone you asked 'em to."

"You don't like dem trooper fellas, do you?" asked Asbul.

Magpie paused before answering, considering his words carefully. He realized that he didn't want to snap an impulsive reply. "I don't like anybody that turns on his own people."

"Didn't you explain that these native troopers aren't from this tribe?" asked Vittorio, puzzled.

"Damn right!" exclaimed Mundil. "We not take 'Governor's shilling' to wear blue coats and wave guns round to frighten folk!"

The Italian was still assembling all the pieces in his mind. "Surely, they're meant to do more than that. They're meant to be the police, aren't they?"

Arnold inhaled deeply and tried to explain, willing himself to put a lid on his natural truculence and be fair.

"Yeah, that's the theory. They got 'em in at first as trackers. Bloody good ones a lot of them. Then some bright spark realized they were even cheaper to employ than most of the white blokes desperate enough to become coppers. And once you get out into the bush a bit, there ain't so many of those white blokes to choose from anyway. Any that are, and can read and write a bit, usually get put in charge. Aw look, some of 'em, white and black, try to do their job properly. They're not all bad bastards, but there's some that definitely are, and plenty more too lazy or just don't care enough to do much about it."

"So where does that leave us?" asked Vittorio, his 'us' already automatically including the Kuthant and Balyarta people. "If someone doesn't make an appearance in front of the sergeant tomorrow, that'll be the Warden's excuse to head straight back here with more guns blazing."

"What if we're not here?" asked Samuel. At Adhilasa's quizzical look he continued, "We've moved before when we've had tae. We can do it again."

"You should not have to," said Adhilasa, firmly.

"No!" agreed Guillermo. "Not when you have done nothing wrong."

James snorted in wry amusement. "You've seen how much difference that makes."

"Yeah. It's obvious Robertson wants rid of them," agreed Magpie.

His usual cheery demeanour momentarily absent, Asbul addressed Samuel, "Running away just give de man what he want den - dat really what you reckon is best?"

It was Mundil who replied on his elder's behalf, "The people mostly don't care about what he wants. They just don't want to be shot."

Pasquale was shocked. "So, they move on, every time they're in someone's way? *Manaya!* This is a big country, but sooner or later you run out of places to run to, si?"

"I know what you mean, but the Balyarta aren't fighters." Magpie had sympathy for both points of view.

The long-time soldier Volkoff was less so. "If you don't fight, you lose," he said.

Guillermo, whose own history had been little discussed but clearly had its own military elements, quietly concurred with the

Cossack. "If you don't fight, you die." The others looked at him. "This man Robertson, he has been challenged - confronted. I think this is something he will not let rest. Even if you move, his pride may well make him hunt you."

Samuel shrugged, though. "It is as Magpie says. We are nae fighting people."

Volkoff tried to respect the attitude, although he truly didn't comprehend it. He sought a compromise. "We can at least not play into his hands and give him an excuse to rouse the troopers and another gang of thugs. Someone must go to this sergeant, and be seen to do so. I do not disagree with you, Guillermo, but let the man not hide behind the law."

"Our Cossack friend makes sense," said Adhilasa. He placed a hand on the shoulders of Samuel and Thonkumundil. "I gave my word - I will present myself to the sergeant and speak on your behalf if you're satisfied with that."

Several of the Balyarta elders conferred quietly, then Samuel answered on their behalf. "Thank ye. Ye speak good, and that might help. I'll go with ye, though. We've been blamed for this sin, and we ought tae answer for ourselves."

Gregori's strategic mind was still ticking over. "I think some of us must stay here on watch, but a few might go with you. If something goes wrong we may be able to help, and let the others know what's happened if necessary."

"Good idea," agreed Vittorio. "I think the opportunity to get some supplies from the town might be welcome, too!"

The Makassar grinned at him. "You sick of blackfellas' tucker?"

"Let's say I'd enjoy the variety."

THE FOLLOWING morning found James Robertson at his desk in his temporary office in the Woolpack. There was always paperwork to be done, he mused. The trick was to make it work in your favour, and the way to ensure that it did was to do it yourself. Trust no-one, and never be disappointed.

Suddenly the door of the office opened. There'd been no knock, no warning of anyone's arrival. Robertson looked up, his hand reaching for the desk drawer which held a loaded revolver. A tall, lean man in a red officer's uniform entered briskly, stopped in front of the desk and snapped off a smart salute.

"Top of the morning, sir. Chap downstairs told me I'd find you here. Captain William Andrews, ex- Queens Own Fusiliers, late 3rd Regiment, now commanding the 1st Riverview Infantry Company. At the service of the Good Lord, and your good self."

The captain smiled broadly and extended a hand. Robertson had been momentarily nonplussed, but recovered swiftly and shook the gloved hand.

"Morning, Andrews," greeted the Warden. "Glad to have you along. No difficulties in getting your men up here, I trust?"

"No, no. Quite uneventful I have to say. How are your plans progressing?"

"My - plans?" Robertson asked cautiously. What sort of intelligence network did this fellow have?

"The new settlement. I assume your presence in this town is only temporary until you get properly established on the goldfield. Which is, of course, where we shall be based."

The Warden kept his relief internal. Just because the mercenaries were one part of his plan, it didn't mean he wanted every detail known by any of his confederates. He already sensed that there was something vaguely disconcerting about this English officer.

"Of course," he confirmed. "I've made a start on organizing my own permanent premises - we'll have to do the same for you and your men. Meanwhile..."

Andrews didn't wait to hear the rest of the sentence. "In the meantime, I've had the lads set up camp just south of the town.

Depending on your immediate plans I may let them into the town itself for a few days - they've behaved well on the journey and I'd like to recognise that. This Louth isn't a cesspool of wickedness and Godlessness, is it?"

James blinked. The question seemed to have been asked in earnest. "Well, I haven't heard it described as such..."

Before he could delve deeper into the captain's concerns, his office door was again unceremoniously opened without warning. This time it was Davinia who flounced in, paying her usual amount of attention to her father's activities.

"I want to go into town today and look for - oh! You have company!"

Davinia started to look the uniformed figure up and down appraisingly, but was taken aback when he met her eyes only briefly before commencing his own appraisal of her. Wordlessly, he walked over to her, adjusted her dress for a better view of her bare shoulder, and with his foot raised her skirt slightly for a better assessment of her legs. The girl looked shocked and appropriately upset, and looked to her father.

Alas for her, James was actually mildly amused by his contrary daughter's discomfort at the reversal of her usual situation, and allowed it to continue for a few moments, increasing her speechless outrage, before he coughed meaningfully and spoke to the captain.

"Captain William Andrews, of the 1st Riverview Infantry Company - my daughter Davinia."

Andrews took a step away, but only because he'd completed his inspection to his own satisfaction. He'd decided he liked what he'd seen thus far.

"Your daughter? Well done old man! Splendid!" At last, he addressed the girl directly, even giving a bow as he said, "Pleasure to meet you. I look forward to seeing rather more of you in the future."

She found herself quite unable to meet his unsubtle gaze as she struggled to reply, "Er... thank you... Father, I must go and... see to some tea..."

It was perversely satisfying to see his willful daughter on the receiving end of the very behaviour she was so notorious for herself. "That's what we have Ali for, my dear," he replied mildly.

"Well... well... I'll go and see to him then!" Davinia stammered, and made a hasty exit.

The mercenary watched her departure with a casual interest. "Nice piece of work," he said. "Where were we? Ah yes - perhaps a day or two of leave for the men before we set up properly wherever we'll be of most benefit."

The notion of 'leave' for his private militia, so soon after their arrival, didn't sit entirely well with the Warden. He had a job in mind for them. Still, it would be shrewd to cultivate the men's loyalty, and not just rely on their commanding officer.

"Louth isn't a big place, Captain. Not a lot to amuse your men, be warned. Of course, if you think it would help with their efficiency... You'd be able to assemble them quickly if required?"

"You think that's likely? Something on the horizon?"

"Potentially. Later today I should..."

James' musing was interrupted by a knock on the door. *Someone* at least had that much politeness, and the squatter was scarcely surprised that it was Ali who entered. He was bearing a tray laden with a teapot and two cups.

"Ah, Ali - thank you. That was quick. Davinia found you, then?"

The manservant looked momentarily puzzled, but quickly resumed his imperturbable manner. "Miss Davinia? No, sir. I've not seen her for some time. When I returned from my small shopping expedition young Hebblethwaite - the lad who supposedly cleans the bar and downstairs area - advised me you had a guest. When he indicated the nature of the guest I presumed tea would be called for."

"The 'nature of the guest'?"

"'One of them brass-buttoned English soldiers - real posh type' were his words, sir."

Ali's impression of the young man's voice, so unlike his own, was remarkably accurate. Mimicry was one of his lesser known talents. He gave a small bow towards the visiting captain, who smiled in response.

"That'd be the little ginger-haired scruff I met on the way in. Posh, eh? Hardly - I'm but a humble soldier and servant of God," Andrews said. He sniffed at the teapot. "Darjeeling? Good quality, too. You're Indian."

"Indeed, sir," Ali replied.

"From the west over Bombay way, I'd say. Spent a bit of time there myself, though I was mostly stationed on the other side, around Calcutta."

"Indeed, sir," repeated Ali as he poured the tea.

"I spent some of my youth on the banks of the Sina," explained Robertson. "My father served in Maharashtra before being relocated to the colony of New South Wales."

"Really? Small world, eh? We must have a good chat sometime. A challenging place to do the Lord's work, India. So many Godless souls."

Ali's reserve was as impeccable as ever. His only reaction was another small bow to both 'gentlemen' before leaving the office, closing the door as he went, of course.

"A good man. Been with me for years," James said.

If there was any hint of reproach in his voice, Andrews didn't react to it. After an analytical mouthful, he only replied, "He makes a good cup of tea, I'll say that much for him."

He stretched his long legs out under the desk. "Now, you were mentioning a potential problem?"

NOT VERY FAR AWAY, out on the main street, five horses were being halted near a small row of shops. Arnold was there as a guide of sorts. Pasquale, Chung and Micah were to obtain supplies. Adhilasa and Samuel shared the diplomatic mission. They also shared a horse, rather to the discomfort of the Balyarta elder, who rode rarely and without enthusiasm. Horses, he thought, were better suited to his younger, better padded relatives.

Arnold finished his directions. "Right, so supplies are easy. Dry goods, your best bet is old man Jones in here." With a thumb he indicated a store over his shoulder. "You'll find a decent little market garden bottom of the next street on the right, and for McCartney's office turn left and go two doors up. You sure you don't want me comin' in there with you?"

The question had been directed at Samuel, but it was Adhilasa who answered, "If you and the policeman get on as badly as you suggest, it's probably best you don't."

"Well, maybe not badly, but diplomacy's not my strong point, I'm told," the teamster admitted. He pointed south and continued, "That intersection's about the best central point. I'll hang around there and try to keep an eye out on all of you. Anyone runs into trouble, give me a bloody loud yell. I'll signal Mundil."

So saying, he waved his hat in the direction from which they'd come. On horseback at the far end of the street, Thonkumundil made a small gesture of acknowledgement. Beside him was Guillermo Buitrito, who made a similar movement. In the event of trouble, their role would be to not interfere unless absolutely necessary, but rather, get word back to the others at the campsite.

"Okay," said Chung, with some eager anticipation, "I'll head for the garden."

Vittorio shared the cook's interest and said, "I might go with you. Micah, you'll be good to get the other supplies?"

"Sure," replied the young man.

"We'll all meet at that intersection as soon as we're able, then? Good," confirmed Adhilasa.

Micah dismounted, and started to lead his horse across to Jones'

store, while the others rode on towards the intersection. Upon entering, he was unsurprised to realize he wasn't the only customer.
However, he wasn't expecting any of them to be quite so attractive as
the young woman standing at the counter, tapping her foot while
Jones folded a length of fabric for her.

Their eyes met, and they both smiled.

"Hello," said Davinia, intrigued. "I haven't seen you before."

The young man gave a very proper bow. "How do you do, ma'am?
Micah Johnson, at your service."

Davinia's smile widened. "My, what a pretty accent! I like pretty
things." Micah was taken aback as she immediately took his arm and
said, "Tell me all about yourself."

"I have these supplies to get..." he tried to explain, although not
resisting her grip.

"Oh, don't be dreary. This place is full of dreary little men. I like
you. Entertain me - tell me your story."

Micah grinned. "Well, I guess the others will be a little while..." he
said.

Two of those 'others' were in McCartney's spare office. Adhilasa
stood in correct 'at ease' position in front of the sergeant's desk.
Samuel was beside him, in a less formal posture. They'd said their
carefully prepared piece.

McCartney stroked his chin. "Boys, I'm inclined to accept your
word. Samuel, you should know Mister McGregor speaks very highly
of you, and whatever our differences I do respect his judgement."

"Thank ye, sir."

"What's more, the description young Robertson first gave me,
before that whole mess in the bush, doesn't seem to fit with what I've
seen of your people," admitted the policeman.

"So, what happens now?" asked Adhilasa.

"I'll have a word with Mr. Robertson, try to settle him down. Folks
in Louth are usually pretty slow to get stirred up - a lot of them are
just pretty slow - and they're not inclined to stay fired up for long.
With a bit of luck, it'll all blow over. Just try to keep a low profile for a
while to be on the safe side."

"But the little girl?" asked the American.

The sergeant only shrugged. "I've already done what I can. Her parents were upset - are upset - but they'll get over it. Frankly, I reckon they're better off with one less mouth to feed, and they know it."

"Suffer the little children," said Samuel sombrely.

"That's the way of the world, I'm afraid," was McCartney's world-weary reply.

"But what if it happens again?" asked Adhilasa.

The policeman fixed him with a cold stare and asked, "Do you think that's likely? Is there something you know you're not telling me?"

"No! I just..."

"Then mind your own business. Do whatever you have to in town, as quickly and as quietly as you can, then be on your way. I don't want any more inconvenience."

"Inconvenience?!" Adhilasa almost spluttered in outrage. "Men have died..."

McCartney cut him off with a gesture. "Mister Johnson, I don't know what it's like where you come from, but round here that's what men do. Personally, I'm trying to delay the inevitable. I notice you don't carry a gun."

"No. I never... not since..."

The policeman held up a hand. "I don't want to know. I don't care. I could wish there were a lot more like you around here, but there aren't. I simply suggest that you don't give any of those others any excuse to shoot you. Samuel, your people are usually pretty good at keeping their heads down. Keep it that way, for their sake. They're not my responsibility."

"Not your responsibility?" The outrage flared again. "You're an officer of the law!"

"Don't tell me my damned job!" the sergeant snapped. "I've told you to keep a low profile. I've tried to suggest to you how to survive here. If you don't like the way things are here, feel free to leave!" He glared at the American. "What the hell *are* you doing here anyway?"

Adhilasa ground his teeth for a moment before replying quietly, "My companions and I heard word of a gold discovery."

"Gold! I might have bloody known! Look, the first I've heard of gold round these parts was when the eminent Mister Robertson arrived to complicate my quiet life."

"So, there is no gold?"

"I honestly have no idea. He must have some clue, or he may be on a wild goose chase for all I know. Quite frankly, I hope that's the case. The prospect of a swarm of gold-diggers descending on my head isn't one I cherish. You can all go back where you came from."

He inhaled deeply, trying to regain his calm equilibrium, but looked seriously at the two men in front of him. "But while he's here, be warned - I'm obliged to recognize and enforce his authority. Clear?"

"Indeed," said Adhilasa.

"Aye, sir," agreed Samuel.

"Wonderful," said McCartney drily. "Now get out of here. Thank you."

While the diplomatic mission was underway, negotiations of a different sort were happening at Louth's market garden. Vittorio was arguing heatedly with a Chinese woman who was waving a rather sorry bunch of kale at him. 'Argument' may not be the right word. They were shouting at each other in frustration, but neither spoke a word of the other's language.

The woman brandished the sad, soggy bunch of vegetation. "These are the plants you pointed at! These are the plants you will buy!"

At almost the same time, Pasquale was waving his hands about and shouting, "I want fresh, crisp leaves! Don't try to foist that old, wilted misery on me!"

Their histrionics had attracted attention of course, but most other buyers and sellers were keeping a discreet distance. One man, however, stepped forward, clutching a cloth bag full of his recent purchases.

He tapped Vittorio on the shoulder, and in good Italian said,

"Pardon me, my friend, perhaps I can help." Then he turned to the woman, and in flawless Cantonese, said, "Excuse me madam, those are the type of vegetable he wants, but he would like fresh leaves."

The gardener was unimpressed. "Pah! He is a Westerner! They all boil vegetables to a pulp anyway!"

The man gave an amiable grin. If she chose to take it as conspiratorial, he wouldn't try to dissuade her. But what he did say was, "Perhaps, perhaps. But consider - this man knows enough to ask for good produce. He would not do so if he did not appreciate the difference."

Now he *did* sound like he was suggesting a cunning plan. "If he enjoys the quality of your vegetables, will he not tell his friends? You will sell more, at the prices you charge Westerners."

The woman peered closely at both men, then thoughtfully answered the mediator, "Hmm... you make sense. Tell him to wait while I fetch some better produce."

As she scurried away, the diplomat reverted to speaking Italian. "Be patient, my friend. I've convinced her that you are a customer worthy of her best - how good that is, of course, remains to be seen!"

"Thank you, sir! Vittorio Pasquale at your service. I hadn't expected to hear my mother tongue spoken here!" The merchant extended his hand.

The handshake was accepted with a smile. "Not my first language, I'm afraid – but happily, not my only one, either. Pierre de la Fontaine."

"Ah! This is an English speaking country - if we are going to live here we should make the effort," exclaimed Vittorio, switching languages.

"A good thought," agreed the Asian Frenchman. "But not one shared by all who've settled here, I think," he said, discreetly indicating that the Chinese woman was returning behind Pasquale.

She held out a very different bunch of kale, green and purple, and more importantly, fresh.

"Oh yes! Much better! With these I can make a sauce and side dish to impress even my Chinese friend!"

Happily, he handed over several coins to the woman, then strolled away, looking forward to chatting with his new acquaintance. Equally sociable, Pierre was intrigued by Vittorio's last remark.

"You travel with someone Chinese?" he asked.

"Oh yes, he's around here somewhere. My travelling companions are a... varied bunch. You remind me of some of them - you carry yourself like a military man."

That got a reserved response from de la Fontaine. "A long time ago. So, what brings you and your friends to Louth?"

Abruptly remembering to be cautious about their prospects, Vittorio replied airily, "Oh, the same as most who travel here I suppose - we're all seeking our fortune. And you?"

Equally non-committal, Pierre answered, "As you say. Are you in town somewhere?"

"We've been travelling with some natives. We're camping for now, a little way out."

"Natives?" asked Pierre, sounding surprised.

"Good people. They've looked after us, in many ways, from a place way north called Palmer River."

"I've heard of it. So - not local natives then." He sounded relieved as he said it.

"No, but we've fallen in with some. I worry we may have... not endeared ourselves with some people in town, including someone powerful."

"Really?" said the Frenchman, cautiously.

Vittorio stopped and looked embarrassed. "I'm sorry - thinking out loud. I shouldn't be troubling you with my concerns."

"Quite all right, mon ami. Sometimes it's good to just let it out. Is there anything I might do to help?"

The merchant took a long, appraising look at his new acquaintance. A well-built man, clearly of mixed parentage, he had a ready smile that extended to his eyes. Vittorio liked to think he was a good judge of character, and this Pierre struck him as a decent man. But under the circumstances, better to be circumspect.

"Hmmm... no, no. I'd like to think things are being resolved and the - misunderstanding will be behind us."

"I hope you're right, my friend. I must take my leave of you here, I'm afraid. Fare well, Signor Pasquale."

"Thank you, Pierre. I hope we meet again."

With another handshake, the two men went their separate ways – Pierre heading for the cheap accommodation he shared with his companions, Vittorio to find Chung, then to their horses.

As they rode away from the market garden, the two were comparing experiences and impressions. They didn't hurry. They could see Samuel and Adhilasa already waiting on foot at the intersection, evidently untroubled.

"You're right about the different treatment! I watched a few people being sold stuff I wouldn't take if it was *given* to me," said Chung, shaking his head. "Nothing like that was even offered to me. Good thing you met this fellow."

"Yes," agreed Vittorio. "Interesting man. A very French name, but he doesn't look it."

"Big French presence in south Asia. A lot of soldiers," observed the cook.

"I got the impression that was his background. Might be a handy man to know, but I hope it doesn't come to that. Adhilasa! How did it go?" he called as they arrived at the meeting point.

"About as well as can be expected. I think the sergeant is as convinced of the Balyarta people's innocence of the crime as we may hope."

"We can only pray that is enough," Samuel added.

Adhilasa nodded. "As you say. And how was the search for fresh vegetables?"

"Enlightening," was Vittorio's unexpected answer. "Some of the Chinese people have a very low opinion of people who are not of their colour. I'm starting to think that's just the way of this country."

Chung raised his eyebrows and asked, "And Italy is different, is it?"

After a moment or two of reflection, Pasquale replied bitterly, "No. Not at all."

"Perhaps that is the sin we all have as men," offered the Balyarta elder.

Adhilasa tilted his chin up and replied, "Perhaps. But we can try to rise above it and be better than that."

"Amen," said Vittorio, with feeling.

"Amen," agreed Samuel. He pointed across to where Micah's horse was still tethered outside the store. "The young man is nae back yet."

"No. Strange - his should have been the shortest of tasks." Puzzled, Adhilasa signalled to the 'lookouts' who'd been joined by James Arnold, who managed to convey by their own gestures that they hadn't seen the young man, either.

Just as Chung started to ride over to investigate inside Jones' store, the missing Micah came running out of a narrow side street, a canvas bag of provisions over his shoulder.

"Hey! Here I am!" he cried, almost skidding to a dusty stop beside his horse.

"Ah - all went well, then?" asked Vittorio, eyeing the heavy bag being tied to the horse.

Micah grinned broadly as he swung himself up into the saddle. "Yes! I met this remarkable girl..."

"I actually meant getting the supplies," said the Italian, good-naturedly.

" Oh that - that was easy. This girl, Davinia..."

Adhilasa had mounted his horse, and helped Samuel up behind him. With a chuckle, he interrupted his young protégé, asking, "Impressive?"

"Oh yes!"

As their horses walked up the street, Adhilasa quietly remarked, "You got out of the store without even Guillermo seeing you."

"Oh - er - Davinia took me out from a back room."

"A back room. I see."

Chung and Vittorio grinned at the note of paternal suspicion in the older American's voice. It was enough to temporarily restrain Micah's enthusiasm, too.

"She's a very... forward young lady," he explained awkwardly.

"I trust you behaved like a gentleman?" said Adhilasa, firmly.

"As best I could! I think that may have - disappointed her somewhat."

Adhilasa wore a look of concern, if not quite outright disapproval, as they neared the three men at the edge of town. "A true lady should never be disappointed by a gentleman behaving properly. Especially one she's only just met."

"It's alright. Davinia's definitely a lady!" exclaimed Micah with more fervor than insight.

"Davinia? Davinia who?" asked Arnold, catching only the end of the conversation.

"Oh, this beautiful girl I met in Jones' store. You know, I just realised she never did tell me her last name! Isn't that stupid? And she asked me to call on her where she's staying, at a place called 'The Woolpack'. Well, I guess there can't be too many Davinias staying there."

"It's not a common name, no," agreed Chung.

"You're right there," said Arnold. "And I'll tell you a funny thing. Magpie mentioned this Gold Warden bloke Robertson has a daughter named Davinia."

Disconcerted, but optimistic, Micah replied, "Well, if she is his daughter, she's nothing like what we've seen of him!"

"You reckon?" muttered Arnold quietly, but otherwise held his peace.

Adhilasa was more forthcoming. "I hope you're right, my young friend. I get the sense that Mister Robertson is a very dangerous man."

～

THE DANGEROUS MAN who was the Warden looked thoughtful as the door of his office was closed behind his latest departing visitor. He drummed his fingers on his desk, and scarcely looked up when the door reopened.

Ali walked in, gave a polite small bow, and handed his employer a small tumbler of good brandy.

"You are troubled, sir?" asked the manservant. "Was Sergeant McCartney's visit unsatisfactory?"

Robertson paused for some moments before answering, collecting his thoughts. Strange, perhaps, that Ali remained probably the only person with whom he might share thoughts 'out loud'. Of course, who would the faithful servant share them with? He was the archetypal 'man alone', after all.

Finally, he replied, "Not so much troubled as challenged, Ali. The sergeant is reluctant to press these particular natives further on this matter. The American was apparently persuasive." Ali nodded solicitously. "I'd expected to have a couple of tribes of aborigines to deal with. Difficult as they can be, I had thought I had things in hand. I have firepower at my disposal. Public opinion was easily swayed. Now there are these men who have allied themselves with the blacks. At least some of them seem to be skilled with weapons..." James swirled the spirit around in the glass, gazing into its clear depths. "Weapons... weapons..."

Suddenly he looked up at Ali and said, "At that campsite, I noticed one of the drunkards died in a most unusual manner."

"Unusual, sir?"

The squatter met his servant's neutral gaze with a wry smile. "Perhaps I should say - somewhat familiar, in its way. A small primitive dart was found in his neck. Judging by the manner of the poor fool's death it seems safe to assume it carried a most effective poison."

Ali raised one eyebrow slightly, his professional curiosity piqued. "Most effective, sir?" he asked, evenly.

"Oh yes - very. I wonder... Ali, you're able to produce something that would have a similarly immediate effect."

"Of course, sir."

"Do so. Carefully, but with all speed. And devise a - delivery system - which will duplicate a dart wound. Perhaps even a real dart? No - not a game I've ever greatly enjoyed," mused the Warden with a grim chuckle.

"Very good, sir."

"Of course, it remains to decide which worthy citizen will be the unfortunate victim of this foreign villain."

"*Foreign* villain, sir?"

The grim smile still played on James' face as he explained, "A poison dart is hardly a white man's weapon - well, not usually - and I've never known it to be used by the natives in this country."

"I see. Indeed not, sir. Although it is my understanding that some natives use poison on their spears."

"Really?" Robertson was genuinely surprised. "That seems excessive."

"Kill quickly with even a glancing blow, sir." Ali could have been discussing comparative recipes for white sauce, so casual was his tone.

"Ah, of course. I'm impressed by your research, old friend."

If the compliment moved the valet, he showed no answering affection, simply replying in his usual even voice, "One does one's best, sir. Another brandy?"

"Mm - perhaps not yet." James continued to muse. "Who in this town is expendable...?" he asked himself aloud.

"A long list, sir."

"Yes, that's true," the Warden replied, with no more trace of humour than Ali had shown. "Someone with profile, though. McCartney? No - I think I'm starting to work him out. His replacement may be less - predictable. That fool who owns the rough bar? Cattenach? No - I suspect the locals would applaud his loss."

"Who here has struck you as particularly significant, sir?"

Robertson laughed without mirth. "In this town? Frankly, nobody! Well, obviously, except for... Mmm... Very attractive woman - it'd be an awful waste."

"Perhaps not the lady, sir."

"The town's best builder? Hmm, he did seem like the best choice for my building projects - but I can't make a start on them until I get the land clear of its current inhabitants... There are other builders."

"I'm sure there must be, sir."

Again, Robertson drummed his fingers on the desk. "Of course, I *am* concerned about the grieving widow. Widow-to-be," he corrected himself.

"Indeed, sir."

LESS THAN FORTY-EIGHT hours had passed between James Robertson conceiving his plan, and putting it into action. The squatter had not made his modest fortune, not all of it inherited, by taking longer than necessary to do what must be done. And, he would admit, one of the most valuable traits of his trusty manservant Ali was the Indian's ability to perform a task with commendable speed.

Yes, the scheme had been quickly devised. Now it was time for execution.

Robertson and Charles Gillespie were riding north, out of Louth, their horses at a gentle canter. The builder was coming to inspect the prospective site of his client's new premises. The way to Hard Rock Creek was, as usual, quiet. Few travellers came this way – as far as most people knew, there was little reason to. Not much here but lots of bush, and some natives - and few folks took much interest in them.

Gillespie was looking around thoughtfully, surveying the road itself as much as their surroundings.

"Not too bad a track for bringing supplies, so far. Does it stay the same all the way to wherever we're going?" he asked.

"Pretty much," his companion replied.

"And is it much further? I'm looking forward to seeing the, um - the source of your eccentricity."

Gillespie was enjoying the thrill of having 'inside knowledge' of the untapped wealth. He was good-humoured by nature, and the prospect of sharing in riches only increased his cheerfulness.

The Warden laughed at the fellow's mood, taking a similar pleasure from imagining the future.

"Not far, my friend. But there's not a lot to be seen. There will be work to be done to extract the - source. Don't worry though. I'm quite confident that we'll all do very well out of this." Robertson changed the subject, to something else he'd been surprised to realize was already, if not dear to his heart, at least of significance to him. "How is the lovely Jade? Looking forward to a life of luxury?"

"Not half!" Gillespie chuckled guilelessly. "I do me best by her, but I reckon any woman would want a life of luxury, as you put it."

James murmured to himself, "She is hardly just 'any woman', I think."

"Pardon? Sorry, mate – didn't catch that."

"Sorry, just talking to myself."

"First sign of madness, my old Dad used to say," replied the builder jovially.

"Really?" said Robertson mildly, giving no sign of offence.

The squatter took one hand off the reins and surreptitiously (and cautiously) removed a hatpin from his broad-brimmed headwear.

Suddenly he exclaimed, "Now there's something you don't see every day!" and with a jerk brought his horse hard alongside Gillespie's. He pointed into an undistinguished clump of trees.

Looking in the direction indicated, the builder managed to utter one startled syllable: "Wha...?" before Robertson jabbed the hatpin into the side of his neck.

With a gurgling sound, Gillespie sat bolt upright, just for a moment, before his eyes rolled up in his head and he toppled sideways from his horse.

Carefully, the murderer wiped the pin on the dead man's saddle blanket, then returned it to his hat. He grasped the loose reins of Gillespie's horse, and looked down at the corpse.

"Oh dear," he said calmly.

MEALS around the Balyarta campfire weren't what they used to be. New ingredients were only a part of it. There were whole new ways of preparing and cooking traditional fare, too.

This evening was a good example. Both tribes, and the men from other lands, were all gathered round the fire feasting – all but the four on the now-standard sentry duty. The meal was fat grubs in something resembling a rich Bolognese sauce.

Cristiano laughed as he licked his fingers. "How good is this? How could you ever imagine a meal like this, in a setting like this?"

"I never known food like this at all, Mister Cris!" replied Mundil gleefully.

James Arnold agreed, saying, "Sure as hell never seen grubs cooked like this before! It's one damn fine sauce you've knocked up, boys!"

The two men responsible – Chung and Vittorio, shared broad smiles.

The Italian explained, "It's based on an old recipe that my family have used for generations. Never quite like this though! Between the local herbs and fruits - these 'bush tomato' things Chung's been experimenting with - and the meat... I never thought of grubs as food until the Kuthant ladies managed to convince me to try them."

"Dis sauce stuff would work real good wit' some of de shellfish I get up home," said Asbul.

"Mm," agreed Micah, imagining something similar. "These white grub things do taste like something between fish and chicken."

"Whole lot better than any sad scrawny chicken you'd find out here," advised Arnold, drily.

"Those big fat pigeon-type birds we had along the way were good," reflected Micah, recalling some particularly fine meals on the long journey south from Palmer River.

"Wongas, they call 'em down south. Yeah, they're good tucker alright. Not many around these parts," said Magpie, between enthusiastic mouthfuls.

Samuel licked his lips approvingly. "Need a lot tae feed this many people. We take too many birds now and there be none at all next time we want some. Plenty grubs round now so they're best for a big feed."

Chung was still grinning. "Talking of big feeds - you better watch yourself, Cristiano. Too much more and you won't be able to reach around your guitar. You're supposed to leave some for your father, too, remember? And Adhilasa."

"A night like this, it seems silly them being on watch. Walan and Biru too," said Vittorio, sadly.

Micah shook his head. "Adhilasa will always insist on taking his

turn at any task, same as everyone else. The 'essence of true discipline' he calls it. A military thing, I think."

Still chewing, Cristiano concurred, "Mm. Papa too - taught me the
same thing."

Vittorio sighed. "I understand, but with all of us gathered here,
and it seems such a beautiful still evening..."

"Bad things can happen even on the best of nights. I think this
Warden Robertson cannot be trusted to respect a tranquil evening,"
warned Gregori, grim as usual.

Samuel sympathized with the Cossack's concern. "It is this gold.
Mister McGregor has spoken often of the evil which greed brings."

"Hmph. I'll bet he has." James made little effort to hide his
disdain for the Church.

Not surprisingly, Samuel defended the preacher. "Mister
McGregor tries tae do what he thinks best by us, James, just as ye do.
He would enjoy this gathering, I think, and this meal."

"Discussions of gold notwithstanding, eh?" said Pasquale, the
diplomat again. "Speaking of which, judging by the Warden's
obvious interest, I think we must be sitting quite near to its source,
eh?"

"He as much as said so, that first time he told us to move on," said
Arnold.

"We should look for it, then!" suggested Micah, with enthusiasm.

Magpie chuckled mischievously. "It'd piss James Robertson right
off if we got to the best of it before he did!"

That spurred Vittorio's eagerness. "All the more reason then, if
any were needed!"

Arnold, though, was unimpressed. "You can suit yourselves - look
for it if you want. I'm with the likes of Samuel and his people. Give
me fresh air, an open sky, food in me belly and I'm happy. I got no
need for anything more."

That earned a sly grin from his teamster partner, who teasingly
asked, "How do you reckon Rebecca'd feel about you sittin' on a gold
mine, mate?"

James only glowered in response, but did then turn away, looking thoughtful. He found an unexpected ally, though, in the young Spaniard.

"I think you got it right, Senor Arnold. You got a good life, you enjoy it, si? You got a life out in this country I could enjoy, I think. Although a bit of gold - she buy some new horses maybe?"

"Nothing wrong with my horses, mate."

"Not at all, senor! But they're not getting younger."

"Fair enough. None of us are," conceded Arnold, before going quiet, apparently concentrating on his meal.

Vittorio took up his enthusiastic thought again. "All I'm saying is, this is the opportunity we came here looking for. I think we should put some effort into looking for the gold."

At just that moment, Adhilasa and Guillermo entered the circle of firelight, both sniffing the air.

"That meal smells delicious!" said the American. "About time someone took over on watch for a little while, I think, while the four of us eat!"

Cristiano looked suitably contrite, and said, "Sorry! I'll go. You take my spot, Papa."

"Gracias. Thank you for saving us some - I know your appetite for good food!"

"Papa!" the young musician exclaimed, feigning indignation before moving off into the gathering darkness with a wave of his hand.

Chung stretched and got to his feet, saying, "I'll take a turn. I'll call Walan and Biru in, too."

"No!" protested Asbul. "Hey, you de cook. No have to do guard duty too! I'll go."

But Chung shook his head. "I'd rather you take the late watch, my friend. I'll sleep better."

The Makassar shrugged, accepting the implied compliment with his usual grin. He exchanged a few words with the natives near him. A Balyarta man and young Kuthant woman stood and accompanied the cook as he walked away. They would change places with Walan and Biru.

Magpie called after the tallest of the departing figures, "Bloody good tucker, Chungy - thanks!"

"Pleasure. Always like an appreciative audience," came the answering voice from the gloom.

"He's always loved to cook for a crowd. Now, what was this about looking for gold?" asked Adhilasa, who'd taken a serve of the Mediterranean-style grubs.

Vittorio replied, "I was saying, we - well, some of us, came here to seek our fortune. We know we're near something good - that Warden's virtually confirmed that for us. If we can make some good finds quickly, well, we can maybe buy him off, or at least have enough to get out ahead."

Adhilasa nodded as he ate. "That makes good sense, my friend. Do you have a plan?"

"Not as such. What's to plan? We're not sitting right on top of the gold - I think one of us would have noticed something by now, so assuming I'm right about us being close, we start looking around."

Volkoff looked thoughtful. "Reasonable logic, but I think a planned approach would help."

Adhilasa turned to him. "You're a strategist, my friend. What do you suggest?"

"Let us think. When the man Robertson first came and spoke of a claim this mining company had, he said the land claimed was here, yes?"

"Yeah. He was pretty definite about that," agreed Arnold.

"He might just have said that 'cos he wanted the tribe out of his way, mind you," added Magpie.

The Russian nodded slowly. "True, but even so, not without a reason. Vittorio, you are right. Were this gold just where we are, I think one of us should have seen some sign of it by now. We may not have been actively seeking it, but gold drew us here and I think it unlikely we would all fail to notice it."

"Of course, someone could be keeping quiet about something he spotted," said James Arnold, cynic.

"Possible, and yet, I think, unlikely," replied Gregori.

"I have more faith in you all than that," declared Adhilasa.

"Spaceeba. Also, there would be few options. Wait until we all leave, then try to come back alone and make oneself rich under the nose of the Warden? I think not." The Azov veteran pondered quietly for a moment or two. "The watercourse we crossed near here, it runs east-west?"

"Pretty much, yeah. Creek winds a bit, and a few miles that way..." said James, pointing west, "it turns south and runs into the Darling."

"Robertson and his group came from the south, we have determined, yes? From the port town. So, we may assume that the gold does not lie in that direction or they would not have come here."

Guillermo nodded in agreement with the Cossack's reasoning. "Sensible, si."

"So, if we accept that the gold is to be found along the creek, we have two directions to consider. And based again on Robertson's interest in this location we might presume that our objective is not a great distance away. Likely no more than a day's ride at most."

"So, we split up and search east and west?" surmised Micah, excited.

"This is sounding like a plan!" enthused Pasquale.

Adhilasa sounded a note of hesitation. "Let us not forget that there are others who've shown an interest in this gold too - a ruthless interest. We must not let enthusiasm get in the way of caution. Nor can we simply abandon our friends here."

Samuel shook his head. "It's alright. We can move on if we have tae."

"But you shouldn't have to!" Magpie objected, again. "The Italian was right when he said that sooner or later you'll run out of places to move on to. Here there's water, food, some shelter..."

"It is a defensible position," added Volkoff, thoughtfully.

"Okay, if you say so," the teamster accepted. "All the better. Samuel, you can't keep letting yourself get pushed around. Doesn't the Lord help those who help themselves?"

Samuel exchanged long looks with some of his tribe. "Mm. We will talk amongst ourselves."

Adhilasa laid a hand on Samuel's shoulder. "For my part, gold or
no gold, I won't abandon you if you choose to stay. Whatever 'claim'
the Warden may try to enforce..."

That prompted a thought for Vittorio. "If we can find gold first we
can afford to tie this company's claim up in court long enough to set
us all up for life, including the Balyarta!"

Samuel smiled gently. He appreciated the sentiment, at least. "I
dinna think ye understand our life yet, my friend. But tis nae my decision tae make alone, and there are many in the tribe with more of
their lives ahead of them than I have, God willing. In any case, thank
ye - all - for yuir support."

"Yeah. You good men," agreed Mundil, simply.

"Don't waste that support, that's all I ask," said Magpie. "Asbul,
what about you and your Kuthant mates?"

"Gold good stuff to trade wit'," said the fisherman, turning to
Walan, who'd quietly sat beside him to eat while the conversation
went on.

"With your people maybe. Never mattered much to us before, or
most people we meet along way," observed the Kuthant.

"Maybe that changing, Walan," said his tribesman Karumbari.
"Maybe. We got no rush to go yet." Briefly he switched to their own
dialect and quietly continued, "We got plants to dry, things to carve,
to weave. We can do that as well here as further along our way. If we
get some of this 'gold' too, maybe that won't hurt." Reverting to
English, he went on more loudly, "Here we got good company,
friends. I reckon we stay for a bit, eh?"

Walan shrugged and nodded. It would be talked about soon
enough, and a collective decision made by the elders. It made sense
to be adaptable, they all knew that. Asbul grinned broadly, radiating
encouragement.

Meanwhile, Micah had leaned close to Pasquale and quietly
asked, "Is that really what you'd do with any gold you find? Pay to
fight for these people in court?"

The Italian groomed some sauce from his beard as he replied,
"I'm not so good at any other kind of fighting. I'd help these people,

yes - they deserve justice." He grinned and added, more audibly, "I choose to think we can find enough wealth to do this as well as ensure our own futures."

Adhilasa looked pleased. "As we give, so shall we receive? A good attitude, my friend. I think that the funding of the New Johnson Hotel could stand the expense of helping with this cause, too. What say you, my brothers?"

Guillermo was first to answer, "I want most what is best for my son, but si, this is right."

"I think there'll always be a place for you both wherever we finish up," Micah told the musician warmly. He turned to his mentor. "I trust your judgement."

"And this girl who has caught your eye?" asked Adhilasa, part teasing but part parental concern.

His protégé squirmed a little and tried to deflect. "I - er - think it's more that I caught her eye..."

Magpie tried not to laugh at the young man's discomfort. "Sorry mate, but don't get your hopes up. I can't see Davinia Robertson as anybody's wife. Certainly not a humble bar owner."

With great solemnity, Adhilasa responded, "I do not expect the New Johnson Hotel to be a humble bar. To honour the name, we should be a grand establishment in a grand location..."

"Well that rules out Louth! Better go south mate!" advised Arnold. Then quietly to himself, as if just realizing what he'd said, "Rebecca'd like that..."

The older American was still in 'patriarch' mode. "If the girl thinks that in any way she's too good for you, young Micah, then that's her mistake, and her loss!"

A non-committal hum was Micah's only response. It was Vittorio who supplied more enthusiasm.

"I am going to enjoy importing fine food and drink just for your hotel! This colony will have seen nothing like it before, I think! And what of you, friend Gregori?"

"I made a promise to do some good. I will help these people make a home here if that is what they wish."

"And after?" the merchant probed. "I sense you need direction, my friend. A purpose. You have a fine mind - I would be glad of you as a business partner."

Volkoff looked unconvinced. "My knowledge is of the arts of war," he said.

Pasquale persisted. "A keen mind is a keen mind. Commerce is simply a different sort of battlefield - one I can teach you your way around. With the gold behind us..."

"We shall see. I have... other assets to realize which were always intended to provide for a new life."

The chassepot rifles remained unknown to anyone but Guillermo, who'd respected the Cossack's secret. There had been too much happening in the recent skirmish for anyone to have paid much attention to anyone else's weaponry.

"So much the better, if that's your choice. I'll put no pressure on you though." Vittorio was shrewd behind his normal hearty demeanour. "Let's focus our efforts on finding our fortunes before the rascal Robertson."

"As you say," agreed his prospective business partner. "Tomorrow I think those who are of a mind to do so, commence an exploration of the stream to the east and west. Set out at early light. An hour, perhaps two, hard ride out, then a slow, thorough search on the return. If need be, we ride out further each day."

Again, it was Adhilasa who counselled caution. "Not all of us though. Someone stays on watch over the campsite, always. And those who do, share equally in whatever we may find. Agreed?"

There were various nods and expressions of agreement all around, even from those who'd evinced no interest in prospecting. It seemed that gold could weave a subtle spell over even the most indifferent minds.

CHARLES GILLESPIE MAY, perhaps, have been pleased by the number of mourners who attended his funeral service. Admittedly, the numbers were swelled by the presence of Captain Andrews and the men of the 1st Riverview Infantry Company. It had been a fairly short, simple ceremony, handled with appropriate solemnity by Peter McGregor.

The preacher stood at the head of the grave, holding his old black Bible, as he finished his formalities.

"Amen. I would ask ye all tae take a minute for silent prayer, and tae reflect upon yuir ane mortality and yuir immortal souls."

Jade Gillespie was standing nearest to the Scot, with James Robertson close by her side. The widow had her head bowed. The squatter put a consoling hand on her shoulder. In response, she took a small step in to lean even closer against his chest and into his arm. Robertson's expression didn't change, although a close observer may have spotted a faint flicker of a smile cross Jade's face.

Neither of James' offspring were that observant. Phillip was giving his sister a disapproving look that she totally ignored. He was unimpressed by her choice of dress. It was the appropriate colour, but that was the end of its suitability. The cut, he thought, belonged in a dance hall or bar, or even a bordello. For her part, Davinia had her attention on the handsome young Turkish ex-soldier who was standing a little distance away.

Eye contact with her was enough for him to discreetly move away from his two companions and toward her. Davinia nodded and gave him a small smile, then stepped away from her brother and raised her arm slightly. Orhan gave a small bow and took the proffered arm. Pierre and Wei Sun had made no move to impede him, but they did exchange concerned looks.

Most of the Riverview Company were standing with heads bowed respectfully. A notable exception was their commanding officer, who was looking around in obvious irritation. His expression was angry, his arms folded, and his fingers tapping aggressively on his biceps. The captain's displeasure was directed squarely at Peter McGregor.

The preacher closed with the solemn words, "Go in peace," as he looked heavenwards. Andrews' response was a low growl through teeth that were clenched to suppress a stronger audible curse.

The crowd started to disperse. Many were preparing to head for the Woolpack, where James Robertson had generously arranged a wake on behalf of the bereaved lady at his side.

Andrews took the opportunity to stride purposefully over to McGregor. He stood right in front of the preacher, looming in obvious threat.

"This is the sort of thing I really object to. I can't be having with this at all!" snapped the mercenary. When the Scot only looked at him curiously, he continued, "This is not the time to go in peace. A man, by all reports a good man, has been murdered by savages and we have a moral - a *spiritual* obligation to do something about it!"

"Ye think so?" asked McGregor, uncommonly mild – a warning sign to anyone who knew him.

"Absolutely! An eye for an eye, the Scripture tells us..."

The interruption was swift. "Aye, and the Devil may quote Scripture for his ane purpose. The Guid Lord Himself brought the Law down tae two very simple Commandments - about love, not vengeance."

"Yes, and look where it got Him." He planted his fists on his hips. "A fine man - a white man - has been struck down treacherously by a godless heathen..."

"So it's been said," McGregor interrupted again.

Andrews' outrage went up another notch. "You're surely not impugning the word of the good Mister Robertson, are you? We should be giving thanks he was spared to bring the remains and the news back to us, and not laid low himself by one of those vile little darts."

"Aye," said the preacher. "The unseen dart."

"Which doubtless fell out in the rush to escape and bring poor Mister Gillespie's body home for a decent Christian burial!" the soldier exclaimed, parroting the Warden's own story uncritically. "I've been told more than once how a man named Hardy was recently killed in the same way."

McGregor's voice got lower, and took on a hard edge. "Alan Hardy died when a pack of men, half of them drunk, dashed off wi' more regard for blood and violence than reason. And now ye'd do the same, would ye?"

Andrews paused for a moment, breathing heavily as he glared at the preacher, who didn't flinch. Finally, he muttered, "No. No, I think not. This is a job for professionals."

Turning briskly on the toe of his boot, the captain strode back to speak quickly to his adjutant. Finlay nodded, saluted sharply, and set about quietly assembling the men. The Company hurriedly followed their commander as he stormed out of the small cemetery.

Watching them go, James Robertson quietly remarked to Jade, "I think the men responsible for your husband's death may shortly find themselves in serious trouble." He didn't sound entirely approving.

"At no risk to you," she said, clutching his arm tightly as he helped her onto the wagon that would take them back into town.

"Happily, no. Thank you, my dear," replied the Warden.

Pleased as he was with his manipulation of events, Robertson was a little concerned about how much of a loose cannon Andrews may prove. The man seemed a little too inclined towards acting independently.

The last of the mourners departed. McGregor remained, removed his coat and took a shovel from the mound of dirt beside Charles Gillespie's open grave. He had no interest in attending the wake, even had he not still one last job to perform for the deceased.

He replayed the heated conversation with Captain Andrews in his head. As he drove the blade of the shovel hard into the earth, he said aloud to the shade of the dead man, "That's a bad yin, that one. Ye'll be having company soon, I fear."

.ooo.

3

HOPES, DREAMS, PLANS, AND REALITY

The sun was little more than a band of colour in the eastern sky. At the edge of the Balyarta campsite, two groups of four horsemen were assembled. Five men stood between them, and together, they all confirmed their plans for the day.

One group of riders comprised Arnold, Volkoff, Pasquale and the younger Buitrito. They were to follow the creek, heading west. The other quartet, riding east, was made up of Adhilasa, Micah, Chung, and an awkward-looking Asbul.

Guillermo Buitrito had his feet firmly planted on the ground, alongside Samuel, Magpie, Thonkumundil and Karumbari.

The Spaniard was reassuring Adhilasa. "Tomorrow it shall be my turn to ride and seek our fortune. Today I shall keep the guard here, and si, watch the ground for any unnoticed nuggets!"

Chung frowned. "Sure you don't want to swap with Asbul now?" He cast a worried eye over the Makassar. "You don't look real comfortable on that horse, my friend."

It was a fair observation, but the fisherman gave as confident a smile as he could muster, and replied, "Eh - I learning. Always good to get new skills."

James patted the neck of his own horse. "This old dog's not much on new tricks, but I'll give this gold-hunting lark a bit of a go. For now, at least..."

"Bueno!" exclaimed Cristiano. "We find gold, we make bigger and better team of horses, eh?"

Arnold's reply was a non-committal grunt. Guillermo glanced thoughtfully at his son, but also said nothing.

Gregori looked at the sky. "The day escapes from us," he warned.

"Indeed," agreed Adhilasa. "Time we were going."

The two groups of riders set off in their opposite directions. In theory, Samuel was responsible for determining who would be on sentry duty and where. But the elder had wisely given that task over to the shrewd Guillermo.

The musician pointed south-east and announced, "I'll set up to watch that way." He put a hand on Karumbari's shoulder and pointed south-west. "You, that way. Senor Samuel, two more good pairs of eyes to the north, gracias. Magpie, Thonkumundil, relax a bit. I'll signal in an hour or so. If we keep to short spells we all stay fresher and more alert on watch, si?"

Satisfied, he walked away, spinning the barrels on his two Colt revolvers, checking that they were loaded. Samuel watched him go. He did not know details of what the 'old hawk' had experienced, but recognized that he had become a wary and canny tactician as a result. He knew that was a valuable asset to his people, and their new allies.

But he couldn't help but lament to himself that such an asset was necessary.

∽

WILLIAM ANDREWS WAS SENSIBLE ENOUGH, and experienced enough, to allow some time for his own temper to cool. Tactically, he knew, rash decisions were seldom good decisions. His sense of moral outrage was undiminished, but by waiting overnight he realized he'd do a better job of leading his men on their mission of swift and bloody vengeance.

Now Michael Finlay rode at the head of the company, alongside the Pole, Kaminski, who'd been convinced, without much difficulty, to lead the way to the "godless heathens". The twenty men of Riverview rode in formation at a brisk canter behind, with Andrews at the rear.

Alongside the captain was the only rider, other than Kaminski, not in a scarlet uniform. Phillip Robertson had chanced to be close by Kaminski the previous evening, when the 'invitation to participate' had been made. He'd made sure he accompanied the guide when he rode out that morning, explaining to his family over breakfast only that he planned to go hunting. Nothing unusual in that.

Andrews wasn't best pleased at having his paymaster's son along for the ride. His Riverview Company had the benefit of long experience together. Discipline happened as a matter of course, from habit. He could envisage this young fellow being disruptive, deliberately or otherwise, and was still hopeful of changing his mind.

"Mister Kaminski is quite able, I'm sure, to lead us to the campsite of these black scoundrels. You really didn't need to ride with us, you know."

"I... appreciate that, but it's my choice. This whole undertaking of my fathers' hangs on Kaminski's knowledge of where this gold outcrop is. Knowledge he so far hasn't shared with anyone. I prefer to keep an eye on him."

Well, at least it was no reflection on himself, or his troops. "Mm. Catholics, a lot of these Poles. Wise not to trust them too far."

Phillip laughed mirthlessly. "Captain Andrews, I'm my father's son. I've learned to not trust anyone. Especially, it seems, when there's gold involved."

His sister, perhaps even his father, might have presumed he was just looking for excitement - a different sort of hunt. But the Robertson heir was, in fact, quite genuine in his expressions of concern.

Andrews tilted his chin up and smiled as he replied, "You're safe with me at least, young man. My calling is to be a soldier of the Lord, not a digger of the earth."

"No offense, Captain, but as I say, I am my father's son."

~

STANDING on the coarse sand that fringed the creek, Asbul flexed his legs and back uncomfortably. His horse stood equably by, helping itself to a tuft of long grass. Beside him, Chung was still mounted on his own horse, watching with a mix of amusement and concern.

"You know, you could have called it quits at either of the first two stops, instead of letting Adhilasa then Micah start exploring."

"Yeah, I know. But I want to get used to dis fella," replied the fisherman, patting the horse's flank.

"But enough is enough, hey?" the cook smiled.

"Man got to know his limits. You okay to go on for a bit?"

"A little while, yeah. Adhilasa was right - makes sense for us to split up and each check out a different section of the creek. Any of us get lucky, we can all get together there tomorrow. I don't mind the peace and quiet of working alone for a bit either, do you?"

The Makassar shrugged. "Spend a lot of time on de boat on my own, fishing and sailing to trading places."

"No family, then?"

"Oh, got family. Got lots of family back on island! Just don't like dem very much." Chung laughed as Asbul continued, "Just cos someone family don't make dem friend."

The cook nodded, reflecting on his own experience. "Better when friends become family."

"You got dat right."

"Yeah - I'm lucky. Well, let's hope that luck holds today." As he started to ride off, he called, "See you later!"

As he waded out into the creek, Asbul replied without thinking, in his own language, "Best of luck!"

Without turning, Chung replied, also in Makassar, "Thanks. Same to you."

The fisherman looked up in surprise. He opened his mouth to say something, then thought better of it. He grinned at the departing figure, and whistled as he began to work.

IT HAD BEEN a quiet morning thus far at the campsite. The people of both tribes had, for the most part, already slipped back into their regular routines: making and foraging. Knowledge was being exchanged, for the benefit of both peoples. The Kuthant preferred their nomadic way to the Balyartas' sedentary lifestyle, but each had skills the other saw value in.

Guillermo watched a group of children from both groups playing together, and smiled. He drank another mouthful of water from the bark vessel just handed to him by Karumbari. It was another hot morning.

"I think I'll go back on watch. Relieve Wiru," said the musician.

"You not long come back. What happened to watch, rest, watch, rest?" asked the Kuthant man.

With a wry smile, the Spaniard answered, "Si, si, I know. I have tried, but I am... restless."

"Wiru is a good man. Good eyes," said Karumbari, reassuringly, knowing the trait that Guillermo particularly valued.

"I don't doubt that. Not for a moment. But sometimes..."

"Ah. Sometimes you must trust your own hand. Si."

Guillermo grinned in surprise at the unselfconscious mimicry. Some of these people just absorbed knowledge, he realized with satisfaction. He handed back the bark vessel, and inclined his head in grateful acknowledgement.

As he walked back to his chosen position, he patted his twin revolvers. People worth protecting, he thought to himself.

THERE WAS a sharp bend in the creek to the west of the campsite. Trees and scrub grew close to the water's edge, but Vittorio was quite glad of the opportunity to doff his boots and socks and wade in the cooling water, leading his horse. He was the 'outlier' of his foursome this morning, and was hot, saddle-sore, and frustrated. He'd stopped several times to examine what he thought – hoped – were promising clusters of rocks, but without success. But maybe, just around this corner?

His face was covered by his large handkerchief as he mopped his brow while he rounded the bend, so he didn't at first notice the scene he'd wandered into. The sound of his and his horses' progress had been noticed though, and when he pulled the sweat-soaked white fabric away from his eyes, the Italian found himself staring at, and being stared at by, three men with various expressions of wariness or even hostility.

Li Wei Sun, squatting a little way up on the bank examining a rocky outcrop, had been first to notice the splashing footsteps. His was the most obviously challenging expression. At the creek's edge, panning for gold, were Orhan and Pierre, both looking cautiously at the new arrival. Then a light of recognition glinted in the Frenchman's eyes.

"My Italian friend! Bonjour - or I should say, buongiorno!" he exclaimed, stepping forward.

The merchant blinked in surprise. "Oh - Monsieur de la Fontaine! Good to see you - if somewhat unexpected."

"Indeed - my very thought," replied the former mercenary. "Come, meet my companions."

At de la Fontaine's invitation, Wei Sun and Orhan approached, both still wary. The Italian bowed and smiled warmly.

"Vittorio Pasquale. Pleased to meet you."

"Li Wei Sun," was one reply, accompanied by a small nod.

Almost simultaneous was, "I am Orhan Keilbren. Pierre spoke to us of you."

"Spoke well of me, I hope!"

"He did," was Wei Sun's careful reply, but he offered a polite smile. "You travel in... mixed company, I believe?"

"Yes, like you. We're camped back along the creek - you should join us for a meal sometime. We eat remarkably well under rough conditions!" said the gregarious Italian.

Pierre clapped an enthusiastic hand on Vittorio's shoulder – he was as naturally sociable as the trader, and would privately admit to appreciating new company. "Thank you. There's much to be said for good food in good company. So - where are your companions? I wondered for a moment if you'd struck out on your own."

"Little fear of that, in this sort of country! They're mostly scattered back along the creek, doing much the same as you." He looked at the pans still clutched by the Frenchman and the Turk, and stroked his beard thoughtfully. "It occurs to me, you might be interested in a business proposition."

Wei Sun immediately looked suspicious, but Pierre was intrigued and gestured for him to continue.

"My friends have come to a mutual agreement. We share the search, covering as much ground as we can, when any of us finds gold we'll share the labour, and together we'll share the benefits. I presume you've agreed something similar?"

The other three exchanged looks. They'd never actually quite discussed this. Suddenly each man realized the extent of his assumptions.

Pierre turned back to Pasquale and admitted, "It sounds... interesting."

"I guess, if we're all working without really knowing where to look, then it makes some sense..." said Orhan.

"It is a question of trust," said Wei Sun, without indicating any.

"Of course," agreed Vittorio. "I've spent enough time - travelled enough, faced enough difficulty, with those men - most of them - to trust them, but you do not have that experience. You've not seen their character."

"Or, indeed, yours."

"A fair point, Signor Sun. All I can do is raise the possibility, and suggest perhaps we all meet? See if we can all work together...?"

"I'd like to keep working here as long as there's plenty of light," said Keilbren.

"As would I," agreed Wei Sun, a little more defensively.

The diplomatic Italian spread his hands. "Well, I can hardly expect you to move on for my sake! And it would seem unfair for me to work alongside you now without us having some sort of agreement in place - that's how fighting starts. I'll go back along the creek a bit, perhaps meet up with my friend James, he's not too far away."

"Gentlemen, I might travel with him - meet some of his comrades at least," suggested Pierre. "I'll make no commitments on your behalf - or even my own. But I can sound them out, and tonight, tell you what I think."

"As you like."

More positively, from the Turk: "Your judgement's been good so far."

"Well, I've trusted you," said de la Fontaine, amiably.

With a sheepish smile, Orhan replied, "That's what I mean."

"Have you a horse?" Vittorio asked Pierre.

"One between us - we kept her as a pack horse. We've been obliged to walk since having to sell our other mounts to afford provisions and equipment."

Orhan gestured expressively. "This Louth is more expensive than Sydney!"

"Some parts, at least!" agreed Pierre.

Pasquale nodded sadly, "And it will only get worse when stories of gold spread. Give the devil his due, James Robertson has kept whatever he knows very, very quiet."

"You know the Robertsons?" asked Keilbren, one particular member of the family prominent in his mind.

"I've... encountered Mister Robertson. Some of my companions have had - more experience of him."

"That sounds ominous," said Pierre, reading the tone of voice.

"Yes..." said Orhan, worried.

"Let's say, he has not endeared himself. Beating him to the gold will add an extra level of delight, if that was needed."

Pierre grinned at that. "Interesting. Come on - I'll walk with you as you ride. Good luck be with you, my friends!" he said to his companions, who waved their acknowledgement.

"Yes – good luck to us all!" cried Vittorio as he set off back along the shallows. In a much lower voice he confided to his new companion, "Huh - precious few places along this stretch of creek where we're not safer on foot anyway!"

THE RIVERVIEW COMPANY still rode in loose formation behind their guide.

Recognizing his surroundings, Kaminski leaned over and spoke to Finlay. The adjutant nodded, then reined in his horse and raised a hand. At the signal, the regiment rode into a close formation behind him. Their captain, accompanied by young Phillip, rode along the flank to speak with the two men at the front.

"We've arrived?" asked Andrews.

"Not far from it," confirmed the Pole.

Phillip pointed ahead. "I think, around that bend up there and through those trees off to the left."

Finlay saluted his officer. "I've halted us, sir, in case the enemy have lookouts posted," he explained.

Kaminski looked around nervously as Andrews replied, "A good thought, old fellow. Not sure how likely that is, but better to be cautious. Men, tether the horses and have your weapons at the ready. We'll continue on foot and approach through the trees with all possible stealth. Following Mister Kaminski's lead, we shall descend on their encampment like a hammer of justice - "vengeance is mine" sayeth the Lord!"

"My lead?" exclaimed Kaminski. "I'm to walk first into a bunch of spear points?"

"You're the one who knows where the camp is. Come on, man - I thought you were a soldier!" snapped Andrews.

"I didn't survive the experience by being a bloody fool! I don't like the idea of walking straight into an ambush!"

"We'll be right behind you..." said the captain.

"Yeah, *behind*."

Phillip rolled his eyes. "Oh, for God's sake..."

"No blasphemy, damn it!"

Phillip ignored Andrews' interruption and continued, "I can find the camp. Just don't be far behind me is all I ask."

"You can bet your life on that, young sir!" said Finlay, impressed by the young man's spirit.

"I am."

Very soon, Phillip was making slow, wary progress through the scrub, his pistol drawn and cocked. Finlay wasn't far behind, rifle at the ready. Young Robertson looked back over his shoulder, reassuring himself of the support, then looked puzzled at the sound of a melodic whistle. That wasn't a birdcall he recognized.

There was a rustle in the branches above the young man's head. He looked up, and amongst the foliage saw a pair of eyes that were surely as startled as his own.

The Balyarta Kumbu hadn't been on watch for long, but it wasn't a responsibility he was used to, and his concentration had wandered. The signal whistle from Guillermo had got his attention, as intended, but the shock of seeing an armed man only a few feet below him had rattled him badly. He fumbled with the unfamiliar handgun he'd been given, trying to aim.

He never got the chance. Finlay's Martini-Henry cracked. Kumbu's gun discharged, but he was dead before he fell from the tree. Phillip had been momentarily distracted by the rifle shot, and was unaware of the falling corpse, even as the dead man's skull smacked into his own. Both figures collapsed to the ground in a tangle of limbs.

Andrews cursed. "That's torn it. So much for subtlety. Right men, steady advance - forward! No prisoners!"

Guillermo was already running at a crouch into the perimeter of the camp, guns cocked.

"Men with guns coming! Men in uniform!" he shouted.

"Where? Damnit!" Magpie had been woken from a pleasant doze by the sound of shots.

"That way!" replied the Spaniard, pointing south. "Protect the camp - I'll do what I can."

The 'old hawk' dashed across the campsite, heading for the large rock that stood at its edge. Guns jammed into his waistband, he scrambled up to take a position atop the monolith. He lay prone, and peered out into the bush.

Magpie threw himself into a shallow depression behind the

shelter of a large branch, and was quickly joined by Karumbari who'd run in from his sentry post.

The half-caste called to his teamster partner, "Mundil! A couple of men with guns to guard the families!"

"I'll go," said Karumbari, and dashed out from their limited cover.

"Be careful!" Magpie called after him as the Kuthant took up a position outside the large shelter.

That was where the women, children and old men of both tribes were scrambling to enter. Two other armed tribesmen set themselves behind such shrubby cover as they could find, supporting Karumbari and the nearby Thonkumundil.

Magpie found himself joined behind the branch by the two Kuthants who'd also been on sentry duty – Walan and Wiru. Other men and women, armed with spears, took up positions of cover wherever they could around the campsite, and waited for hell to break loose. It wasn't a long wait.

Up on the 'high ground', Guillermo heard, as much as saw, the approach of the troops. He got up into a crouch to aim, fired two shots, and dropped flat again.

In the vanguard of the Riverview, Finlay dived down. Now behind cover, he got to one knee to aim his rifle in the direction from where the shots had come.

"You okay, Murphy?" he called to the soldier who'd been beside him a moment earlier.

"Aye sir. Close, but no - aargh!"

Finlay fired as Murphy fell wounded. At this range, the Martini-Henry was considerably more lethal than a pair of Colt pistols.

Crouching to aim over the edge of his rocky vantage point, Guillermo suddenly looked shocked as the bullet slammed into his chest. The impact took him off his feet. Guns still tightly clutched, he rolled off the edge of the rock, and landed dead in the scrub below.

As Finlay tended to the wounded Murphy, trying to staunch the bleeding, several soldiers advanced past them, firing as they went. Kaminski was in their midst, torn between a desire to kill, and an impulse to stay behind a uniformed shield.

The three men in the shallow ditch were mostly pinned down by the soldiers' fire. Only rarely could any of them rise up or out to get off shots of their own. The defenders in front of the large shelter had a similar problem. One of the tribesmen, sheltering behind a low bush, died as Martini-Henry bullets ripped through the foliage. Panicked, his friend stood to fire frenziedly at their attackers.

Too late, Karumbari cried, "Keep your head down!"

A fruitless gesture – the would-be revenger was struck by several bullets at once, and pitched forward to quickly bleed to death.

Thonkumundil, at least, was able to respond to the warning, muttering, "Too bloody right!"

He winced at the sound of screams from behind him, as bullets hit the shelter and penetrated weaker sections of wall.

The soldiers, well-disciplined, were kneeling, firing , and advancing in a slow but steady rhythm. As they neared the campsite, spears started to fly. One of the throwers smiled with satisfaction as a soldier screamed, but it was a short-lived victory. He was still smiling as he died.

Realizing the danger to those in the shelter, Wiru tried to run over to aid Karumbari. He only managed a few paces before he was struck by several bullets at once, and fell in a dying heap.

"Damn it!" swore Magpie. "This is a slaughter!" In Burundji he called, "Mundil! Can you get those people away?"

The part-time teamster rolled his eyes in response, and tried to edge closer to the entrance of the shelter. Karumbari shifted his own position, and fired a volley of shots towards the attackers. It wasn't much protection, but it was enough for a fast-moving Mundil to make a low dive and roll into the shelter.

He came out of the roll into as low a crouch as he could manage. 'Just as well', he thought, as a couple of bullets tore through bark at what have been shoulder height. The women, children and elders were keeping their heads down. Most were huddled into a slight depression near the back wall. A few moaned softly and clutched injuries. The bodies of a woman and a small boy lay on the floor.

Giving little more than a glance to the bodies, Mundil maneuvered himself into a position to kick out a section of the rough back wall.

In Burundji he snapped, "Come on, move! Don't just lie there!"

Samuel looked up through haunted eyes. "They are afraid, Thonkumundil! The Balyarta have had enough..."

"The option is to lie here and die! These soldiers will clearly not show mercy to anyone," he said, indicating the bodies.

Samuel sighed and nodded. "As you say. Go – hurry!" he chivvied his survivors.

As Thonkumundil hustled people through the gap in the wall, out into the scrub as quickly as they could, Samuel gave himself up as a diversion. He walked to the entrance of the shelter, hands raised. Mundil shook his head and followed the last of the women. The elder caught Karumbari's eye, and with a quick movement of his head indicated that the Kuthant should try to follow the others.

As Samuel walked out into the clearing, Karumbari ducked behind him into the shelter, immediately diving out of the hole in the wall, hidden from the soldiers.

Magpie looked back over his shoulder, saw Samuel slowly walking with his hands above his head, and cursed under his breath. "You bloody fool..."

The elder called to the attackers, "Please! This must stop! In God's name..."

It was Andrews whose shot hit the grey-beard, and who said casually, "Damned heathen."

In a red haze of rage, Magpie stood up to shoot at the captain, who was kneeling just to the left of Kaminski.

"Got you now, you half-caste bastard!" cried the Pole, but his rushed shot missed.

Magpie returned fire, far more successfully. Kaminski's body clipped Andrews just as the soldier was firing at the teamster. It was enough to save Magpie's life, although he fell clutching at his left shoulder and chest.

Andrews looked down disapprovingly at his dead guide. "Not

with shooting like that. Tsk tsk." He signalled his men with a wave, and started to advance slowly into the clearing itself.

Walan attempted to run across to protect Magpie, but he too was shot, his gun skittering across the ground as he fell.

Just then there was an inarticulate roar from the eastern edge of the clearing. The men of Riverview turned, raising their rifles, as Adhilasa burst from the bushes and ran to where Samuel was lying.

"No-o-o!" he cried as he crouched beside the elder.

Unexpectedly, Andrews held up a hand to stop his soldiers from firing. He strode forward to stand beside the fallen Wiru. He looked impassively at the new arrival, close enough to spit on him, had he been so inclined. In his hand was his Tranter double-action revolver, an immaculately-maintained pistol which had been his favourite since his days serving in India.

"I was wondering about these 'allies' the black scoundrels were supposed to have. Explains the guns." Staring into Adhilasa's red-rimmed eyes, he gestured around the campsite. "Consider this a message."

The growl came from deep in the American's throat. "I'll give you a message..." But even as he moved to leap at the uniformed man, Andrews very calmly shot his left kneecap. Adhilasa collapsed and rolled, clutching at his leg. The captain holstered his revolver, turned and walked away.

As his commanding officer approached, Finlay asked, with surprise, "Not finishing him off, sir?"

Andrews waved a casual hand. "Let him rot here. If any others turn up and want to carry him around, let them. He can be their cross - their reminder of this day of retribution."

"As you wish, sir." The reply was accompanied by a salute.

"Casualties?" asked the captain, without breaking his slow stride.

"Limited, sir. Limited. Murphy and Dallas walking wounded. Billington, a spear to the foot, unlucky. Smith caught a bullet in the head - died immediately I'm afraid. Blears took a spear and looks finished. The Pole and young Robertson also went down."

"Pity. Ah well - the fortunes of war. Back to the horses, we'll be off and break the news to the Warden," he said mildly, his signal bringing his men into formation around him.

His adjutant still looked concerned. "No decent Christian burial, sir?"

"I rather think Mister Robertson will want to know what's happened and then relocate in here as quickly as possible. We move only with those who can move themselves." He paused to look back at the bodies lying around the clearing. "I don't think they're going anywhere any time soon. We can bury them when we return. Tally ho!"

The Riverview Infantry Company made their way through the bush, north, to where their horses had been tethered.

For a minute or two, the only sounds around the campsite were the groans and whimpers of wounded men. Then came a distinctive musical whistle. Adhilasa jerked himself as upright as he could.

"Cristiano – be careful!" he gasped.

The Spaniard emerged cautiously from the scrub at the western perimeter, closely followed by Volkoff. Both men had pistols at the ready.

"Told you I heard shots!" exclaimed the younger man.

The Cossack shook his head in frustration with himself. "Age!" he muttered bitterly.

Micah came bursting through bush opposite them, rushing with far less caution to Adhilasa's side.

"What happened?" he asked urgently. "Robertson and his gang?"

Adhilasa shook his head and answered through gritted teeth, "No. Soldiers. English. Cold vicious bastard in charge of them."

Cristiano approached, peering around warily. "Where's my father? Where's everybody else?"

"Don't know. Not long got here myself," said Adhilasa, his voice a strained whisper.

"Let me see your leg," ordered Micah, then he blanched. "Oh, that doesn't look good..."

"Doesn't feel it. Tourniquet. Stop bleeding..."

Micah took the belt from around his own waist and wrapped it tightly around his mentor's upper leg. He started tearing at the trouser leg to expose the ugly wound. Meanwhile, Gregori had knelt to examine Samuel.

"He's still breathing," he reported.

"Good," said Magpie, with some surprise, as he propped himself up on his right arm.

"You're alive?!" Adhilasa said hoarsely. "I saw you fall just as I got here - I'd heard shots and ran as fast as I could. I'm sorry..."

"No apology necessary. Already too late..." the half-caste grunted through his own pain. The Cossack had moved to inspect his injury. "Ouch! Don't think there'd have been any stopping those soldiers."

Volkoff had wiped some of the blood away. "You're lucky. Much higher and the bullet would have shattered your shoulder. Lower and you would be dead."

Meanwhile, Cristiano had been going from body to body around the clearing.

"Walan is still alive, but I think he may be the only one. Where is my father? Where is everyone else?"

Wincing, Magpie replied, "I think - I hope - Mundil got a lot of the families to safety. Some of the men with them, I hope. Don't know about your father but..."

As he spoke, three more figures dashed into the clearing, from the north-west. James Arnold, with Vittorio and Pierre at his heels.

"Jesus, what the hell's happened here?" asked Arnold, skidding to a halt beside his long-time friend and business partner.

Magpie grinned up at him as Vittorio and Pierre started to move among the dead and wounded. "James! Not like you to miss the fun!"

The older teamster was cursing himself, and the world in general.

"I bloody thought I bloody heard something! I was just about to down tools and head back when these two trotted up and distracted me. We were coming back to grab some tucker and meet up with everyone..."

"Sorry mate - not quite the everyone you expected," said Magpie ruefully.

James snarled, "That bastard Warden again..."

"Not this time. Soldiers," Adhilasa corrected, through pain.

Arnold looked down at the speaker, seeing him properly for the first time.

"Jesus - your leg!"

"Officer of the soldiers. Said he was leaving a message..." Adhilasa's voice trailed off, as pain and blood loss took their toll.

"Know who it was from," said a grim Magpie.

Pasquale's voice came from an area of dense scrub. "Can somebody help?"

"On my way!" shouted Cristiano.

"No!" The Italian's reaction was immediate.

Volkoff read the merchant's voice, and grabbed the musician's shoulder. He held the young man in place, kneeling at the side of a wounded Kuthant who he'd been tending.

"Let me," said the Cossack, and ran into the scrub behind the large rock outcrop.

As he expected, he found Vittorio kneeling by the body of Guillermo, tears in his eyes. He stood for a moment at Pasquale's shoulder, then crouched beside him, pulling the Colts from the dead man's hands. Wordlessly, he slipped the guns back into their holsters. With an exchange of nods, the two men carefully lifted the corpse and began to carry it back to the clearing.

By now, Cristiano was propping up the wounded tribesman against his own leg, using a torn piece of his shirt to staunch some bleeding. He looked up as the two men emerged from behind the rock. He crossed himself, and closed his eyes for a moment, but didn't let go of his patient.

Pasquale and Volkoff carefully put the body on the ground, Vittorio drawing his hand over Guillermo's eyes to close them.

"I'm sorry..." he began, but Cristiano cut him off, hoarsely.

"Let's help the living." Suddenly he turned sharply to the north, drawing his gun as he warned, "Someone's coming!"

Nobody doubted him. Arnold, Micah and Volkoff immediately had their own weapons aimed in the direction he'd indicated. Magpie winced as he reached for the gun he'd dropped. At the sound of branches rustling, Micah blasted a shot into the green without aiming. It whizzed about head height through the foliage.

Crouched low, Thonkumundil emerged from a point only just to the left of where the bullet had flown.

"Hey! We on the same side, mate, aren't we?!" he cried.

"Oh God - I'm sorry! I thought you were..."

"Ah – it's alright. I was watchin' out. I got the families hidden away safe as I can back in some real thick scrub. Karumbari's with 'em. I been listening - heard the shooting stop, but thought I better wait for a bit. Circle round an' check. Sorry Magpie - didn't want to risk an ambush."

The half-caste shook his head. "Hey, makes sense. You were the last line of defence, mate. Enough good people died today."

"Lucky you weren't one of them." Adhilasa summoned enough energy to admonish his protégé. "Lucky for you, too. Don't want that on your conscience. Damn guns."

Vittorio knelt by the fallen American. "They've done enough damage here, for sure. Not least to you."

But Micah stood a distance away, and replied bitterly, "At least if you'd had a rifle or something you could have defended yourself - made a difference."

"I've told you before. I will not use a gun. No more."

"I know, I know. What you saw in the war..."

"What I saw. What I did."

Gregori interrupted the family dispute. "There is honour, yes, nobility perhaps, in fighting man to man, face to face. But not all men have such honour."

"I will not lower myself to their level."

The Russian understood his point, but answered dispassionately, "Then you must accept the consequences."

"Consequences?" raged Micah. "How many more people have to die around you to make you see sense? Do I have to?"

His mentor couldn't answer that. He closed his eyes in pain, not all of it physical. Magpie came to his defence, though.

"One more gun wouldn't have helped. And it was hardly face to face. They were picking us off. Keeping lookouts gave us a bit of warning, that's all."

"Might have lost everyone otherwise," Mundil added.

Magpie exhaled deeply as he flexed his fingers. "Don't know how much damage we were able to do," he admitted.

"I saw the old hawk fire two, three shots before he went down," said Mundil.

"My papa would not miss! He has to have been outmanned."

Gregori was contemplating the dead Spaniard's Colts. "Outmanned. Outgunned. A very fine marksman has done this. With a very fine weapon," he observed, looking at the fatal wound.

Pierre was casting a similarly forensic eye over the body. "Something accurate, at range. The handguns would have left your friend - your father - at a considerable disadvantage."

Nobody noticed the look on Gregori's face. Pierre addressed the young Spaniard whose relationship he'd quickly discerned. "I'm sorry. I don't mean to sound so... dispassionate."

"It's alright. What you say is true," Cristiano replied. He gave himself a momentary shake as he lay the wounded man down as comfortably as possible. "Who else was on watch?" he asked.

"Wiru..." answered Magpie.

"He's here," said Vittorio. "I've done what I can but I don't think it's enough."

The half-caste closed his eyes. "Damn! I was afraid of that. Kumbu was over that way - the direction the bastards came from."

Mundil added, "The old... Guillermo was shooting that way to back him up."

"I'll go," said Arnold, immediately moving in that direction.

"I'll go with you," said Micah. The tone of his voice made it clear he was still angry.

Weapons at the ready, the pair made careful progress through bush disturbed by the soldiers' advance. The white man pointed ahead, seeing Kumbu's body at the base of a tree. They were both about to dash forward, when Arnold held up a hand.

"Wait. Cover me," he said, and crept forward.

As Micah watched, the teamster gently moved Kumbu's body to reveal another, almost hidden from view beneath. He whistled softly.

"Well - what have we here? He's still breathing," he said to Micah as the young man approached.

"That's easily fixed," came the reply, as the gun was pointed at Phillip's head.

Arnold reached over and gently pushed the barrel away.

"Maybe not the best idea," he said thoughtfully.

Davinia Robertson had never been inclined to disguise her irritation. More usually, she broadcast it, in voice, behaviour and body language. Presently, she was pacing around the Ladies Lounge of the Woolpack Inn, radiating annoyance.

The only other occupant of the room was the recently-widowed Jade Gillespie, who sat comfortably in one of the comfortable chairs. She held a slim book of poetry, but made little effort to read it. The younger woman was a persistent distraction.

"Don't play the grieving widow around me," snarled Davinia. "I know why you're sniffing around here. You know my father has money - I know your type."

"You do not have a generous spirit, Miss Robertson," said Mrs. Gillespie, with calculatedly infuriating calmness.

Davinia sniffed affectedly. "I have a very giving nature, thank you," she replied haughtily.

"Really? Well, you can hardly be surprised by your father's kindness to me then, can you? Clearly, it's a family trait."

The careful diplomacy put Davinia in an uncomfortable spot. She did place a high value on her position as a Lady, even in this rough community, and was obliged to acknowledge her father's part in that status.

"I'm obviously more... discerning than him. And considerably more than you. I mean - my father?" she said, with no effort to keep the sneer of distaste from her voice.

Jade only smiled. "You do him an injustice. James Robertson is a fine man, and a fine figure of a man."

"Who's thirty years older than you!" the girl snapped.

The smile didn't slip. "I think you may underestimate my age. And there is much to be said for older, more experienced men. You may learn this for yourself one day. But really, you misjudge us - him. Your father is offering me nothing but comfort."

"Oh yes, I'm sure," was the sarcastic reply. "I know his taste for the - exotic. I do understand that." She scowled at the knowing glint in Jade's eyes. "But I don't recommend you try to take advantage of it."

"I wouldn't wish to come between you and your father's affection."

"Never mind that! You're not going to come between me and what's rightfully mine. Be warned. My mother tried that - she wanted to leave us, take "her share". Half of everything we owned."

"Surely not...?" said Gillespie, with transparent sympathy that Davinia completely missed.

"A preposterous idea. But I found there'd been instances like that already, where judges were fooled by fluttering eyelashes, winsome smiles and protestations of injustice." Her voice took on an even more sarcastic edge. "*Brave* women thrown over by *heartless* men. That was not going to happen with us."

"Your mother...?"

"Fortunately for all concerned my mother passed away before her plan could come to anything."

"Not fortunate for her," Jade corrected mildly.

With a grim smile, Davinia conceded, "Well, no. We grieved, of course. Then moved on."

The widow looked searchingly at the girl. "Miss Robertson, what did your mother die of?"

Davinia looked off into the middle distance. "A sudden illness?" she offered, her voice vague. "It appeared to be quite natural causes. This is a harsh country. These things happen."

"Yes, so I've seen."

Davinia shed her vagueness like a cloak, and stared coldly at Jade. "I'm sorry about your husband, Mrs. Gillespie. I suggest that you grieve and move on."

Before the exchange could progress any further, there was a knock at the Lounge door, which immediately opened before either woman could respond.

Ali entered and walked directly towards Jade. He gave Davinia a perfunctory nod as he passed her, but a more courteous bow to the widow as he stood by her chair.

"Mrs. Gillespie, Mister Robertson has asked you to join him in his office, please."

Jade smiled and stood, closing the book and laying it on the seat. "Thank you, Ali," she said, following the servant towards the exit.

The two exchanged smiles as Ali held the door open for her. Davinia watched grumpily, fists on her hips. As Ali went to follow Mrs. Gillespie out, the girl called out to him.

The servant stopped, and without turning responded, "Miss Davinia?"

She looked down her nose. "I have need of your services," she said. At his questioning raised eyebrow she continued, "I'm sick of this bloody backwater. I'm bored, I'm restless and I'm not sleeping well. The only liquor here in any quantity is the dreadful rotgut I'm sure they use as horse liniment when they're not drinking it. I want you to prepare something to relax me."

"Yes, Miss," was the polite response.

"Not too strong. Just enough to take the edge off living here."

"Yes, Miss," he repeated, going to leave.

"And Ali!" He paused at her bark. "Father is *not* to know!"

"As you say, Miss," came the dispassionate reply, as he closed the door behind him.

Swearing under her breath, Davinia went to sit down. Realizing that it was the chair that Jade had occupied, she stopped herself. The curse was a little louder as she paced over to a different chair. She threw herself down and closed her eyes.

She folded her arms and stretched her legs out. She'd have looked quite relaxed, if not for the sour expression on her face.

THE MEN of the 1st Riverview Infantry Company rode in their regular well-drilled formation, even with a couple of holes in the usual positions, and some injuries being nursed. The native encampment was behind, and Louth lay a little way ahead. Their two officers rode in the midst of the group, but towards the rear. They spoke quietly as they rode.

"Any thoughts on how to break the news to Mister Robertson about his son, sir?" asked Finlay, concerned about how it may affect the Company's standing with their new employer.

Andrews was typically dismissive. "Fortunes of war, old chap. I'm sure the Warden understands that."

"I suppose so, sir. But to lose his only son..."

"God's will, my friend. Not for mortal men to question - we are but instruments of the Divine Plan."

"As you say sir," Finlay replied, diplomatic but unconvinced. "I have to observe, though, the Warden hasn't struck me as sharing your spiritual outlook."

"A man of more secular persuasion, you think?" the commander asked wryly.

"Worldly is the word I'd use, sir."

Andrews looked thoughtful. He trusted Finlay's instinct, probably more than he let on. It's why he'd made the man his adjutant. "Mm. Good observation," he mused. "When we get back to camp, have Eaton see to the horses and Matthews attend the wounded men."

"Sir."

"You and I will make ourselves presentable, then pay a call on our employer, as men of the world, one to another. I shall offer such comfort and spiritual guidance as I can."

After some consideration he gave a predatory smile. "I think Mister Robertson will understand the concept of a vengeful God."

"Indeed, sir."

PHILLIP ROBERTSON HAD RECOVERED CONSCIOUSNESS. His head was still spinning, but only a small part of that could be attributed to the corpse that had fallen onto him. He'd actually woken while being carried over the shoulder of a grizzled white man, his ankles and wrists tied tightly with torn strips of his own shirt – fabric which had since been supplemented by stout cords.

He'd been dumped casually in the middle of the campsite. At first, he'd mostly been left alone, trying to gather his wits while activities blurred around him. He'd been aware of voices, in a bewildering array of accents and languages – presumably native ones that he didn't understand, and fragments of European ones where he caught a smattering of dimly familiar words.

It dawned on him that this community that the regiment had ridden to attack was more complex than expected. Clearly, they'd survived the raid, although it was equally clear that substantial damage had been inflicted. He had no great hopes about his own prospects of survival. Indeed, he was more surprised than relieved not to have been killed out of hand. Phillip didn't know what to expect next, but if these people were anything like what he'd been given to anticipate, surely his future held nothing but vengeful pain.

Two dark-skinned men stood nearby. Dark-skinned, but not native. One looked vaguely Asian – Phillip had never heard of Makassar, so explanation of Asbul's origin wouldn't have helped much. The other was Caribbean, and looked about his own age. But his expression and body language were menacing, and Robertson suspected his own continuing survival was not this young man's idea.

Pierre was still with the group, having introduced himself quickly while offering such help as his battlefield experience allowed. Now he walked alongside Gregori and Vittorio, trying to reconstruct the details of the recent events.

The wounded were being tended, as best as possible, around the campsite. Thonkumundil was kneeling in such a way as to support the heavily bandaged Samuel, who sat staring fixedly at the young prisoner. Several members of both tribes were being looked after by women of either. Few of the patients were awake. Among the unconscious was Adhilasa, presently having the rough dressing on his knee checked by a weary Chung. The cook had been at the forefront of most of the treatments, and had probably saved more than one life.

Of course, there were armed sentries posted. Karumbari stood by the bark shelter, eyes scanning the fringing scrub. Walan and James Arnold had taken positions back in the bush, the Kuthant dismissing his wound after Chung had cleaned it and applied a handful of pulpy crushed eucalyptus leaves. Cristiano sat atop the rock outcrop where his father had died, his eyes clear and alert even as he spoke with Magpie, standing below.

The half-caste first nodded, then shook his head in bemusement as he walked away. He approached their prisoner, still musing, and said, "He's a better man than I am."

"Cristiano, you mean?" asked Pasquale.

"Yeah. Man's father's just been killed. Son of the bastard responsible lands in his lap. Wouldn't blame him for shooting you like a dog, would you? No - 'keep him, he might be useful' he says."

Pierre de la Fontaine approved. "Impressive - he's thinking tactically."

Anger clouding Phillip's consideration of his vulnerable position, the young man scoffed. "Tactically? No tactics in the world will keep my father from getting what he wants!"

Beside him, Micah had just enough self-discipline to not reply with a well-placed kick. Instead, he growled, "We've seen what your father's prepared to do."

The Italian merchant was also thinking tactically as he pondered aloud, "I wonder - if the warden knew his son was alive? Could we use him as a shield of sorts?"

Magpie gave the idea no credence. "Hah! Robertson'd shoot straight through him!" he said.

"Really? That's a shame," replied Pierre mildly.

Such a cynical assessment was harder for Vittorio to accept. "But worth a try, surely? Unless it provokes him to mount a rescue mission... I suppose that's no more or less likely than an attack in revenge for the loss he thinks he's sustained. He knows where we are."

The prospect of another attack moved Samuel to express his concern to, and for, his allies. "Ye should nae be here with us. This is nae yuir fight," he rasped, wearily.

It only got a shake of the head from the Cossack, who replied, "I think that it is, now. It has become personal."

"We've already talked about this, Samuel," Vittorio said gently. "And there is still the gold."

"Of course..." muttered Phillip, thinking he now understood everything.

Thonkumundil was still propping up the Balyarta elder, watching the old man's injuries. He was perhaps shrewdly changing the subject as he observed, "We gonna need medicine - more than what we got - I reckon."

"No chance of any white doctor comin' out here to help, mate, you know that," Magpie replied. "You and Chung and the women are just gonna have to do the best you can. Use the native stuff."

Placing a grateful hand on his tribesman's supporting leg, Samuel managed to gasp the suggestion, "Mister McGregor."

"Reckon so," agreed Mundil.

"The preacher man? I'll go into town and get him," offered Micah, suddenly keen to be somewhere else.

Volkoff raised a cautionary hand. "Right idea, wrong man. You're too recognizable."

"I don't think too many of Robertson's men got much of a look at me," Micah protested.

Pasquale understood the Russian's reasoning, though. "Si," he said, "But his daughter did. You think she wouldn't give you away if she spots you?"

Phillip sat up, startled. Not quite shocked, but surprised. He stared at the West Indian. "You? God - she's impossible!" Everyone ignored him.

It was Pierre who proposed a solution. "I'll go find this McGregor," he offered.

The small handful of people in Louth who might know his face had no reason to associate him with the Balyarta or their allies. It was a sensible idea.

"Try the little church house out on the west side of town. If he's not there he'll be out doing some good somewhere," said Magpie, the last wry observation made as he exchanged meaningful looks with Samuel.

"Oui," confirmed Pierre. "I know this Gold Warden by sight, but I doubt he knows me - and certainly he wouldn't associate me with any of you." He paused for thought before continuing, "I'll call into my camp afterwards and talk to my companions about what has happened here. Should I tell Monsieur McGregor, or anyone else in town, about your - guest?"

"Not yet, I reckon," said Magpie. "We gotta agree on what to do with 'im. Mister Mac'll find out when he gets here." He stared down at the young Robertson as he added, "If you're still with us."

Briskly efficient, Pierre replied, "That makes sense. I'll go now - ah - can I borrow a horse?" he asked, suddenly embarrassed.

"Sure," said Magpie.

"Take mine. I'm not going anywhere just now," offered Vittorio, an unenthusiastic rider in any case.

"Just bring her back, right?" cautioned Magpie.

"A promise!" said Pierre, taking the saddle that his Italian acquaintance held out to him.

~

THERE WERE four people in the Gold Warden's temporary office in the Woolpack. None of them were comfortable, or even seated. The adjutant of the Riverview Company, Michael Finlay, stood at attention just beside the open door, carefully expressionless. His commanding officer stood in the centre of the room, in a similar pose, if a little less correct, such was Andrews' natural insouciance. James Robertson stood angrily behind his desk, clenching and unclenching his fists. His daughter was at the other side of the doorway to Finlay, radiating a distress that was more the product of anger than sorrow.

She snapped at her father, "I told you we should never have come here! You should never have made me come with you!"

Andrews made a show of apology to his employer. "Sorry - perhaps I should have broken the news more gently - spoken to you myself, privately."

"Absolutely not!" the girl shouted in response, before storming out of the room and slamming the door behind her.

The regiment's commander resisted the impulse to leer admiringly, instead saying, "My apologies, sir. She's clearly close to her brother."

Robertson was dismissive of his daughter's reaction. He was used to her temper, and she was less of a priority to him than usual at this moment.

"Not especially. By this time tomorrow she'll have figured out that she'll get his share of my estate," he replied, with what would be admirable prescience. He addressed the real cause of his anger, demanding, "Captain, what were you thinking, charging off on a raid, taking Kaminski and Phillip with you?"

"With all due respect, sir, I was undertaking to address the problem you've commissioned me to resolve. I needed the services of your man only to locate our quarry - I made no other request of him to become involved. When our attack started he participated enthusiastically of his own accord. As to your son - well, I did counsel him to return to you, but he's - *was*, sorry, a resolute young man."

The squatter considered Andrews' defence. He knew both the individuals in question all too well, and with some reluctance conceded, "Kaminski always had a temper - too damned fond of a fight. Phillip - stubborn, yes, I know. Damn. Damn and blast. What the hell do I do now?" he asked, addressing the question more to himself than the other men in the room.

"I'll regroup the men," suggested Andrews. "Now we've an understanding of where we're going and what we're up against I can arrange a sortie to collect the bodies for a decent Christian burial..."

The Warden cut him off impatiently. "That's not what I'm talking about, you fool. Kaminski seems to be the only man who knew exactly where the gold was. I think he's done a damn good job of disguising or hiding the outcrop - if any of those characters living out with the blacks had found it I reckon we'd know by now." He sat down heavily, and steepled his fingers on his desk.

"I want them gone - all of them. Black, white, any other damn colour, I want them gone. Then I'll turn over every damned rock in a ten mile radius if I have to."

"Very good, sir," said Andrews, while Finlay nodded obediently, if not enthusiastically.

"We'll hit them," continued Robertson. "Hit them hard. Drive them off, kill them off, I don't care."

The Company commander didn't keep the excitement from his voice as he exclaimed, "Right you are, sir! I'll start rallying the troops."

James slapped the desk hard, even as the two mercenaries started to move off. "I said we, Captain. *We* will hit them. I want McCartney's boys and their guns, such as they are. I want any man in this town that will shoot for a handful of coins."

Andrews didn't hide his disappointment, although his adjutant was able to conceal his own quiet relief even as his officer protested, "Sir, the Riverview Infantry is more than capable..."

"I appreciate your capabilities, Captain," Robertson interrupted. "Consider this to be reinforcement. You're a commander - use your organizational skills. I want this to be one, final effective rout."

"Right, sir." Andrews knew where the money was coming from,

knew better than to argue. "How soon do you wish the hammer of God to fall on these heathens?" he asked.

"The ham...? Ah. I want nothing left to chance. No one is to be left on that patch of dirt when we're done, clear? However long it takes to devise your plan, and assemble the manpower to carry it out - that's how soon. And make it soon."

"Very good, sir. Finlay and I will go and have words with the police chappie, instruct him to put his boys at my disposal."

The man behind the desk wrinkled an angry lip. "He won't like that. Damn him. Tell him – no, ask him - to come see me." He considered what he already knew of McCartney, and how best to handle him. "I'll explain the situation. He's been instructed to put himself and his troopers under my authority. I'll be riding with you."

"If you insist, Mister Robertson," said Andrews without commitment.

"Oh, I do, Captain, I do!"

$\sim$

IT WAS evening by the time Pierre de la Fontaine had finished the tasks he'd allocated himself. Peter McGregor had been located, and the news delivered. The preacher was unhappy, as was to be expected, but was an intensely practical man. He undertook to pull together such medical supplies as he could buy, beg, or otherwise obtain (diplomatically not mentioning how) and deliver them to the Balyarta and friends himself, most likely at first light. He dispatched Pierre to advise those at the campsite of his plan.

Having done so, while returning Vittorio's horse, the Frenchman had returned to his own camp. Micah had ridden him part-way there, but the mercenary wanted to complete the journey on foot. He explained to the young man that there was much he needed to think about before he reported to his own comrades, and would welcome a short spell of solitary contemplation as he walked.

Frayed as Micah's temper was, that made sense. He'd been raised to self-discipline. So, he'd ridden back to his own camp while Pierre made his quick but cautious way through fading light to the glow of a fire, tended by his two companions.

A wok was now perched on a small circle of stones surrounding another, smaller patch of flames. Pierre was stirring the contents, having expressed his desire to cook as he told his story – not least so he could enjoy using a small handful of herbs he'd been given by the Italian.

"So, what do you think, my friends?" he asked at the end of his discourse.

The Turk was first to reply. "My heart goes out to a girl who will believe she has lost her brother, but you're right - the actions of her father who must have sent these soldiers - they are not to be tolerated!"

Wei Sun, however, folded his arms and looked away into the gathering darkness before replying flatly, "This is not our fight."

"Not our fight?" exclaimed Orhan, outraged. "Look at what's going on. What did you once describe? 'Men used for target practice! Women used for that and worse!' Well here it is again! What would you do? Wait and hope to scavenge among the remains to find the gold? You said you tried to stand up against it before - try again!"

The Chinese man was unmoved by the emotion of youth. "You've seen as I have seen as we've journeyed. Some of these blacks see men of our colour as no better than pigs, fit for slaughter and feasting on. I do not wish to risk my life for a people who hold me in no regard."

Pierre didn't look up from stirring the wok, but his voice made his disagreement plain. "Some. Not all. Far from all. These people are clearly different - I've seen the men they travel and live alongside. And tell me, my friend - when we marched against Hong Xiuquan, how much regard were we truly held in by the Qing leaders?"

"That was different. Then we followed orders and fought because we were professional soldiers."

As he started to scoop fragrant stew onto three tin plates, Pierre continued to calmly press his case. "So - maybe now it's time we fought for a better reason. Orhan has a point. In Nanjing events were too big for us to prevent. Now, we can't undo what's been done here, but we might be able to help prevent any more abuse." As he handed Orhan his meal, he smiled. "Well said, my young friend."

Wei Sun received his own plate with a small polite bow, and a thoughtful look on his face. For all his cold reserve, he was a fundamentally decent man. He may not react with Keilbren's fervor, but he did understand the moral affront. In truth, he shared it, but he'd kept his emotions in check for so long that he had to struggle with himself to admit it.

"Mmm. Perhaps. If we fight with honour, and for honour, then we may teach honour," he said, more cautiously than he truly felt.

The Frenchman grinned approvingly. "So, tomorrow we go together eh? You can meet these people, the natives and the others, and if you both agree, perhaps we will join the little army, eh?"

They ate, in thoughtful silence.

Hours later, the campfire had burned low. De la Fontaine and Wei Sun were deeply asleep – it had, in different ways, been a long day for both.

Keilbren was ostensibly on watch. Certainly, he was wide awake.

He sat fidgeting, restless, looking agitated. Suddenly he stood, very quietly, and took a few noiseless steps towards his companions, checking that they slept.

Satisfied, the Turk crept into the bush. With the stealth of his training and experience, he approached their pack-horse. He kept the animal quiet as he untied the reins, mounted and rode away ghost-like, with only a backward glance to confirm he hadn't disturbed the others.

Only when he adjudged himself to be safely clear, he rode with more speed than silence, and made his way to Louth, and the Wool-pack Inn.

It would be an exaggeration to say that Orhan had a plan. At best, he had a vague, brain-fogged hope. But it seemed that fortune was with him. As he reined in his mount in the street outside the Woolpack, he looked up. One window was lit, dimly illuminated by a kerosene lamp. And in its faint glow he recognized a pretty feminine silhouette – the very one he'd hoped to see.

Alighting from the horse, he waved, resisting the initial urge to shout out.

Restless as ever, Davinia had been staring out into the darkness. Not watching the street, but in her mind's eye playing out different scenarios of what she'd do when *she* had control of the Robertson estate.

For a moment she was quite oblivious to the impassioned signalling from below. Then she saw him, and smiled mischievously. She threw a robe over her nightdress, and silently left her room to go downstairs.

The squatter's heiress slipped out of the Inn door and quickly scampered over to Orhan, throwing her arms around his waist. She put a finger to his lips, and led him into a dark side street.

"My dashing Turk - what are you doing here at this hour?" she asked softly.

"I had to see you. I hoped, prayed you'd be awake."

"I haven't been sleeping well - good thing for you, eh? I was just about to take something for it when I saw you wave, you impulsive boy. You don't sleep either."

Orhan squirmed a little, discomfited by the blunt truth. "Not well, not often, no. But why I'm here..."

"Yes?" she asked, taking one of his hands, and perhaps hoping for some reckless declaration of passion, or perhaps the announcement of a fabulous gold strike he wanted to share with her.

"Your brother - I have news of him."

"Phillip's dead, I know. That dreadful Englishman told us," the girl replied, just keeping the disappointment out of her voice.

"No! He is alive. He is with... with a group of natives and - others."

"The ones Andrews' soldiers attacked," she said, quick to grasp the situation and already analyzing how to use it.

"Yes! I don't know how badly hurt he is - not much I think, but he..."

"Thank you! That's - good to know," she interrupted. "What are their plans for him?"

"I don't know. I don't think they've decided, but I imagine they'll try to use him to bargain for some settlement with your father."

"Hmph! Good luck with that!" she said, as much to herself as to her would-be swain.

"I..."

Again, she cut him off before he could say, or ask, anything inconvenient. She sensed an opportunity here, and considering how best to take advantage of it was suddenly more important than any amorous possibilities. Although it wouldn't do for the boy to know that, would it?

"You've done well, my brave Turk. What can I do to reward you?"

"I... I wanted no..." Orhan stammered. He'd been a soldier, yes, and a mercenary, but he was young and idealistic. His knowledge and experience of women was scant. "Just... being here, seeing you again is reward enough."

"Sweet boy!" She embraced and kissed him passionately, then broke away suddenly. "Out here in the street is a little indiscreet at this hour, I think. Perhaps if you tie your horse behind the Inn, my room...?" she suggested coyly.

That sounded good – temptingly so. "Mmm. But your father?"

"Sleeps soundly - a skill I've never had." She had her excuse planned, though. This was a tease, not an intent. "But that wretched servant of his, I think he sleeps with one eye open, and both ears." Orhan suppressed a giggle at the image as she continued, "Ah, but there's my reward for you, handsome boy. Wait here - I'll fetch you the sleeping draught he made up for me. I can get him to make me more."

Davinia planted a quick kiss on Orhan's lips, then ran back to the Woolpack, leaving him to keep the horse quiet while nervously watching up and down the street. Nobody in Louth seemed to be stirring, to his relief.

The girl picked up a small folded paper packet of powder from her bedside table. She had genuinely been about to try it only minutes earlier, only the distraction of a particularly juicy fantasy keeping her from chemically-assisted slumber.

If Ali was as supernaturally alert as she'd suggested, years of practice must have given her powers of stealth beyond even his talents, as she again slipped out of the Inn, apparently unnoticed. She found Orhan with his hand over the horse's muzzle, restraining a startled whinny as the girl ran up.

She slipped the packet of powder into his shirt pocket. "Here. Dissolve some of this in water before you lie down, and you'll sleep the sleep of the dead, so I'm told."

The young man grinned and said gratefully, "Sleep would be a blessing, thank you! But your brother - what should I do?"

Davinia looked thoughtful. In truth, she wasn't sure herself, yet. "Nothing for now, I think. See what happens. You might try to prevent your friends doing anything... hasty. But at no risk to yourself, understand?" He *was* potentially useful, as well as undeniably attractive.

"They are not my friends - well, most of them, but I'll do what I can. I should go before I'm missed," he said reluctantly.

That convenient remark won him a lingering kiss. "If you must."

Orhan almost leapt onto his horse, but was noticeably slower to actually ride away. He did so while looking backwards as much as he could, imagining more than truly seeing the smile on her face, even as she crept back to her room.

Yes, Davinia was smiling. Shrewd, calculating. There was nothing wistful nor romantic in her expression as she turned out her lamp.

THE MORNING SAW a buzz of activity around the Balyarta campsite that was quite different from their routine of many generations. One thing, though, hadn't changed. Food was still being prepared, now by women of both tribes.

Chung, who would otherwise have been helping, was engaged in another pressing task, along with the Balyarta woman Koolwunnung and two of her friends. They were tending to the wounds, with Chung especially relieved to be using dressings and salves just delivered by Peter McGregor. The preacher, too, was an active part of the 'medical team'.

Wide-eyed children watched as the tall Chinese man knelt and gently massaged the arm of the Balyarta woman Keewuk – mother to three of them – resetting the bone fractured by a bullet from an infantry rifle. At his side, Koolwunnung pressed an ointment to the wound that inevitably reopened as he worked. Then she held in place the hard sticks that would act as splints for the limb, while he wrapped a firm layer of bandage. At one point, as she assisted him, Koolwunnung's hand brushed Chung's, apparently by accident. Although there was a look on her face hinting that may not have been so.

Also watching their efforts was James Arnold, although his eyes just as often darted about the surrounding bush, and his hand rarely left his gun. He knew there were, as usual, a quartet of sentries on duty, one at each compass point, but Arnold hadn't stayed alive as long as he had in a harsh environment without becoming very, very cautious.

Micah was considerably younger, but fast becoming no less cautious. He was one of the designated sentries, along with Cristiano, the Kuthant man Bowra, and the Balyarta woman Wittarkee, both of whom had shown some aptitude with a gun. The young West Indian had chosen to stay at the fringe of the scrub, looking outward but also listening intently to the activities of the campsite. His temper had cooled somewhat since the aftermath of the attack, but his nerves were still taut.

In other parts of the camp, damaged bark structures were being repaired or replaced. Weapons were being fixed, or constructed. Spears had been gathered up and examined. Shafts and points were restored to effectiveness wherever necessary and possible by members of both tribes. It was a good opportunity for some younger folk to be taught these skills, too.

Among the wounded who'd already been seen to were Samuel and Adhilasa. Freshly bandaged, they sat together near the fire. Both were drowsy, but enjoying a quiet, deep conversation as they continued to explore each other's philosophies.

Nearby, McGregor was tending to Magpie's wound. The half-caste had insisted on being among the last to be seen to. Thonkumundil and Karumbari sat cross-legged, watching with interest, Asbul standing alongside, doing the same. Vittorio paced about, clearly distressed by the various injuries to people he already considered his friends.

He was also distressed for those who'd been more than injured. A makeshift mortuary had been set up at the edge of the encampment, several bodies lying covered by blankets. A well-trussed Phillip Robertson had been sat, very deliberately close by, propped against a tree with Gregori Volkoff standing guard right in his line of sight.

Magpie winced as the Scot managed to extract what he hoped was the last bullet fragment. He looked over towards the corpses, perhaps seeking to distract himself. "Thanks padre. Y'know, I've known priests who'd have insisted on doin' the funerals before takin' time to patch up those as didn't need it right away."

"A guid Christian ceremony awaits them for whom it's appropriate, but ma first responsibility's tae the livin'. They others are wi' the Lord or not as the case may be, and owt I say is only tae comfort those are left behind. Ye're aye lucky, Magpie - inch or two lower and ye'd have been amongst them we're tae bury."

"Yeah, so I was told. Must have been spared for a reason, eh?" he replied, with a pained smile.

"Aye, well. Ye make sure it's a guid one," was McGregor's grim response.

Pasquale stopped his agitated pacing near the preacher, and addressed his patient. "We must consider our plans."

"Plans?" asked McGregor.

"Now you soundin' like de Russian fella!" Asbul told Vittorio with a grin.

"There are worse men I could learn from," came the reply.

The fisherman was quick to agree. "He smart fella, yeah."

The preacher was intrigued, and concerned. "What sort of plans do ye have in mind?"

"Well for a start, everyone is agreed to stay here," Vittorio explained.

McGregor looked around, at the small group near him, and at others he could see at their various activities. There was no evidence that the Italian was wrong.

With a determined pride, Magpie gritted through his pain, "Like the old hawk said, you don't fight, you die."

"Yes, but he died anyway," Vittorio answered softly.

The teamster was undeterred. "But he made a choice, and he died fighting for the choice he made - for something - someone he believed in." Asbul and Karumbari exchanged thoughtful looks as the half-caste continued, "The only bloke I can speak for is me, but I'll stay and fight alongside anyone that wants to."

After a contemplative pause, Thonkumundil observed, "Don't reckon Samuel's in no state to make a decision."

The old man gave a nod of acceptance, both of Mundil's observation and the younger man's growing into a position of authority within the tribe.

Acknowledging the gesture, Mundil went on, "I talk to the other old men, if we can make the kids and women safe, them as want, some of us stay and try to fight if we gotta. We try to make this place good. What you reckon, Mister Mac?"

"You can't expect the padre to fight, Mundil!" exclaimed Pasquale.

But McGregor rocked back and forth as he knelt. He'd been watching, listening, and thinking deeply as he worked.

"I took an oath tae be a man o' peace, aye. But, sometimes..." He felt the need to explain himself to these people, perhaps to himself, at last.

"I had a wee kirk on the island o' Mull. Maybe a hundred in the flock. Crofters and their families mostly - folk who'd scratched a puir livin' out o' hard ground and gardens ye could throw a wee blanket over, but it was home and they clung tae it. Laird o' the estate, lived in England all his life, never sae much as visited the lands he inherited frae his drunken sot o' an uncle. He heard tell o' how much mair money he could make frae the land by runnin' sheep on it so he drove the rents up. An wi' his tacksman and some bully boys he drove the crofters out. Beggin' and scrapin' their way on tae boats tae God knows where."

"Even to Louth, eh?" observed Magpie wryly.

"Tae wherever any scrappit tug or hulk would take them on God's green earth. It was that or stay and either starve or be beaten tae death, that was all the choice they thought they had."

The Scot paused, remembering. His voice was bitter as he continued, "And ma kirk... ma kirk Fathers, in their wisdom, said 'ye must render untae Caesar what is Caesars. 'The laird has the right o' it' they told me, frae their comfortable homes. And so, I watched as ma flock were scattered, like stones flung out across the bay, tae fall or sink where they may. And I raised neither hand nor voice to stop it. And o' course, in the end, I was moved on like the rest. And right enough - who had I left tae preach tae but the sheep? And what could I have said?"

There was general uncomfortable movement among the group. Few of them had much experience of organized religion, virtually none among the natives. The co-ordinated evil known as the Clearances in Scotland's highlands and islands was unknown to them all, but the impact on Peter McGregor was obviously profound.

"I'll nae fight wi' ye, gentlemen, but I will do such else I can tae support ye, whatever ye decide," he declared. "I've over much runnin' away on ma conscience as it is," he said firmly, finishing Magpie's wound dressing with a decisive movement.

"So, we stay..." said Thonkumundil, confident of the support of his elders.

"I stay wit' you too," answered Asbul quickly.

The Kuthant Karumbari nodded. "My people too, for now. Our women with your women. Our fighters with yours. Our people not start this fight but our men and women die with yours. Our law says we owed blood."

Pasquale looked alarmed. "I don't want to start a war..."

Magpie interrupted. "No-one here started anything."

"We have the boy," the Italian mused.

"I'll nae be a party tae murder!" snapped McGregor.

"That's not what I meant!" protested Vittorio, although Karumbari's sideways look toward Phillip suggested that the thought had crossed at least one other mind.

"It's enough that ye have him tethered beside yon mortuary..." the preacher admonished, but Magpie cut him off.

"And I hope he's breathin' deep of the damage he helped do!"

"Aye, well, I see yuir thinkin'."

"Padre, can you - will you, convey a message to Mister Robertson?" asked Pasquale.

The Scot looked cautious. "Aye," he said carefully.

"What we want is his agreement, in writing, officially as Gold Warden so it'll stand up in court, to register a claim on this land here."

"In whose name?" McGregor asked.

"Well, he won't recognise that Samuel or any of his people have any rights, so we discussed it and came up with New Johnson Hotel Holdings," explained the merchant, as Adhilasa smiled weakly and raised a hand in acknowledgement.

"And who is that?" asked McGregor, puzzled. He'd not heard the details of the Americans and their blighted ambitions in the new country.

"All of us," Magpie replied. "Black, white and in-between. Balyarta, Kuthant, Cossack, Italian, American..."

"Even Makassar!" added the grinning native of that old port.

Vittorio continued his explanation. "It's the same agreement we already had - if anyone finds any gold here it's shared by all. But we guarantee the Balyarta a home, and anyone else that wants to stay. The offer is open to anyone who'll stand beside us," he said, giving McGregor a significant look. "I'm hoping Monsieur de la Fontaine and his friends will join us. Robertson signs that claim, and we'll let his son go."

"Hmm... an honourable offer if, I think, an optimistic one. Aye, I'll tell him, but dinna get yuir hopes up."

Samuel's voice was weak as he said optimistically, "The man is a father."

"Not all fathers are guid ones. What will ye do if he doesnae agree?"

Vittorio sighed sadly, and replied, "Cross that bridge when we come to it, I suppose. That's why Gregori wants us making plans."

"Canny. Aye, I'll deliver the message for ye, and pray that it doesnae fall on deaf ears. But first, I have other responsibilities."

Over the next couple of hours, McGregor set about meeting those responsibilities he'd taken upon himself. First to the living, tending and dressing wounds, quietly talking and counselling, listening to those expressing their grief, anger or confusion. Then to the dead, respectfully cleaning bodies and discussing with kinfolk the appropriate means of treating the corpse. Most of the Balyarta dead were to be placed in trees, as per their long tradition. A couple were to be buried, as were the Kuthant victims, and Guillermo Buitrito.

In the course of the morning Pierre de la Fontaine arrived with his two companions and introduced them around. Wei Sun and Keilbren were both quiet, reserved, and watchful. Both ex-soldiers, though, were soon impressed by the *esprit de corps* they saw around the campsite.

They had stood respectfully during the services for the dead, first the burials, then the tree depositions (which frankly baffled them – feeding bodies to the worms was one thing, but to birds?). All three had willingly joined in the rotating sentry party personnel as the solemn ceremonies continued, appreciating the implicit trust in them that this conveyed.

The graves were filled, rough crosses raised.

Kumbu was the last Balyarta to be carried aloft. Two brothers, Cooterah and Coreel, had shared this honour for all their kin. The nimble Cooterah climbing up into the branches, and his bigger, burly brother sombrely handing up the blanket-swathed body to be wedged securely in the branches of a tree, a little way beyond the fringe of the clearing. The corpses were far enough away from daily activity for health and hygiene, but near enough to be regularly respected.

The hostage Robertson was well-secured, and stood silently among the group of mourners. They stood, or sat, as their injuries permitted. He looked around frequently, watching the expressions on people's faces and contemplating what he saw.

There was the raw grief of Cristiano, Samuel and men and women of both tribes, the open anger of Arnold and Micah, simmering reserve from the likes of Karumbari and Koolwunnung, bitter self-recrimination from Volkoff. There were expressions of respect, and resignation, and sorrow. On Magpie, tight-lipped resolve. If he could have watched his own face, Phillip would have seen puzzlement, and the dawning of deeper thought.

Cooterah dropped down from the tree, handing the blanket to his brother. Coreel folded it neatly, and with a respectful nod handed it back to McGregor. The preacher returned the gesture of respect and laid the blanket at his feet.

He clutched his worn Bible, but spoke entirely from the heart. At first, he spoke in peculiarly-accented Burundji: "And so we commit the soul of oor brother tae his rest, with oor thanks for his sacrifice, oor blessings, and oor sorrow..."

There were audible sobs from some of the women of Kumbu's tribe, not all of them family.

McGregor continued, now in English, "Lord, I would ask yuir protection, and yuir guidance, of these yuir children. For whether they know the ways o' yuir Scripture or not, they are aye all yuir children. Amen."

The mourners started to disperse, singly or in small groups. Robertson shuffled awkwardly, flanked by Micah and the Cossack.

Still mulling over what he'd just witnessed, Phillip said, "That was... different. Never been to a funeral like that before."

"Me neither," admitted Micah. "Different people, different ways. I reckon not a lot of preacher-men would do what the Scots fella did, respecting all those differences."

The Warden's son shook his head. "I don't get that either. You blokes - well, a lot of you - you don't talk, or act, like hired guns."

"Hired guns?" repeated Micah, with a laugh. "Is that what you think we are? Who'd hire us? Samuel's people? Why? And what with?"

"It's the gold, isn't it?" asked Phillip, his eyes narrowing.

Micah shrugged. "Yeah, that's why most of us are here, one way or another. But you know, some things are actually more important."

Phillip looked at him blankly, then turned his attention to Volkoff, on his other side. "What about you? Are you here for the gold, or something 'more important'? You never seem to say much."

In a low voice, Gregori answered, "I learned long ago that when any breath could be your last it is better not to waste any of them."

With a firm, but not unduly rough shove, the Cossack directed Robertson to sit in front of the large bark shelter, in the most exposed position possible.

～

THE ATMOSPHERE in James Robertson's temporary office was more than usually tense this morning. That was entirely due to the Warden's visitor, and the news he'd delivered. And the incautious reaction of Phillip's sister Davinia.

The Warden himself stood behind his desk, scowling at his offspring. She, meanwhile, stood by the window, half turned away from her sire, a similar expression on her face.

A pace or two in front of the desk stood Peter McGregor, arms folded, looking bemusedly back and forth between the pair.

The older Robertson's voice was only a little below a shout as he addressed Davinia. "So, you knew he was alive, and didn't think to mention it to me?"

The girl tossed her head back and replied, "Well, you'd already made it clear you were more concerned about the loss of that Polish horse thief. I didn't think you'd be interested."

"Losing Kaminski is about business! Of course I was concerned - it's important!"

The Scot was frankly amazed by the behaviour of both generations. "More important than yuir son?" he asked.

"I didn't say that!" snapped the squatter, defensively.

"But we both know it's true," answered the girl.

"Look ye," McGregor tried again to intercede, "Look, yuir boy is alive, and bein' well looked after by these people..."

"Who are occupying land that I own," insisted Robertson.

"And that's all that matters to you, isn't it? That and that painted widow who's caught your fancy. You're not letting her get ideas above her station, are you? You remember what happened with Mother?"

James glared, but replied coldly, "Davinia, any interest I may have in Mrs. Gillespie is absolutely none - I repeat *none* of your concern. My business is exactly that. *My* business. Not yours." He took a deep breath. "You may go to your room."

"I'm not a child..." Davinia replied, in a petulant voice that belied the words.

"You are my child. Indulged perhaps, spoiled even, but I have my limits and you, young lady, are pushing them. Go to your room!"

Her face flushed, but head held high, Davinia flounced out of the office. She stood outside the doorway, just out of her father's view, clenching and unclenching her fists.

Coming from downstairs, Ali approached her quietly. Neutral as ever, the servant asked, "Is something the matter, Miss?"

"My damned father..." she hissed, then had a 'not in front of the servant' moment. She sniffed, then explained, "I am a little... tense, Ali. I've told you, I'm not sleeping well."

The Indian contrived to look concerned. "I note your - powder does not appear to have worked."

"I tried a pinch before retiring last night," she lied smoothly. "Didn't seem to do much."

Ali nodded solicitously, and said, "The famous Robertson iron constitution. A greater dose, perhaps?"

"It's all gone. One of the staff must have stolen it this morning while I was at breakfast."

"Staff? Ah - the hotel staff. Mm. How... unfortunate. I shall prepare something new for you, shall I?"

"Something that will work! Deliver it to my room," the girl ordered.

Ali gave his usual small, formal bow as he replied, "Of course, Miss. Er - I may require a day or two to obtain some of the pharmaceuticals I require."

"As quickly as you can!" she snapped.

"As you say, Miss. Might I suggest you may also wish to try taking the powder with something stronger than water? If you wish it, I may be able to procure a small amount of your father's good whisky. For medicinal purposes."

"Better still, procure some of that lovely French brandy." Her voice softened slightly.

"The cognac? As you wish, Miss. I'm sure that will work."

The fire returned to Davinia's voice. "It better. I'm sick to death of - all this!"

While this exchange was taking place, back inside the office James had forced himself back into some calmness. He'd sat down, and motioned McGregor to do the same. They faced each other across the desk.

"I won't lie to you, Mister McGregor. I think the proposition is ridiculous. A claim already exists on the land, which I am empowered, indeed obliged to enforce."

"I think ye've a verra clear view o' yuir authority, Mister Robertson, and o' what ye can and cannae do. And I will nae bandy words wi' ye, sir, aboot the rights o' the people already livin' there. Ye've made yuir opinion abundantly clear. But yuir son?"

"Is a complication, yes. " The Warden paused, apparently deep in thought, before continuing, "Mister McGregor, can I ask you to please go and occupy yourself elsewhere until - let's say, tomorrow morning? I wish to consider my options."

"Tomorrow? But yuir son..."

"Is, you assure me, in safe hands. I expect he should remain so overnight?"

"Aye, alright. As ye wish." The preacher was suspicious, but could see no room to maneuver.

"Indeed. Thank you. Ali!" called Robertson.

Realizing the interview was over, the Scot stalked out of the office, Ali politely nodding and taking a step out of his way before gliding in to answer his employer's summons.

McGregor caught a glimpse of Davinia storming up the stairs. He sighed in exasperation and headed in the opposite direction.

"Sir?" said the servant, standing before the desk.

"Ali, that girl is really becoming a vexation to me."

"Sir." The impassive tone could have signified anything, or nothing. Each man knew how the other's mind worked. It wasn't trust, but each understood and respected the other man's capabilities. And how dangerous they could be.

The squatter steepled his fingers as he reached a decision. "Mm. Get a message to Mrs. Gillespie, will you? I'd like to see her after I'm done with Andrews and Sergeant McCartney. I'm going to draw up papers advising Amos of my decision to install her to look after the property at home if she's interested."

Ali raised his eyebrows in some surprise. "Not a little... precipitous a decision, sir?" he asked carefully.

"Mm, perhaps a little. But no, I've considered it fully. I'd like Mrs... I'd like Jade to be in a safe environment well away from painful memories of her late husband, and it may encourage me to expedite matters here even more quickly." His thoughtful face hardened. "And it won't hurt to remind Davinia of the limits of the authority she imagines she has. Mm. Off you go, Ali."

"With pleasure, sir."

As his servant left, Robertson dipped a convenient pen into an inkwell, and began to write on a sheet of his private letterhead paper. If he'd noticed Ali humming faintly as he departed, he gave no sign of it.

GOLD PROSPECTING HAD CEASED in the area of the campsite. The raid and its aftermath, and the prospect of more to come, stood too heavily at the front of everyone's mind.

Chung and Koolwunnung had prepared lunch – a hearty stew of hunted possum meat and purchased potato and carrot. The Balyarta woman was taking pannikins of the steaming meal out to the sentries: Baza, Arnold, Micah and Vittorio.

The Italian was perhaps least suited to the role, but had insisted on taking his turn. He was certainly alert enough, and even if he wasn't comfortable with a weapon, his voice could be loud and would carry if necessary.

Asbul perched atop the large rocky outcrop, eating and watching. As gregarious as he was, he was used to long spells alone at sea. Like all of them, his life had changed suddenly and dramatically. For all his jovial, almost comical manner, the Makassar had been greatly moved by recent experience. Behind his grinning façade, he thought more deeply than his new companions realized. Just for now, he wanted solitude. He understood how close he felt to these people, especially the tribe who'd first 'adopted' him, and was considering how best he could contribute to resolving their troubles.

Sitting in a small cluster near the low fire were Mundil, Pierre, Wei Sun, Volkoff and Cristiano. The latter had taken some time earlier to teach rudimentary music lessons to a few tribespeople. One in particular, a Balyarta man named Pirrewuy, showed signs of natural talent with the guitar before he'd gone off to take his 'shift' as a sentry. It had been a good, positive distraction for the grieving Spaniard.

The Cossack grumbled impatiently as he ate. "We cannot afford to sit and wait."

"Si," agreed Cristiano. "There's clearly no point in 'hoping for the best', I'm afraid."

"Expect the worst, and never be disappointed," was Wei Sun's gloomy rejoinder.

Pierre chuckled, though. "You are a cynic, my friend! But I have to agree - better we be as well prepared as possible."

Magpie and Phillip, connected by a length of rope tied securely around their waists, walked over with pannikins in hand to join the group.

"Prepared? Prepared for what?" asked Robertson.

"For your father and his friends. Perhaps I should say, allies," the Frenchman replied.

"You've got no chance," said the prisoner, grimly.

Magpie turned to look at him, almost amused. "You reckon they'll come along to spring you any time now, eh?"

The young man gave a small, bitter laugh. "I might be a lucky bonus for them," he said. Pierre scooped some stew into his pannikin from his own. "Thank you. No - I'm not stupid enough to think I'm their first priority. But you've all made a fatal mistake. You're in my father's way."

"All the more reason to get our defences in order," said Cristiano.

Phillip snorted disdainfully. "Defences? Come on, what have you got to build defences with?"

"What build? We have the land," replied Thonkumundil, calmly.

That only puzzled Phillip. "What do you mean?"

Enjoying his meal, Cristiano only got as far as answering, "We..." before Volkoff cut him off sharply.

"Not in front of the boy. The less he knows, the less he can warn his father of, if he gets the opportunity."

"He's not gonna get the chance," declared Magpie.

"Better safe than sorry," said Pierre. He spoke amiably to Phillip, though. "Enjoy your stew. When you're done we'll put you in the shelter with the wounded and someone to watch over you."

Satisfied, Gregori watched the bereaved Spaniard with the admiration of an old soldier. "You are, resilient, my young friend," he said.

The musician shrugged, but did smile. "For years, my father and I expected to die in a war. Both of us. The only question was, which war? I was born and raised on a battlefield."

"I understand," replied the Cossack. "It was much the same for me. But, you grew tired of fighting? You, or your father? Perhaps both?"

"Not exactly. Papa taught me to consider why we fought. We were never professional soldiers. Oh yes, we were paid, but that was incidental. We talked long about it. The cause was more important than the fight, and one day, well, we ran out of causes. Ones that we believed in. So, we found a new life, that we were happy in." He looked around. "And then, we found a new cause. Papa will be content. And so am I."

The others in the little group ate in respectful silence.

Inside the large bark shelter were the wounded, together with some of the tribes' children. They all lay on rough mats or blankets. A very tired-looking Orhan Keilbren sat cross-legged by the entrance, a rifle in his lap. He jerked into at least semi-alertness as Chung arrived with pannikins and a wok full of stew.

"Wha...? Oh – food!" stammered the Turk.

Chung looked at the youth, concerned. "Yeah. You don't look much healthier than some of the patients - you okay?"

"Sorry. Yes, yes. I'm just not sleeping well."

"Perhaps we can help ye," offered Samuel, struggling to sit up and accept a small meal. "There are some roots we sometimes use."

Orhan gave him a grateful smile. "Thank you. I... have something. I've just been reluctant to try it. I thought I should try to - keep my head clear."

Chung continued to ladle out food, but kept one eye on Keilbren. "Good idea. Pity it's not working. You better do something, I reckon."

The young man nodded, "Yes. I want to be a help, not a burden."

"You are not a burden," said Adhilasa, wearily and perhaps a little bitterly.

Chung looked sharply at his old friend, and said pointedly, "Nobody here is a burden."

Samuel reached out to rest a hand on the American's shoulder, saying, "Especially not ye. Ye teach our wains, and their parents. Ye teach strength, compassion, loyalty."

"Thank you, my brother," sighed Adhilasa, accepting a plate of stew from Chung.

He managed a few mouthfuls, smiling his enjoyment and gratitude before slumping wearily back down to his mat, eyes closing in pain.

Chung's face reflected some of that weariness, but also a steely resolve. With a decisive squaring of his shoulders, he went back to the fireplace to finally have his own share of the food.

IT WAS LATER that afternoon when Sergeant McCartney faced James Robertson over the latter's desk. He'd been irked that, again, he was expected to go to the Warden instead of being able to meet the man in his own office, and his unhappiness was only growing in the course of the meeting. Sufficiently so that his cup of tea sat untouched on the desk.

"I'm not especially comfortable with this, sir," the policeman said.

"Bluntly, Sergeant, I don't care. It's an order."

He tried to protest again, "Mister Robertson, there are limits to your authority..."

The Warden was resolute, but determinedly patient. He'd already worked out that this man would only be made more difficult by a show of anger, and he wanted his co-operation. It would be more effective if it was willing. He played the bureaucratic card.

"In fact, Sergeant, as regards the securing of gold-bearing property in the name of the Crown, there are very few. I have determined that these - people - represent a clear impediment to the establishment of the settlement I am charged with responsibility for. They're to be removed, and you and your troopers are to assist with that."

McCartney sighed. "Whatever you say. Sir."

"Sergeant, I don't want you and I to be at odds over this. The skills of your troopers - bushcraft, local knowledge - they're very important to me."

Slightly placated, the uniformed man replied, "Alright. Alright. We're at your disposal. I know what you want. When do you want this to happen?"

"Soon is the best I can say. I want to talk to Captain Andrews - his firepower is essential. I also would like to speak to some of the local men. I think that it would be appropriate to involve the community in this exercise."

It took an effort for McCartney to restrain a laugh. "Involve the community? Never heard a posse described quite like that way before."

"I prefer to avoid that expression," said Robertson rather primly.

"Yeah, I can see that. Call it what you want." The policeman wasn't happy about the idea, and didn't disguise it. "Vigilantes bother me - I have enough trouble with discipline with my lads. Remember the last time?"

The Warden was implacable though. He knew exactly what he wanted, and he intended to get it. "Yes, I remember. That's one of the reasons I want this exercise to be planned. Can you be here tomorrow - say, midday?"

McCartney nodded, gave a salute so unenthusiastic as to be little more than a wave, then turned and left the office without another word from either man. It seemed he'd barely closed the door behind him when it was opened again, this time by Ali.

"Captain Andrews is here, as requested, sir. Shall I...?"

The servant's offer to fetch the mercenary in wasn't finished, the Indian simply being bullocked past by the man in question.

Andrews did at least acknowledge his presence, remarking, "Good man, thank you. You can go now."

The squatter's long-time aide raised an eyebrow towards his employer. He knew where his orders came from, and where they didn't.

"Thank you, Ali. It'll be fine," Robertson said, with a small smile to acknowledge Ali's concern.

"Very good, sir," came the reply, with no audible expression of uncertainty.

As Ali exited the room, Andrews sat down, unbidden, opposite the Warden.

"Now then, Mister Robertson, I..."

James cut him off sharply. "Are you aware that my son is still alive?"

"Really? Well, praise the Lord for that..."

Caught off-guard, the Captain wasn't sure how to take the news, or his paymaster's reaction. The fellow didn't seem especially pleased.

"He's being held hostage by that motley bunch you failed to take care of when you attacked them without my permission!"

"Ah..."

"They say they'll not release him until I grant a claim for the blackfellas' land to some Holding company I presume they've concocted."

The soldier was suitably outraged. "Well, we can't be having that! I'll..."

Robertson interrupted him again. He'd worked out that the key to dealing with Andrews was to out-bluster him, and was more than happy to adopt that strategy.

"You'll listen to me. We're going to eliminate this problem once and for all. I said we. Midday tomorrow you and I will sit here with Sergeant McCartney, and we'll assess our resources. Our weaponry. What we know of where we're going and who we're up against. Our manpower. Tonight, I'm going to offer a cash incentive to any man in Louth who'll join us."

"Civilians, sir? Hardly necessary."

"Do you know exactly how many we're up against?" the Warden quizzed.

Reluctantly Andrews admitted, "I didn't do a precise head count. I saw one white man, who we dealt with, one very dark tall chap with an American accent..."

"We've met," recalled Robertson, who'd been warily impressed by Adhilasa.

"Well, he'll be rather less active now. Beyond that, perhaps a dozen, fifteen native men, some women and children."

"I want them all gone."

Andrews nodded, satisfied. "Eliminated, as you put it."

"If they haven't the sense to run away, then damn it, yes. Now, at the same time as I encountered the American I'd say there were maybe half a dozen other armed men, including whoever uses that blow-gun, and the half-caste."

"Half-caste?" echoed the soldier, a little disconcerted by news of an opposition he hadn't encountered or expected. Still, nothing that couldn't be dealt with by superior firepower.

"Goes by the name of Magpie. We have - a history. That's not important. What matters is we know we're dealing with more than a handful of natives with spears. I don't know how much more - not a lot, I expect, but every man with a gun who I can bring to bear is one more man advantage."

"Well, I can't argue with your reasoning," Andrews admitted.

Robertson leaned on his desk, fingers steepled, as he replied coldly, "Mm. That's correct, Captain. You can't. Tonight, I'll muster some reinforcements. Tomorrow we'll determine exactly what to do with them."

THE THREE MEN who'd come to Australia with the villainous Master Wu had relocated to the Balyarta campsite. It was a decision based on a certain amount of convenience, and a greater amount of mutual security.

In conversation, the trio had realized that when another attack came, as seemed inevitable, even had they not agreed to side with the natives and their allies, they'd be in jeopardy. The raiders had not seemed likely to respect any declaration of neutrality. And nor did they wish to abandon their hopes of wresting a future from the wealth reputed to be in the ground here somewhere.

It was late at night when Wei Sun, returning from sentry duty, silently entered their shared tent. He went to rouse Orhan to take over his position, but found the Turk already awake. The young man sat up sharply. Realizing that de la Fontaine was still asleep, they conversed in whispers.

"You are keen to start your spell on watch," Wei Sun observed wryly.

"Not especially, but I wasn't sleeping well. Again."

The older man was more sympathetic than his companion would have expected when they first met. "The dreams? Or - the need?"

"The dream. The memory. It's never far away," admitted Orhan, wearily.

The Chinese ex-soldier understood, all too well. "Some never leave us, no."

Keilbren by now knew something of Li's experiences, and the trauma shared with their other companion in China. "How do you live with yours?" he asked.

"With difficulty at times," Wei Sun admitted. "But I have learned... Think of the mind as a house, with many rooms. The horrors I saw, they are locked in a room I choose not to visit."

"Unless someone takes you there," said Orhan, with a nod towards the Frenchman.

"Mm. Someone or something that takes me by surprise, catches me off guard. I wish I were better at steeling myself," was the rueful reply.

The Turk gave a supportive smile, his teeth just visible in the light of the fire that still burned low outside. "You do pretty well! I wish I could do as much."

"Discipline is not the natural state of men. It takes time to learn. For some longer than others. You are better than you were, I think."

"A little, maybe, yes. The meditation you've taught me - you and Pierre, now even the American in the last days - that has helped."

As he lay down, Wei Sun asked, "Is it tomorrow you are not on the Russian's "roster" for night watch? Perhaps the opportunity of a full night's sleep will make it easier to settle your mind."

"The night after. But maybe you're right. I think those soldiers are unlikely to attack in darkness, though I understand the precaution. Maybe I can allow myself a good, deep sleep. But now it's your turn. I'll see you in the morning."

Orhan took up the 'sentry gun' – one of the repeating rifles, and quietly left the tent. Wei Sun stretched out, beginning a silent meditation preparatory to sleep. He was surprised by a low voice from nearby.

"Sorry I opened a troublesome door for you, Wei Sun," said Pierre softly. He'd been awake for a little while at least, evidently.

Wei Sun was silent for a moment, then replied, "It is not your place to apologise. It was my discipline which failed."

"Like the boy said - you do pretty well." His companion grunted uncertainly, so Pierre persisted. "As well as mastering yourself, try to befriend yourself."

"I do not make friends easily."

"You've managed with me. And the boy."

"Perhaps you are easier to like than I am."

Pierre grinned in response, although his expression couldn't be seen. "Give yourself a chance," he suggested, and rolled over. "Good night, my friend. I'll see you in the morning."

Li Wei Sun lay quietly for some time. For a man much given to introspection, it was rarely a particularly positive experience. But he had, unexpectedly but undeniably, developed friendships with these two. He'd developed respect and regard for them both, in their very different ways. What were they seeing in him?

Slowly he closed his eyes, and drifted off into his meditation, perhaps a little wiser in his self-awareness.

By MID-MORNING, Peter McGregor had returned to the campsite, the bearer of tidings that were no better than all but the most optimistic had expected. He sat by the low central fire, in a circle with the 'senior' members of the various disparate groups in the alliance – those who weren't on sentry duty.

The two native tribes had designated Thonkumundil and Karumbari as their representatives and spokesmen in the matter of conflict. It was a situation the putative elders of the two groups had little familiarity with, and they recognized their lack of strategic insight. The two men were expected to consult with their people before any final decisions were reached, but there was a fatalistic resignation that confrontation seemed inevitable. There seemed no way out, including surrender or retreat, so what was to be the best option for the survival of as many of the people as possible? Especially the next generation.

Seated with the preacher and the natives were Magpie, Gregori, Adhilasa, Vittorio, Wei Sun and Asbul. A tightly-bound Phillip Robertson was also sitting in the circle, since he was central to at least some of their discussions. Volkoff never took his eyes off the young man, nor moved his hand from the rifle on his lap.

The Scot finished his report. "If ye dinna have the message back tae him by noon Friday that ye've left this place, he'll remove ye by force. I asked aboot the lad - that's who he'd prefer tae have the message delivered by, he says. The lassie quietly mentioned tae me she's sure that's less important tae him, and I have tae say that's how it seemed tae me."

"What sort of a man *is* this Warden?" asked Pasquale, who had been one of the most optimistic of a better resolution.

Adhilasa's nostrils flared as he replied, "A ruthless one."

"He's a businessman," said Phillip, his voice neutral. It seemed less a defence than a simple statement of fact.

The Italian shook his head. "So is my father, but I don't think that he..."

"Not all fathers are the same."

It was the normally taciturn Wei Sun who had interrupted. Expressions of surprise flitted across faces in the circle, and other, deeper looks were exchanged in the momentary pause.

It was McGregor who broke the brief silence. "So, he's calling yuir bluff, ye think?"

"Who says we're bluffing?" asked Magpie. "I'm not keen to run."

"We talked this through before, remember. This time we stay," said Mundil decisively.

His Kuthant counterpart Karumbari concurred, "It was agreed."

"By all of us," added the Cossack, grimly.

Sensing the need for some sort of positive progress, it was Adhilasa who spoke next. "So - the young man. What do we do with him? Holding him hostage seems to have had little influence on the Warden."

Magpie gestured dismissively. "Ah, Phillip was only a lucky catch. We wasn't gonna let Mundil's people get run off anyway. No surprise Robertson don't care if we got him here."

"Not even much good as a shield, eh?" grinned Asbul.

"I think not," said Wei Sun, apparently seriously considering the practicalities but assessing that the youth would offer scant cover for all but the leanest members of the group.

"We let him go?" wondered Mundil, uncertainly.

The former Chinese mercenary, now adding more to the conversation than anyone could remember, asked, "Would that be wise? Could he compromise us?"

"What's to compromise?" responded Magpie. "No great plans or strategies here. Robertson already knows where we are."

"There is an alternative," said Volkoff, still gazing fixedly at young Robertson, and making a small movement of his gun.

"No!" answered Adhilasa sharply.

"Well, for his own sake we should get him out of the line of fire," suggested Vittorio.

"I think that's preferable," agreed the American.

"I can take him back wi' me..." said McGregor.

Phillip was meeting the Cossack's gaze squarely, and asked, "Do I get a say in this?"

"What do you want to say?" Vittorio replied.

The squatter's son looked around the campsite. His eyes particularly lingered on those areas of the surrounding bush where he knew Cristiano and Micah were out on guard somewhere. He also looked for some moments at the large shelter where most of the injured, the elderly, and the children sat while the future was being discussed. Finally, he brought his gaze back to meet Volkoff's still unwavering stare.

"I'd like to stay, if you'll have me. Look, I know about the agreement you've got - if anyone finds any gold here it's shared by all. My father wouldn't understand that, but I think I do. I've seen how you work together."

"There's rather more to it than that now," Pasquale pointed out.

"I know. You want to protect the natives. Give them a home." He paused, trying to read the faces around him. "I heard you say the offer is open to anyone."

"You ain't exactly 'anyone', mate," observed Magpie, drily.

"You would fight against your father?" asked Adhilasa, suspicious of such a sentiment.

"One way or another I've been fighting my father for years."

That forced a smile from Magpie. "Yeah, well - he does kinda inspire that," he conceded, before scowling again. "But you never sided with no black folks, neither. You rode out here with that damned soldier."

"I could point out I never fired a shot. But I couldn't prove that," Phillip admitted.

The half-caste was unmoved. "Don't matter - you led the bastard and his men here, didn't you?"

"Yes," the young man admitted, dropping his head. "I didn't trust the Pole. I was trying to look after my father's interests - and, I thought, mine."

"And now?" asked Vittorio.

"It looks like my interests aren't my father's interests. No, Magpie,

I never 'sided with black folks' as you put it. I was raised to... to... think they were different."

"Not so good, hah?" said Asbul.

"That's right! It's how I was brought up! I didn't know any better!"

Volkoff was expressionless. "Now you do."

"Yes, I do."

"It wasn't a question. An observation." The Cossack's thoughts were unreadable.

Thonkumundil watched the old soldier thoughtfully. He'd developed a high regard for the veteran's instincts.

"You trust him?" he asked.

"I watch him," was the reply.

Phillip persisted with his declaration. "And I've watched you. All of you. I've never - met men like you. And these people are - not what I expected. They're..." He paused, looking at Mundil and Karumbari. "... *you're* not savages. Even in a couple of days I've learned that much."

"Big of you," said Magpie, drily.

"All learning has to start somewhere," said Adhilasa.

"Maybe," admitted the teamster, recognizing the prevailing sentiment. "But Phillip, I'm gonna be watching you. We're gonna have to get working on some kinda defences, and if I get any hint of you runnin' back to yer father tellin' him anything..."

"No! I give you my word - padre, you can be witness to this - I swear I will not betray you. I'll work beside you, and if it comes to a fight I'll fight beside you."

The designated 'witness' was intrigued. "And yuir father?" he asked.

"Tell him. Tell him what I've sworn. He's shown how concerned about me he is."

The young man looked earnestly around the circle of men. "You've had every reason to shoot me out of hand, I know that, but yet you've fed me, looked after me - even argued to protect me. I think that from you I can learn to be a better man."

"I'm thinking ye already have," said the preacher.

As a ripple of cautious agreement went around the circle, Phillip sighed, "Thank you. Thank you all."

Moving to assist Gregori in releasing the ineffective hostage's bonds, Magpie said quietly, "Yeah, well, don't let us down."

WITHIN AN HOUR of McGregor's delivery of the Gold Warden's ultimatum, the campsite had become a hive of activity. In addition to the usual food preparation, maintenance and child-rearing tasks, there was much effort going into planning.

Just outside the large shelter, a map had been scratched into the dirt, depicting the layout of the campsite and the surrounding area. Terrain and particular features were marked in, with more added as their potential was identified by someone in the group who were working on it.

There were over a dozen people in that group. At other times that might have been unwieldy, a committee often being one of humankind's most inefficient constructions. But each of these had their own skills and perspectives to offer, and the urgency of the situation prompted any potential ego issues to be subsumed by the need to make the most of their resources.

The group comprised the ex-soldiers: Volkoff, Adhilasa, de la Fontaine, Keilbren and Buitrito; from the Balyarta, Thonkumundil and the canny woman Koolwunnung; Karumbari and Baza of the Kuthant; Magpie, the shrewd Asbul, Chung, Pasquale and Phillip Robertson. It was hoped that the latter's insights into his father would prove valuable, and so it was proving.

Declaring themselves better suited for action than strategizing, Wei Sun, Micah and James Arnold had taken on sentry duty. Samuel had excluded himself from the discussion, too. He felt he could contribute little, and frankly was heartbroken by the necessity for it.

Almost from habit, the old Azov commander Gregori had slipped into the role of coordinating discussion of strategy. It had been his whole career, after all, and while the others may not know much detail of his past, there was no debate about his ability.

"We cannot be sure the next attack will come from the same direction as the last two. We must cover all directions around the campsite," the Cossack said.

"It's the only way in my father and Andrews know," Phillip asserted.

Vittorio was unconvinced. "They're not stupid men. There must be maps, others who know their way around."

"Nobody as well as Mundil's people," replied Magpie. "Or James and me." He paused for thought. "McCartney and some of his lot might have some ideas though."

Robertson dismissed that concern with a grunt. "Hmph. Small chance of my father paying much attention to them."

"Is your father a military man?" asked Cristiano.

Phillip shook his head. "He's a businessman. His father was in the British army in India."

"Did he learn anything from his father, I wonder?" mused Pierre.

The squatter's boy considered the question for a moment. "Much the same as I did from him, I think. How to ride, how to shoot, how to give orders. How to treat people badly."

"You think, military strategy he will defer to the English captain?" asked Vittorio.

"I can't imagine my father deferring to anyone. But I think he'll be guided by him, yes."

"Good," replied Volkoff, to the surprise of some in the group. In response to several puzzled looks he explained, "A British officer - he thinks in lines. Lines of men, lines of guns. We defend in small clusters. Ones and twos - no more than threes or fours. At strong points." He tapped the map with the long branch he held. "We have to identify such points. Thonkumundil, we'll need your help – you and your people. The small groups use terrain, camouflage, height. Break the lines, cause chaos and confusion."

"Break the lines?" asked the Italian merchant, already feeling out of his depth.

"Hit and run. Hit from a distance, hit from behind," Gregori explained patiently. "To stand and fight face to face - that is a last resort."

Adhilasa looked unhappy. He still held to ideals of honour in warfare, despite his experiences, and the tactics Volkoff proposed offended him. But he had to admit, under the circumstances, they were the best option. "I see the sense in it, but I don't like it," he said.

The Turk had other concerns. "There's not just the soldiers, though. What if those troopers come back? You think they'll fight in British lines?"

"Perhaps. If the captain has command of the operation," suggested Gregori.

"Command will be my father's job," Phillip said.

"Mmm... if the Englishman directs the operation..." said Volkoff, rephrasing the point he was trying to convey. "How good is the discipline of those troopers, I wonder?"

The assessment offered by Magpie was harsh, but backed by experience. "Huh! Near as damnit to none. They take orders, sorta, from the likes of McCartney cos they're paid to. But rattle them hard and they'll go to pieces I reckon."

"They do have local knowledge though," warned Adhilasa.

The teamster shook his head. "Not that much. They're not from round here remember - none of the local boys would take the job. Balyarta know the area a lot better."

That puzzled Vittorio. "I thought they'd not long set up camp here."

"Yeah, but we hunt and gather stuff all round dis place," explained Koolwunnung, who'd participated in, or even led, many of those expeditions.

Magpie agreed. "Yeah. That's why they headed for here when their last place got shot up. Knew enough to know it'd be easier to defend, even if the ground itself's too hard to grow much just here. A lot of the troopers, they're good in the bush alright, but they don't know the shape an' feel of these trees and this ground - the land. It's not their place."

The Makassar fisherman looked thoughtful. "Dey trooper fellas know about pitjuri?" he wondered aloud.

The teamster shrugged. "Maybe. Dunno. Dunno too much about it meself."

Asbul grinned, his eyes twinkling. Karumbari's reflection of that grin was somehow more menacing.

"We're learning," stated the Kuthant.

His fellow tribesman Baza agreed. "Bad stuff – good stuff for hunt," he offered.

It was clear that Karumbari saw an active role for his people in the inevitable conflict, as he said, "And we startin' to know this ground too. We been watchin', learnin'."

The Russian had come to respect this tribe of wanderers. "I have no doubt of that," he said. "Alright. What else? What have we got that they do not? And vice versa."

Pierre counted off points on his fingers. "They may or may not have more men than us. Probably do. They have more guns, and better."

That prompted Gregori Volkoff to draw himself to his full height. A determined look on his face, he said, "More, to be sure. Better, I think not. Wait, please."

He briskly walked away from the group, heading for the small tent where he dwelt alone.

Adhilasa stepped into the task of steering the discussion, starting to consider their assets. "We have handguns. We have two repeating rifles. At twenty rounds a minute I think they will fire faster than our enemies, for as long as our ammunition lasts."

In his tent, Gregori was unwrapping an oilskin from around a long box. With a pocket knife, he prised off the lid of the crate. From a protective nest of paper and rag he withdrew a rifle. He gazed at it for a long moment, then closed his eyes as he sighed, picturing the face of his beloved Christina.

Resolute now, he strode back to the group around the map. He extended the rifle for inspection.

"Chassepot," he said. "I – *we* have four of them."

"In the hands of a good marksman, deadly over as much as twelve hundred yards," assessed de la Fontaine, approvingly.

Cristiano had taken the gun and was examining it carefully. "With a weapon like this my Papa would not have been outgunned."

The Russian looked downcast. "I know. I am sorry," he replied, deeply apologetic. Determinedly, he pulled himself up, explaining, "Christina and I... took possession of them after fighting the Prussians alongside Garibaldi. They are valuable. We intended to sell them, use the money to start a new life here. I - obsessed about preserving them. I did not..."

His faltering apology was cut off by the bereaved Spaniard, who shrugged and said, "You didn't know we'd be attacked by well-armed soldiers. We only knew about troopers and fools no better equipped than us. It is what it is."

"You are gracious," replied Gregori.

"I'm realistic. My father and I fought in Paraguay. I was young then, but you learn to be realistic in a war."

"A war. Is that what we're in?" asked Pasquale sadly.

"Si. What else would you call it?" replied Cristiano evenly.

The half-caste agreed. "You're right there. We didn't start it, but like your father said, you don't fight you die." He turned to Volkoff. "How much ammunition you got for these?"

"Less than I would like under the circumstances. Those who use them will have to shoot well. We will need more than bullets. More than these four rifles and the other guns we have," answered the Russian.

The sometime aide to the teamsters rapped Magpie's undamaged shoulder and gestured. "Scrap stuff on the wagon you and James got back dere. Stuff from Mr. Sutherland's place."

His half-caste working partner caught on. "Some mangled corrugated iron, rusty baling wire, a few busted plough blades. Metal - right, we can use that."

"What? You want to make suits of armour or something?" asked Vittorio, bemused at the idea.

Magpie scoffed. "Nah - that'd be stupid. Be too hard to move in unless you didn't cover the legs. Then anyone with any sense would just shoot them legs out from under you. Nah, not armour, but shields, mebbe."

"*Da.* Protection," agreed Volkoff. "Shoot from behind it. The wire, perhaps we can do something with that, also."

"How bad rusted is it?" asked Asbul, an idea forming.

"Pretty crook. Won't hold much weight, if any," warned Magpie.

"Long as I can sharpen bits of it," said the fisherman.

"We have blades, Pierre and I," offered Keilbren, thinking of their dao and ninjato.

Volkoff smiled, a little wistfully. "Good at close range. I could wish I still had my sabre."

"As might I," agreed Adhilasa, who'd also carried an officer's sword.

Talk of bladed weapons prompted Chung to point out, "I've got knives - several, all sharp." He was also doing some lateral thinking. "We've got some kerosene too, and a bit of cooking oil. Some bottles."

"You're thinking fire bombs?" presumed Pierre.

"Not good. Not here," objected Gregori. "This bush - grass, trees, they're our allies. We should use them, not destroy them."

But Magpie saw another possibility. "Yeah, but not everything here is bush," he said, and pointed to the map. "Cover all directions you said."

"Alongside the creek," said Chung, seeing where the teamster was indicating on the map.

De la Fontaine considered the landscape in that area. "Big track other side of scrub that way. Creek through worse scrub that way. Scrub all round."

But Koolwunnung shook her head. "Scrub not worse, just different. Got to know way through is all," she said in a voice that made it clear that she did.

Mundil gestured at the map, nodding. "Hunting traps all around. Us in the middle."

"Agreed," declared the Cossack. "Time is against us. Noon Friday, McGregor said. Does anyone believe Robertson will wait that long?"

"Not likely," replied Phillip, saying aloud what most of the others were thinking.

Magpie was more specific. "He says Friday, expect Thursday. Maybe sooner."

"Maybe him an' his army on dere way now," suggested the Makassar, but Adhilasa shook his head.

"I think not. What would be the point of sending the padre to us with a message?"

"Catch us off guard?" said Pasquale, trying to think treacherously – not a natural attitude for him.

But Adhilasa didn't consider that likely. "I believe he's confident that wouldn't be necessary. Asbul, you mentioned his 'army'. I suspect he's trying to assemble something very like that. Even if he's relying on the Englishman, it will require some time for planning and strategy, communicating and preparing."

"So. It falls to us to be better at it," declared the veteran Cossack commander. He reached out to receive the chassepot that was held out to him. "Come, we have work to do."

CAPTAIN ANDREWS CUT a relaxed figure in the lounge of the Woolpack Inn. He sat cross-legged in a chair, reading his Bible, and whistling 'Onward Christian Soldiers'. He broke off the tune at the sound of voices from the staircase. He recognized them as belonging to Ali and the preacher McGregor. He had no interest in engaging with either man, but eavesdropping could sometimes be a useful source of information.

The pair were conversing politely after the Scot had paid another frustrating visit to the Gold Warden's office. Neither noticed the mercenary who'd slipped down slightly to be hidden by the back of the chair.

"I dinna understand that man. I dinna ken how ye put up wi' him," said McGregor.

"Years of practice, sir," replied Ali, without rancour.

The preacher was struggling to make sense of the interview he'd just endured. "I tell him his son wants tae take a stand agin him. That he's learned tae respect the people already on the land - why cannae he? He looks at me like I was frae another planet."

"Mister Robertson is single-minded in his approach," said the Indian, diplomatically.

With a sigh, McGregor replied, "Aye, I understand it's yuir job tae defend him, or at least not tae criticize..."

Irked beyond the narrow limit of his patience, Andrews suddenly interrupted, exclaiming, "I should say not! Servant has to know his place. The good Book tells us that!"

To the soldier's chagrin, Ali seemed unperturbed. The manservant acknowledged his presence with his usual small nod. "Sir. I shall advise Mister Robertson that you are here to see him," he said, and went back the way he'd just come.

McGregor glared at the mercenary. "Captain, ye claim tae be a man of God, but ye've nae regard for yuir fellow man at all, have ye?"

Andrews waved the Bible, brandishing the pages he'd been reading like a regimental banner. "The Book of Hosea – 'I will be unto Ephraim as a lion, and as a young lion to the house of Judah. I will tear and go away. I will reduce them and none shall rescue!' This is my sort of God! Strong, powerful!"

The soldier's rhetoric outraged the Scot. "Men like ye are the reason why I left ma kirk on Mull. Men who'd hide behind the Lord - use the Scripture as a cloak for their bastardry, their villainy. I ran away once, tae ma everlasting shame. I'll nae do so again!"

"You'll fight me then? This shouldn't take long," said Andrews, amused, as he drew a pistol from his waistband.

"I'll nae take up arms, ye blackguard!" answered McGregor defiantly. "I swore tae live by the Lord's commandments, and live by them I shall. But I will stand beside those who will fight ye. Aye, and do so proudly."

As the preacher turned to leave, he saw Andrews cock his pistol. Undeterred, he strode to the door of the lounge, growling as he went, "If ye choose tae shoot me in the back - aye well, tis yuir immortal soul..." Unseen, the soldier flinched fractionally as the Scot walked out, muttering, "...if there's owt left."

Peeved, Andrews was just about to squeeze the trigger, when the familiar figure of Michael Finlay appeared in the doorway, inadvertently but effectively blocking his shot.

"Captain?" asked the adjutant, puzzled by the raised pistol.

"Damn!" Uncharacteristically discomfited, the regimental commander lowered the weapon. "Ah well, damn fool can't do any harm anyway. What is it, Finlay?"

"The body of civilians Mister Robertson required has gathered outside. I won't use the word assembled."

"Ah. Cannon fodder, so to speak, at least. Very good." Not waiting to speak with the Warden, Andrews led the way out of the lounge and out to the street. "Let's see what we've got. If we're very lucky one or two will be able to shoot straight."

The two mercenaries surveyed the small mob milling about at the front of the Woolpack. Some of the group had been part of the ill-fated earlier assault on the Balyarta, and bore the scars, visible or otherwise. That number included Norman Heath, and even the injured Swede, Jansen. His arm was in a sling, but in his other hand he held a big, battered old musket pistol, the replacement for his ruined rifle.

Robertson's financial inducement, and a certain amount of peer pressure, had attracted a few more recruits. They scarcely lifted the overall standard of men. Their number included some of the worst of Louth – Kev Seiman, Lewis Heath and regular 'guests' of McCartney's cells like Raymond Foster and 'Stone' Murray.

The Captain frowned. He'd expected little, and still was disappointed. "Hmph. Straight shooting? Maybe not. Finlay, pop upstairs and ask Mister Robertson to come and inspect his rabble, would you? Sorry, his 'volunteers', I suppose you should say."

BY THE FOLLOWING MORNING, the campsite had steadily gone from a hive of activity to something like a primitive but well-tuned factory. Anyone who could work, did - men, women and children, well or wounded. Overnight, jobs that could be safely done by firelight happened in short, disciplined shifts.

Spears of different lengths were crafted, their points hardened in the ashes at the edge of the fire. Clubs were shaped. Blades were sharpened. Tough grasses and plant fibres were split and rolled in patient hands, ready to be plaited and woven as needed.

As few people as possible were spared for food preparation – just enough to keep the workers fuelled. It was a good chance for young-sters who'd been learning from their mothers (and recently, the patient Chung) to apply some of what they'd been taught. Nobody complained.

Once the morning light was good enough, a group of women from both tribes busied themselves grinding a dark, evil-looking plant paste. They'd already produced a far greater quantity than even the oldest of them had ever seen, yet they knew more was required. This was the pitjuri that Asbul wanted. Its properties were well-known, but not often employed, not least because of its toxicity. The subtle variation the Makassar had taught only increased the danger.

One of the Balyarta children wandered over, intrigued. He reached out a curious finger towards the dark pulp, but jumped back as his questing hand was slapped away by one of his aunties.

"You touch that and your little brother will be looking for someone new to chase wallabies with!" she warned, raising a laugh from others who shared her Burundji dialect.

The other women laughed. Even if the words were still unfamil-iar, the gist of the warning was clear.

"This pitjuri is real bad stuff, hey?" said one of the Kuthant women in her own tongue.

The auntie who'd just warned off the child looked at her, turning the syllables over in her head. The Kuthant woman tried again, in a broken attempt at Burundji.

"Pitjuri. Bad stuff. Thanks for teaching us how to make it."

"Thank Asbul. He makes it better than us," replied another of the Balyarta, better comprehending the mangled speech.

Another Kuthant woman mused aloud to her kin, "Maybe good to trade when we move on. We will, I reckon, when the men settle the blood debt."

A Balyarta woman, a quick learner whose knowledge of the other dialect was a little better, replied, "You be careful. Only pass it on to folks you're sure won't use it against you!"

The other Kuthant women nodded sagely. It was sensible advice.

In another part of the camp, Asbul, Adhilasa and Vittorio sat on the ground beside the tangle of rusted wire from the teamsters' wagon. The American winced frequently, his maimed knee troubling him badly, but determined to work. The three were twisting, sawing and snapping short lengths off from the curling strands.

At Adhilasa's direction, they knotted the lengths into four-pronged caltrops – roughly pyramidal skeletal 'burrs', each point to be sharpened at the next stage of the production process. They weren't especially robust, but if well-honed, they wouldn't need to be. Each finished caltrop was dropped into one of several shallow bark basins. As each of these was filled, they were taken to the group of elders and wounded folks who were handling the sharpening stones.

Asbul held up one of the little weapons to admire. "I was just t'inkin' of usin' de wire for fish-hooks. Dese are real clever!"

"We used to use something similar on the Confederate cavalry," explained Adhilasa.

"Tough on the horses!" said Vittorio.

"Unfortunately, yes," the former Union soldier admitted. "Painful enough to stop them in their tracks when ridden over. Not fatal though."

The Makassar laughed, without his usual geniality. "Heh - not like dese will be."

"Should we scatter some on the ground, too?" asked Vittorio.

"No," replied Adhilasa. "They won't get horses that close. And Robertson's men will be wearing boots."

"Some of dem troopers won't be," Asbul pointed out.

"True. But neither will a lot of our people," replied the American, with a gesture towards some of their native allies. "At least with your plan, we'll know where the caltrops have landed. Watch where we walk. Well, probably not including me, I'm afraid," he said, looking at his leg.

Asbul nodded, as Vittorio shuddered slightly.

Elsewhere, Samuel was propped against a tree, assisting and encouraging elders and youngsters alike who were doing the plaiting of long, slender cords of plant material. The old man had been awake and working for much of the night. He'd led communal singing or even humming to maintain a rhythm as they laboured.

Tired as he was, much as his wounds throbbed, he persisted. To keep himself focused, he kept repeating the words he'd been told best described the lines that they were making.

"Thin, but strong. Thin, but strong. Thin, but strong." He looked around the campsite. The people he'd grown up with, watched them grow up, spent his life with – these other people, some of whom who'd already become friends, all so busy, doing their best to prepare for a fight for their lives. Their own, and each other's.

Samuel was proud and terrified all at once. He'd spoken truly when he'd said his people were not warriors. There had been some problems with the vexing Beeargah, yes, and the occasional squabble within their own tribe had come to blows, but fighting was simply not the Balyarta way. But now, it seemed, it had to be.

"Thin, but strong. Thin, but strong. Thin, but strong."

Over in the shadow of the rocky outcrop, Volkoff was distributing the chassepot rifles. Three leaned against the rock, and the Russian held the fourth. Beside him stood Cristiano Buitrito, James Arnold, and Orhan Keilbren.

Only Cristiano had met the Russian's late wife, but the others had been quietly apprised of relevant details by those who'd sailed to Cooktown with the Volkoffs. They understood, at least a little, the emotional investment which Gregori had in the weapons, and respected the solemnity of the moment when he handed them over. There was no ceremony about it – the Cossack was too much the

professional soldier for that – but there was a wordless acknowledgement of what had been the couple's shared hopes for a better future.

Characteristically efficient now, Gregori tapped his rifle butt on
one of the four boxes of ammunition he'd also been discreetly trans-
porting. "We cannot spare the ammunition to test my judgement.
Senor Buitrito, I have seen enough to trust your skill as I trust my
own. More, I think. Gentlemen, I will take you and your colleagues at
your word and accept that you can also be numbered as our best
marksmen."

Arnold nodded in appreciation, and the Turk stood a little
straighter as the Russian continued. "These, and the repeating rifles
Micah and the Frenchman will hold are our best weapons. We must
set them in the strongest positions."

"Cover all directions," said James.

"*Da*. But also be able to support one another. I doubt that attack
will come from all sides at once, but we cannot say from which it will
come."

"No good sticking us out on the fringes then, eh?" reasoned the
veteran teamster.

Orhan, too, had a shrewd tactical sense. "But if the range of these
is as you say, we can be effective from this central position. Here or
near to it. Perhaps two atop this rock, facing north and east, but able
to turn if needed."

"Such is my thinking," agreed Volkoff. He turned to the Spaniard.
"You know these guns - you concur?"

"From what I know by reputation, sure. I've never used one."

The Cossack, remembering the elder Buitrito's reaction when
he'd accidently seen the distinctive weapon, was puzzled. "But your
father..."

"My father was, shall we say, a career soldier. I fought alongside
him in Paraguay, and elsewhere. But he had rank, and experience. I
followed in his footsteps, and when he made the decision to walk
away from that life I was glad to follow him still."

Gregori nodded his comprehension. "Yet you have his skills," he
acknowledged.

"Thanks. And here I will use them. But I hope for better for myself."

All three men indicated their agreement, although it was clear that the thought processes of each differed.

Some distance away, a small group were making their way through a cluster of trees, a few of which had corpses secured in their branches. Magpie and Mundil led the way, Pierre and Phillip close behind with the Kuthant Walan and the Balyarta brothers Cooterah and Coreel. They looked up frequently as they walked and talked.

"See and not be seen, eh?" said Magpie, and gestured to Cooterah, who nodded, and quickly clambered up the nearest tree.

Looking up, the others confirmed that from ground level, neither the tribesman nor his dead kinsman were more than barely visible among the foliage – and that was when they knew to look for them.

"Good. But hit and run, the Russian said. Hard to run up there," mused the half-caste.

Walan already grasped the plan, though. "Man below dead. Other men on ground can't see where come from. Maybe man above no need to run."

"Balyarta good with trees!" declared Thonkumundil.

"I've... had some experience," agreed Phillip, ruefully.

Appreciating the idea, but also diplomatic, Pierre asked, "Thonkumundil, would you and your people - er, accept your dead being used as camouflage?"

Coreel looked at him blankly. His brother's similarly baffled voice came down from above, "Camo-flage?"

Magpie explained, in Burundji, as best he could. "Disguise. A way to hide." In English, he acknowledged de la Fontaine. "Good o' you to ask, Frenchie, thanks."

As Cooterah dropped back down from the branches, he and his brother exchanged looks with Thonkumundil. All three men shrugged, an oddly synchronous gesture.

"Sure," said Mundil. "Dead is dead. Body anyway."

"Spirit important," added Coreel.

That intrigued Phillip, who asked, "Is that the Scottish preacher speaking, or your people themselves?"

It was Mundil who replied, much more comfortable with English than his kinsmen. "Both. Same. Body is meat - that's why we use trees. Give food back to birds and animals. They eat us, we eat them, spirits go on."

"A conversation for another time, I think," said the Frenchman sincerely, but turned back to the task at hand. "We have to pick out some good trees, right around the camp. And the right men to put in them."

The group working by the bank of the creek were furthest from the campsite. But as soon as Li Wei Sun had looked at the spot through his soldier's eyes, he'd realized the appeal it could have for potential attackers. At first, he'd admonished himself for not recognizing the risk sooner. With an effort though, he reminded himself that he'd been in the area looking for gold, not expecting a military operation. It was a step on the path of self-forgiveness.

He'd been part of a group comprising mostly Kuthant men and women. With a few small axes, of both iron and stone, and with his own application of the dao he'd gratefully borrowed from Pierre, they'd been thinning out carefully selected areas of scrub. Dry, ageing bark, twigs and branches were being collected. Clumps of dead or dying grass had been reefed up by hand, and added to the pile.

Laden with the browning hoard, the group emerged from the bush onto the crescent-shaped beach at the bend of the creek. Another crew of natives were working with Chung, with shovels and branches to scrape sand and small stones into heaps.

Many of those with the cook were female. He and Asbul fascinated them. Both men willingly took on tasks traditionally done by women, as well as those of the men, and usually did them well. Whereas the Makassar tended to be extroverted – genial and chatty in his interactions, Chung was more reserved. A listener, as much as a talker. Learning as much as instructing. Intriguing.

Wei Sun crossed the little beach, approaching his countryman.

"We are done. The low brush is thinned, but not cleared so much as to appear too obvious, I think."

"Good work. If they come following the creek bed that should catch their eye as an entry point. Even if they're suspicious, they should stop here to at least think about their next move. You get much dry grass?"

The former soldier looked at the cleared area of the bank, pensively. "Some," he said. "We need more."

He gestured to one of his Kuthant companions, indicating that they'd need more of the long dead stalks and reeds he carried.

"Small thin branches and twigs are good, too," Chung said, holding up a couple of useful examples. "Pile what we've got here. I'll start getting it spread. You want to spread grass, or cut it?"

Wei Sun looked back and forth between Chung and the group he'd just been working with.

"I will stay with - my team," he announced.

Chung grinned. The taciturn newcomer was learning, he thought.

"Okay. See you soon," he replied.

∽

THE MANAGEMENT of the Woolpack Inn had taken a certain amount of pride in offering '*Louth's Finest Accommodation Option*'. Admittedly the standard of competition wasn't very high, but the Woolpack did try, allowing for staff whose interest in their jobs extended no further than the next pay-packet.

Certainly, there had been few complaints from their visitors. Until recently, anyway. Mister Robertson himself wasn't the problem. He seemed mostly content to accept things as they were, perhaps conscious of the temporary nature of his residence. There had been a few critical comments passed on from the man's servant, when some matter of disorder went beyond what he was prepared to correct himself. No, the main source of negative reports was the daughter.

In truth, there was little wrong with her accommodation. The shared facilities were serviceable enough, especially with Ali's attentions, and her own room was as comfortable as Louth's resources allowed. Not as large as she'd enjoyed "at home", but adequate for most women of her age.

"Well, I suppose when Papa gets this whole messy business resolved, he can get on with having a proper house built, and I can have some room to stretch out comfortably again," she said, lying on a couch and watching Ali dust and tidy the room.

"Indeed, miss. On the subject of comfort, I have been able to procure more - medicine."

With that, he reached into a pocket, extracted a small packet of powder, and held it out, subtly just a fraction out of her reach. The act of reaching for the packet was all that got the girl to move, at least partially, off the couch. That meant Ali could quickly wipe crumbs from where she routinely lay.

"This should help, miss," he assured her.

"About time. I could do with a good long sleep."

The Indian gave a single nod as he continued with his tasks, not looking at her, and said decisively, "You will rest."

ONE OF THE places offering no competition to the Woolpack's standards was Bob Cattenach's bar. Accommodation wasn't an option anyway, but pandering to the comfort of the clientele would never have occurred to the publican. He was greedy, but clueless when it came to good ways to improve his profits.

This afternoon his customers were mostly regulars, including a few who had already publicly agreed to take Robertson's money, and were spending it in anticipation. The Warden had still managed to keep his official position secret. For most of the population of Louth, he was just an unusually public-spirited fellow with deep pockets. Probably an aspiring politician.

The drinkers included the Heath brothers, Lewis and Norman, ratty Kev Seiman, and the sometime dock labourer John Rourke. Both of the latter two wore rough slings. The four were sharing a table and a bottle of Cattenach's rotgut rum.

"So, you reckon this Robertson bloke's money is good?" Rourke asked the brothers, his interest piqued by the prospect of being a 'hired gun'.

Lewis shrugged. He certainly hoped so. "Paid up alright on the last bunch of blokes he got together, I hear."

"Better'n this bastard of a publican pays," observed Norman, past events still in his bleary memory. "It ain't just about the money, but."

Rourke looked thoughtful. "Yeah, I know. I'd love to go with ya, fellas, but, y'know..." He indicated the sling, and the shoulder injury that was proving remarkably slow to heal, and was keeping him from taking on anything he considered heavy or difficult work. "Bit of a problem."

Seiman sneered at him, "That's bull, John. I'm goin'!" Ironic, since his own 'disability' was, in truth, scarcely more troublesome any more.

The belligerent Rourke was prepared to say so, too. "It's alright fer you, you just got a whack on yer mitt - I copped that bloody teamster's bullet."

"You could shoot with yer other hand if ya wanted to. If you were game," suggested Kev, emboldened by the rotgut.

"You callin' me gutless?"

"Got a whole army fer back-up this time. Really stick it to the black bastards," mused big Norman, more to himself than his companions.

The now angry Rourke didn't take it that way, though. "You sayin' I need an army to back me up? I..."

Lewis Heath was the peacemaker. "Ah, simmer down, John. We're all on the same side, ain't we?" He was turning a coin over and over in his hand. "All after the one thing?"

Kev looked at his sling, thinking of the men responsible. "Yeah."

Norman swigged at his rum, clenching and opening his other fist. "Yeah."

THE WORK in the bush around the campsite proceeded at a good pace.

Adhilasa was lying on the ground beside a tree, boring a small hole through the bark near the base with the point of his knife. Several of the natives watched, some holding coils or lengths of the thin plaited or woven plant fibre rope.

"So, you see," explained the American, in a determined mix of English and such of the two native tongues as he could communicate in, "the cord comes down the trunk, so no-one will notice it. Then through this hole and across the path, tie it tight to that tree over there."

"Aye, right," said Wittarkee, showing off some of the little English she'd mastered.

Unable to suppress a double take in reaction to the woman's incongruous language, Adhilasa carried on. "Er - yes. When you're sure this end is tight and secure, then the bowl - what did you call it, coolamon? That goes up and rests in the branches, with the other end of the rope attached to it."

There were various signs and sounds of understanding from his audience.

"You're sure you can get back down the tree without disturbing either the coolamon or the rope?" he asked.

"Told you before - Balyarta good with trees," affirmed Cooterah.

"You'd better be, my friend. You don't want to be under a shower of Asbul's little treats if they fall!"

Back in the campsite itself, Asbul and a small group of natives were very carefully applying pitjuri to thorns on spiky branches that had been cut from plants that grew in the surrounding bush. Volkoff sat beside them, watching approvingly. On his lap was a paper copy of the map that had been originally scratched in the dirt. Micah sat beside him, studiously completing a second copy of the map. It was a good use of some secretarial skills he'd learned in the Johnson household.

"I reckon we got just about enough to make a little line of dese round de outside of de camp, Mister Gregori," said Asbul.

That thought bothered Micah. "A bit too close for comfort, I think, Asbul," he said, worriedly.

The Cossack was inclined to agree. "Mmm. I'd like to keep our enemies as far from our inner perimeter as possible. Reduce the number of their guns before they can make the most of them." He ran his finger around the map. "I'd actually like them laid as well away from here as we can."

"Not laid," corrected Karumbari, who was heavily involved in this element of the defensive strategy. "Trooper fella, he spot dead branch on ground where no tree like it. Keep away." Volkoff nodded his understanding. "Gotta put them back in same kinda bush they came from."

Asbul was enthused. "Dat's good! Mebbe clear some trail leadin' near enough to dem to lure soldier fellas in. Like baitin' a hook!"

Volkoff liked their thinking. "Good plan gentlemen. Just so long as *we* know which bushes to avoid. Two parties to set these out, I'll be with one, Mister Johnson here with the other. We'll have to note the positions as accurately as possible on these maps so our own people don't run into them."

"Same with the other snares. Whoever set them, Adhilasa, Magpie, whoever, will have to mark them on here," observed Micah.

"Or guide you or I to each one," agreed the Russian.

Their discussion was interrupted by the approach of Samuel. The elder was being heavily supported by Thonkumundil and Magpie. His wounds had been treated as well as possible, but he wasn't a young man, and he felt quietly pessimistic about his recovery. 'Whatever God wills', he thought to himself.

"Mister Volkoff, Karumbari - can we talk please?" he asked.

Karumbari nodded, as the Cossack replied, "Of course, Samuel. This is your community - you are in charge here."

Samuel looked ruefully but not resentfully at the two supporting him as they helped him sit down.

"I think not, but it's kind of ye tae say so. I want tae ask about our women and children. As I've said, we are nae a warrior people, but we will fight when we must, as seems to be the case now."

"Not a fight we started, or wanted," averred Thonkumundil, for his elder's benefit.

"But no backing down now. We fight - we win!" declared Magpie.

The older man made a gesture of acquiescence. "As God wills. But we have never made warriors of our women as some do, and as some of them now seem tae want. Karumbari, I do not know about your people...?"

"Kuthant traders, not warriors. But if we fight, all who want to, can. Some look after others - sick, very young."

"That's ma concern," said Samuel. "Ye are making plans for a battleground - what of those who cannae fight for themselves?"

Micah indicated the centre of the map he held. "Here in the middle, with all our defences around them? We're putting in shields - we could concentrate them in a circle."

He gestured over to activity some way to their left. Phillip and Pierre were working with two burly tribesmen to prop a piece of plough blade at the edge of a shallow dug-out depression and disguise the metal with dirt and foliage.

The half-caste shook his head. "We ain't got enough metal to make something of any size."

Volkoff was thoughtful. Military man as he was, he had some sympathy for the elder's concerns. He pondered how to accommodate those concerns in the overall strategy. "It will be, as you say, Samuel, a battleground. Bullets will fly. There can be no guarantee of safety anywhere, but yes - certainly not here."

It was Thonkumundil who reached over the Russian's shoulder and indicated a spot on the map. "Place I took them last time. Deep bush, hard to get into, even for them troopers. Not big, but big enough."

"That could work," agreed Samuel. "Someone must be there tae defend them. Mundil, would ye...?"

"No! Not this time! My place to stand and fight alongside my brothers."

Magpie looked earnestly at the Balyarta leader. "In all honesty, Samuel, I don't reckon it'd make much difference. Robertson and them bloody soldiers get as far as the women and kids, they'll shoot 'em down - we know that. And if they get to them they'll have already gone through us anyway."

Samuel grimaced. "Aye. Not a happy thought, but true. And perhaps if they were tae be found unaccompanied by any armed men, there may be a chance of mercy. If there is mercy in the hearts of such men."

The Cossack looked grim. "Think on what evidence we've seen," he warned.

The elder could only sigh unhappily.

IT TECHNICALLY WASN'T his job, but professional pride had Ali cleaning and tidying the lounge of the Woolpack Inn. The force of his personality now routinely kept guests and other staff from interrupting his work. He looked up as Jade Gillespie walked into the room from the stairwell, returning from the Warden's temporary office upstairs. He greeted the widow with a smile and a bow.

"I trust your visit was pleasant?" he asked.

"Mister Robertson is being a great comfort to me," Jade replied diplomatically.

"I'm glad. You certainly seem to have made an impression on him. I've not seen him so - taken - with a lady since his dear wife died."

"Yes - Davinia told me of her passing." The voice was carefully neutral, much like Ali's so often was.

"I'm sure she would have," he said wryly.

Jade's studied neutrality slipped for a moment. The bitterness was undisguised as she said, "I confess that my visits here are more enjoyable without an encounter with young Miss Robertson."

The Indian looked more than sympathetic as he replied simply, "Indeed." After a pause in which the two searched each other's eyes deeply, he continued, "I have papers which Mister Robertson asked me to give to you."

Ali drew an envelope from his pocket and handed it to Jade. Intrigued, she immediately opened it and briefly scanned the contents.

Her sense of intrigue only deepened. "A letter of introduction? Yes, he mentioned it. And directions to reach the family property?"

"Yes. Rather more than introduction. Mister Robertson has given instruction to the foreman Amos that you are to be regarded as the new mistress of the house. An interesting turn of phrase," Ali mused wryly. "Miss Davinia would not be pleased if she knew."

"She doesn't?" asked the widow in surprise.

The servant moved closer to her and spoke softly. "I would know if she did. No, I think Mister Robertson is holding back this news as a... surprise, for such an occasion as his daughter's behaviour may warrant it."

"That's rather cynical."

"I am merely familiar with Mister Robertson's methods."

"I didn't mean you were cynical," she corrected, gently touching his hand. "I meant him."

"Ah." Ali sounded pleased, although as restrained as ever.

As she read further, Jade said, "James has suggested I set off for the property as soon as possible. Do you agree?"

The Indian considered for some moments before replying, "I think that there are - events in motion. Would you wait a day or two?"

"I would be guided by your wisdom."

"Gracious lady. I will be..." He looked down at her hand, still resting on his. "...in touch."

They exchanged smiles and courteous bows. Both recognized that a bond had been created. In truth, it had probably existed for some time. The pair were closer in age and life experience than anyone realized. Ali was certainly her senior, but Jade was hardly a girl, despite first appearances and her late husband's starry-eyed description of her.

The widow departed, leaving Ali to continue tidying the room. Yet again, he grumbled to himself about the inadequate job the Woolpack staff were doing. His input was a double-edged sword. Some, like the young Hebblethwaite, had improved, stung by criticism or better informed on how to do certain tasks. Others had realized their shortcomings were being covered for by 'that dark-skinned bloke' and were trying even less hard than usual.

It was scant minutes later that the police sergeant and the mercenary Captain walked into the room. They'd evidently passed the bereaved Mrs. Gillespie out in the street as she left.

"Damned fine looking woman, that," observed Andrews.

"The colour of her skin doesn't bother you, then?" asked McCartney, drily.

"Not at all. Dark women are more submissive."

The policeman shook his head, but said nothing. He had to work with this bloke, however bloody appalling he found him, in so many ways. Ali had stood stiffly and silently throughout the exchange as they entered. If either man had noticed him, there'd been no acknowledgement. Now he stepped directly in front of them.

"Gentlemen. Please remain here. I shall inform Mister Robertson that you have arrived as requested," he said, and smartly left the room for the staircase.

Andrews watched him go, with an arrogant air of approval. "Make bloody good servants, these Indian chaps. Almost wish I'd brought one back with me. Almost."

Under his breath, the sergeant muttered, "Why doesn't that surprise me?"

Soon after, they'd been summoned into the presence of the Gold Warden. All three men were seated around Robertson's desk, studying a hand drawn map. It was rougher and far less detailed than the one Gregori Volkoff had prepared, not that they could know that. The road and the relative position of the campsite were the only significant features clearly marked.

"So, you and I know basically the same route to the blighters," observed Andrews to his employer, drawing an arrow from the wide track to the campsite. "There must be other options."

Robertson agreed. It was a logical assessment. "Sergeant, you're the local. What do we have?"

"We have a lot of trees. We have a lot of scrub. Most of it dense. Bloody poor place for white men if you want to be quiet making any sort of approach."

"Could your troopers do it?" the Warden asked. "Coming in from any of these directions?"

"Maybe. They'll certainly reckon they can."

Andrews ran his index finger around the map and asked, "Could we get them in from the east and west flanks? Get them to draw fire and attract enough attention for us to then launch a main assault from the path we already know?"

"Put my boys in the line of fire first?" clarified McCartney, clearly unimpressed.

"Well, yes..." Robertson began to admit, somewhat reluctantly, but the soldier talked over the top of him.

"Common sense, yes. Best use of resources for best chance of success."

The sergeant's voice was cold. "Mm. Yes. I see." He considered the map. "There is the creek to consider."

"How so?" asked James.

"Well, they wouldn't have made camp very far from water. We know the creek runs along here somewhere. There's a point..." He drew on the map. "...here, where we know the creek runs quite close to the road - there's a track used to water horses sometimes."

"Do we know the course of the creek?" asked the commander of the infantry.

"I certainly don't," McCartney replied. "Never seen it marked on anything. No-one's bothered with it as far as I know."

"So, it could lead us straight to the natives' camp?" suggested Robertson.

The soldier frowned. "Or it could meander all over the place and take hours to get near it. I'd be reluctant to send my men that way."

The Warden raised an eyebrow. "Captain, does your regiment have to be deployed as a single unit?"

"I do prefer to keep my men under my own direct command. No offence, gentlemen."

"Oh no, none taken," replied the policeman, his sarcasm either unnoticed or ignored.

Robertson persisted with his thought. "Mm. Given the superiority of your armaments perhaps a few men could be spared to support the other lines of attack? I'm sure their training and discipline would be up to it."

Reluctantly the Captain admitted, "Yes, yes... I can see how that would strengthen our overall assault. Very well."

Now that some actual planning was underway, the squatter's enthusiasm was firing up. "I want this to happen as soon as possible. Gentlemen, are your men ready for battle?"

"My lads are always ready," replied Andrews with prim pride.

McCartney shrugged. "My boys never are. So, it makes no difference. Name a time."

"Right," said Robertson. "Sunrise tomorrow we set off."

The policeman looked surprised. "That soon? You know some of your 'volunteers' are already lodged in Cattenach's bar spending the money you've promised them? I don't know how much use they'll be."

Robertson was unmoved. "That would be the case any time we chose, wouldn't it?" he asked.

McCartney shrugged, and the Captain chuckled.

"As I thought," said the Warden.

The mercenary was sanguine. "They're not our main strength anyway. Expendables."

"Aren't we all?" asked the sergeant, bleakly.

The Warden ignored the comment, now fully focused on planning an assault strategy. He started drawing lines and arrows on the map. "Sergeant, at this point here one or two of your men will lead some of the volunteers to the creek, accompanied by as many of the Captain's troops as he feels he can spare."

Andrews added his own indicators to the paper on the desk. There were arrows drawn from three directions, question marks and arrows from others representing the creek.

The Riverview commander didn't look up as he spoke. "At this point we send two parties of your black boys to the flanks. We give them time - how long we'll have to determine - to engage the enemy. Then the rest of us attack on all three of these fronts. If we are supported by the squad following the creek, all to the good. My men will make up the main body of the attack here. The rest, with regimental support, will follow the flanking parties."

The Captain drew a heavy emphatic X over the campsite. It was an unspoken declaration of intent: the intent to eliminate the people who'd affronted and opposed him.

∿

THE DAYLIGHT WAS FADING, but out on the track from Louth to the campsite, Peter McGregor was still able to read as he rode. A swag on his back, he held the reins loosely in one hand, his mount moving at little more than a gentle plod.

What he read, of course, was the Bible he held in his other hand. One of the Epistles of Paul.

Aloud, he read, "For brethren, ye have been called untae liberty. Only use not liberty for an occasion tae the flesh, but by love serve one another. For all the law is fulfilled in one word, even in this: thou shalt love thy neighbour as thyself. But if ye bite and devour one another, take heed that ye be not consumed one of another."

He shook his head sadly as he mused aloud, "Ah Paul, Paul... did yon Galatians listen tae ye, I wonder?"

QUITE A BIT LATER THAT EVENING, McGregor was sitting by the campfire, together with most of the multinational cohort of 'allies'. Nearly all of people of both tribes had long since retired for the night The exceptions were the Balyarta woman Wittarkee, and the Kuthants Karumbari and Bowra, two of whom were due to go on sentry duty.

Another watchman-to-be was currently strumming his guitar quietly. The young Spaniard had spent some time earlier teaching elementary skills to a few interested natives, but now he played for his own relaxation.

The final sentry was to be Pierre, who'd been enjoying the music, but now reluctantly signalled to Wittarkee and Bowra.

Turning to Vittorio he said, "Most of the people are already asleep. Wonder if they know something we don't, eh? Ah well, time for us to change watch, I think."

He stood up and stretched, before addressing the others by the fire. "My friends, I bid you goodnight."

As the foursome walked out of the circle of firelight to relieve the current shift, Cristiano called over his shoulder, "Sleep well, mi amigos."

"Not too well," counselled Volkoff. "At first light we must have all our defences manned."

"Or womanned," added Vittorio, with an eye on where Wittarkee had departed. "They have fire, these people. I do still wonder if we're over cautious?"

Phillip shook his head. "No. My father shouldn't be underestimated. I'm pretty sure he won't try to attack at night - Andrews doesn't seem keen to move his men through bush in the dark. But any time outside of that..."

The Cossack agreed. "*Da*. But we will be ready."

"Ye're sure the bairns and such are safe?" asked the preacher.

It was Magpie who tried to reassure him. "As much as can be. Mundil's got them settled in a place that's hard to spot and hard to approach without bein' seen."

Arnold added his endorsement. "And he covers his own trail bloody well."

The other sentries were arriving back – Thonkumundil among them, just in time to hear the teamster's words of praise.

"Thanks, James," he said.

"Hey, I'm just telling truth. I've tried to track you, remember? Even with Magpie's help it was a bugger of a job!"

Magpie was looking concernedly at the preacher, still thinking of the vulnerable tribespeople. "You sure you shouldn't be with them, Mr. Mac? Help Samuel?"

"I've thought about it, aye, but I believe I'm led tae stay wi' all o' ye."

Pasquale looked surprised. "You'll carry a gun?"

Magpie offered a pistol to the preacher, but McGregor waved it away. "I've one o' ma ane, thank ye, Magpie." He pulled a small revolver from his vest pocket. "Guid for close range only, but ma job will be tae tend the wounded, not add tae the number slain."

Adhilasa was frankly shocked. "I hadn't pictured you holding a gun, brother Peter."

"I've nae problem wi' guns, Adhilasa. They're tools. It's the hands and hearts o' too many of the men as hold them that trouble me."

"Amen," agreed the American.

Micah turned to him, still bitter about his mentor's wounding. "I think you should have gone with Samuel and the others. You won't use a gun, what good are you here?"

There was more than the pain of his shattered knee in Adhilasa's voice as he answered, "You know there are other ways to fight."

"You're on one leg. And that wound has weakened you badly," Micah snapped.

"I have eyes, and ears, and two good arms. I will stand by my friends, my family, and fight with them!"

"You can't stand!"

Appreciating the older man's sentiment, McGregor cut into the argument, declaring, "A pure spirit may stand mightily, even when the body is failing."

Volkoff had considered options. "We keep you here," he said, pointing to the large shelter. "In the best defended position, with the padre. As best we can, we bring our wounded to you."

"I think not," said the former Union officer. "Set me near the big rocks. I can keep watch, and maintain some guard over the gap near the shelter. I believe Chung can spare me a good knife or two."

The Russian shrugged. "As you wish. It is a point which does need defending."

The last of the retiring sentries joined the group. It was Orhan Keilbren.

"It's all quiet out there this evening," he reported.

Wei Sun had been sitting quietly, watching and listening, as usual. He rested a hand on the Turk's shoulder. "You have no more duties tonight. Sleep. Be ready for the morning."

Orhan nodded. "Yes. Yes, I think I can sleep deeply tonight."

"It'll make a world of difference, my young friend!" said Vittorio, warmly.

He and the Turk exchanged smiles as the young man replied, "Ah yes, a different world. Now that is what I have longed for."

The return of the last sentry seemed to act as a signal for the group to break up, and soon nearly all of them had retired to their various tents or swags, to catch whatever sleep their whirling imaginations of what was to come would allow.

Last to leave the fireside was Li Wei Sun. He was allowing his tent-mate Keilbren an opportunity to get to sleep without feeling any obligation to converse. It was also a time of peace for himself. He enjoyed the fire's warmth, and gazed up into the sky. The sweep of stars had a certain majesty he enjoyed.

A few nocturnal noises were around him. The passage of small animals, or the odd night-active bird. The rustling of breeze in the bush, louder when a stronger gust pushed briefly through. Sleep sounds from some people. Snores, or the mumbles, even whimpers, of dreaming.

He was by nature and by choice a solitary man, he'd long told himself. His wartime experiences had only reinforced that, he believed. This last little while had been confronting, challenging, but in the end, positive. He'd said more than once that he didn't make friends easily. That had been true, and usually very deliberate. Pierre de la Fontaine had stubbornly persisted with him though, perhaps seeing something the farmer no longer saw in himself.

And so too, in his own sometimes desperate way, had the Turk. Behind the fragility, Wei Sun had seen an admirable character, and had been silently pleased to find that this was what Keilbren saw in him. He'd never been a role model before, and the experience surprised him.

Now these others – the natives, and the men from different parts of the world – had welcomed him into their company. Accepted his skills, his experience and his character, however different to their own.

He looked once more into the depths of the heavens above. Stars, too numerous to count. Each one different, he was sure, each one independent and apart from the others. And yet, how magnificent was the whole? Imponderable but majestic. Mysterious, perplexing, and wonderful.

Yes. The threat to these people was real, and intolerable. It would be his honour to help combat it. But he knew now, honour was more than a cause. It was *people* he would fight for, and do so with pride.

DAWN'S early dim light filtered through tendrils of smoke still drifting from the chimneys and stovepipes of Louth. Men were gathered, some still arriving blearily, unused to being active quite so early in the morning.

The men of the 1st Riverview Infantry Company were fully and correctly assembled. As was to be expected. All had served in the regular British army – Andrews would consider no-one else for his Company, and most had served under him in the Queen's Own Fusiliers 3rd Regiment. They knew his foibles, but knew he was a good field commander. And they knew he was good at finding them work.

They'd left service with few prospects, and few skills beyond following orders and a preparedness to kill on demand. Andrews' proposal to form a mercenary platoon was a lifeline for some men who'd most likely soon have found themselves dead or in jail, and they knew it. They were disciplined, but it was the discipline of habit, not conscious self-discipline. But such a distinction didn't matter to their commander. He gave an order, it would be obeyed, he was happy.

Content with the Company's assembly, Andrews snapped off a smart salute.

Michael Finlay returned the salute, and at a gesture from the adjutant, all of the men of the company did the same. The commanding officer nodded, pleased. Too much to hope that the rest of his 'force' could be so efficient. Walking beside him, James Robertson shared the same thought.

To be fair, Sergeant McCartney had tried. His troopers had been mustered into a rough approximation of the mercenaries' formation. McCartney gave a correct salute to the Warden, pointedly not looking at Andrews as he did so.

Possum and a few other experienced troopers like Meataxe and Big Billy did the same. Others were too busy looking around to notice the inspection. Mostly, they were admiring the shiny new guns held by the Riverview Company to their left, or snickering at some of the more obviously hung-over volunteers gathering on the other side of them.

Robertson returned the sergeant's salute with a wry smile. The man was a professional, he had to concede. In other circumstances, he could be worth cultivating. As it was, he provided a useful asset. He walked on, to assess his civilian 'posse'.

They were an untidy rabble – no more generous description could be applied.

Norman Heath was actually dozing in his saddle, only jerking awake when kicked in the shin by his brother Lewis.

Robertson managed to get the attention of the men, and directed them to gather in some sort of formation alongside the police troopers. They complied, some with an attempt at efficiency, others more sullenly. Most weren't used to taking orders.

A few were particularly uncomfortable with the direction to assemble so close to the troopers. They'd had unhappy experiences with the police, or simply didn't like the colour of their skin. The Heath brothers, Raymond Foster and John Rourke were prominent among those keeping as far away from the uniformed natives as possible. The dockhand Rourke had finally been shamed into volunteering by his drinking partners. For all his image of 'toughness', he was a weak man, easily pressured by his peers. That, and a deep-seated dislike of the local "darkies", had gotten him here this morning.

The feeling of antipathy was mutual for some. The troopers Burracan and Little Billy looked warily at the broad figure of 'Stone' Murray. It was barely a week since they'd had to haul him into a cell on a charge of 'affray', and they were still feeling the bruises.

There were wounded men among his volunteers, Robertson noted. Motivated by revenge, or too greedy for money to care, he wondered. He looked questioningly at the men in slings – Swede Jansen, Kev Seiman and Rourke. Jansen gave a determined nod and squeezed the antique musket he'd found to replace his damaged rifle. Seiman curled his lip angrily and patted the hilt of the knife in his waistband. Rourke didn't meet the Warden's eye, instead looking around furtively. Or perhaps nervously.

As satisfied as he could be, which wasn't much, Robertson took a final look around his 'civilian volunteers'. He barely suppressed a small sigh of resignation before walking back to stand beside his horse, between Andrews and McCartney.

The three 'commanders' exchanged a few words, with Robertson holding up four fingers. At a signal from Andrews, four of the Riverview contingent split from their comrades, and rode into positions at the corners of the rough rectangle formed by the troopers and volunteers. As they took their places, the soldiers Thornton, Taylor, Layton and Billington saluted to both Andrews and Robertson.

The latter noted with some concern that Billington had one foot unbooted and bandaged, but admired the fellow's resilience and discipline. He returned the salute with satisfaction, climbed into his saddle, and signalled the group to move off. Andrews and his company led the way, a look of anticipation on the officer's face.

AT THE SAME time as James Robertson had been silently lamenting the standard of his volunteers, and being privately relieved that they were there to be expendable, their soon-to-be foes were starting their day in their own seemingly casual way.

Chung was stirring a hearty, sustaining stew in his wok. Vittorio was beside him, serving pannikins or coolamons of food to anyone who had the appetite for it.

Nearby, Cristiano was caressing the strings of his late father's guitar, while teaching the Balyarta man Pirrewuy to play what had been his own instrument. The Spaniard patted the body of the guitar contentedly.

"Time we ate, I reckon," he said. "You keep that - it's yours now."

Pirrewuy smiled and gestured around the campsite to his kinsmen, involved in their various tasks and distractions. "Belong all, okay?" he said, to Cristiano's answering smile.

Chung scooped another serving of stew into a coolamon held out by the Italian, and said, "Glad I kept a little bit of oil back to cook with, eh?"

"Aye lad - it's grand!" agreed McGregor, sitting nearby, grateful for one of the best meals he'd eaten for a long time.

Magpie took four pannikins from Vittorio. "Give me some tucker and I'll take it out to James and the others already on watch. Eat up, folks, time we were all gettin' settled into our spots for the day."

From his position, seated on a small rock, Gregori called out a warning, "Remember, check the map before you go! No walking into our own snares."

"Could be a long day of doing nothing," said Vittorio hopefully. "Ah well, plenty of time for prospecting when this is all over, eh?"

"I'd like to pray that's so," said Adhilasa.

The preacher agreed through a mouthful of breakfast, "Aye, so would I, especially on the first count, but I'm nae so sure."

"I'm afraid you've read my father too well, Mister McGregor," said Phillip Robertson, ruefully, as he sat enjoying his own small coolamon of stew.

The last of the pannikins for the sentries was being filled as Wei Sun walked slowly towards the fire, holding a water canteen and a skerrick of folded paper.

"We have lost one of our warriors already," he said sombrely. In response to the puzzled looks, he continued, "Orhan Keilbren is no longer with us."

"The young Turk?" said Adhilasa, surprised.

Magpie was more cynical in his first thoughts. "He's skipped out on us?"

"No. I woke to find his soul had fled during the night."

Pasquale was startled by Li's carefully chosen words. "What? How?"

The former farmer's voice was low. "I had thought he had won his private war, but beside him I found these," he said as he held out the objects he held.

"He said he wasn't sleeping well..." recalled Vittorio.

Wei Sun nodded. "Yes. A drastic step too far to remedy that, I fear."

"But where did he get the drug?" asked the Italian. "Surely none of us here...?"

Wei Sun and Magpie both looked straight at Phillip, who, although his conscience was clear, shifted uncomfortably. He had a hunch.

"Could I see that packet, please?" he asked.

Wei Sun handed him the folded paper. Phillip examined the traces of powder still caught in the creases. He tasted a very tiny sample on a cautious fingertip.

"This looks like something my father's manservant Ali would prepare," he declared.

"Is that sly old bugger still around? Dangerous bloke, I always thought," said Magpie.

"You'd be right," agreed the squatter's son.

Volkoff had stalked over to stand alongside Phillip. He was not pleased to have lost an experienced fighting man. There were too few to begin with. He wondered if they'd not adequately searched young Robertson when he was first taken as a hostage.

"Is this yours? Did you bring...?"

"No! I never..."

Unexpectedly, Wei Sun interrupted Phillip's protest. "I think our late companion may have - spent some time with your sister."

With a sigh, Phillip rolled his eyes and nodded.

"I thought she'd taken an interest in Micah," said Adhilasa, puzzled.

That brought a sneer from Magpie. "Davinia's never been the sort to confine her interests to one bloke at a time."

"Magpie! Not in front of the lass's brother!" admonished McGregor.

"It's alright. No point in my getting angry when I know he's speaking the truth," the young man admitted.

"I must find de la Fontaine and break the news. He rose early to 'check the perimeter', he said. He thought well of the young man," said Wei Sun.

"As did we all," agreed Gregori.

"Have we time tae gie him a proper burial?" asked the preacher. "I ken he wasnae of ma faith, but still –"

"Burial, yes, but a ceremony best wait until this is all over," replied the Cossack strategist. "I do not dare weaken our defences. Which we must attend to. Someone must take the fine rifle put aside for the young man."

"May I?" asked Phillip, hoping to atone in some way for his sister's actions. "I shoot well."

Magpie conceded, "He does, I'll say that."

Volkoff was satisfied that their former hostage wasn't complicit in Keilbren's death. He'd been quietly impressed by the efforts their newest 'recruit' had made to actively assist.

"Very well. To our tasks..." he said. "And you, Mister McGregor, to yours."

As various people started to move off, Adhilasa approached the Scot. "I'll help you, as best I can, Brother Peter."

Wei Sun also approached the preacher. "Let me speak to de la Fontaine. Young Keilbren was with us. We will assist." He looked to Volkoff. "At least one of us will."

"Both, if you see fit," conceded the Russian. "But don't take too long, please."

Phillip looked up at the late Turk's tent-mate. "Li Wei Sun, I'm sorry."

"It is not your place to apologise. You are not responsible for your sister's debts."

"Nor those of your father," added Volkoff.

"Thank you. But I aim to try anyway," the young man replied, as Magpie extended a hand to help him to his feet.

THE WARDEN'S SMALL PRIVATE 'ARMY' had stopped at the side of the broad track from Louth. Most of the men of the main force were still in formation.

Five of them, though, had been extracted from the group.

The infantryman Street, the volunteers Foster, Martin and Heffernan, and the trooper known as Big Billy were assembled a little way apart from the others.

"Right, off you go," snapped Andrews, who'd rattled off a quick order.

The white men prepared to ride off, looking expectantly at Big Billy. The trooper blinked at Andrews. The Captain had spoken directly to his trusted rifleman Street, so the burly bluecoat hadn't really been paying much attention. He looked to his sergeant, helplessly.

McCartney rode over to him, and sympathetically explained in a slow voice, "Find the creek, Billy. Follow it. Find the campsite. Meet up with us there, as quick as you can."

The big man grinned and nodded.

Captain Andrews waved his revolver in warning at the five men. "If you find the enemy before we do, do *not* engage them before us! Your role is to support, not destroy the element of surprise."

Street, nominally in command of the little group, saluted and led his men off, waving the trooper up to ride beside him.

As they rode, the dockhand Martin growled, "Hope I get to put a bullet in one of them yellow bastards I hear's with them."

Rumours of the assortment of 'allies' the local natives had acquired were circulating in Louth. The three Asian men who'd been briefly seen around the town – the trio brought to Australia by Master Wu – had been mentioned suspiciously.

"Hunh – I don't care who I get to shoot," replied Raymond Foster, riding alongside him.

Heffernan, an older man, an ex-soldier himself, who'd volunteered out of a sense of duty to the missing child, shook his head. The girl seemed to have slipped everyone else's mind, he thought. He steered his horse a little further away from the other two volunteers.

The rest of the party, their formation slightly adjusted for the extracted men, started to continue along the road.

MILES AWAY, Ali was doing his morning round of cleaning the Robertsons' suites in the Woolpack Inn.

He was dusting Davinia's room, walking leisurely with a contented smile on his face. He got to the couch.

The squatter's daughter seemed to be half-reclining across it, but her eyes were open and glazed. Ali casually moved her body like a large cushion, and dusted behind it.

He turned to the small table beside the couch, and picked up a small paper packet from beside an almost-empty brandy glass. He carefully folded the packet and put it in his pocket, then continued the dusting routine. Only his habitual self-discipline kept him from a cheery whistle as he worked.

.ooo.

4

A SMALL, PRIVATE WAR

The raiders had dismounted at the point their commanders had agreed was the best place to commence their stealthy approach. The horses were tethered just off the track, and left in the care of the wounded soldier Murphy, and the oldest of the volunteers, Leo Holt.

Organized into a few small squads in a line advancing ahead of the main body, the Warden's men crept into the bush, most of them wary and alert.

One small group was led by a couple of native troopers, followed by the limping soldier Billington, Kev Seiman and John Rourke. The lead trooper, a bushman named Cooree, from the Victorian high country, suddenly stopped and held up his hand.

He pointed down at one of Adhilasa's 'trip wires' and grinned. Carefully, he and the other trooper stepped over the thin length of fibre.

Sneering, Seiman knelt to cut the 'rope' with his trusty knife. As he tugged at the cord, there was a rustling from above. Alarmed, the troopers looked up, just in time to see a coolamon tipping. They and Seiman were showered with caltrops, several of them sticking in faces and hands. All three fell and died without a word.

Rourke, horrified, barely managed to stifle a scream. He went to pick a single caltrop off his sling, thought better of it, and then turned and ran through the bush, shoving the soldier out of his way.

Grabbing the tree trunk to keep his balance, Billington looked down at his bandaged foot, then at the ground around him. He began to very carefully sweep caltrops away with the butt of his rifle.

SOME DISTANCE AWAY, the infantrymen Grey and Matthews were backing up through scrub they'd just traversed, worried looks on their faces. Grey stifled a yelp as they almost backed into Robertson and McCartney at the head of a party of troopers and volunteers.

At the Warden's questioning look, Matthews pointed back the way he and Grey had just come. Reluctantly, the two soldiers accepted Robertson's wordless order, and led the way back along where they'd just retreated.

Grey pointed. Two troopers and two volunteers lay dead, sprawled in front of and leaning into a thorn bush. Robertson's lips tightened into a thin line as the sergeant cursed silently.

Very carefully, Robertson stepped forward to examine the bush. He wasn't surprised to find dark smears of poison on some of the long thorns of the fatal bush. He'd suspected as much as soon as he saw the dead men, having not long ago used something similar himself.

McCartney nodded his understanding of what had befallen the four men, and signalled the following party to wait.

Annoyed, Robertson pointed back in the direction they'd just come from. As the group moved off, the Warden started to veer away, cursing to himself.

AT ANOTHER POINT of the broad advance, the troopers Possum and Narby were making slow, careful progress. They'd already dodged one of the deadly trip wires. The Irish soldier Barrett and the volunteers Boyd and Medlin followed, equally watchful and appreciating the caution.

Suddenly John Rourke came crashing through the bushes. Boyd grabbed his shoulders. He shook the dockhand, calming and quietening him as best he could.

Breathing hard, Rourke nervously joined their slow advance. Unbeknownst to any of them, though, his blundering arrival had shaken a shallow coolamon, precariously balanced above. Narby suddenly stiffened. He made a grab for his bare foot but before he could reach it, collapsed, already dead.

White-faced, Rourke turned and ran again, into another section of the bush. Medlin took a few steps after him, hoping to calm, or at least restrain the charging man. A trip wire snapped. There was no way to know which man was responsible, but it was Medlin who caught the load of fatal caltrops. Rourke ran on, regardless.

Possum, Barrett and Boyd stood frozen between the two bodies. The trooper checked the soles of his battered boots, suddenly very glad he was one of the few of Louth's native policemen who bothered with footwear. Grunting with satisfaction, he started to advance again, slowly and steadily, musket at the ready.

Boyd and Barrett copied his movements and followed.

ROURKE'S headlong run through the scrub almost brought him crashing into another of the small raiding parties. The troopers Burracan and Little Billy had been picking their way carefully forward, ahead of the soldier Thornton and the two volunteers 'Stone' Murray and Tim Barnes. It was the mercenary who was nearly collected by the frightened man.

Thornton threw his arms around the dockhand – no mean feat. In his panic he was babbling.

"Little spiky things! They're deadly! On the ground. In the bushes. Up in the trees..."

The soldier slapped him, hard, in the hope of both bringing him to his senses and shutting him up. Rourke rocked back from the blow, inadvertently looking up into the canopy. He whimpered and pointed. "Look! Look! Up in the trees!"

Thornton couldn't help but look up, and was more than startled by what he saw. There was a black man lying in the branches several feet away, almost directly above his head. He was already rattled by Rourke's fear. Thoroughly spooked now, he swung his rifle up and fired two rapid shots.

Not far away, their sound was heard by Andrews and Robertson, who'd only just arrived at his side. They looked in the direction of the shots.

"Contact! Come on!" exclaimed the Warden.

The mercenary commander grinned maliciously, "Right lads, on with all speed!"

At his command, the group of soldiers accelerated their advance, hurrying the two troopers ahead of them. A couple even applied rough shoves with the hands of rifle butts to emphasize their haste. The two natives, Purrahmirre and Gimbi Gimbi, exchanged worried looks. They both knew this was not good territory for rushing. In his agitation, though, the leading Purrahmirre missed spotting a trip wire, slung low through tussocks of grass. He stumbled, but more importantly, the end of the cord jerked loose a coolamon balanced precariously above them. The bowl, and its deadly load of caltrops, dropped.

The luckless Purrahmirre took most of the little weapons, and was dead before he hit the ground. It was perhaps fate that ensured that the two soldiers who'd been responsible for pushing the trooper – Rackman and O'Connell – both caught caltrops themselves. O'Connell stared at the back of his hand as he fell forward, his vision already going dark. Rackman just had time to turn towards his commander, but couldn't speak before the poisoned fragment of wire stuck in his face did its work. Gimbi Gimbi shrank back, staring wide-eyed.

Andrews glared angrily. "The cunning sods!" he breathed.

Other small groups had heard Thornton's wild shots. Meataxe and Kundewung had already successfully navigated one trip wire, unaware of the caltrop fate they'd avoided for themselves and the men following – the volunteer Penfold, and the soldiers Taylor and Dallas, the latter still bandaged from the Company's earlier raid.

But at the sound of nearby gunfire Meataxe spun suddenly in that direction. Off balance, his heel caught another low slung cord. No caltrops this time – the cord dislodged cunningly arranged supports, and a large rock fell from overhead. All that saved Meataxe was, in fact, that he'd been reeling off balance. The heavy stone landed where he otherwise would have been.

Both troopers grinned at the narrow escape. Kundewung patted his old friend's shoulder. Another shot was heard, from some way off. Blood spurted from Kundewung's neck. Reflexively, his hand clutched at Meataxe's blue coat, even as he slumped to the ground. Taylor, Dallas and Penfold all dived for cover. It took a moment for Meataxe to react, but when he did, it was to do the unexpected, leaping up into the branches from where the rock had dropped. Another bullet whizzed by his feet as he hoisted them up.

Many yards away, Phillip Robertson lowered the chassepot rifle and smiled mirthlessly.

Dallas was cursing and clutching at his leg. The recent wound to his thigh had opened up as he'd hit the ground, and he realised he was bleeding heavily. He grabbed Taylor's arm.

"I don't reckon I can bloody well stand on this, chum," Dallas gritted. "See if you can join back up with the C.O., eh? He's over that way."

Taylor nodded. Penfold said nothing, but figured it made sense to stay near as many of the better-armed soldiers as possible. One trooper was dead and the other bloke seemed to have vanished, anyway.

∽

THE CAUSE OF THE CHAOS, Thornton, was staring up at the body he'd just shot. Burracan had grabbed his arm, though, and pointed up at the dark figure.

"He's already dead! That's what they do with their bodies!" the trooper exclaimed.

"Ah, don't be bloody ridiculous," snarled 'Stone' Murray, shoving the dusky policeman's shoulder.

"Bloody hell..." swore Thornton, taking a step away.

Behind and above them, the nimble Cooterah rose from his prone position atop the corpse which had stopped Thornton's bullets. With a fluid movement he hurled a short spear that impaled the reeling Burracan, then quickly dropped back down out of sight before being spotted.

Thornton, Little Billy, Barnes and Murray fired wildly up, but with no target to aim for. From the cover of another tree, Asbul fired his blowgun, selecting who he figured to be the most dangerous adversary. Dropping his gun, Thornton clutched at his throat. As the soldier's knees buckled under him, John Rourke once again took fright, and plunged away into the scrub.

While Little Billy and Murray were distracted, watching him go, three Kuthant warriors – Ugeree, Nalloor and the woman Pummirri – rose up from the bushes ahead of them and charged. Tim Barnes raised his pistol, but couldn't get a clear shot past the other two. Little Billy propelled 'Stone' forward with a shove between the shoulder blades, straight onto the point of Pummirri's short spear.

Horrified, Barnes fired, but the shot passed Billy's ribs harmlessly, and sailed over the heads of the three attackers. The trooper turned to run, leaving Barnes to his fate. He didn't get far. Kuthant spears didn't fly far, but they were deadly, especially when pitjuri was applied to their tips.

∽

ROBERTSON HAD FOUND ANDREWS, and had managed to reunite with Sergeant McCartney. Together with Andrews' adjutant, they were conferring behind the main body of remaining soldiers, troopers and volunteers.

The advance of that group had been temporarily halted. Shots and screams from some of the small squads sent out gave eloquent testimony as to why.

"I don't think clearing fire will work in this instance, do you Sergeant?" asked Andrews, evidently serious, but perhaps talking more to himself.

"Not bloody likely!" agreed the policeman, only to be ignored as Andrews addressed Finlay.

"Get the men to advance at a crouch - use their packs for cover from above. Eyes peeled but move as fast as they can. They're relying on these traps – I think we have them outnumbered. Warden, we should extend the front. Look for a safe way through and try to link up with the flanking sorties."

The Warden was staring ahead, in the direction of the campsite. "No. We drive one wedge straight through, straight ahead. I think you're right about the numbers. They don't know our resources though, we can still surprise them. Moving the way you just said - your men in front since they're best protected. We send some men to join the east and west flanks and use the same approach there. I'll take men east. Sergeant McCartney, you take a group west."

The Company commander began to protest. "I'd rather we... "

"This is not a debate," said Robertson, sharply.

"If you insist..."

"I do, Captain."

Robertson and McCartney hastily assembled their two small groups of troopers and volunteers, and each drew a couple of soldiers from the main body of Riverview men, the rest of whom were to comprise the central attacking force.

The Warden and the policeman led their teams east and west. Andrews watched them go, hands on hips and a sour look on his face.

"I really do detest working with civilians, Mister Finlay," he said. "They will not render unto Caesar the authority that is Caesar's. Ah well - onward, my soldiers!"

JOHN ROURKE WAS STILL BLUNDERING through scrub. Miraculously, he'd missed poisoned thorn bushes, caltrop traps, and falling rocks. He spotted furtive movement a little way ahead and stopped suddenly. To his enormous relief, he then recognized Norman Heath, swaggering near the cautious policeman McCartney.

He rushed forward, shouting, "Sergeant! Sergeant! Norm! Ya gotta watch out! There's traps everywhere! They…"

McCartney gestured to try to stop the fool's shouting but their stealthy advance was ruined.

"Bloody hell! Move it, men!" growled the sergeant.

A coolamon trap was triggered, but the caltrops landed on the packs of the two soldiers in the lead – Dundee and Layton. It was Dundee whose foot had caught the tripwire, and he fell heavily. In the tree above, the Balyarta man Kurrawarah rose up from atop a corpse and threw his long spear.

A volley of shots killed the tribesman almost instantly, but the damage was done. The spear had flown over the prone figure of Dundee but embedded itself in Layton's belly. He staggered and collapsed heavily, his knee cracking into the head of his regimental colleague. Dundee lost consciousness without knowing what hit him.

But Kurrawarah's action was the spark that inspired a little band of his fellow tribesmen and women to attack from cover with guns, spears and clubs, killing and being killed. McCartney managed to get behind a substantial tree. He checked his pistol and reloaded his rifle but stayed standing unseen by the attackers.

"What a bloody mess," he muttered to himself.

Not far from him, Norman had been about to fling himself to the ground when Possum grabbed his shoulder. The trooper pointed down at a couple of the deadly caltrops which the big man had been about to throw himself onto.

Heath grunted and shook off the dark hand. His response was to wipe his shoulder as he ran, ducking and weaving into the bushes, away from the skirmish unfolding around him. Barrett went to go after him, but the local man Boyd stopped him. They were better off without the big fool.

The small bloody melee was almost over already, not that John Rourke would know, having fled the scene, yet again. The Balyarta attackers lay dead or wounded, as did several volunteers and troopers. Possum busied himself checking on the latter, tending to those whose wounds weren't fatal. His sergeant moved from cover, nodded at his efforts, and moved away through the scrub with the remains of his complement.

Norman's flight was random, thoughtless. He'd actually trodden on the body of his brother Lewis, barely noting the upright spear and oblivious to the man skewered by it. But now, his retreat had provided him with an unexpected bounty. He'd spotted the back of a white man, perched up in the fork of a tree. It was Gregori Volkoff, engrossed in watching activity in another direction, where Andrews' squad of soldiers were advancing.

As Norman raised the barrel of his rifle to sight on the man's back, another movement caught his eye. One of the local natives was at the base of the tree, and had shifted slightly so his back was now visible. Irresistible. Norman lowered his aim. Grinning maliciously, he took a step forward. His foot crunched on a fallen branch.

Alerted by the sound, Magpie stepped out from the cover of another tree and shot the big man in the belly.

As DIRECTED, the little patrol led by the infantryman Street had followed the creek. The sounds of gunfire hadn't yet reached them, muffled by the dense bush. The most recent patch of that scrub had forced them to move on foot, their horses trailing awkwardly behind. They rounded a sharp bend, and were met with the sight of a broader crescent of sand, stones and driftwood branches.

Street sniffed the air with a puzzled look on his face. He'd been laboriously explaining to the trooper what they were looking for, so hadn't at first noticed the odd smell. Big Billy was aware of it, but it wasn't something he'd been told to look out for, so didn't mention it. He was keen to do exactly what this soldier fella asked, then maybe he'd get a go with that flash new gun. He'd noticed something else, though, and signalled a halt.

Billy pointed into a patch of the scrub fringing the bank, and said, "Men been through dere. Mebbe dat's de spot."

They didn't hear the barely breathed words, "Oh, it sure is."

Far closer than the would-be raiders realized, Chung and Koolwunnung watched and listened. She had a pistol looted from one of the earlier attackers jammed in the battered leather belt she wore. But more importantly, in her hands was a thick wadding of kangaroo skin, in which nestled some glowing embers.

From that handful, Chung lit the short wick of a bottle in his hand. As it flared, he tossed it low and hard at the gravel where the party of five stood at the edge of the creek.

Glimpsing the movement, Street fired in their direction, winging Koolwunnung's arm. But it was too late. As the firebomb landed, the fuel-soaked grass under the thin layer of sand and small stones erupted in flame.

The soldier was immediately lost to the fire, as was Big Billy. Martin managed to stagger out of the inferno, his clothes, skin and hair burning. For a brief instant, he caught sight of Chung standing amongst the bushes. His last thought as he fell, dying, into the creek, was something like, "Bloody Chinaman - I shoulda known..."

The horses managed to bolt back the way they'd come, suddenly more sure-footed in their fear. Foster and Heffernan had dived away, making it to the creek. Heffernan scrambled and splashed his way after the horses. The veteran knew that he was out of his depth in a fight like this.

But Raymond Foster managed to struggle ashore from the waist-deep water at a spot some way distant from where the flames were already subsiding, their fuel spent. He, too, saw Chung, and threw his hands up.

"Don't shoot me! I'm an injured man!" he cried.

Having checked that her injury wasn't too serious, Chung motioned to Koolwunnung to stay hidden and cover him. He stepped forward, hands spread.

"Shoot you? What with? I don't have a gun."

That was good enough for Foster, whose 'injury' was entirely fictional. "Yeah?" he replied. "Well I reckon I kept mine dry!"

Hampered by his wet heavy coat, he fumbled to cock the pistol he'd managed to hold up out of the water as he'd jumped into the creek.

The cook was walking toward him, casually. "Oh? So, it's a fair fight then."

He drew one of his knives from the special belt he wore around his waist. His hand barely seemed to flick, but the blade flew unerringly. Foster was still trying to get his gun organized when the knife struck him at the base of his neck.

The pistol dropped into the creek as he tried to grasp the protruding hilt. His mouth moved, but nothing more than a gurgle came out as Foster fell, first to his knees, then sideways into the shallows at the edge of the creek.

"You quick!" said Koolwunnung, impressed. "Quicker than me." She looked at her gun and smiled. "But I shoot straight."

"I hope so, when you have to." He helped the Balyarta woman out of cover, checking her arm as he did so.

They maintained their grasp on each other's hand for a few moments as they carefully scanned their surroundings. Heffernan was lost to view. The bodies of Foster and Martin polluted the creek.

The remains of Street and Big Billy still smoked on the charred beach.

"Looks like that's it from this quarter," announced Chung with some satisfaction.

The words were barely out of his mouth when a volley of shots and screams could be heard from the direction of the campsite. "I'm gonna hope so - sounds like we're needed elsewhere." He unconsciously squeezed the Balyarta woman's hand. "How are you?"

"Hurt. Alive. We go, yeah?"

Chung nodded. He retrieved his knife, then turned and ran into the bush, one hand steadying the wounded woman running at his side.

~

NOT FAR AWAY, the sounds of shots and screams caused Peter McGregor to look up sharply from wiping dirt from his hands over a fresh grave. The same reaction came from the men with him – Wei Sun, Pierre, and Adhilasa, the latter leaning heavily on a shovel. His ruined knee was extremely painful, but he was beyond stubborn.

"It's done, and it begins," said the preacher.

The Frenchman looked down, and raised the chassepot rifle in salute. "Goodbye my friend - we've work to do!" To the others, he said simply, "Come on."

The quartet started out for the campsite. Adhilasa was trying to hobble as quickly as he could using the shovel as a crutch. De la Fontaine took the shovel and positioned himself under Adhilasa's arm to half support, half carry him.

Embarrassed, the American snapped, "I can manage!"

Wei Sun quickly got under the other arm and completed the lift. "No, you cannot, and we are needed quickly."

Their speed increased considerably, McGregor following the other three with his Bible in one hand, and the shovel in the other.

Suddenly Chung and Koolwunnung emerged from the scrub on their left. Wei Sun almost dropped Adhilasa as he reached quickly for Orhan's ninjato. He'd chosen to carry his late companion's weapon at his waist as a mark of respect.

Chung threw up his hands, calling, "Easy - I'm on your side!"

He quickly assessed the situation, and clapped the Frenchman on the shoulder where the chassepot was slung. "Pierre, you get going - they're gonna need that big gun. I'll take over."

"I do not need..." Adhilasa again tried to protest, but Wei Sun interrupted brusquely.

"Yes, you do! And we will not abandon you - accept it."

As he took over Pierre's position, Chung spoke quietly to the American. "You know he's right, old friend."

Adhilasa's shoulders slumped for a moment in reluctant agreement, then he steadied himself, and stood erect. There was no shame in accepting the help of men such as these, when it was truly needed.

Koolwunnung gripped Chung's arm, and offered, "I do this."

He smiled, but shook his head. "No, you've only got one good hand right now, and you need that to hold the gun."

Pierre went to hand his dao to Chung. "Know how to use this?" he asked.

"Reckon so, but I've got my knives," replied the cook.

Adhilasa reached out a hand. "May I?" he asked.

There was only a momentary pause before de la Fontaine handed over the weapon, saying, "Of course. An honour."

He gave a small bow, then unslung the chassepot from his shoulder, ready for use as he ran on ahead.

McGregor watched him go. Squeezing his Bible, he said in a firm voice, "Onward, ever onward!"

Unbeknownst to the burial party, they were spotted by McCartney's contingent. With none of the soldiers left after the luckless Irishman Barrett had blundered into a poison-laced thicket of thorns, the sergeant had placed two of his most experienced troopers at the front of his 'wedge', and it was Kurracar who first saw the tall Adhilasa and the others.

A trained soldier might have signalled silently, and so retained an element of surprise. Kurracar didn't have that discipline – he called loudly to alert his fellows behind him.

Even as they raised their muskets, some heard a strange whistle, that came from no bird. A shot rang out, from some distance away. Cristiano's aim was true, and Kurracar fell, dead. Spooked, but angry, four of the troopers broke ranks and charged at the strangers before McCartney could stop them. They didn't realize that the fatal shot had come from a different direction.

Reluctantly leaving Adhilasa to stand as best he could, Chung used one hand to chop upwards, upsetting the aim of Trooper Wombi's long musket barrel. Instantly closing in, his other hand lodged a knife between the bluecoat's ribs.

Also stepping away from the American, Wei Sun slashed at the advancing Yirrawon with Orhan's ninjato. The blade tore open the trooper's face, but as he fell backwards he managed to fire his anti-quated musket. It hadn't been aimed, but the worst of the blast caught Wei Sun in the chest. Both men collapsed, badly wounded.

A shot from Koolwunnung ricocheted from a tree, causing the other two troopers to duck before they could fire. Even from his crouch, though, Neenan was looking to finish off the injured Chinese man, not realising it was already unnecessary. But Adhilasa threw himself forward, springing with all the considerable strength in his good leg. He caught Neenan a hard, fatal blow with the dao before crashing painfully to the ground himself.

It had all taken seconds, during which McCartney was frantically shepherding his survivors, troopers and volunteers, to slip away quietly to their right, seeking a better position. So, he didn't see Pindi lunge to attack the fallen American. Nor did he see the preacher step forward and slam the flat of the shovel into Pindi's skull. The trooper wasn't dead, but he wouldn't regain consciousness for long while.

"Keep low, Young Joey!" ordered the sergeant, as another bullet from the distance whipped past at shoulder height.

Barely more than a lad, he shouldn't have been brought on this fool's errand, thought McCartney bitterly. Blasted Warden had wanted "every available man", though, hadn't he?

The wounded soldier Dallas, hearing the nearby shots and cries of Wei Sun and the fallen troopers, realized that the action was suddenly much closer than he'd thought. He was a brave man, and knew his responsibility to the Company in which he served. He hauled himself painfully to his feet, hobbling a few paces then bracing himself against a tree. He loosed off a shot in the direction he'd heard the ruckus, and set himself to fire at any target that presented itself.

No such target appeared. The soldier's movement had caught the attention of Pierre de la Fontaine, and any thoughts that Dallas may have had of an ambush were dashed when two chassepot bullets hit him. The shock robbed him of consciousness as he fell, and he quietly bled to death with a smile on his face, duty done.

By capricious fate more than design, Dallas' single shot had been effective. The Martini Henry bullet had struck Adhilasa, just as he'd been awkwardly trying to stand with McGregor's assistance. The American was dying in the Scot's arms, just as his old companion Chung reached his side.

"Fight... the good fight... my brothers," were his last words.

McCartney's phalanx had just encountered Taylor and Penfold. While Penfold was welcomed by some of the other volunteers in the group, the policeman was even more pleased to see the soldier and his rifle. The Martini Henry was a welcome addition to their reduced firepower.

Realizing that they'd stumbled upon an area of reasonable cover, the poisoned thorn branches identifiable by the bodies of a trooper and a volunteer who'd walked into them a little earlier, the sergeant arranged his resources.

'Dug in' as best they could, they turned their attention back in the direction of the melee they'd just fled. As the first of their bullets started to fly, Chung, Koolwunnung and McGregor threw themselves to the ground. Not far away, de la Fontaine dropped to one knee, and started to fire in the direction that the threat was coming from.

"Come on!" called the Frenchman. "I'll cover you as best I can!"

The trio scrambled up and moved at a crouching zigzag run as bullets flew around them. McGregor felt one tug at his black shirt as it whistled close by his ribs, and said a silent prayer of thanks.

They reached Pierre, who rose to his feet and joined their rush towards the campsite. Together the four made it to the gap in the rocky outcrop that was to have been guarded by Adhilasa.

It was as well for them that McCartney, reluctant to risk more casualties, had not yet ordered his men to advance from their position. Andrews wouldn't have approved. Probably, neither would the damned Warden. 'To hell with them,' thought the sergeant to himself. 'I won't disobey specific orders, we'll do our job, but with all bloody caution!'

~

ATOP THE LARGE ROCK, Cristiano and Micah had been directing their shots towards wherever they saw or heard a suitable target – the sound of the Martini Henry rifles was quite unlike anything else on the battlefield.

They saw the surviving members of Orhan Keilbren's burial party break from the scrub and dash towards them. Micah looked down questioningly as the Spaniard provided covering fire. The padre shook his head, even as Pierre clenched a fist over his heart. The West Indian clenched his teeth and resumed firing. Stone chips flew around him and Cristiano as bullets hit the fringes of the rock before ricocheting upwards.

Pierre threw himself behind the stones that were to have been Adhilasa's scant protection, and shot back in the direction they'd come from. The increase in lead from that direction indicated that the policeman had started to cautiously advance his force, Taylor and his rifle near the front. The Frenchman's metronomic shooting gave his three companions some opportunity to dash across the expanse of the campsite, heading for the large reinforced bark shelter.

Bullets whirred at them from other directions. The preacher's shirt acquired another hole, this time in a billowing sleeve. Directing Cristiano to cover the west, Micah wriggled to shoot more southerly, where the majority of other shots seemed to be coming from. He raised himself up from his prone position, eager to improve his angle of fire towards some red uniforms he'd caught sight of.

Suddenly, his rifle jammed , perhaps the result of him trying to fire too often, too quickly for the mechanism. In the moment that he looked down at it, a bullet from Taylor's Martini Henry smashed into his left side. The impact pitched him off the rock, and he landed heavily at the base of the outcrop.

Chung heard his cry and saw him land. He'd helped raise the young man – of course, he turned back to help if he could. He was only dimly aware that Koolwunnung was at his side, until together they managed to drag Micah to the shelter, under the protective fire of both Pierre and Cristiano.

As they reached the shelter, Pierre seized the moment to make a quick dash to the most protected face of the large rock. It wasn't the easiest ascent, especially with the rifle slung over his shoulder, but adrenaline got him to the top quickly. Both acutely aware of Micah's fate, the Frenchman immediately dived to lie full-length alongside Cristiano.

At first, they both concentrated their fire towards the west, where the burial party had come from, but quickly realised that the threats were increasingly widespread. The Spaniard wriggled to face the south. Both men worked their weapons in a deadly rhythm, both in grim silence.

WITHIN THE SHELTER, McGregor was trying to stem the bleeding from Micah's wound, while Chung knelt, guarding the entrance. Both were trying to keep down behind the protection of the old plough blades and corrugated iron lining the walls. The latter was no protection against the Riverview rifles, but was at least proving effective against some of the less potent weapons of troopers and volunteers, especially those fired from a long range.

Micah groaned softly. "Can't move legs. Funny - know how Adhilasa must have felt. Damn gun jammed. He'd have said 'I told you so'. Guess I wouldn't blame him..."

"I doubt he'd ha' said that, laddie..." said the Scot gently, then he winced and ducked lower at the sound of a bullet striking their metal barricade. "That was close, eh?"

There was no response. "Micah?" the preacher asked. With a sigh, he closed the young man's sightless eyes.

He turned his attention to Koolwunnung's injury, only for her to wave him away as Thonkumundil arrived, gasping, at the entrance of the shelter. In his arms was the wounded Yallaroi, mumbling in Burundji through his pain. Chung ushered them in.

"Glad you here, Mister Mac," said Mundil.

"Doin' ma time in hell, lad - doin' ma time in hell. Bring him here."

A LITTLE WAY apart from any of the main attacking groups, the little sortie led by infantryman Ted Clapham moved cautiously, resisting any temptation to rush into the fray escalating around them.

Trooper Yarreel understood and appreciated Clapham's lack of urgency. He didn't want to get shot, either. The same could be said for the two volunteers in the party, Miller and Dalton. Their well-meant enthusiasm for the just cause that the Warden had 'sold' them on was disintegrating in the face of so much bloodshed.

The quartet suddenly found themselves in a little clearing, trampled flat by a recent scuffle. The evidence was chilling. Each of the four men knew at least one of the bodies strewn in front of them: Riverview's Thornton, troopers Burracan and Little Billy, Tim Barnes and 'Stone' Murray. The Kuthant man and woman, Nalloor and Pummirri, were anonymous to them, but their role in what had transpired was obvious by the weapons each still clutched.

Swearing, Clapham knelt by the body of his old comrade. Captain Andrews had led them into, and out of, tough situations before. They understood difficult conditions. But this type of warfare, it was a new experience. Hidden enemies were one thing, but this was like fighting phantoms. Traps that could kill at a touch. Weapons they'd never encountered before. Ted had to struggle to hold his nerve.

Yarreel squatted beside him, and pointed to the dart embedded in the infantryman's neck. Suddenly the trooper grabbed at the side of his own face. It had felt like a wasp stung him. His eyes rolling up in his head, Yarreel keeled sideways, toppling into Clapham as he fell.

The soldier had time to spot Asbul, but couldn't shoot, tangled as he was with the trooper's body. Miller and Dalton also saw the fisherman, though, and fired instinctively. Miller's rushed shot missed its mark, but some of the pellets from Dalton's shotgun caught the Makassar's leg as he tried to clamber back up into the tree. Wincing, Asbul managed to complete the climb, covered by the rifle fire of Phillip Robertson and, near him, the Balyarta Baza.

One of Robertson's shots did for Dalton, who collapsed with a chest wound that, if not fatal, ended his involvement in this or any other battle. Clapham and Miller fired towards this new threat as they drew back. The tall tribesman fell with a cry of pain as Miller's shooting improved.

"Hold on, I'm coming," exclaimed Phillip, seeing their two adversaries retreating. Lowering his rifle, he went to assist Baza.

IN THE MIDST of his main central body of soldiers, William Andrews was becoming all too aware of the cost of this exercise, and was righteously vexed by it. His own role in provoking the violence was ignored. Gingerly, he stepped over the body of Bertram Connor, another man who'd served alongside him in India.

He stopped and picked up Connor's rifle. As an officer, he still preferred his beloved Tranter revolver, but having invested in the Martini Henrys, it seemed wasteful not to use one.

The bodies of more of his Company lay nearby, along with those of troopers and tribesmen. Andrews couldn't have identified Balyarta from Kuthant, and wouldn't have cared to. They were all to be exterminated, as far as he was concerned.

With a series of signals, the commander arranged the Riverview men, himself included, into formation, most of them kneeling, rifles directed into the heart of the campsite.

Turning his head to watch his men, Andrews called in a low voice, "Right, lads - sweeping fire, on my mark. One, two..." A chassepot bullet ricocheted off a tree beside him, causing him to duck automatically as it whistled past his ear. "Hell!" he shouted impulsively.

His regiment, confused about whether that was a command or not, and not fully prepared if it was, fired a disorganized volley. Many of their shots thudded into dirt or pinged off from hidden plough blades. All they achieved was the unwanted effect of drawing attention to themselves. With that attention came more fire from the unexpectedly effective resistance. Near the front of the hastily arranged formation, Moir and Clark collapsed – one dead, the other dying. Sprawled behind a tree, Andrews swore again in anger.

Away to the soldiers' left, Magpie grinned at Volkoff. The Cossack had just fired the shot that narrowly missed Andrews.

"Boss cocky soldier didn't expect that, eh?" said the half-caste.

Gregori's gaze didn't shift. "Concentrate. Task at hand."

He fired again, as did Magpie. Positioned between their rifles, the Balyarta woman Wittarkee fired her pistol in the same direction.

Andrews could barely glance up from his prone position as he heard another one, two of his Company fall. This was intolerable! He managed to catch Finlay's eye, and signalled for an attack to be launched in what was the direction where Magpie, Volkoff and Wittarkee were currently placed. The adjutant responded by pointing towards the campsite with eyebrows raised in question.

Frustrated, but understanding the thinking of his long-time comrade, Andrews chewed a lip for a moment. Then he pointed a hand in each direction before having to duck again as one of Wittarkee's shots ricocheted off a tree and over his head.

ON THE EASTERN FLANK, Robertson had his party advancing towards the campsite, spread out behind the deadly rifles of Matthews and Grey. The soldiers were brave, but neither were natural bushmen. Another tripwire was caught, bringing a large rock down to hit Grey's pack. Not a big man, he was knocked down and winded.

From one of the shielded depressions dug in the campsite, Vittorio saw the soldier fall. He raised his rifle to take advantage of the situation, but realized that he couldn't. Slowly, he lowered the barrel.

Beside him, Karumbari looked at him, puzzled, and shrugged. Grey struggled to his feet. Perhaps still groggy, he injudiciously cocked and pointed his rifle while standing. Karumbari promptly shot him.

Vittorio closed his eyes and shuddered. Then he opened them again, and nodded acknowledgement to the Kuthant beside him. Karumbari shrugged again.

~

DESPITE THE TRAPS laid so effectively about the perimeter, the fighting had nearly reached the fringe of the campsite. From their position atop the rocky outcrop, Cristiano and Pierre could see flashes of the red coats of the remainder of the Riverview Company. As much as possible, they directed their fire that way, but conscious of shots still ringing from their east.

At least the especially dangerous rifle fire from that quarter seemed to have abated. Unbeknownst to them, one of Pierre's shots through dense foliage had killed the soldier Taylor. While his Martini Henry had been enthusiastically picked up by the trooper Tooracle, the bluecoat was far less effective with the unfamiliar weapon.

Another of the small armoured ditches had been dug in the cover of a low acacia bush some yards distant from the bark shelter. It had been reinforced with an almost complete plough blade, the top of which was propped amongst the wattle branches. It was providing cover for James Arnold, whose attention was fixed on activity from the west.

He'd been being supported by the Balyarta men Biru and Pirrewuy, and from adjacent similar ditches, the Kuthants Bowra and Moolbong, and Walan and Dendendaloom. The latter was a small woman, who was proving remarkably effective with the pistol she'd much earlier lifted from the body of Alan Hardy – the first victim of Asbul's deadly darts. Unfortunately, she was fast running out of ammunition, a problem also confronting the other Kuthant shooters.

As to Arnold's own immediate support, Pirrewuy had been shot in the arm, and while he was ordinarily competent with a rifle, he was fumbling with James' pistol in his 'wrong' hand. Biru lay behind them both, unconscious at least. There'd been no time to check on him properly since a bullet struck his skull. He'd been breathing when they'd moved him into the deepest cover of the bush. Beyond that, they could only hope.

Thonkumundil sprinted from the bark shelter, and dived full length to roll under the acacia bush. He'd seen Biru fall, and hoped to get him back for McGregor's attentions. Just as he'd been in motion, the lost and bewildered John Rourke had staggered out of the scrub into the open campsite. Seeing the running dark figure, Rourke fired. His bullet clanged into the plough even as Mundil dived behind it.

Rourke cursed his sling as he struggled to reload. Arnold recognized his old adversary and rose slightly from the bush. This time he would, and did, more than wound the man. But his rash action had its own consequences. Both Clapham and Miller spotted their chance and fired. The teamster fell, blood welling from his head and his side.

Pasquale saw him go down. He briefly put a hand on Karumbari's shoulder, then broke from their cover and ran to the fallen teamster. Clutching his rifle in one hand, the Italian managed to grab and lift James with the other, helped by Mundil. The Kuthant quickly dropped back into position to give some covering fire as the merchant turned to half-carry the staggering James to the shelter. Such aid also came from the nearby Kuthant shooters, and others in and around the campsite.

The infantryman Clapham repositioned himself to get a clearer shot at the two men. Pasquale glimpsed his movement and clumsily fired his rifle in that general direction. Ted Clapham fell dead. Whose bullet did the deed was a matter for conjecture, but in Pasquale's racing mind, there was only one possibility. As he half carried, half dragged the teamster into the waiting arms of McGregor and Chung in the shelter, he fell to his knees, throwing down the rifle.

"I killed a man! Padre! I killed a man - God forgive me!"

McGregor looked up from his immediate task, cleaning the head wound of the softly groaning Arnold. "Ye saved James' life," he said simply.

"Do they balance out? Is his life worth more than the man I shot?"

"I pray so. Only God knows."

The wounded teamster looked over at the shocked merchant, and managed to gasp weakly, "Well, I reckon so. To me, anyway. Thanks, mate..."

Vittorio nodded gratefully and crossed himself, trying to reframe his thoughts.

Chung was back near the entrance. He quietly called back to the preacher, "There's more wounded out there. You want me to get them?"

"Yuir call, my friend. It's yuir life tae risk."

The cook grinned, then dashed out at a low crouch, a couple of bullets whizzing over and around him. Koolwunnung watched him closely as she reloaded her gun from a dwindling box of bullets in the shelter. Vittorio also watched him go, threw down his rifle, gritted his teeth and ran out after him. Still in shock, he was much less cautious as he ran.

Sheltering in the shadow of a large tree, Andrews saw the trader emerge from the shelter. An easy target! "Now there's a man who's no soldier!" he said, smiling to himself as he killed him.

There was a crash from some distance to the Captain's right, as Gregori Volkoff jumped down from the tree where he'd been perching, picking off targets.

"You want soldier, I give you soldier, bastard! Azov soldier!" he snarled, shooting as he hit the ground.

The impact of his landing jarred his aim, and Andrews was only wounded, clutching his shoulder as he fell. The Cossack advanced to finish the job – right into Finlay's line of fire. The adjutant's rifle didn't miss, although the man himself had to dive quickly behind a tree himself as Magpie fired at him.

The Martini Henry bullet spun Volkoff, who crashed heavily to the ground, his chassepot still clutched tightly. As he fell, the stock of the rifle, firm in his grip, hit hard on a rock. A small piece broke off the stone. Sunlight glinted off a thin seam of gold, suddenly exposed.

The tiny sparkle caught Gregori's eye, and he smiled at the irony as he died, sighing, "Ah – Christina, *kotchinka*..."

Magpie had other priorities. He'd seen events unfolding elsewhere. He ducked through the scrub, then sprinted across the campsite to take over Arnold's position.

PHILLIP WAS HEADING in the same direction, making for the shelter, with the wounded Baza supported by his left arm. It was the tall Kuthant who realized their danger and tried to warn the youth, pushing at him.

Oblivious, Phillip tried to reassure him, "It's alright - I'll get you to McGregor."

They'd stopped momentarily, the tribesman fractionally in front of his would-be rescuer, as James Robertson emerged from the scrub on their right. Without a word, the Warden shot and killed the wounded man.

Phillip tried to turn quickly, his effort to bring up the chassepot hampered by the dead weight still on his arm. He had no choice but to let Baza's body fall. He looked up and realized who stood before him. Father and son's eyes locked.

"Damn you, father! He was a good man - these are all good people!"

James' face was impassive. "So, you've decided to join them, have you? Are you willing to die for your cause?"

"Yes, I –"

The elder Robinson fired before a third word could be uttered. Shot at such close range, Phillip died instantly.

"That's good, because I'm willing to kill for mine," said his father coldly, stepping around the two bodies and advancing without a backwards glance.

~

MUTTERING words that wouldn't be found in the Bible, Andrews had crawled to sit with his back against a sturdy tree trunk. He'd reluctantly dropped the expensive rifle he'd so prudently salvaged. His damaged shoulder couldn't bear the weight. Now it was hampering him as he struggled to reload his revolver with one hand.

Suddenly a shadow fell over him, and the trusty Tranter was smashed from his hand by a clubbing boomerang. The Captain looked up into the face of a large Kuthant woman, Pooloongearn. It was a face that wore a vicious grin. She'd seen a soldier shoot her son only minutes before.

"You're a bloody woman..." Andrews just managed to say, as the boomerang clubbed down again. Pooloongearn put all of her considerable weight into the blow. This was vengeance.

Finlay turned at the sound of his commander's voice. There'd been no shot to alert him, and his attention had been focused on the stubborn resistance from around the centre of the campsite. Immediately he put a bullet in the broad back of Pooloongearn.

"Damn it! Sorry Captain - I was watching the campsite - didn't spot her till too late."

He rushed over to where the Kuthant woman's body lay over that of the officer he'd served faithfully for years. The mess that now was Andrews' skull left no doubt that he was dead.

The adjutant leaned wearily on the trunk of the tree, and looked around for the remains of the Riverview Company's disciplined formation. It was now mostly a formation of corpses. Men who'd done their job, as ordered, to the last. There was Billington, bandaged foot ignored as he'd made his way back to fight alongside his comrades. Eaton. Bain. The rest. Men he'd fought alongside, lived alongside, for years. If they, or others unseen, weren't dead, it was beyond his power to help them. It was over, Finlay suddenly knew. This fight, and the efficient mercenary company he'd helped forge. He saw two red coats moving.

"Matthews! Dundee! Are you the last? Dear God... Come on, let's get out of here! Let's just hope Murphy's still back there with the horses!"

The last two mobile soldiers joined their surviving officer without demur, and together they carefully retreated under sporadic shooting. They very soon crossed paths with Sergeant McCartney.

"Going somewhere, Mister Finlay? I think the Warden expects you and your army to be in at the finish," said the policeman.

"Me and what army? Look around! Sod the Warden." He jerked a thumb over his shoulder, in the direction of the lifeless Andrews.

"Abso-bloody-lutely!" agreed Matthews.

Dundee managed to nod. He'd not long recovered consciousness, and was functioning solely on instinct. Luckily for him, he had a good survival instinct.

The adjutant shook his head. "We've already had our finish. You're not going to try to stop us, are you?"

"No bloody chance - I want to find Robertson and hope he's got as much sense as you do!"

"Yeah, well, good luck with that," returned Finlay bitterly.

The three survivors continued their withdrawal.

McCartney called after them, "Hey! Leave us some horses!" then moved off in the opposite direction.

The shooting was now sporadic. Neither side realized how low the other's stock of ammunition was getting.

Chung had run from the shelter to flatten himself by the large rocky outcrop. He called up to the pair on the high ground, "Hey! How's it looking?"

Hearing the cook's voice, but not seeing him, the angle of the rock obscuring the view from his spot under the 'armoured' acacia, it was Magpie who first answered. "We've got 'em on the run I reckon!"

Still cautiously prone, Cristiano fired another shot at a flash of blue coat he'd spotted, and was satisfied by an answering scream. "I think you're right, amigo."

Beside him, Pierre said softly, "I hope so. I don't know about you but I'm nearly out of ammunition."

"We got plenty of wounded out there," called Chung.

The two marksmen atop the outcrop exchanged looks, then

nodded before de la Fontaine replied, "You want to go get them, we'll try to cover you as best we can."

"Okay. Thanks." With that, the cook sprinted through the gap in the rocks back out into the bush.

Behind their now battered and dented plough blade, the two dark teamsters watched him run off.

"I go do the same," said Mundil.

Magpie nodded. "Right. I will too." He grabbed Arnold's chassepot then called up to the outcrop, "Hey! Keep an eye out for us too, okay?"

The two teamsters split left and right as they ran into the western scrub.

From his position crouched in a thicket of scrub, Miller saw Magpie running towards him, still some distance away. Good. He wasn't a man to shoot someone in the back. He fired, but he'd misjudged the distance and the shot missed. Magpie's chassepot was a considerably superior weapon. Although the half-caste's return fire was rushed, he still managed to wing the volunteer.

He tried to fire again, but discovered he was out of bullets, just as Miller went to ground. "Damn! That doesn't help!" muttered the teamster.

He crouched low, dropping the rifle and pulling a pistol from his belt. Quickly, he checked it. "This is bloody empty too!" he swore, starting to pull shells from a pouch on his belt.

Miller rolled, gun raised, at the sound of a foot cracking a branch on the ground behind him. Just in time, he recognized the police sergeant. McCartney saw him, and moved quickly to kneel beside the wounded man.

"You okay?" asked the policeman.

"Been better, Sarge, but I'll live."

"If you're lucky. Stay down!" ordered McCartney, recommencing his slow, cautious advance in Magpie's direction.

Much closer to the teamster, James Robertson emerged from the bushes to find his quarry still loading his pistol. Magpie stood, and stared at the squatter's cold eyes.

"You gonna to kill me, Mister Robertson?"

"I've already shot one son. Why would you think I wouldn't shoot you?"

But even as he began to raise his gun, Robertson's body was jolted by a sudden impact. He looked down and was surprised to see the sharp end of a spear protruding from his chest. Fascinated, he watched the bloodstain spread across the fabric of his shirt. The light faded from his eyes as he toppled forward, crushing bracken and breaking the spear's point as he landed.

Magpie looked across the body into the impassive face of Thonkumundil. The Balyarta man tugged his spear loose, frowning as he realised the tip was broken. Damn – he liked that spear. Ah, it was only the point. He could fix a new one of them. Without a word he turned and walked away.

The half-caste stood motionless for a moment, seemingly unde-cided. Was that it? Even as he wondered that, there was a rustle of branches and Sergeant McCartney stepped out from heavy scrub. If he'd seen or heard anything of the previous few minutes, he gave no immediate indication of it.

Magpie had at last gotten the pistol loaded. He raised it threaten-ingly. "You next?"

McCartney didn't raise his own gun. "No. I've seen enough. I've heard enough." Loudly he called, "Troopers! Any of you men, or soldiers that are left out there - put up your guns!"

The sergeant holstered his pistol and walked into the campsite with his hands raised to shoulder height.

"No more!" he demanded, as loud as his tired voice could muster.

The last of the shooting stopped as first Magpie, then Thonku-mundil, followed McCartney into the campsite.

So too did Meataxe, who had just dropped from the safety of his tree after watching all that had gone on around him. He'd quickly worked out that he was fighting on the wrong side, but also knew that his uniform would make him a marked man. No, Meataxe wasn't mad.

Others emerged. Miller, hobbling. The Swede Jansen, whose anti-quated gun had proved useless, but who wouldn't desert his companions. Several troopers, led by Possum. The sergeant was briefly relieved to spot Young Joey among them.

Magpie and McCartney faced each other warily.

"What now?" asked the half-caste.

"I've got a lot of dead and wounded men. Daresay so have you."

"Reckon so. You want to take your wounded and clear off." It wasn't a question.

"I do," the policeman agreed.

"Right then."

"We'll come back for our dead."

Magpie shook his head. "We'll put 'em where you can find them. You don't come back here."

"Believe me, I'd rather not. But I can't promise anything. I can tell the truth - the Warden turned out to be a mad bastard and there was no sign of any gold." The teamster snorted wryly at that as McCartney continued, warningly. "But that doesn't mean there may not be hell to pay. Like I said, no promises."

"Fair enough. You better get going."

McCartney nodded solemnly, turned, and signalled for the remains of Robertson's private army to follow him.

"Wait," called Chung. "We'll find your wounded. Together."

McGregor remained in the shelter, patching up the injured natives who were brought to him. Cristiano remained near Magpie, a rifle in each hand, watchful in case any hot-headed or grief-maddened raider should change their mind.

To find and gather up such casualties as could move with some assistance, Chung and Pierre led Possum, Young Joey, and a strong man named Graham through the surrounding bush. They were trusting their memory of Volkoff's meticulous map of their traps.

Quite soon, McCartney had his survivors gathered at the edge of the campsite. A few were to be carried. Graham held the blue-coated cousins Toorarcle and Toorang, one in each powerful arm.

"Thank you," the sergeant said quietly to Chung and de la Fontaine, who were standing beside the silent Magpie.

"Too late to say 'go in peace', I'm afraid," said the Frenchman.

"Damned right," agreed McCartney. "Still, that was a gesture of good faith. It might help when I put it into the report I'll have to write."

Pierre smiled grimly. "You can do no more, I'm sure."

The beleaguered policeman looked back at the campsite. "No. There'll be local feeling, but there's not many left to act on it, even if they're stupid enough. Official reaction though... Mind you, that has to go through bureaucracy. Paperwork. Takes some time, usually." He met Magpie's gaze. "Can't say how much, though."

There was a slow nod in response. "I understand."

THE AFTERNOON SUN shone with indecent brightness on the sombre scene. Carefully laid out under a canopy of shading branches were the bodies. Balyarta and Kuthant. Chinese, Russian, American, Italian. The betrayed son of the squatter. Men and women.

Another array of corpses, many in red or blue uniforms, had been laid out near the main track to Louth, a little way into the bush so as not to alarm unwitting passers-by. Some of them were particularly unpleasant sights - the men burned at the creek, the shattered head of William Andrews.

No sentries were posted. McCartney was being trusted, after a brief discussion.

Those most badly wounded were being attended to again, now there'd been an opportunity to look after those less hurt.

Cristiano finished bandaging the arm of Pirrewuy, the Balyarta man who'd received his guitar earlier. The native flexed the fingers of his wounded arm then moved them on an imaginary fret board. The two men exchanged grins.

A handful of Balyarta and Kuthant, some wounded, stood together discussing and exchanging their different types of weaponry. Comparing stories of their effectiveness or otherwise.

Several coolamons piled with carefully collected caltrops were on the ground beside them - Micah's map laid over one.

Magpie squatted at the side of Arnold, who was propped against the large shelter, his head bandaged. McGregor knelt at James' other side, changing the dressing on his ribs, where the bullet wound persisted in oozing.

Asbul limped up to them, his leg bandaged. In his hand was a sheaf of papers. He spoke enthusiastically for a minute or two. Magpie shook his head, and the senior teamster glared at him. The half-caste made a placatory gesture towards his injured friend. The Makassar spoke again, but McGregor shook his head without even looking up.

Several of the wounded from both tribes were sitting or lying in the lee of the rocky outcrop, together with others miraculously unscathed. Some were already swapping stories of the morning's battle, the way some fighters do. Others already wanted nothing more than to forget, or at least be distracted by other things.

The Kuthant Ugeree was proposing to Karumbari and Walan that he'd go and hunt for some food for the group. There'd be no game nearby – birds and animals would surely have fled so much gunfire. But there were plants that could be foraged, good enough for this evening. Mere days ago, he'd have been amongst those who dismissed this as women's work. But he'd seen some of these women fight. His perspective had changed.

One of those women was little Dendendaloom. She was now almost unrecognizable as the feisty shooter who'd wreaked havoc from a shallow ditch. She was tenderly wiping sweat from the forehead of the much larger Balyarta man Yallaroi, who sat rocking on his haunches, appreciating her effort to take his mind off the elbow that had been smashed by a soldier's bullet. It had been his throwing arm. He faced the dreadful prospect of not being able to hunt again if he couldn't relearn his skills using the other hand.

Equally formidable with a gun in her hand was the Balyarta woman Wittarkee, but now that hand coyly held that of the Kuthant Bowra. It was far too early to know if, or how far, any relationship between them might develop. But if they did have a son, that offspring would probably be a natural marksman.

Similarly tired of fighting, Cooterah and Moolbong had sat close together, side by side. As exhaustion overcame them, their eyelids drooped – the side of the lithe Balyarta's face landing on the taller Moolbong's shoulder. The Kuthant's head soon nestled in Cooterah's lush hair. Both sleepers were smiling, at last.

In the centre of the campsite, Pierre was building up the fire they'd need that evening. Near him, Chung was preparing his large wok for the scant supply of fish and tubers he'd kept aside to feed them all. That element of pre-planning had slipped amongst the preparations for battle, with the usual hunters and gatherers either absent or otherwise engaged. Anything that Ugeree could find would certainly be welcomed.

Standing beside the cook was Koolwunnung. She spoke, hesitantly.

""I think... I think, I better be with my people. Reckon they need me more'n you do."

If she hoped for an argument, it didn't come. Chung drew a clear distinction between 'need' and 'want'.

"I'm sorry. I reckon you're right, though. Been a lot of losses to make up, whatever you all do, wherever you all go. You take these to remember me by, eh?" he said, and handed over two of his knives to her.

"Hah! You reckon I gonna forget you?" Koolwunnung laughed, and ran her fingers through his long hair. "I put these somewhere safe and come back soon. We not gone just yet!" she said, teasingly. With that, she strode away.

"You've made an impression, my friend," said the Frenchman tactfully.

"A good one, I hope. But I can't stay with the tribe, however much I'm... interested in... them. Too many memories, of old friends and family, dying in my arms." His voice trailed off for a moment. "Funerals at first light - can't call them all 'burials' I suppose. Then I think the tribes are taking off."

Pierre poked at the developing fire. "Can't blame them. Not much chance of peace for them here - too much blood spilt."

"Don't know that everybody's looking for peace," said Chung, and both men looked towards the shelter where the teamsters were in animated conversation. "You're a soldier. You gonna ride with them?"

"Was a soldier," de la Fontaine corrected. "No, I'm done with fighting. What about you? Go with Magpie? Stay and look for gold maybe?"

"Hah! You think there ever was any? I know what young Phillip said, but maybe that Polish fella was working a con all along." The Frenchman nodded in agreement. "Nah - I'm no more looking for a fight than you are. Reckon I'll try to make my way south. Get to somewhere decent sized and maybe start a business."

"The New Johnston Hotel, after all?"

Chung chuckled. "Maybe. Why not? That'd be a nice mark of respect. Something where I can cook for folks, anyway."

"I'll ride with you, if you'll have me."

"Thanks."

There was a promising, companionable silence for some moments as the two men worked.

Then Pierre said, thoughtfully, "You're going to need some starting capital. What about Gregori's rifles? He wanted them to go to a good cause."

"Magpie's gonna want those."

"No. I asked him. No use to him without the bullets to go with them, and the right sort are in short supply out here."

That made sense to the cook. He pondered the suggestion. "They're a bit second hand now, but even without ammunition they should be worth some money."

Asbul had limped over to talk, and now stood beside the pair. He'd heard the tail end of their conversation.

"You want money? Dis do?" he asked, proffering a handful of creased Bank of NSW fifty pound banknotes from a wedge of them that he carried.

Pierre stared. "Where did you get these?"

"Dey was folded up all neat-like inside de coat of dat Captain Andrews."

"How did you find them?" asked Chung, suspiciously.

The fisherman grinned guilelessly. "When we was all movin' de bodies out nearer de road, like Magpie promised dat trooper fella. I went to drag de Captain. His coat fell open an' a bunch of dese fell out. Pockets was full o' dem!"

"Must be what he was paid. For this job, and maybe others," surmised Pierre.

He was correct. Andrews had never really trusted banks, and had preferred to keep the Riverview Company's finances close at hand. *His* hand.

"Reckon so," agreed the Makassar, who didn't really care.

"It should be shared around. That was the agreement with the gold," Chung pointed out.

"Eh, I know dat. Dat Magpie, he not want any. Says paper money ain't no good to him or his people."

De la Fontaine nodded as he tossed a few more branches on the fire. "That makes sense. Poor Vittorio - his idea of hiring a lawyer for them... well, things are past that, now."

Continuing his mental 'checklist', Asbul continued, "De preacher man, he want no part of it."

"Not surprised," said Chung, not disappointed to hear it, though.

"Mister Arnold, he take his share. Plenty left for you fellas, and de music man."

Pierre looked at the cook. "Makes business sense. Better than the rifles."

"Right enough. What about you, Asbul? You want to ride south with us, or are you gonna go with Magpie?"

"Neider, I t'ink. Some of dey Kut'ant, dey not gonna go wit' Magpie, or any udder Balyarta fellas. Dey reckon it past time dey was headin' back to near where dey found me. Dey got some good stuff to trade, but need more, dey say. I go with dem, try to get home."

The Frenchman smiled as he pocketed banknotes. "Home, eh? Sounds nice. Where *is* home for you, Asbul?"

The smile didn't leave the fisherman's face, but his eyes seemed to lose focus, as if he was staring at something a long, long way distant. "I miss de smell of de sea. An' how it feels underneat' you when you sail."

Chung put a hand on the Makassar's shoulder. "Take the long rifles if you want."

"Maybe you can trade them for a boat," suggested de la Fontaine.

That seemed to snap Asbul back to the present. His grin grew even wider. "Hey yeah - some dumb pirate, he not gonna know, you put de wrong bullets in one of dem, you blow off your own hands, eh?" He winked theatrically.

Pierre and Chung exchanged looks of surprise, then broke into laughter. Asbul joined in.

The sound brought a smile to Peter McGregor's face as he changed the dressing on James' head wound. There'd been too little laughter recently.

Even Arnold found himself smiling. "Reckon I was lucky, padre," he said.

"Aye. More than most."

It was true. Neither bullet would have had to strike more than a fraction differently to have been fatal.

Magpie and Thonkumundil stood watching. There was an air of tension around both men. Not quite impatience, but suppressed agitation. A kind of excitement, even.

The half-caste squatted beside his oldest, closest friend. "James - I'm sorry. I've said my thanks and goodbyes to Cris and Chungy and Frenchie. They ain't ridin' with us. Pity, they good men to have on your side, all of 'em. We can't wait for you. Mundil wants to catch up with the people quick in case they've panicked and scattered too far. I know Samuel wanted to keep 'em together but, like he said, this sorta fight was new to 'em. Them as weren't here, well, they mighta run at the sound of guns."

The grizzled teamster managed a painful, but sympathetic nod.

"You gonna stay with them, then?" he asked.

Magpie offered a wry smile of his own. "They're gonna stay with me, I reckon. A lot, anyways. Them and maybe more. I'll try to get a message to you, how to catch us up when you're better."

The preacher put a warning hand on the half-caste's arm. "Risky. Ye want tae be very careful who knows how and where tae find ye."

"True enough," agreed Arnold. "Listen, old friend - I don't reckon I want to push my luck much further. I reckon I'm done with fighting."

He brushed his hand across his head wound. Magpie nodded as James went on. "There's a young bloke there'll look after the team since it seems you got other ideas." He pointed over at Cristiano. "I'll talk with him. Reckon he's alright with horses. Might even get one or two of the tribe to work with him, if you can spare them."

He gave a tired smile. Magpie tilted his head, smiling in response – he understood and appreciated the idea.

"Better if he moved on from here," advised the Scot.

James agreed. "Yeah. With some of that bastard Andrews' money to help him, he'll be right. As for me, reckon it's time I headed for new pastures, too. Put my share of the bastard's blood money to good use. Take Rebecca with me if she's up for it."

"We'll get ye somewhere safe tae rest up, then I'll talk tae her for ye," offered the preacher.

"Thanks padre. Magpie - I'm sorry, mate..."

"No need to be sorry, mate. You've stood beside me for a long time. You been family - you'll always be family. Be good to not have you die on me. Look after yourself, you old bastard."

"Same to you..."

The two clasped hands, then James lay back, closing his eyes.

Mundil squatted beside him to say his own quiet words of farewell, as Magpie stood and stepped away. McGregor also stood, and with a hand on the now ex-teamster's shoulder, shepherded him away a few paces.

Quietly, he said, "Ye know there'll be more trouble when word of this gets out."

"Trouble, Mister Mac? This is just the start of trouble. Thonku-mundil and me - we're gonna catch up with the rest of the people, then see how many of them wants to fight and how many wants to keep running. Come back in the morning to pay our respects. Then them as want to, Balyarta and Kuthant together, we're gonna find the Beeargah, and Murrong, and any other people we can. I'm gonna gather any and all that's willing to fight beside us. That crazy Meataxe, he reckons to come along. Too damn many men like my... like *him*..." He gestured in the direction where Robertson's body had fallen. "They don't respect nothing but strength."

"Men like him respect nothing at all."

That accurate statement got a wry chuckle. "Too true. So, we teach them. Me and my brothers - all of them. Like these brothers that died beside me. Will you ride with us?" he asked, unexpectedly.

McGregor was surprised. Perhaps flattered, and even fleetingly tempted. "Be Friar Tuck tae yuir Robin Hood? I cannae. No, ma friend. I can... understand ye, but I cannae condone, or be a party tae, any more killing. There's been far too much already."

After his brief conversation with Arnold, Mundil had slipped away into the bush. Now he emerged again, leading two horses. He stood near.

Magpie nodded respectfully at McGregor's decision. "I don't wanna be a killer, but I'll do what I gotta. Whatever I have to, to get respect. I'll be what Robertson and men like him have made me be. You tell them that, Mister McGregor."

"Aye - that I can do, Magpie."

"No. Not Magpie. Not any more. Tell them my name is... is..."

"Moograbah," offered Thonkumundil.

"Yeah. Tell them my name is Moograbah."

After a final exchange of handshakes with the preacher, the two dark men mounted and rode away into the scrub.

They'd find Samuel and the others, and send those who didn't want to ride as outlaws back to the campsite. The sojourn there would be very temporary. The Balyarta would find a new home. Adapt. The tribe was good at that.

Peter McGregor stood and watched the two men go. "Moograbah. Balyarta for 'magpie'. Hmmph. Aye, I'll tell them. But God only knows who'll care."

-xXx-

ACKNOWLEDGMENTS

Mixed Blood began with a conversation. A conversation between several very talented men - as interesting a group as those assembled in these pages. Sailors of the Royal Narnian Navy flagship the *Dawn Treader*. We were working together on the third in the *Chronicles of Narnia* series of films.

One day between takes, the question was asked "Why hasn't there ever been a Great Australian Western?" That sparked discussion of what defines each of those terms: 'Great', 'Australian' and 'Western'.

Talk came around to formulas. What makes certain movies memorable? *The Magnificent Seven* kept coming up. Ideas swirled. Guys created characters for themselves, and those characters created threads of a story. Somebody wrote stuff down.

Then they gave it to me.

My first response was "What do you expect me to do with it?" Then I read the scribbled notes, and realised that there was a story in there.

A story that could say a lot about Australia as it was, as it is, and as it could be. A story that could say a lot about Australians as we were, are and could be. Australians of many and varied origins and colours, beliefs and histories.

My name is on the cover, and yes, I own the copyright. After more than ten years of researching, writing and rewriting, revising and refining, I don't reckon that's unreasonable.

But I do want to acknowledge the story's origin.

With my greatest respect and gratitude this goes out to:

Cooper Ali-Shabazz, Basheer Ally, Alex Batschowanow, Andre

Boiteux, Kamran Fulleylove, Paul Gosselin, Robbie Harrison, Ryan Holding, Agung Igusti, Mark Kaminski, Vic Leto, Gerardo Maluenda, Salvador Maluenda, Boon Thie and Andy Williams.

A fond remembrance to the late, great Ross Price, a determinedly grumpy old bastard, who's much missed.

In the course of all that research, I've also had help from other sources. The staff at the South Australian Museum, who provided a lot of help with native Australian aspects of the story. Any inaccuracies of fact (interpretation is subjective, remember!) are my fault, not theirs.

Armaments questions were cheerfully and helpfully answered by John Lehoczky. Thanks, old friend.

Others to help along the way have included Greg Shevtzoff, Karl Johnston, Ross Kelly and Doug Broad. Much appreciated, gentlemen.

Finally, love and thanks to my darling Meredith, without whom I couldn't have got this project this far.

Peace, love and magpies to you all.

RENOIR - BALLINA 2022

ALSO BY RENOIR

www.ingramcontent.com/pod-product-compliance
Lightning Source LLC
Chambersburg PA
CBHW070049120726
47909CB00002B/334